Archangels II:
The Grigori

Archangels II: The Grigori

STEVEN L. FAWCETTE

ARCHANGEL GROUP, INC.

Archangels II: The Grigori
Copyright 2008 by Steven L. Fawcette
Archangel Group, Inc.

For further information contact:

Archangel Group, Inc.
910 Chester Avenue
Bakersfield, CA 93301

Book design by MacGraphics Services

Cover Illustration by Marty Petersen Artwork and Design

Printed in the United States

Steven L. Fawcette
Archangels II: The Grigori

1. Author 2. Title 3. Fiction
Library of Congress Control Number: 2008902835
ISBN: 978-0-615-20021-7

AUTHOR'S NOTE

Archangels II: The Grigori is not only a sequel, but a direct continuation of the novel *The Archangels of Dreamland*. The characters, motivations and plot development of this story are identical to the previous book. As such, the numbering of chapters begins where the first novel ends. Both books are intended to be read as one seamless story.

Acknowledgment

$\mathcal{I}$ would like to take this opportunity to acknowledge my business associates in Archangel Group, Inc. It is your dedication and passion for this project that has made it possible to share this continuing story with readers around the world. In particular, I wish to thank Scarlett, Jorge, Elias and, most importantly, my best friend Moses, who has believed in this project with all his heart and soul from the first day I set pen to paper. I am indebted to you all.

Dedication

$\mathcal{I}$t isn't often that an author is at a loss for words, but this is such an occasion. I would like to restate the dedication from my first book: "She is my gift from God and my love for her is eternal." That heartfelt tribute has only grown more resolute with time. But, I will add something else. This wonderful woman is *my* archangel. Once again, thank you Eva...for everything.

"And there was war in Heaven:
Michael and his angels
Fought against the Dragon;
And the Dragon fought and His angels."

Revelation 12:7

CHAPTER TWENTY-SIX

WASHINGTON, D.C. — MAY 8th — 3:32 AM EDT

$\mathcal{T}$he body of Richard Stern grew cold, purged of a soul that had rendered it lifeless years before. A gruesome, eight-centimeter entry wound splayed the forehead, channeling blood and cranial fluid down jagged fissures in the skull. A coroner's report would not be necessary. The hollow point bullet had left little doubt that death was instantaneous.

Steven Yeager, the President's Secret Service bodyguard, prepared the corpse for disposal. He convinced himself to accept this situation, refusing to venture into the ethical minefields of conscience or integrity. The President's life had been threatened and he'd responded with necessary force, just as his training and duty demanded. But, now he was involved in the cover-up of a murder. Yeager felt no legal obligation to report the incident, for doing so would compromise and politically harm the President. He could not allow that to happen. Susan Webber was his assigned charge, as well as his secret lover. Knowledge of their affair might leave the Chief Executive open to endless blackmail and threats of disclosure. The ensuing scandal would topple the Administration and irreparably tarnish the Presidency. Yeager knew he was in way too deep, but there was no turning back. He vowed to protect her at all cost. *After all, it is my job.*

A body bag, secured from the White House infirmary, now became a thick, plastic shroud. As Stern's face slipped behind the airtight zipper, Yeager sighed at the daunting task ahead. The removal of the body would have to be executed with stealth, a fact made all the more difficult by his current location. The White House was one of the most secure facilities in the country. Dozens of office staffers, housekeepers, kitchen employees and maintenance workers were present; not to mention military personnel, District of Columbia Police and United States Secret Service agents constantly on alert for suspicious activity. Security cameras monitored the hallways on a 24/7 basis. Eyes were everywhere. *This won't be easy.*

He grasped a two-way radio and summoned his friend of 17 years, Secret Service Agent Glenn Marrero. The 41 year old, former Navy SEAL Captain had served with Yeager on many special ops missions and personally vouched for him when he joined the Secret Service, lobbying the Director to have him assigned to Presidential protection.

Marrero had been making his rounds on the second floor of the West Wing and arrived at the National Security Advisor's office moments after Yeager's call. In an instant, he understood the severity of the situation as only a trained agent would. The disorientation of objects in the room, the odor of cleaning agents masking those of bodily fluids and the sullen demeanor of his partner could only mean one thing.

"Holy shit."

Yeager spun Stern's chair around to reveal a seated body bag. "He threatened the Client at gunpoint."

A more emphatic exclamation followed. "Holy shit!"

"I did what I had to do," the agent reasoned. "He would've killed her if I hadn't responded."

An additional pause stalled their conversation. "Holy shit!"

"Is that all you're going to say?"

"What else do you want me to say?" he stammered. "Holy shit."

"I need your help. The Client wants this kept secret for obvious reasons. How do we get him out of here?"

Marrero soon freed himself from shock and began to focus on the problem. "There's a dozen agents on duty now," checking his watch. "Should be two in the East Wing, two in the residence, a couple in the Command Center. The rest are on the grounds. Where's the Client?"

"Oval Office. She's with the Press Secretary and her speechwriter. They're going over her address to the nation."

His partner nodded in apparent relief. "Good. Tell her to stay there. If this thing blows up in our face, she's going to need an alibi."

The agents discussed their limited options. They both agreed the emergency egress tunnel was the answer, burying Stern in an area that almost no one knew existed. In spite of countless rumors and Hollywood conjecture, there had never been a secret underground entrance that led into 1600 Pennsylvania Avenue. But, that was before the terrorist attacks of September 11, 2001. After that date, a decision was made to construct a half-mile long subway spur underneath Lafayette Park, linking the District of Columbia METRO Red Line with the White House, thereby providing the President with a final means of escape in case of disaster. The Army Corps of Engineers spent nearly three years on the clandestine project, constructing the tunnel at a cost of over $480 million. Stern's body would soon be placed inside the world's most expensive crypt.

A message was sent to the Secret Service Command Center. "This is Marrero in the West Wing. Over."

A duty agent responded. "Go ahead, West Wing. Over."

"We had a little accident over here. Client's toilet overflowed. Over."

"You need maintenance? Over."

"No, we've got it fixed. But, we went through a shitload of towels and I do mean a shitload. Can you have someone from laundry bring us a cart? Over."

A momentary pause, presumably for their laughter to subside. "Will do, West Wing. Out."

Within ten minutes, a maintenance employee exited the West Wing service elevator pushing a 3 x 4 foot laundry cart. Marrero intercepted the man in the hallway outside the Oval Office. "Thanks. We'll bring it down later."

The orderly left with a perfunctory nod. Now alone, he quickly deviated course, wheeling the cart inside the Presidential Study to avoid security camera detection. Interior doors linking the work areas of the Chief of Staff and White House General Counsel, provided labyrinth-like access into the National Security Advisor's Office where Stern's body awaited transport. Both agents placed the corpse into a fetal position within the cart and covered their unpleasant cargo with several soiled towels. They looked at each other in unified disbelief.

"We'll never get away with this," declared Marrero. "People are going to wonder what happened to him."

"Why can't he just disappear?"

"From what? Alien abduction?"

His partner snickered. "Not even aliens want this asshole."

"I suppose he could've been in Vegas…fell into a canyon of molten lava."

"What a tragedy. Couldn't have happened to a nicer guy."

"The Client owes us big time for this."

Yeager cast a nervous eye toward Marrero. "So, what's your price for keeping shut?"

"Haven't really thought about it. I guess she could name me ambassador to Tahiti. Of course, I'd want it to be a lifetime appointment."

"Yeah, like that's going to happen. Let's get this done."

They backtracked the route and emerged from the Presidential Study into full view of the hallway security cameras. Their movements appeared casual, but were tightly choreographed. The agents had the advantage. They knew who was watching and from which angles they could watch. It was imperative to remain calm and execute their plan without hesitation.

The two entered the service elevator. Once the doors closed, they took a moment to breathe and collect their emotions. During their descent to the White House basement, they said nothing, both choosing to stare directly at the laundry cart. Yeager nervously repositioned some towels that had shifted in transit. A security camera awaited their arrival. Getting past it would require a good amount of guile and some superior playacting.

The doors opened. As they wheeled out the cart, Yeager glanced inside the nearby Situation Room. Several members of the MAJIK-12 were seated at the conference table, monitoring live television broadcasts of the devastation in Las Vegas. He immediately recognized them as the people he'd been ordered to strip search weeks before. *That's the group Stern was with... probably waiting for him to arrive. Oh, well...*

They continued down the corridor, aware of their closing proximity to the camera. The laundry room lay directly ahead. Access to the emergency egress tunnel was to the left down a side hallway. It was time for some artful deception. Marrero began waving his hand over the laundry cart, behaving as if the smell was too difficult to bear.

"God, I can't take this anymore."

Yeager stopped to confront his partner. "Oh, come on. Stop being such a wuss."

He backed up, further showcasing his distress. As they surmised, their comrades in the Command Center were gleefully watching the proceedings.

"What's the problem, Marrero?" an agent radioed. "Having a bad day?"

The man feigned agitation. "Hey, if you think it's so funny, come down here and haul this crap yourself."

A few seconds of broadcast laughter. "No, thanks. We'll let the experts handle it."

Marrero grabbed a towel from the cart and walked in front of the camera. "I'm serious. Take a whiff of this..." He placed the towel directly over the lens, obscuring their view of Yeager as he headed down the side corridor. "Go on. Get a good, long sniff."

Their laughter continued. "Man, you're too much."

Marrero lowered the towel and let slip an ironic truth. "No shit."

He walked out of view, entering the laundry supervisor's office. The agent traversed two interior storage rooms and joined his partner in the side hallway. Access to the tunnel was before them. Yeager was already at work, sliding a business card into place through a crack in the doorjamb.

"I've got the electric eye covered. Open it."

A five-digit code was entered on a nearby keypad and the door sprung free. They secured the business card with tape, ensuring the alarm in the Command Center remained silent. The cart was pushed through the portal and the door locked behind.

Yeager activated the emergency lighting. Before them was a single rail car, detailed to appear identical to any METRO system passenger car. On the left side of the concrete platform rested a maintenance locker from which two shovels were appropriated. Transfer of the body onto the train was swift, since time was of the essence. Marrero made his way to the operator's console and brought the rail car to life. It moved slowly at first, creaking forth into a higher speed as the agent pressed down on the throttle. The train's headlight flared against the rough-hewn walls, revealing the tight clearance afforded the rail car. At times, a shrill noise would announce the skirmish between rock and metal. Yeager gazed down at the body bag and vented a sigh of relief, knowing this nightmare would soon be over.

The secured hatch leading into the METRO Red Line was now in sight. Marrero brought the rail car to a stop and followed his partner into the tunnel with shovel in hand. Standing in the headlight's beam, they selected an appropriate spot and began to dig. A stray sound echoed briefly, followed by the deafening roar of a passing train on the other side of the hatch. The noise, much louder than both had imagined, failed to deter them from their task. Soon, the only thing heard was the feverish churning of dirt. A slight shiver caused Marrero to pause.

"Cold in here."

Yeager agreed. "Just like a tomb."

His partner rested for a moment, peering into the light. Something then caught Marrero's attention. He couldn't be sure at first, but it soon became obvious. "Steve...it's moving."

"What is?"

"The rail car...it's moving."

Yeager gazed up from his labor and shuddered at the sight. Slowly, the train was drifting away from them, initiating a backward retreat down the rails. "That's impossible," he cried, dropping his shovel. "There's no one at the controls!"

The men began to run. Without warning, the engine revved to full power, increasing the train's reverse acceleration. Yeager was in full flight, grasping hold of a metal handlebar that aided his ascent into the cab. Before he could reach the controls, he heard Marrero's desperate plea.

"Give me a hand!"

Yeager leaned back and extended an arm to his partner. The agent still had not gained a foothold. Exhausted from the run, he clutched Yeager's hand in an awkward attempt to board the train. With his feet flailing in midair, their tenuous grip began to loosen further.

"I can't hold you! Pull your feet up!"

Marrero tried to swing his legs into the cabin, arching his back in the process. It would prove to be a fatal maneuver. In an instant of unfathomable horror, the agent struck the tunnel wall and fell between the car and the rails.

Yeager's voice squealed in shock. "Glenn!...Glenn!...Oh, fuck!"

He shut his eyes, hoping there was some way his partner had survived. The train was now at full throttle, hurtling back toward the White House basement. Yeager forced himself to the controls, cut power and applied the emergency brake. A lengthy shriek of grinding metal echoed through the tunnel, showering the undercarriage in a riot of sparks. The train came to a reluctant stop less than 300 feet from its base platform. He bowed his head in atypical prayer, scarcely believing what had occurred. After an extended period of reflection, he beheld a sight that chilled his soul. *Oh, my God...*

Stern's body was gone. Vanished without a trace. The corpse had been removed from the bag with the plastic shroud laying flat across the floor. A handwritten note was pinned to the front. Yeager didn't need to bend down. He could read it from where he stood. It said: WE'RE WATCHING YOU.

The agent pulled out his gun and began searching the rest of the car. He found nothing. Yeager stepped off the train and into the cold expanse of the tunnel. The echo of another METRO subway reverberated through the darkness. He searched one way then another, keeping his hand firmly on the trigger. *Who the hell's in here? What do they want?* The agent held his breath, scanning the area, listening for anything that would signal a presence. A creeping sense of unease made him feel vulnerable, but not alone. Several minutes passed. Nothing was seen or heard. At last, Yeager marched back along the tracks. There he found the severed body of his friend. As he crouched down in grief, a slight movement of air caused the hair on his arms to rise. Something was coming up on him from behind. Before he could turn, the agent was struck on the back of his head. Yeager keeled over, noting the blurred image of a hooded figure, before fading into unconsciousness.

CHAPTER TWENTY-SEVEN

N. SCOTTSDALE, ARIZONA — MAY 8th — 5:24 AM MST

*T*he children of Mary Ellen Hart arrived exhausted after their five-hour trip from Nevada. Forced to drive south into California because of the Hoover Dam deluge, they stopped briefly in the town of Needles to purchase food, fuel and diapers for the baby. It was here Kevin suggested a detour, offering his six-bedroom, eight-bath North Scottsdale home as a welcome haven for the extended family. The spectacular, three-acre property backed to the 5th fairway of the exclusive Troon North Monument Golf Course, providing ample landing room for Major Osborne's UH-1 helicopter. The craft touched down near a stand of picturesque saguaro cacti. An early sunrise over the high Sonoran desert revealed striking vistas of natural ravines, foothills and rock formations. Kimberly and the Major exited the chopper and strolled through the manicured grounds to join the others now entering Kevin's residence.

"Whoa!" exclaimed Moses, awed upon sight of the ornate interior. "Get a look at this place."

The house was meticulously decorated in a southwestern motif with dramatic reds and earth tones. Oversized furniture attempted to fill the cavernous, marble-floored great room. A two-story wall of glass provided spectacular views of Kevin's Olympic-size swimming pool, the desert landscape and majestic Pinnacle Peak beyond.

"Okay. We've seen the Country Club...now where's your place?" Osborne teased.

Kevin managed a tired, but prideful smile. "Make yourselves at home."

After gazing at the décor, Barbara and Shannon shared a common, thoroughly female thought. *This is way too nice for a bachelor to have done himself.*

"Très chic, Kevin," complimented his eldest sister. "Who was your decorator?"

He refused to lie. "An old girlfriend helped me with it. Or, was it two girlfriends. No, I think it was three...it's been awhile."

"Well, whoever's responsible, it's very nice," Shannon added. She struggled with the babe in her arms, who was starting to squirm in discomfort. "Hope's wet. Where I can change her?"

He pointed down an adjacent hallway. "Main bathroom's second door on your left."

She escorted the baby to the room. Kevin closed the front door, locking the dead bolt almost as an afterthought. "I was told the Feds were watching the house."

"That was weeks ago," Casey whined. "They'd have given up by now."

C.J. agreed. "Bank on it. After what happened in Nevada, they want no part of us. They're probably running for their lives."

An anxious pause was shattered by Kimberly's unexpected chutzpah. "If I see any Feds, I'm going out there and kick their asses."

Her family erupted in a chorus of laughter. "That's my girl," beamed the Major, enveloping her in a hug.

The first few notes of Frederic Chopin's Concerto #1 in E Minor began to echo through the room. Kevin led the others into the nearby parlor where Benjamin was seated at a beautiful Victorian rosewood piano.

"Please, kid. Don't play with the furniture."

"Oh, Kevin. Leave him be," Barbara chided.

Her brother was resolute. "No. I really don't want him playing with the furniture."

The music ceased. "This is a Steinway & Sons Concert Grand Hamburg Model D," stated the perturbed musician. "It's not furniture."

"Yes, it is. It takes up space in the room. That's what furniture does."

"This is one of the finest pianos in the world. It's worth over a 100 thousand dollars."

"I know," Kevin responded. "That's why I don't want you playing with the furniture."

Benjamin stared at his brother in bewilderment, wondering how anyone could disrespect such a precious instrument. He gently replaced the wooden keyboard cover and eased himself off the bench.

"Thank you," relief evident in his voice. The tyke left the room as Kevin turned to the others. "I guess we could all use some sleep."

"Not me," Roberta declared, eyeing the pool outside. "I see a lounge chair with my name on it." She departed the group in haste.

Moses' thoughts were with his girlfriend, Atali. "I need to make a personal call. I'll probably be awhile."

"I want to check out these CDs," Casey declared, still holding the box of top-secret discs recovered from Dreamland. "There's a lot we need to know."

"We'd like to get to bed," Osborne admitted. "Though I can't say how much sleep we'll get." Kimberly playfully elbowed him in the side.

Kevin felt a little foolish. He seemed to be the only one who was tired. The former NFL star had pulled many all-nighters in his life, but over the years the novelty had worn thin. Although desperate for rest, his role as host required him to remain awake.

"I'll show you to your room."

Upon leaving the parlor, they now spotted Benjamin in the expansive, gourmet kitchen with his head half-buried in the freezer. He withdrew from the Sub-Zero clutching a gallon tub of vanilla ice cream.

"Can I help you?" asked Kevin, wearily.

"Yeah. I want some root beer with this."

"Do I look like a soda jerk to you?" His brother's impish smile spoke volumes. "All right. Don't answer that." Kevin came to the refrigerator and removed a can of root beer from the top shelf. "There. Knock yourself out." The child took his spoils to the counter, soon to devour his ice cream float.

Kevin resumed his duties as escort, showing Kimberly and Major Osborne to the largest of his five guest bedrooms with private bath. After obligatory praise for his choice of décor and thanks for his hospitality, the two left no doubt of their desire to be alone. At first, Kevin failed to take the hint, but Osborne flashed him the look. It was that centuries-old, non-verbal communication between human males, informing one that the other was about to get some.

Kevin backed out of the room as Osborne closed the door. His protective nature finally surfaced. "All right, you two. Don't make too much noise…and try not to get any on the walls."

He then witnessed Benjamin conducting his own self-guided tour, carelessly spooning ice cream out of the gallon container. "Kid," squeaked his fatigued voice. "The carpet." The child continued on his trek, oblivious to his brother's concern. Kevin faced reality, aware that each member of the family had their own agenda. His brothers and sisters could fend for themselves. *I've got to get some rest.* Without notice, he slipped inside his private sanctuary, the master bedroom, and dove into the massive four-poster. Soon, he'd find sleep and make yet another descent into dreamland.

For several minutes, he perceived nothing more than optical floaters and non-descript shapes. Typical phenomena associated with gradual retinal relaxation. An ebony canvas began to form, slowly fusing into high-definition slate. The palette of the mind was now ready to receive images. He saw a sunrise over an open sea. He heard seagulls chattering above, holding position in the brisk wind. He felt his feet wading through the surf. Unable to identify the beach, other representations developed. Most integrated seamlessly. Some overlapped. A few were completely out of context. Youthful laughter. Children playing around a swing set. His mind shuddered as his brother Benjamin walked by, still holding the same container of ice cream. *Oh, no! Can't I have a better dream than this?*

Kevin had plans for an attractive female to saunter by naked. A woman confident enough to throw his body on the sand and use him as her boy toy. He concentrated, trying to conjure the object of his desire. Frustration mounted as the image remained elusive. A wistful sigh followed. Looking back at the swing set, the children began to drift out of focus. Soon, they all disappeared...except for one. It was a newborn baby, strapped securely in a swing. She held her head upright, physiologically impossible for an infant so young. Her eyes were like that of a doll's, vacant and devoid of soul. The image disturbed Kevin on a primal level, for he knew this child. It was his day-old sister, Hope.

Their silent communion was as intense as it was persistent. Her gaze penetrated his inner defenses, leaving him spiritually exposed and stunned by vulnerability. Kevin made an attempt to change the scene. Look away. Take whatever action he could to sever the connection. The image was indelible and never wavered. When all else failed, he tried to reason with the infant.

What do you want?

Her telepathic ability made vocal communication unnecessary. *Fear me, Raphael. Fear me as you would thy enemy, for that is what I am, and shall be throughout eternity.*

Kevin raged against the thought, countering with his own. *That can't be. We were told you were Immanuel...the chosen one. Why would God be my enemy?*

Remember the travail, Raphael? The excruciating agony you

endured at Dreamland? It was I who was responsible for your every scream…every gasp…your death a million times over.

Fear rose with Kevin's response. *That's not true. God had nothing to do with that.*

The infant smiled in a satanic manner. *Who said I was God?*

Mother, he answered in terror. *Mother told us.*

A tense pause, made unbearable by her revelation. *Your mother was my mother. But, how little she knew. I have now become breath and skin…and this body will be used to vanquish all that oppose me. Fear me, Raphael. Fear me well. For I am Lucifer, the Bearer of Light…*

"No!" Kevin cried out, his face damp with sweat. He was alone in bed, trying to calm an accelerated heart rate. It took him a moment to understand what had happened. *Just a dream…Just a bad dream.* Once more his eyes grew heavy. He drifted back into a fitful sleep, muttering the same plaintive words over and over. "Oh, God…Oh, God…"

Barbara and Shannon agreed to be roommates, having located a spare guestroom with two twin beds. Their newborn sister was resting comfortably in Shannon's arms, pressed against her chest. Her loving hand rubbed the baby's back, soothing any gas pocket that might have formed during her recent feeding. A burp rag was strategically positioned, just in case. Barbara closed the window blinds and sat on her bed across from them.

"She's got a lot of hair."

Shannon acknowledged with a smile. "Kind of reminds me of Ben."

They both giggled. Their sudden laughter triggered a loud burp from Hope.

"Aww. That's my girl," Shannon cooed. "You feel better now, don't you?"

It was not lost on Barbara that her sister was taking extreme pleasure in her newfound motherhood. "How long have you wanted a child?"

"Longer than I care to remember," she admitted. "I tried for years. It just wouldn't happen. I wanted it more than anything... even more than my life."

Barbara became lost in reflection. "Sometimes people want things too much. I know I did. I couldn't stand the thought of God laughing at my pain... taking away the ones I loved. So, I ignored Him. Treated Him like He didn't exist. The more I did, the more He made Himself known. I wanted to hurt Him so much, but all I did was end up hurting myself."

Shannon embraced the irony. "Strange. I was yelling at God because He wouldn't hear me...and God was upset because you wouldn't hear Him."

"I'm a different person now," Barbara confessed.

"Aren't we all?" She repositioned the baby who appeared to have drifted asleep. "I mean, look what's happened. Whether we like it or not, our lives will never be the same. Each of us lost something, which once meant everything to us. Our friends. Our families..."

"Our mother," came the soulful lament.

Shannon paused in mourning. "I think she was the bravest person I've ever known. All she went through. Everything she suffered. The last few minutes were so hard to watch, but she did what she had to do. She died just seconds before the quake."

"What was that like?" her sister inquired. "The earthquake?"

Her mind recalled the frightful memory. "Mother said it best. 'Annihilation beyond comprehension'. That's what it was. But, if you weren't there...you couldn't possibly know."

Barbara understood, noting the symmetry of events. "Like what happened to us at Dreamland. Mother said something about 'unspeakable travail'. And, that's just what it was. But, if you weren't there..." She ended her train of thought, realizing they'd both experienced a level of horror that neither should revisit.

In Kevin's home office, Casey and C.J. were placing the first of the Dreamland discs into a high-speed computer drive. The two huddled before a monitor, unable to conceal their restless anticipation. Soon, an image appeared on screen. It contained an official FBI warning that read as follows:

> *These documents contain sensitive intelligence information affecting national security and defense of the United States within the context of Title 18, Section 793 and 794 of the U.S. Code, as amended. Access, transmission or revelation of the contents herein to any unauthorized person can result in a Federal prison sentence of no less than 500 years, an undisclosed fine, and/or "other punishment deemed appropriate".*

Casey expressed amusement. "Uh, oh. We're in big trouble now."

His brother dismissed the threat with equal sarcasm. "Don't worry. We can mail it back to them with postage due."

They scrolled down to an abbreviated list of contents, which categorized each of the remaining discs. The first CD was a historical record of all high-level Government correspondence pertaining to the 1947 Roswell crash. Another CD announced the findings of the alien autopsies. A third addressed the advanced technology that had been recovered from the craft. Other CDs contained data about the Dreamland facility, the MAJIK-12, the construction of Socrates, as well as peripheral military programs that had been compartmentalized for security. These secret programs used code words such as GRUDGE, TRINE, MOONDUST, SNOWBIRD and ZODIAC. There was another program mentioned that was even more cryptic: JEHOVAH.

C.J. and his brother shared a foreboding glance. They were about to embark on a journey of incredible consequence. After decades of U.S. Government lies and disinformation, the truth would finally be known. The data stream was rapid, as both selected choice excerpts, trying to read ahead as the other spoke.

Casey began. "At 23:21 Hours on 4 July 1947, Roswell Army

Air Field in New Mexico initiated an investigation of a bogey which fell off radar approximately 23 miles northwest of the base during a severe electrical storm. Upon arriving at the crash site, military police discovered a technologically advanced craft capable of high altitude flight and, what were initially thought to be, three EBEs, or Extraterrestrial Biological Entities."

C.J. followed. "It was later determined that the craft and occupants were from Earth's future, circa 2953 A.D., and their designation should be changed to IBEs, Intertemporal Biological Entities, or time travelers. Initial autopsies were performed on 5 July 1947 at Roswell Army Air Field, New Mexico. Advanced autopsies and pathology was conducted the week of 9-15 July 1947 at Ft. Worth Army Air Field, Texas. The IBEs are currently stored in cryogenic freeze at Hanger 18, Wright Field, Dayton, Ohio."

It was Casey's turn. "Two civilian eyewitnesses were at the crash site prior to the arrival of military police. Robert Alan Kirke, age 19, of 351 N. Virginia Avenue in Roswell, was killed while attempting to escape custody. The other witness, Mary Ellen Hart, age 18, of 1704 W. Matthews Street in Roswell, escaped a military dragnet and is currently being sought."

C.J. again. "The debris from the crash site was codenamed ULAT, Unidentified Lenticular Aerodyne Technology, which baffled Army metallurgists with its tensile and shear strength. The craft's cold fusion engine used heavy water and deuterium pumped through plasma coils and phased electromagnetic arrays for propulsion. The onboard computer was reverse engineered and the technology shared with select Government contractors. Bell Telephone Laboratories patented the solid-state transistor in late 1947 and so began the modern computer age." He channeled a breath of disgust. "Unbelievable."

Another document captured Casey's attention. "The crash has allowed discovery of a new virus and bacterial agents so lethal, no known serum can affect a cure. The blood samples extracted from the IBEs have yielded a genetically-engineered strain of retrovirus not totally understood, but gives promise for development as the ultimate biological weapon."

C.J. related additional information. "It is the belief of the Joint Chiefs that if the Roswell incident were made public, insecurity and mass paranoia would ensue, along with communist infiltration; incitement of disorder and chaos threatening the global economy; the undermining of popular support for the Government and its leaders; and a general disintegration of morality, religion and public law."

Casey continued. "On 24 September 1947, President Truman signed an executive order establishing a 12 member panel of top military, scientific and intelligence personnel to coordinate all activities associated with the Roswell incident and any future contact with IBEs. This panel would possess the highest security clearance in the Government and be autonomous, without any Congressional oversight. Codename: MAJIK-12."

C.J. read a far more incendiary paragraph. "MAJIK-12 security is of utmost importance. It is with official regret that 'contract killers' in the employ of FBI Director J. Edgar Hoover have been dispatched on numerous missions to silence former MAJIK-12 members who have either threatened to speak publicly or those who were considered to be unacceptable risks. Among the notables terminated were Secretary of Defense James Forrestal, General Hoyt Vandenberg, Professor Albert Einstein, Dr. Enrico Fermi, Dr. J. Robert Oppenheimer, Dr. Wernher von Braun, Attorney General Robert Kennedy and President John Fitzgerald Kennedy." C.J. collapsed in his chair. He was astounded by the disclosure and horrified by the document's cavalier tone. "Jesus. What a nightmare. What an incredible, goddamn nightmare. Everything we've been lead to believe. Everything we thought was true. It's all been a lie."

"No wonder they came after us," Casey declared. "We represent a significant threat to the U.S. military and intelligence establishment. Now, more than ever."

Silence became their sanctuary. The computer hummed

patiently, but additional revelations would have to wait. The two were in no mood to continue. Casey suggested that they both get some sleep. Later on, the family could decide the best way to make the Roswell information public.

C.J. sat stoically, the future rendered clear in his eyes. "We were wrong. They're not going to give up. They can't afford to," his voice warbling in fear. "They're going to hit us with everything they've got."

Moses retired to another room, watching the clock and wondering what he'd say when he got the chance. He didn't want to call Atali before 8:00 am, for she was not an early riser. The last time he'd spoken with her was a few hours before the Vegas earthquake. Moses knew it was silly to wait, but the last 48 hours had left him at a loss for words. The fortunate survivor of three separate apocalyptic events, he hadn't had a chance to sort through his emotions. He did so now as waves of visceral impressions left him shivering in awe. Time continued to pass. It was a necessary transition, allowing Moses to honor the memory of his beloved Madre while immersing himself in the warmth of her spirit.

He called once the appropriate hour arrived. Atali wasted no time, answering the phone on the very first ring.

"Moses! My God, I've been so worried. Are you all right?"

"I'm fine, babe. I haven't had a chance to call with all the cell lines jammed. I'm sorry."

Her words trembled with relief. "I thought I'd lost you forever. Oh, Moses. It's so good to hear your voice."

"I'm OK," he assured her in somber tones. "I've just been through a lot. I'm really tired."

They spoke briefly of the earthquake, the nuclear explosion in the desert, and the deluge at the Hoover Dam. When Atali heard that Moses had been present at all three incidents, she collapsed to her knees, praising God for his miraculous deliverance. Moses also informed her of his mother's fate. After expressing heartfelt sympathy, she had news of her own.

"The Padre Superior called yesterday morning. He wants you to contact him as soon as you can."

"What about?"

"I don't know. But, he was very insistent."

Through a nearby window, Moses noticed a car pulling up in front of Kevin's property. "OK, babe. I'll call him. Look, I'll get back with you when I've got more time to talk."

"When will I see you again?"

A lone figure emerged from the vehicle and approached the house. "I don't know. Soon. I've got to go."

"I love you, Moses. Stay safe."

"Love ya, babe."

He hung up, assuming a defensive position behind the front door. A key was inserted. The knob turned wide. Moses waited for the right moment and pounced. The intruder was female. She struggled against his hold, her screams muted by his hand-over-mouth tactic. The woman tried to kick him from behind and bit down on one of his fingers.

"Hey!" jabbing her in the side. "Knock it off."

Muffled screams continued to flow, forcing the soldier to state the obvious. "Lady, settle down. This ain't no water pistol in your back." Her vocal distress fell to a whimper. "Now, I'm gonna let you go, if you promise to keep it shut. Deal?"

She nodded and was released unharmed. The woman jumped away, spinning around to face him. It was Kevin's girlfriend, Lynda Knight.

"Who the hell are you?" she demanded to know.

"I could ask the same thing."

"I'm the one with the key," holding the piece of metal as proof.

"And, I'm the one with the gun," keeping it leveled at her chest.

This Mexican Standoff was clearly a one-sided affair. "I'm Lynda Knight. Kevin's fiancée."

"His fiancée?" Moses smiled. "Now, I know you're full of shit."

She corrected her romantic leap of faith. "Well, soon-to-be

fiancée. I've been watching the house while he's been gone. Taking in the mail. Watering the plants. Normal stuff." Lynda took note of Roberta and Benjamin by the pool outside.

Perceiving no danger, the soldier holstered his sidearm. "I'm Moses Castaneda, Kevin's half-brother. He's asleep in the master… at the end of the hall."

"I know where his bedroom is," snorted the woman. "I've been there many times."

She strode away in a huff, quickly traversing the distance to Kevin's room. Slinking inside, she glided over to nudge her sleeping beau.

"Hey, wake up."

He twitched in surprise. "Huh? What?" adjusting his eyes in the dark. "Oh, it's you." Kevin rolled over, giving her the cold shoulder.

"That's a fine how-do-you-do after all these weeks."

"Let me sleep," he groaned.

"Kevin, who are these strange people? They're all over the house."

He buried his head in a pillow. "They're my family. Leave 'em alone. Leave us all alone."

"Family?" she whined. "They don't even look like you."

"Don't be a snot, Lynda."

"That Moses whatever his name is. He assaulted me with a gun."

"Too bad he didn't use it."

"What?"

"Never mind," he sighed in exasperation. "Go away."

Lynda took the initiative. She joined him in bed, spooning her lithe body against his bulging physique while draping a hand across his chest. "I saw a young girl out by the pool. She was wearing this thong bikini I wouldn't have been caught dead in." Kevin failed to give her the benefit of a response. "And, that nasty little boy. I saw him take his pants off right in front of her."

"He didn't happen to have tub of ice cream, did he?"

"Don't you think these people are obnoxious?"

"No, I think you're obnoxious," he countered. "Now, leave me be. I've got to get sleep."

Her hand slid to a more provocative area, eliciting a response she clearly hadn't anticipated. "Don't grab the hose if you can't start the fire."

An awkward silence fell, causing her to remove the wayward hand. "I'm just playing around, Kev."

"We can play later...right now...I just...I just wanna...try and...rest..."

He mumbled a few extra words before drifting back to sleep. Lynda came to her feet, disappointed at the failed tryst. The woman chided herself on her bedside manner. *Too much talk, too little action.* She left the room depressed, hoping she'd get another chance to display her sexual prowess.

The hallway was empty as Kevin's family gained the shuteye they so desperately needed. Lynda entered the office, anxious to check her morning emails. The Dreamland data was still displayed on the monitor. Ever curious, she began digesting the secret reports in exponential amazement. *Holy shit! What the hell is all this?* Lynda was a speed-reader, able to scan information at an impressive rate. Minutes morphed into hours. Making full use of her talent, the woman surfed through the majority of discs in record time. She was left astounded by the experience, achieving an epiphany she could scarcely believe or contain. Lynda now knew what the Government had done. She was aware of how Kevin and his family came to be. And, after much soul-searching, she became convinced of what she needed to do next.

Fear me, Michael. Fear me well. For I am Lucifer, the Bearer of Light... C.J. awoke suddenly, as if suffering a convulsion. Sitting up in bed, it took him several deep breaths to grasp what had happened. Shaken by the nightmare, he forced himself to his feet. Across from him was Casey, sleeping soundly and unaware of his brother's distress. C.J. took note of the time, having been asleep less than three hours. He made his way to the bathroom, splashing water on his troubled face. The image of the newborn continued to haunt him. It was etched indelibly in his mind, present whether he closed his eyes or not.

He returned to the bedroom, encountering his brother who was now awake. "What's going on?" Casey asked.

"Nothing. Just a bad dream." C.J. climbed back in his bed.

"Want to talk about it?"

"Not really," he sighed. "Let's get some sleep."

The room went silent and remained that way for a significant period. Then, Casey spoke. "Was it about Hope?"

The light flashed on, both of them now sharing a common horror.

Within minutes, the entire family had been roused and assembled in the great room. The topic of conversation was obvious. C.J., Casey, Kevin, Barbara, Kimberly and Roberta all confirmed having remarkably similar dreams. They were the six who'd been held captive at Dreamland.

"It's Lucifer," C.J. theorized. "He's in control of the nanobots... and they're still inside us."

"So, how do we get 'em out?" railed Kevin.

Shannon didn't foresee a medical solution. "I'm not sure hospitalizing you would help. Surgery's out of the question. There's just too many of them, all attacking different parts of the brain. Plus, they're intelligent. They'd have defense mechanisms to survive an injection of antibodies."

"She's right," Casey concurred. "We've got to find a way to block the signal...either at the source, from the relay satellite or locally. Until we do, we're all at risk."

Roberta appeared confused. "But, why's it only happening when we're asleep?"

"That's the most suggestive time," he continued to explain. "We're no longer in the sensory deprivation tank. There's too much going on while we're awake."

Kimberly came to understand. "Lucifer's trying to turn us against Hope. Tricking us into doing His dirty work. He can't get to her, but knows we can."

The news caused Shannon to hold the newborn a bit closer than normal.

"And, it's only going to get worse," predicted Casey. "More pressure. More subliminal suggestion...until one of us snaps."

"We've got to make certain that doesn't happen," C.J. insisted. "Shannon, Moses and Ben are in the clear. But, the six of us are compromised. None of us can be trusted with the baby. Not alone. Not for a second. Understood?"

The others nodded in agreement.

"One more thing," Casey added. "Falling asleep puts Lucifer in control of our thoughts. No matter how tired we get, we've got to stay awake for as long as we can."

CHAPTER TWENTY-EIGHT

WASHINGTON D.C. — MAY 8th — 8:39 AM EDT

*T*he surviving members of the MAJIK-12 were thrust into silence. Cloistered within the White House Situation Room, they sat motionless, their lungs laboring for breath. Before them was a wall-mounted, 72-inch plasma monitor. Captured upon the pixels of that screen was the final visual representation of Dreamland. In a thermonuclear instant, the entire military complex vanished from our world. A physical manifestation obliterated from existence, consumed in a roiling sea of flame.

Defense Secretary Roth gasped. "My God," his voice quaking in disbelief. "How many people were in there?"

Checking his notes, Air Force General Stevenson responded. "At the moment of detonation, there were 5,176 military and contractor personnel within a 20-mile radius of the base. All lost."

"Not all, General." CIA Director Langlois expressed his wrath by crushing a lit cigarette between his fingers, welcoming the pain. The intelligence agency that provided these top secret satellite images had already briefed him.

Once the fireball began to dissipate, a piece of ejected matter emerged through the swirling debris. They gazed in wonder as it defied the force of gravity, performing a mystic aerial ballet. After a controlled descent, the metallic object landed intact, finally coming to rest upon the melted charnel house.

DARPA Chairman Blau recognized the craft. "That's the X-91. An experimental Armored Personnel Carrier with flight and anti-grav capability. I've been waiting to see the next round of test results."

The recording was sped forward to reveal nine individuals standing outside the APC. "You don't have to wait, Professor," scowled Langlois. "The damn thing works."

NASA Director Leonetti was incredulous. "Those people... survived?"

His words were left unanswered, cursed by those who could offer no rebuttal. The indisputable visual evidence nullified any possible debate. General Stevenson took the remote in hand and cued another image. "This was taken by another satellite approximately three hours later..."

Another high-resolution digital image appeared. It was a night scene over the Hoover Dam, rendered from an obtuse angle. The satellite in question, an advanced KH-13, was tracking the area in an elliptical polar orbit that allowed for long dwell times over a particular target. By using low-light image intensifiers and electromagnetic spectrum enhancement, it was able to provide clear pictures at night even through dense cloud cover.

As the assembled members watched intently, events unfolded as before. The erupting geysers triggered audible gasps. Withering sighs accompanied each of the four helicopters after their explosive demise. They then leaned back in their chairs as the massive 300-foot wave struck the dam, sending the entire Army battalion into the darkened abyss. The haunting images left them speechless. Confounded by the eye and betrayed by the mind. Langlois came to his feet, pointing at the monitor.

"There they are," calling attention to a group of individuals on the near side of the dam. "Just standing there. They didn't run. They didn't even think about it." He paused for a bitter breath.

"After everything we've done. After all we've tried. They're alive." His voice suddenly thundered in rage. "They're still alive! What in the name of God are we dealing with?"

Professor Blau offered an explanation that was clearly at odds with his scientific background. "You may have answered your own question. It could be in the name of God."

He shook his head in confusion. "What are you saying?"

"Any statistician will tell you random chance can only last so long. For these people to have survived after all this, you'd have to be a fool to think there wasn't some sort of...divine intervention."

"Oh, please," rubbing his eyes in fatigue. "You're the scientist. I expected something better from you."

"I'm sorry. There is no logical reason."

"So, now we're chasing shadows? Fighting the boogeyman?" He sighed in exasperation, climbing upon an invisible soapbox of paranoia. "If there was a God, He'd be on our side, not theirs. We're the United States Government. We honor Him by holding our bibles high and shouting 'God Bless America'...and we don't even need His blessing. This is our world. Our domain. And, we control the lives of all those therein." He pointed back at the monitor. "Including them."

"Amen to that," added Admiral Holliman, providing an appropriate end to the demagoguery.

It was the sound of approaching footsteps that curtailed further discussion. President Susan Webber entered the room, flanked by six members of her Secret Service detail. Their robotic demeanor made it clear this was not a social call. The others rose to their feet from involuntary reflex.

"Madam President," stated Langlois, displeased by her presence. "How may we help you?"

Charles Wolff, head of White House security, promptly led the interrogation. "Secret Service Agents Glenn Marrero and Steven Yeager are currently missing. The President has informed us that one or more of you might have knowledge of their whereabouts."

Langlois' eyes drew thin, clenching his jaw as though biting through concrete. "You can inform the President that we know nothing about this. Furthermore, perhaps she'd like to use her prescient skills to explain what's happened to National Security Advisor Richard Stern."

Wolff approached, barely containing his ire. "I think it would be wise to show a little more respect...and be less dismissive with your tone." He turned to the other MAJIK-12 members. "What about the rest of you? Does anyone know what's happened to our agents?"

Negative responses were obtained from all. An oppressive silence took hold before the CIA Director restated his concern. "The question remains, Madam President. Where is Richard Stern?"

Webber was a consummate politician. It was well within her nature to lie. "Mr. Stern was confronted with evidence of his culpability in several egregious crimes against the Government. Instead of tendering his resignation as asked, he fled in disgrace."

Langlois sneered at her lame cover story. "Or, was eliminated. Perhaps your missing agents could shed some light on the situation."

The President approached him with resolve. She refused to show her emotional distress over Agent Yeager's disappearance, nor share the truth of Richard Stern's fate. "If you've done anything to them," her voice rich with threat. "I'll make sure you never take a breath in this world again."

Surprised by her bravado, he issued a veiled warning of his own. "Madam President, don't say things you may not live to regret."

The tense exchange was extraordinary, widening every eye in the room. Webber was convinced of their guilt, but had no substantive proof. She realized now was the time to strike boldly, without fear of consequence. "The Attorney General just tendered her resignation. She's been granted immunity from prosecution, in exchange for her testimony, as a material witness against the MAJIK-12."

He shook his head in denial. "I find that very hard to believe."

"She was present at every meeting," the President continued. "She witnessed firsthand your criminal conspiracies and cover-ups. Whether you believe it or not, you're about to be prosecuted to the fullest extent of the law." Webber secretly rejoiced, sensing a palpable wave of defeat washing over those present. "The MAJIK-12 is finished. Your reign of terror is over."

General Connolly blurted forth a rebuttal. "Madam President, what one might perceive as a reign of terror, could be seen by others as patriotism."

"I want nothing to do with your type of patriotism, General," offended by his remark. "Save your rhetoric for the jury."

Langlois was adrift in confusion. His lips fluttered, selecting a response only to reject it before the words were spoken. He moved toward her, causing Agent Wolff to interpose himself between the two. His voice found life, resonating with malicious intent. "You can't do this to us."

"On the contrary. It's already done," she insisted. The President turned to address them all. "Your White House passes have been revoked. I've instructed the Secret Service to escort you from this facility at once." She motioned for the agents to proceed. "I'll accept each of your resignations, effective immediately. Now, I have a Press Conference to attend. Good day, gentlemen."

Their departure was swift. The men stood outside the White House portico waiting for their limousines to arrive. Still seething in mutual humiliation, they agreed to share one vehicle to privately discuss their limited options. They entered the Joint Chiefs' stretch limo and informed the chauffer to drive them to 'The Club', a secure facility used by the MAJIK-12 on the grounds of Fort Meade, adjacent to NSA headquarters in suburban Maryland. After the privacy slide was raised, the members of the secret cabal began to foster a plot.

"There are seven of us here," Langlois declared. "We still have a quorum."

"As long as we're all in agreement," General Stevenson added.

Professor Blau issued a defiant snort. "What are we going to argue about? Who gets to go down the toilet first?"

Leonetti spoke with misguided concern. "Do you think we'll lose our pensions?"

"Pensions?" Admiral Holliman bellowed in disbelief. "Wake the fuck up, man! You're going to a Federal penitentiary."

"We're not there yet," cautioned General Connolly. "But, we have to take action. The longer we wait, the harder it'll be to fight back."

Defense Secretary Roth turned on the limo TV and adjusted the volume. The President was just assuming the podium for her nationally televised press conference.

"Haven't you had your fill of this bitch yet?" whined the Admiral.

Langlois rose up in his seat, holding forth a hand to quell the discussion. "No, let's listen. If she's going to sack us publicly, she'll do it now."

President Webber appeared most somber, trying to convey appropriate decorum as she addressed the nation. "Good morning. I'd like to make a brief statement before I take your questions. My fellow Americans, the devastation in Las Vegas, Nevada has eclipsed our darkest fears. It is, without question, the single greatest calamity in our nation's history. The city has been completely leveled. Fires are still raging out of control. The death toll will be in the hundreds of thousands. We cannot help those who have perished. They are now with God. But, we must turn our nation's attention, from one of shock and awe, to that of help and healing for the thousands left alive in the ruins. Food and potable water are in critical demand. Diseases, such as cholera and dysentery, are spreading. Medical supplies are urgently needed. Temporary housing has to be erected. Electric power and phone service must be restored. Americans have always risen to a challenge and I have no doubt we shall do so again. But, this disaster is so massive in scope, so horrific in scale, the Government cannot do everything that needs to be done. I have instructed FEMA and the National Guard to make arrangements for private citizens from across this nation to enter Las Vegas and lend whatever support they can. If you are a doctor, nurse, paramedic, policeman or fireman, we are asking for your help. If you are a construction or utility worker, carpenter, electrician, plumber or mason, your nation is calling you to duty. I am asking all Americans to donate as much blood as they possibly can to their local blood banks. Please provide whatever canned food and bottled water you can spare to your local Red Cross or charitable religious organization, so that your fellow countrymen may have a chance to survive. It is our sacred duty as Americans to put aside our petty differences and rally together in this effort, our most trying hour. With God's help, we shall prevail." She acknowledged the reporters before her. "I'll now take a few of your questions..."

"Good," Langlois stated in relief. "She didn't mention us."

"There's too much on her plate with the earthquake," Roth reasoned. "She won't announce our fate for a few more days."

General Connolly continued with the thought. "That buys us some time. We have to move...with all possible force."

The military men went silent, staring at one another, having arrived at a most radical and deeply troubling conclusion. Military honor was now in direct conflict with self-preservation. There was a sense of foreboding unease, a portent of the future unknown. In spite of their fears, they knew what they had to do. The date was the eighth of May, but it felt much more like the Ides of March.

NASA Director Leonetti expressed his naiveté, wondering why the discussion had ended so abruptly. "What is it? What are we talking about?"

Langlois understood, finding himself in total agreement with the unspoken decision. "It's about taking over the Government," he explained. "A coup d'etat."

"Oh, my God," cried Leonetti, his nerves on edge. "You can't be serious. You can't be. Murder's one thing, but...but this is treason. What makes you think we could ever get away with something like this?"

"We're the Joint Chiefs of the United States military," General Stevenson responded. "Once the President's out of the way, who'll be left to challenge us?"

He felt a cessation of breath, his amazement expressed in a single word. "Jesus." He looked over at Blau and Roth, neither of whom returned his incredulous gaze. "I don't want to hear anymore of this. We're in too much trouble as it is." He began twisting to the side, grasping at the door release. "I need to get out of here."

"You're not going anywhere, you spineless turd," snapped the Admiral. "You're in this as deep as we are. So, shut the hell up and do as you're told."

Defense Secretary Roth cleared his throat. "I'm afraid I also have a problem with this plan. Susan's family and mine go way back. She's been like a niece to me."

The CIA Director taunted him. "Well, isn't that sweet. Maybe you didn't notice, but she just threw you under the bus. I think it's fair to say that you don't owe her squat."

He nodded in acceptance of the fact. Langlois eyed DARPA Chairman Blau who had thus far remained reticent. "Any objections, Professor?"

He spoke, having plotted out every move in his mind. "If it has to be done, I want it done right. It's not just the President. We have to stop the Attorney General before she gives her testimony. I'm afraid it also means silencing our good friend at GG&E."

"Dr. LeClerke?" uttered Leonetti, in shock.

"With Dreamland destroyed, Pierre's become expendable. He could also be forced to testify against us. No one outside of this car can know what we know, or be aware of what we've done."

Without further debate, the seven came to an agreement. Nothing was left to chance. The President of the United States, Attorney General Ortiz-Bennett and Dr. LeClerke were now targeted for assassination. In order for the plan to succeed, the three could no longer be allowed to live. The military would take over the Government and declare Martial Law throughout the country. All that remained was to determine where and when.

The conspirators captured a stray sound bite from the President, still addressing the media on TV. "Yes, I'll be traveling to Las Vegas to personally survey the devastation. I intend to leave right after this press conference."

A decision was made. Without her knowledge, Susan Webber had rendered it for them. The decisive coup would happen during her trip out west. Las Vegas would not only be a graveyard for untold humanity, but for our democracy as well.

CHAPTER TWENTY-NINE

SIERRA VISTA, AZ. AND JUAREZ, MEXICO — MAY 8th

*A*s promised, Moses called the Padre Superior at the Nuestra Senora de Guadalupe Mission in Juarez. While mourning over the death of the Madre Superiora, the Padre shared some unexpected news. The Pope had previously scheduled a pilgrimage to Mexico to coincide with the birth of the baby. He was currently in Mexico City and requesting a secret audience with Mary Ellen's children at the Juarez Mission. The family agreed this was an opportunity that should not be forsaken. Enlisting the aid of a respected world leader such as the Pontiff would be enormously helpful in their bid to expose the events of Roswell. Forced to remain awake from Lucifer's insidious dreams, they informed the Padre they would make the six-hour trip to Juarez, arriving later that afternoon.

Major Osborne flew on ahead, making an unscheduled stop in the desert of southeastern Arizona. Fort Huachuca, home to the U.S. Army's Signal Intelligence (SIGINT) Center, was located along the Mexican border near the town of Sierra Vista. It was the military's main listening post in the Western Hemisphere, intercepting all telecommunications originating from Central and South America. The Deputy Garrison Commander, Captain Charles Parnell, was a long time friend of Osborne's, having served with him during Operation Desert Storm. While the Major's helicopter was serviced and refueled, the two engaged in light banter.

"Chuckster! How the hell ya doin'?"

"You're putting me in a bad spot, Oz," answered the wiry, 48 year old. "I'm supposed to arrest you on sight."

"So, why don't you?"

He flashed a rebellious smile. "Never could follow orders. Reckon that's why I'm still a Captain."

"I got a favor to ask."

"On top of gassing up this Huey you stole?"

"Yeah," came the sheepish response. "I need to hire about a half dozen mercs for a security detail in Juarez. They need to be the best, man. The absolute tits."

He furrowed his brow in thought. "You still read *Soldier of Fortune*?"

"Not as much as I used to."

"Last month they had an article on these three assholes...so crazy they got drummed right out of the SEALs. Formed their own little A-Team. They once rappelled into an active volcano for kicks. Sounds like your kinda guys."

Osborne was impressed. "Guess I just found me three cases of bad ass."

"I also know a couple of Mexican dudes that might help. I trained with them at Fort Campbell. They're bilingual and know that area inside out. They work with the DEA on occasion, tracking the cartel."

"Where are they now?"

"Not real sure. Let me check."

After obtaining a phone number from his office computer, Captain Parnell placed a call. The soldiers were currently assigned to the Fuerza Aerea Mexicana, Escaudron 110, in Chihuahua, Mexico. The air base was located approximately 230 miles from Juarez. Once the need to hire mercenaries was made clear, Capitan Primero Ramon Tejada and Capitan Segundo Jorge Garza negotiated their fees with Major Osborne over the phone. They were now in his employ. He made plans to pick them up at the air base on his way to the Juarez Mission.

Parnell dug out the copy of *Soldier of Fortune*, leaving a message for the ex-SEAL team to contact him as soon as possible. He agreed to relay any message if and when it was received. Osborne thanked his friend and departed without further delay.

The helicopter roared to life and executed a sharp turn toward the border. Flying nap-of-the-earth to avoid radar detection, the Major's Huey banked and swayed mere feet above the contoured terrain. The danger was not only from natural obstructions, but man-made objects such as towers and wires. This type of flight was mentally and physically taxing on a pilot, leaving no room for error. Fatigue soon became a factor. Once well within Mexican airspace, the chopper finally climbed to a less stressful level.

An hour and a half of boredom came to an end as he sighted the Chihuahua Air Base on the horizon. Much to his surprise, the field was small, only accommodating a squadron of Cessna 182s used for drug traffic surveillance. Two men stood alone on the tarmac, away from the aircraft hangers and Quonset huts. He set the Huey down nearby, allowing the men to board. They were each in their early-40's, with muscular builds and black, short-cropped hair. Osborne would have guessed they were brothers had one not been six inches taller than the other. The two introduced themselves in English, without the slightest trace of an accent.

"Major Osborne, I'm Captain Tejada. Glad to meet you." They briefly shook hands.

"I'm Captain Garza, sir. Hope we can help."

"I'm sure you can," noting their canvas satchels stuffed with firearms. "Strap yourselves in."

The helicopter again took flight, now on its final leg into Juarez. Major Osborne used the time to brief them on the nature of their assignment. They absorbed the news with a professionalism expected of their military training, but expressed disbelief over a stray revelation.

"The Pope?' stammered Tejada. "The Pope is coming to the

Mission? The Pope who's head of the Catholic Church? That Pope?"

Osborne nodded, amused by his choice of words. "The one and only."

The Mexican officers glanced at each other, awed at the prospect of meeting the Pontiff in person.

Mary Ellen's children arrived at the border crossing between El Paso and Juarez. After a brief discourse with Mexican Customs officials, they were granted entry into the country. The Major awaited their arrival outside the Mission, having coordinated the rendezvous via cell phone. His soldiers-for-hire were busy securing the helicopter at a nearby elementary school playground. Captain Garza's cousin was a caretaker at the site and promised to guard the Huey during their visit to Juarez.

Osborne pushed open the wrought iron gate, allowing the U.S. Government van onto church grounds. Benjamin and Roberta jumped out, racing each other inside with childish glee. The older siblings were less enthused, expressing their fatigue in a stream of colorful dialogue that was highly inappropriate given their current location. Hope had become fussy, alerting Shannon that a change of diaper was in order. She and the baby remained by the van while the others trudged up to the Mission entrance.

Moses led the group inside, first greeting the Padre Superior. Sisters Josephina, Diana and Victoria were one step behind, forming a tearful reception line. These were Maria Elena's sons and daughters. The babies they had placed up for adoption many years before. A cruel truth enslaved them all, stirring bittersweet memories. Her children had found their way home, but the Madre was now lost forever.

Names were exchanged. Physical gestures of welcome were rejected by the nuns in favor of a respectful bowing of the head, their hands clasped in prayerful tribute. The display of adoration was uncomfortable for the family, not knowing exactly how to respond. Some answered by nodding their heads in return. Others mumbled a brief greeting under their breath. They shuffled to the end of the line and congregated in a tight group within the main reception area.

Roberta was standing next to Sister Lupe, having already embraced her with a long and loving hug. Moses was happy to see that she'd fully recovered from her wounds. Two young nuns soon joined the others from the adjacent orphanage, replacements for the late Sisters Juanita and Alicia.

"This is Sister Carmen and Sister Raquel," introduced the Padre. "They recently transferred here from a convent in…"

His voice suddenly failed. Shannon stood in the entry, cradling the babe in her arms. The sight left them breathless as though a Renaissance painting had come to life, vibrant and full of color. For the Catholic faithful, this was a reverent moment. A holy scene, framed by an image everlasting. They fell to their knees in tribute, maintaining silence, refusing to look directly upon the child. The spiritual was now physical. Each of them truly believed they were in the presence of God.

Shannon appeared stunned by the reception, quickly striding past the genuflecting worshippers. Failing to understand their servile response, Roberta reached down to tug at her friend. "Get up, Sister Lupe. It's only my sister."

An embarrassed C.J. nudged Moses to action, having him end the heartfelt tribute. "Please, Padre," helping the elderly priest from the floor. "We appreciate the gesture, but we've done nothing to deserve it."

"You are above all others who have graced this Mission," he proclaimed, as the nuns also found their feet. "It is our honor to receive you. Make this humble sanctuary your own."

"Thank you, Padre. That's kind of you," C.J. replied, echoing the thoughts of the others. "When will the Pope arrive?"

"The Holy Father is holding an open air mass today at the Estadio Azteca in Mexico City. After he returns to the Basilica de Guadalupe, he will secretly fly to Juarez this evening. The Papal Nuncio said we should expect the delegation around 10:00 pm."

The Padre paused, noting his guests' obvious fatigue. "Perhaps, you'd like to take a siesta first. We've prepared quarters for each of you."

C.J. managed a weary smile. "We'd love to Padre, but we can't right now. It's a long story…" Muddled thoughts now betrayed his ability to speak in a coherent manner. "We just can't," his voice staggered onward. "Don't ask me why, but we've got to stay awake."

It didn't require a psychoanalyst to determine their faculties were being impaired from lack of sleep. The Padre was rightfully concerned, but chose not to pry further. "Well then, how about a cup of coffee or tea?"

Acceptance of the offer was swift and unanimous. The nuns broke formation, scurrying toward the kitchen to prepare the caffeine-laden beverages. The others followed in a slower gait, taking time to admire the ancient religious artifacts that lined the walls of the Great Hallway. They stopped to peer into the chapel, the Padre taking pride in discussing its reconstruction after the fire. The guided tour also stopped in front of the Madre Superiora's study. It was undisturbed, just as she had left it.

"Maria Elena saved many things," the Padre informed them. "Letters… photographs…all of which are still here. I once asked her why she kept these memories. She told me that one day her children might want to see them. I hope that day has come."

They appeared deeply moved by the disclosure. The group at last made their way to the kitchen, where the nuns served coffee and tea to the guests. Some took seats at the center table while others remained standing. Sister Raquel refilled Kevin's cup, sharing a furtive glance with the former NFL star. He then sidled over to Casey to engage in a whispered discussion.

"I hate to say this, but they've got some serious tail here."

His brother looked upon him, aghast. "This is a Catholic Mission. These are nuns."

Kevin delayed his response, attempting to rationalize his comment. "That's why I hated saying it."

Casey took a gulp of hot tea to quell a sudden spasm of amusement. The time was now approaching 4:30 pm and dinner had to be prepared. Sister Diana addressed the guests, asking if they'd like anything special to eat. She was assured that their scheduled meal of beef tamales, beans and rice would be perfect. As Shannon provided the baby with a bottle of warm milk, her siblings shocked the nuns by lending a multitude of hands in the kitchen. At first, they were surprised by the amount of food on display, but were reminded of the 26 children in the orphanage, a fact reinforced when they witnessed all of them march single-file into the adjacent dining hall. Dinner was served, with the honored visitors eating alongside the Mission residents. It had taken a few hours of adjustment, but Mary Ellen's children were now beginning to feel at home.

After dinner, the daughters of Mary Ellen congregated in their mother's study. They were in search, but for what they did not know. Maybe they'd find a window into the past. Perhaps, hidden truths would be revealed. Hopefully, emotional closure would at last be theirs. What they did experience was intense spiritual satisfaction, the ephemeral caress of their mother's touch. This was a chamber of love and there was no other place they wanted to be.

Roberta proved adept at locating the Madre's secret stashes of memorabilia. Yellowed newspaper clippings, magazine articles, personal letters, diaries and photo albums were spread across her desk for review. It became a journey of discovery, one which they all took time to savor.

"Mother wrote several letters to her priest in Roswell," informed Kimberly, as she sifted through decades-old correspondence. "She had him contact New Mexico Senator Carl Hatch to see if he could find out what happened to her family. He deferred the request to a State Representative who probed into the matter, before he was killed in a freak car accident…August 1947."

Such disclosures were no longer surprising. But, a letter written by the Madre to President John F. Kennedy in November 1963 raised collective eyebrows. "Mother warned him about travel," Barbara related the chilling details. "She said there were forces in the Government that were aligning against him. Apparently, he knew who she was and shielded her identity 'til the day he died."

"But, why didn't he listen?" Roberta wondered. "Didn't he believe her?"

"That's the problem," added Shannon, balancing Hope on her lap. "How does someone believe the unbelievable?"

More letters were read. Correspondence with former Popes, foreign dignitaries, philosophers and scientists were all addressed anonymously, but clearly expressed her passion and pain. Entries in her diary revealed the depth of her tortured soul. She agonized over the fate of her family in Roswell, day after silent day eating away at her heart. Their tears poured forth as she fondly discussed her children. How she sang to them safe in her womb and how she feared for their future. The adoption dates were circled in red, as if bathed in her blood. She prayed to God that she was doing the right thing, but her spirit suffered, receiving no solace. With each child taken from her arms, she begged their forgiveness, confident they would one day share this written account. Her daughters each had a singular thought, communing with the Madre through the power of mutual love. *Don't be upset, Mother. There's nothing to forgive.*

"It's like she's still alive," blubbered an emotional Kimberly. "Like I could reach out and hold her."

The baby cooed softly, stretching her tiny hands toward one of the albums. Shannon wiped a lingering tear and began scanning the black and white photographs within. There were pictures of their mother, before she and youth had parted. The images captured a beautiful girl, unable to shroud her fear. Mary Ellen's eyes were laden with concern, sporting a grim countenance, stripped of her ability to smile.

"This is so sad," observed Shannon, shaking her head. "She was still a child and had to bear the weight of an entire world. It wasn't fair. It just wasn't fair."

Echoing her sentiments, Barbara flipped further through the album. Before her were several faded pictures of a miracle. It was a tiny infant, her ebony skin pressed lovingly against the pale flesh of the Madre.

"Oh, my God," she cried, adjusting her eyes on the image. "It's me. It's...it's me..." She removed one of the photos from its cellophane housing, allowing the joy of this discovery to fully consume her. Tears soon flowed over her cheeks. "I never saw myself as a baby. I thought my life started when I was six months old."

Shannon burst into a nervous giggle, triggering the others to do the same. Before long, each had found visual evidence of their first days on Earth. They were now awash in a sea of emotion. Their voices carried freely, warbling with glee. Kevin appeared in the doorway, trying to determine a cause for their revelry.

"What's going on? Are you guys into the sacramental wine?"

Kimberly waved him inside, holding a photograph to his face. "Who do you think this is?"

He looked briefly at the infant's image and expressed ignorance. Assured that it was a picture of one-day-old Kevin Reese, he sought refuge in denial. "No way. I was never that small."

The phone rang in the Padre's office. It was the Papal Nuncio, sharing news that the Pope had secretly landed in Juarez and would be at the Mission within minutes. Although they'd anticipated this visit for some time, there had always been a chance he'd have to cancel. Any lingering doubts were replaced with a flurry of activity. Candles were lit throughout the sanctuary. An intricately carved, golden censer was prepared to burn granulated incense. The Papal Court of Arms and the flags of the Holy See were strategically positioned down the length of the Great Hallway and inside the chapel. After the Padre had slipped into his ceremonial robe, the vestry was readied for the Pontiff's use. Sister Diana began playing the new church organ, ignoring Benjamin's jealous frustration. She was quite talented in her own right, performing several advent hymns and Gregorian chant harmonies to set the desired mood. Major Osborne went outside to check on his security detail, alerting Captain Tejada and Captain Garza of the Pope's imminent arrival. Sisters Raquel and Carmen had agreed to split time watching the orphanage children, now asleep in their beds, so each could experience a brief audience with the Holy Father. The elder nuns assembled in the chapel. They worked efficiently, moving the priest celebrant's chair to a central location in front of the choir dais. The Madre's offspring assumed positions along two separate pews, but did not seat themselves out of deference to the guest of honor. An air of electric anticipation began to build, along with escalating heart rates. Palms were dried and breaths went shallow. Headlights soon flared through the stained glass windows. The Papal entourage had arrived.

Outside the Mission, two rented Land Rovers rolled to a stop on church grounds. The iron gates were secured and both Captain Tejada and Garza dashed over to open the vehicle passenger doors. Emerging from the first car were seven men, all middle-aged to elderly, none of whom were clothed in the traditional accoutrements expected of high ranking Catholic officials. It was evident that the party had been traveling incognito. Although darkness helped to cloak their features, one individual was instantly recognizable to the soldiers. They had seen his face countless times on television, newspapers and magazines as was appropriate for a renowned world leader. Overcoming paralysis, they fell to their knees in respect, each kissing the Pope's ring. He graced both with a silent blessing, then turned to Osborne who remained standing, a product of his mid-western Protestant upbringing.

"Hello, your Holiness." He offered a hand in awkward greeting.

Dispensing with decorum, the Pope smiled, graciously returning the gesture. The entire 14 member entourage was now ushered inside, while the astonished Tejada and Garza remained by the vehicles as sentry.

The Padre Superior welcomed the Pontiff, showing him

and the others to the Mission vestry. There they would have an opportunity to don ceremonial apparel that had accompanied them from Mexico City. After a few minutes of fevered activity, the party now looked the part. The Pope was clothed in sartorial splendor, his ornate vestments forcing every eye to widen. They were led through an anteroom and, sorting themselves by protocol, emerged through a side door into the chapel.

The candlelit sanctuary now became a grand stage with a performance bordering on the sublime. A single-file procession began with five monks, each wearing hooded, brown robes shrouding the occupant within. They were devout members of the Capuchin-Franciscan friars, a monastic order founded by Saint Francis of Assisi. The five kept their hands pressed together in prayer, stepping with purpose, in concert with the baroque music played by Sister Diana. At a prearranged moment, they turned to face the Madre's bewildered children. The monks then took two strides back and halted their march, as if part of a precision drill team. There they remained, stoic and immobile, while the others assumed positions in front of them. The lineup of Church dignitaries consisted of Monsignor Guiseppe Peluso, master of papal ceremonies; Cardinal Felix Morales of Mexico City, official host for the Pope's visit; Cardinal Jose Aquino, Vatican Secretary of State; Papal Nuncio Joaquin Sandoval, the Pontiff's traveling secretary; Dr. Franco Manneri, the Pope's personal physician and three members of the elite Swiss Guard, the Vatican security force.

Mary Ellen's children found it difficult to remain still, their anticipation getting the better of them. At last, the Pontiff entered the chapel to a chorus of subconscious gasps. His movements were fluid, walking toward them with an almost magisterial presence. Shannon, who was holding Hope in her arms, met the Pope's eyes and immediately came to ease. This was a warm and decent soul, one that she and her family could trust.

Instead of taking a seat to formally receive his audience, he broke with tradition and directly approached the Madre's offspring. What happened next sent shockwaves through the assembled faithful. Upon sight of the baby, the Pontiff dropped to his knees, clearly overcome with emotion. His sudden tears were genuine, some of which pooled onto the floor before them. It wasn't palsy that made the man shake, but a soulful reverence for the Divine. His mind trembled at the thought that resonated above all others. *God is now with us...*

He cupped his hands over Hope's head, never daring to touch. The proximity to the newborn imbued him with spiritual energy. It was a harmonious sensation of infinite love and contentment.

The Pontiff came to his feet, blessing his audience with sweeping hand gestures and a few hushed verses in Latin. At last, he addressed them in their native tongue. "This child is the Holy one," he proclaimed in awe. "The one foretold in scripture. The one destined to save humanity from itself."

C.J. took a step forward, making it clear that he was the family's appointed spokesman. "We appreciate this time with you, your Holiness. Your words were heartfelt and sincere. But, none of us warrant this kind of adulation. We're just not comfortable with it."

The Pope's voice quavered with passion. "Did your mother not tell you? Did she not share the secret of who you truly are?"

The inquiry caught C.J. off-guard, preventing a timely response. "We're aware of who she believed us to be."

"You are the Archangels," confided the Pontiff. "The Madre Superiora made the Word of God become flesh. How you came to this world and your purpose on Earth, were prophesized by the Blessed Virgin...Our Lady of Fatima."

Most of them knew the well-publicized story. Many years ago in Portugal, a trio of shepherd children had seen an apparition of the Virgin Mary. Three secrets were confided to them, two of which were eventually made public. However, the third remained a mystery and was deemed so apocalyptic, it was known only to a chosen few within the Vatican.

"It was disturbing and made little sense…until the events of Roswell." The Pope now sought to empower their spirit, speaking from a well of incontrovertible faith. "Do not doubt your divinity. You have been formed from the seed of God. Let His strength become your own. He provided you the breath of life for a holy purpose. Trust in Him and you will never fear your future."

The Major's attention was distracted by the monks' odd behavior. They glared at the family with stealth, paying no mind to the Pontiff's sacred plea. Ten hungry eyes devouring all they could capture, assimilating every sight, watching intently behind thick, hooded cloth. Osborne returned their stares, trying to understand what could possibly be of such interest. Their steely gaze was obsessive and resolute. He could sense that something wasn't quite right with these servants of God and decided to address the situation as tactfully as he knew how.

"Excuse me, your Holiness," pointing to the five. "But, who are these assholes?"

Although the others recoiled in horror, the Major remained unapologetic for his outburst. Kevin added to the dismay by whispering a few choice words to Casey. "Now there's a line I never thought I'd hear."

The Pope fell speechless, further compounding an already awkward moment. Hoping to spare the Holy Father the indignity of a response, the Papal Nuncio came to the monks' defense, chiding the Major with an acidic tongue.

"These men are from the Capuchin Order of Friars Minor and are devout servants of the Lord. They teach Jesuit studies at the University De LaSalle in Mexico City."

"They can't speak for themselves?" Osborne challenged.

He received a less than subtle rebuke. "It is part of their monastic code. They'd prefer not to say anything that would dishonor God in His house."

"Why are they hiding behind those hoods?"

Cardinal Morales smiled, aware that the Major was simply an uncultured heathen who didn't know the ways of the Church.

"For the Capuchins, wearing the hood is a sign of respect. In fact, they were invited to this gathering, for they have spent many years researching the events of Roswell and documenting the prophecies that have now brought us together. As a reward for their labors, we granted them the right to join the Pope's party in celebration of the newborn."

While the explanation left him wanting more, this was no time for a protracted debate. Osborne dipped his head in mock regret. "Forgive me."

The five acknowledged his courtesy, reciprocating the hollow gesture. But, their eyes remained restless.

If the Pontiff was offended by the Major's colorful vocabulary, he hid his resentment well. In fact, the needs of the baby were foremost on his mind. He again turned to C.J. to plead his case. "The safety of this blessed child is our utmost concern. There are forces in this world that will stop at nothing to harm her. Just as we provided refuge for your mother in her time of need, the Catholic Church is now offering a safe haven for the newborn. We respectfully ask that you place the infant in our charge. Let us provide for the care and security of the messiah."

C.J. craned his neck toward Shannon, curious as to her reaction. His sister's face swelled in cartoonish angst, wondering why it was taking so long for him to respond. Visibly amused, he turned back to their honored guest. "Your Holiness, that's a very magnanimous offer. One that I'm sure all of us appreciate. However, I'm afraid we can't accept."

"I assure you, she will want for nothing. We will give her our deepest respect and devotion."

"But, only we can give her the love she needs," C.J. countered. This time, he didn't have to check with Shannon. Her incandescent smile now lit the room.

The Pope paused, hoping the delay might give them time to reconsider. It soon became clear that there would be no change of heart. "Very well," he sighed in regret. "Please know that the Church stands ready to assist you, however we can."

C.J. saw an opening and took full advantage. "There is something you could do to help. For many years, the knowledge of Roswell has been kept from the masses. You have the power to change that."

Cardinal Aquino interjected. "Other Popes have faced this dilemma. They deemed it too radical a concept for the Holy See to embrace. The faithful might not be able to deal with such a startling revelation. It could destroy the Church."

Indignant, Barbara voiced her concern. "You call yourselves men of God? What kind of religion hides from the truth?"

"If you're so afraid of what might happen," C.J. added, "then perhaps you don't have the faith you profess."

The Cardinal was stunned by their bitter condemnation. Initially, anger flared over what he perceived as insolence. But, soon he felt betrayed by his words and humbled by theirs. The Pontiff was also moved, chiding himself for turning a blind eye.

"I will address this matter with the Roman Curia, our legislative body, upon my return to the Vatican," promised the Pope. "Hopefully, they too will see the wisdom in disclosing the facts. You have my assurance that I will do what I can."

C. J. smiled. "That is all we can ask, your Holiness."

The hour was late. After the Pontiff had blessed all in attendance, the delegation prepared for their return to Mexico City. The procession left the chapel in reverse order, with the monks exiting last. As the final friar approached the anteroom door, Major Osborne seized the initiative. He yanked back on the monk's pointed hood, exposing the person within. The subject was male, late 40's, with jet black hair and even darker eyes. His pupils dilated in silent fury, almost becoming weapons in themselves. It was a haunting image that would linger long after the hood was replaced. The encounter instilled a degree of anxiety in Osborne that he had not thought possible. There was something else. He felt a spiritual presence of incomprehensible evil.

As the monk left, Kimberly came to the Major's side, placing a gentle hand on his shoulder. "What was that all about?"

He paused in reflection. "Oh, I just wanted to see what we're going to have to deal with."

Approximately 20 minutes after departure of the papal entourage, the Major's walkie-talkie squawked with life.

"Tejada here, sir."

"Go ahead, Captain," directed Osborne.

"There are two individuals here by the Mission gate. They say they need to speak with the head of security."

"What about?"

"Don't know, sir. Both of them say they have information that you'll find useful. They don't appear to be a threat." A period of silence, as the situation was assessed. "Want us to get rid of them?"

"No, not yet. I'll be out there in a minute."

"Roger that."

As Osborne approached the perimeter fence, two men emerged from the shadows beyond, stopping less than a foot from the rusty metal bars. Captain Tejada brandished an Uzi 9mm automatic, keeping the weapon's muzzle elevated. He made brief eye contact with the Major, silently assuring him that he was prepared for any eventuality. The meeting took place with the four bathed in the pale yellow glow of an aging street light.

Osborne wasted no time gathering his impressions of the pair. One was older, perhaps by more than a decade, and his bald dome topped out a full head shorter. There was an aura of gamesmanship about him as though his very existence was dependent upon endless manipulation and deceit. The other appeared more refined, well groomed, with a tightly-cropped salt and pepper beard. He had the look of an intellectual. A scholarly, pipe and jacket type that would be the smartest person in any room.

The Major was mystified by this late night encounter. *Who the hell are these clowns? Government officials? Paparazzi? Papal groupies?*

"What do you want, gentlemen?" he inquired.

The older man spoke for both. "There is nothing we want. But, we have something that you may."

"And, that is?"

"Information. For example, the identity of those Capuchin Monks that accompanied the Pope."

Osborne had traveled extensively in the Middle East and detected tonal inflections in the man's voice, characteristic of a native Semitic speaker. "That accent of yours...Israeli?"

A counterfeit smile. "You have a finely tuned ear. We're on a special mission for our Government."

"Secret Service? Mossad?"

"Very good," confessed the man. "Well done, Major Robert Osborne, formerly of the United States Army. Fugitive at large on charges of tax fraud and embezzlement."

It was the Major's turn to smirk, aware he was confronting a particularly venomous creature. "Are you trying to threaten me, pal?"

"Not at all," came the specious reply. "I'm merely stating the facts."

A stream of sarcasm suddenly bubbled forth. "I think you have me at a disadvantage. You seem to know all about me, but for some reason, you're still quite the mystery. As head of security, that's not giving me a nice, warm woody."

"I believe we could solve that situation...by inviting us in."

Osborne's retort was immediate. "Absolutely not. It's late and I don't have the time or desire to run background checks on you." The Major's demeanor quickly turned dour. "So, why don't the two of you hit the road and forget you were ever here."

He turned, beginning his march back to the Mission. However, he froze when the younger man spoke. "Tell the Archangels, we're just trying to help."

A moment later, the gate opened and their entrance was granted.

After a thorough frisking, Osborne escorted the Israeli

nationals into the main reception area, ordering them to take a seat on a nearby couch. He gathered members of the Madre's family and explained the situation. Prior to approaching the men, Barbara pulled her brothers aside to recommend extreme caution.

"I've dealt with the Mossad before," warned the worldly diplomat. "These guys are shrewd. They're experts at disguising their true intentions. You can bet they want something in return."

"So, we shouldn't listen to them?" questioned Casey.

"I didn't say that. Just be careful. We could end up giving them more information than they give us."

Reaching agreement, the siblings grabbed chairs and formed a tight semi-circle in front of the pair. C.J. again took the lead. "Suppose you begin by telling us who you are."

The elder agent obliged their curiosity. "As I confirmed for Major Osborne, I am an operative for the Israeli Mossad. My name is Moishe Gehrin. Lieutenant Colonel Gerhin, at your service."

Several eyes now drifted to the other man. "And, you are?"

"We all possess multiple identities," he stated cryptically. "Here in the physical world, as well as the spiritual. I'm sure you've come to realize this."

C.J. feigned amusement. "Well, let's start with what they call you here on planet Earth."

"I do not have a given surname," he insisted. "But, if you require an identity, you can refer to me as Ariel."

"All right, Ariel. So, what do you know about the Archangels?"

He took the time to scan each member of the family. His inspection was exhaustive as though he were probing their flesh, peeling back layer upon layer until their inner essence was revealed. "I should not have to tell you that which you already know. You are the physical manifestations of Heaven's greatest spirits. The trusted warriors of Elohim."

"Elohim?" asked Casey, striving for clarification.

"In the Jewish faith, we have many names for the Creator. Some of which are so sacred, they must never be uttered by human voice. Elohim is a variant of the ancient Canaanite word for the Almighty." He paused while they digested the information. "Regardless of our religious differences, we all honor the same God. I am but His humble servant...and yours as well."

He closed his eyes, reverently bowing his head. C.J. was impressed by the man's erudite manner and what seemed to be his genuine piety. He now facetiously addressed Gerhin.

"Are you also our humble servant?"

"I serve only the Government of Israel," the man declared. "For the past 23 years, I have been their lead agent collecting secret intelligence on the Roswell crash and the shadow organization known as the MAJIK-12."

"We read about the MAJIK-12," Casey affirmed. "That and a lot more."

The disclosure ignited the man's interest. "You have a copy of the BLACK MAJIK data?"

Casey nodded his head imperceptibly. "On CDs"

"In a secure location," added the Major, just to discourage any wild ideas the Mossad agent might have.

"Then you possess something the U.S. Government will most certainly kill you for," Gerhin admonished. "Take the information and go public. It may be your only chance."

"We still need to go through it ourselves," confided Casey. "There were several codenamed programs: GRUDGE, TRINE, MOONDUST. What can you tell us about them?"

It was soon apparent that Gerhin was privy to much more than they realized. "GRUDGE was the name assigned to the covert program that hid the truth about Roswell. TRINE involved the back engineering of the craft in three key areas: metallurgy, propulsion and flight dynamics. MOONDUST involved the physical examination of the IBEs and analysis of how the human genome mutated from what it is today...to what it will become."

"Tell us about JEHOVAH," C.J. probed.

Gerhin leaned back on the sofa, exhibiting unease. "JEHOVAH was a concept, proposed by Albert Einstein. He correctly theorized that the events surrounding Roswell might cascade into a fourth dimensional paradox, disrupting the future timeline. Possibly even altering God's plan for humanity."

"Since July 1947, we all exist in a different reality," explained Ariel. "One that was never intended. With every decision made, with every choice selected, the laws of causality are creating new temporal paths, lines of confluence...even parallel worlds. Our concept of the space-time continuum is no longer valid."

The siblings eyed each other, wondering who would respond. Their bewilderment was understandable, due to the mind-numbing news and compulsory lack of sleep.

"So, you're saying the universe is screwed," warbled Kevin. "If that's the case, what are we supposed to do about it?"

"Well, that brings us to another secret program," continued Gerhin. "It was called Project Destiny. Using technology recovered at the crash site, the Government attempted to make contact with the future human race. In August 1963, they succeeded in this quest. Roswell wasn't their only visit."

His disclosure was of such magnitude, they could scarcely draw a breath. Random thoughts circulated amongst them. *How could this have happened? What the hell was the Government thinking? After what was done at Roswell, they went ahead and made matters worse?*

"Are you certain of this?" challenged Moses.

Gerhin sighed. "I'm afraid I am. Once the second contact was made, the Government proposed a fertilization program, purely for research. Several females were selected as breeding stock and rendered pregnant by the IBEs. They bore a handful of hybrid humans who possessed an extra pair of chromosomes, identical to your own genetic code. The U.S. Government raised these children in the thought they might be able to conduct psychological warfare against the Soviet Union. But, the experiment failed. The subjects went insane. Only one managed to escape and preserve his mental faculties. That person now sits before you."

Their gaze fell back on Ariel, who acknowledged them with

a humble nod. "Since my mother was Jewish, I decided to defect to Israel. I felt it was the only chance I had to hide from the Americans."

"What happened to the IBEs?" wondered Kimberly.

"They were held prisoner by the Government," Gerhin stated. "One actually survived ten years in military captivity. President Kennedy found out about Project Destiny and planned to go public with the evidence. He was assassinated for that very reason."

It was incredible. Though this revelation caught them off-guard, they knew it shouldn't have. Nothing the Government had done should surprise them. Their emotions ranged from anger to disgust. They were more convinced than ever that the truth about Roswell had to be exposed.

"So, why are you here, Ariel?" Casey inquired.

"We came to warn you. Those five monks that accompanied the Pope are not who they claim to be."

Major Osborne actually fist pumped the air, congratulating himself on his intuition. "How do you know this?"

He hesitated briefly. "Because they're the ones I grew up with. The ones who went insane."

An oppressive silence halted the conversation. C.J. struggled for his words, eyeing the man with compassion. "Why did they lose their minds, Ariel? What was it that came over them?"

He scrunched his face with a pained expression as he took a torturous look through the prism of the past. "I don't know. It settled upon us slowly. A kind of creeping malevolence. Changing our moods. Affecting our thoughts. I realized something wasn't right. At first, it occurred to me the Government might be conducting another psy-ops experiment, using us as human guinea pigs. But, this time it felt different. There was some sort of entity trying to force its way inside us. It scared me and I had never known fear in my life. Our only hope was escape. I tried to reason with the others, but they were too far gone. There was nothing else I could do. So, I ran like a coward. That was the day I lost my honor…but not my soul."

Barbara watched in empathy as a tear traveled past his cheek. Normally, it would be difficult for her to generate an emotional connection with a stranger, but Ariel's depth of spirit was remarkable. His anguish had somehow become hers. "Self-preservation isn't cowardly," consoling him. "But, it is human. You did what you had to do."

He regained his composure. "And, that is what I'm doing now. I felt compelled to be here. To reach out to you at this time."

C.J. fought the urge to yawn, his eyes red with fatigue. "How do you propose to help us?"

His demeanor changed, becoming less emotional and more focused on esoteric matters. "We are all special children, conceived by a paternal IBE. Our chromosome structure is different from all other humans. These extra strands of DNA are not without purpose. Their function is to allow the mind to open, revealing an alternate reality which you have yet to experience." He leaned forward, lowering his voice to reveal a secret. "If I were to tell you that you had the ability to manipulate space and time, allowing free movement within those constraints, would you want to learn how to develop that skill? Control it at will? Use that power…for the glory of Elohim?"

Their silence grew, strengthened by collective confusion. They looked at one another, sharing neither word nor thought. Did they just hear what they thought they heard? Was their sleep deprivation causing them to hallucinate? Sifting through a maze of abstract mental images, C.J. could only muster a vacuous response. "I don't understand."

Ariel attempted to explain. "The Roswell craft came from the future. Our fathers were able to warp space and time into a loop, known in quantum physics as a Closed Timeline Curve. This creates a wormhole that opens in three dimensional space. It allows physical matter to transit to another place or another time. Our fathers had this ability…and so do we."

Their empty stares slowly began to fade. At last, the message had been received and understood. In the midst of their personal

discovery, Kevin's cell phone rang. He answered gruffly. "Hello?...
Yeah, right. Whatever you say." He hung up with stunning
abruptness. "Just a crank," he explained.

"I ask again, would you like to learn how to use this power? If
so, I am offering myself as an instructor. A spiritual guide. I will
show you that the world you perceive is but a small part of a larger
reality. It is time for the Archangels to take the next step. Let me
lead you to your destiny."

A significant period of silence followed. Kimberly finally
addressed the family. "Well, I don't know about you guys, but if
there's something that'll give us an edge, I say we go for it."

Before the others could answer, Kevin's phone rang once
more. He was even less courteous this time. "Look, girl. Let me
give you the scoop. I'm sure we had some fun times, but it's over.
You and your vibrator have a nice life, OK?" He disconnected the
call, satisfied there'd be no further interruption.

"Who's trying to get hold of you at this hour?" asked
Barbara.

"Just some nutcase," he whined. "Must've banged her too
hard. Kept saying she was the President." Kevin quickly became
conscious of every eye upon him. "What? Wait a minute, you
don't think..."

The phone rang again, but this time the call was treated with
the serious attention it rightfully deserved.

CHAPTER THIRTY

FT. MEADE, MD. AND EL PASO, TX — MAY 9th

$\mathscr{T}$he MAJIK-12 conspirators embraced a bunker mentality. Alone in their headquarters on the grounds of Fort Meade, they bore the weight of their actions and dared not contemplate failure. The time had come to ignore Executive Order 47-142. They could no longer risk informing future Chief Executives of the Roswell cover-up, then be forced to assassinate them in endless succession. Only a military coup d'etat would ensure the MAJIK-12's continued survival. It would mean the death of yet another President and the termination of freedom in America. But, they reasoned such sacrifices had to be made for the collective good. *Didn't the end always justify the means?*

It occurred to them that this might be their final stand. In case the coup failed and the plot was uncovered, loaded handguns were placed on nearby tabletops left within easy reach. There would be no trial for treason. No apologies. No justice. They were determined not to be taken alive.

The seven had prepared for a lengthy stay, having fed their families official cover stories. Their high-tech lair was a gutted former officer's club, equipped with three wall-sized plasma displays; secure voice and data communications; real-time satellite tracking imagery; banks of computers linked to Pentagon and CIA mainframes; as well as enough food, water and purified air for 30 days of sustained living…all contained behind 18-inch thick, strike-hardened blast doors.

The plot had been agonizingly slow to develop. Frustrations flared with each passing hour, since time was not on their side. Every military base commander within 500 miles of Las Vegas had been contacted and each articulated the enormous logistic and support nightmare which they currently faced. President Webber had ordered the military to assist FEMA and the National Guard with the distribution of food, water and medical supplies for the Las Vegas disaster relief effort. As such, assets and manpower were spread too thin over too wide an area. The MAJIK-12 had no desire to attempt a premeditated attack upon the President without first securing the necessary resources to ensure success. The Joint Chiefs continued to work the phones, as they had for the better part of the past 24 hours, trying to cobble together a sufficient armed force from disparate units within the operational theatre.

Until now, fortuitous circumstances had protected President Webber allowing her to elude the MAJIK-12's grip of death. Air Force One was a Boeing 747-200B aircraft and required a runway length of 10,000 feet to safely accommodate landing and take-off procedures. The two Las Vegas airfields that met these requirements, McCarran International Airport and Nellis Air Force Base, were left inoperable due to the earthquake. Air Force One traveled to Reno-Tahoe International Airport, where the President met with the Governor of Nevada and other emergency management personnel. They boarded Marine One, the Presidential helicopter which had flown ahead on a C-5A cargo plane, and headed south toward Las Vegas to survey the damage from the air.

The horizon soon parted, casting them into the breach of Hell. The smoldering ruins of the great city left those aboard shivering in awe. Miles upon miles of devastation lay below, still shrouded by a wafting haze of smoke and particulate debris. It was impossible to fathom and equally so to ignore. Never had President Webber felt more helpless or doubtful of her ability to lead. She knew this was a pivotal moment in time, one that would determine how she'd be perceived by historians and the American people for generations to come. But, none of that mattered now. Her thoughts were reserved for the thousands of lives lost and the millions more who'd been physically and emotionally scarred forever. She briefly closed her eyes, trying to commune with a higher power, beseeching guidance from any possible source.

As they hovered above a crowded triage center, the President ordered the pilot to land the craft. Her Secret Service detail immediately objected, citing unsafe conditions on the ground and the possibility of contracting airborne disease. However, her insistence won out. The helicopter swooped down, coming to rest upon the ruptured asphalt of a shopping mall parking lot.

Wearing surgical masks, the official entourage disembarked and fell aghast at the scene. Medical personnel were hurriedly tagging the survivors, identifying those who could possibly be saved and the others who were too far gone. Surgeries were being performed without the benefit of anesthesia, using crude instruments that had yet to be sterilized. Screams of agony overlapped in a loathsome chorus, echoing through ubiquitous clouds of filth. Pools of congealed body fluids created an otherworldly stench, exceeding tolerance and belief. The survivors didn't know that the President was amongst them nor did they care. Nothing she could say or do would comfort them. Webber and her entourage reboarded Marine One, leaving these unfortunate souls in the hands of God.

That evening, the President addressed the media and spoke to the assembled Nevada State Legislature. Thwarting the MAJIK-12's plans, she accepted an invitation to stay the night at the Governor's mansion in Carson City. It was here where she called Kevin Reese, using the number written on the back of Agent Steven Yeager's business card. Overcoming initial miscommunication, she arranged to meet with Mary Ellen's children later in the morning at El Paso International Airport. Before fading to sleep, Webber caressed the card, stroking the paper with a loving touch. Until Yeager was found, this tangible object would keep him foremost in her thoughts, receiving her secret affection and concern.

The pressure was mounting. Unable to secure sufficient forces for the coup attempt in Nevada, the MAJIK-12 knew the attack had to occur no later than the President's return to Andrews Air Force Base in Maryland. They'd never get another chance if she made it back to the security of the White House.

It was 10:24 hours Eastern Time when General Stevenson was informed by his subordinates of an unscheduled deviation in Air Force One's flight plan to Washington. "They're stopping in El Paso," disclosing the news to the others. "E.T.A. 53 minutes."

"What the hell for?" Admiral Holliman whined. "Why in God's name is she headed there?"

CIA Director Langlois engaged in some mental gymnastics, attempting to transpose his thoughts with those of the President. The true purpose of her visit soon became clear. "It's not El Paso that interests her...it's Juarez. She's meeting them."

"Who?" Secretary Roth wondered.

"Who do you think?" nearly gagging on his words. "Those bastard kids. The ones who keep slipping through our fingers." A minor delay allowed additional reflection. "Has the Secret Service made preparations for a motorcade?"

"No," General Stevenson assured him. "The Presidential limo's on a C-5 headed back to Andrews."

Langlois surmised the unfolding scenario. "They're coming to see her aboard Air Force One. This just keeps getting better by the minute." Flashing a tenuous smirk, he addressed General Connolly. "That Field Commander at Fort Bliss...what the hell's his name?"

"Colonel Wright?"

He bobbed his head in recollection. "Get him on the line. They have less than an hour to get ready."

"What's your plan?" probed Roth.

For the first time in days, his smile brightened considerably. "General Stevenson, contact your people. Tell them to deliver a gift to the President...as a token of our love."

Susan Webber was embarrassed by her actions and conflicted by her thoughts. Since her visit to the triage center in Las Vegas, she tried to fend off a series of oppressive psychological effects. Feeling soiled by her exposure, three separate showers had done nothing to cleanse her concern. Visceral images still haunted her memory, but it was what she hadn't seen that caused her the most distress. The Presidential helicopter had landed in a pervasive mist, clouds of microscopic particles coating their clothes, hair and skin. She feared it was the vaporized remains of countless humanity. If so, no amount of bathing would separate the living from the dead. She'd become a part of them...and they her. The President's guilt was compounded by her relief at leaving the area. Webber had experienced the unspeakable horror for only a few minutes. The survivors were not so fortunate. They had no option to escape, trapped within a lingering miasma of disease and carnage. She chastised herself for being so preoccupied with her own well-being, that she could turn her back on the suffering of others. It was an all-too-human reaction, but one that shamed her nonetheless. *What kind of person am I? Why did I leave those people like I didn't care? Have I lost my principles...my sense of what's right and wrong? How can I get a nation to respond to this tragedy when I have trouble doing so myself?*

Tamara Sheldon, the White House Press Secretary, entered the President's private quarters aboard Air Force One, finding Webber adrift in self-doubt. Tamara was just three years younger than her famous aunt. Their familial relationship was no secret. In fact, the President had received ample criticism after appointing her niece to the post. The only daughter of Webber's eldest brother, Tamara was a former correspondent for a cable news outlet and had championed Susan's nomination as President Petersen's running mate years before. She was eminently qualified for the position, always maintaining a professional rapport with Webber despite their kinship.

Sheldon announced her presence by gently tapping on the door. "We'll be landing in a few minutes." Webber nodded, her expression set in stone. "Madam President, members of the Press would like to know why we're going to El Paso."

It was a question that had been anticipated. More surprising was the fatigue which forced her mind to labor. "Tell them...tell them I'm here to visit a sick relative."

"We don't have relatives in El Paso."

"You know that," she sighed. "But, I doubt they would."

A smile briefly emerged. "So, you want me to lie?"

"I want you to do your job," setting firm eyes upon her. "Don't forget the first rule of politics. Disinformation can be just as important as the truth."

Webber's niece had never been afraid to speak her mind. "Then, give it to me straight and I'll handle the rest."

The President allowed herself time to answer, lifting strands of auburn hair away from her neck. If she were to confide in her, then Sheldon would also become a target of the MAJIK-12. That was reason enough to remain evasive. "I have to meet some people... some special people I need to apologize to." She paused to sip some bottled water. "I'm sorry, Tamara. I really wish I could tell you, but I'd be dragging you into something you'd want no part of. Believe me..."

"Still trying to protect me, Auntie Sue?"

The long forgotten moniker rekindled childhood memories. "Well, us Sheldons have to stick together, don't we?"

Their smiles grew broader. "You know, I think you're amazing," Tamara confessed. "I've always looked up to you, but never so much as I did yesterday."

"Why's that?"

She spoke with a passion Webber had seldom heard. "My career's taken me all over this world. I've witnessed things no one should ever have to see. War...Famine...Terrorist attacks.

But, nothing could've prepared me for what I saw in Vegas. I don't mind telling you, I was scared. So was the Secret Service. Nobody wanted to be there. We wouldn't have blamed you for flying on and leaving those people behind. In fact, I was hoping you would. You had the courage to make them land. You forced us to experience the horror of it all. I wanted to run away and never look back. But, you showed us what was important. That no matter how bad things get, as long as there's life, there's hope. Now it's real for me. I can tell the rest of the world what has to be done. The aid will come. We'll get them the help they need. And, whoever's still alive after this, will have you to thank for it." She paused, left emotional by a random thought. "I think you're the bravest person I've ever known."

Humbled by the tribute, Webber opened her arms to receive her niece. They held each other as tightly as they could, basking in the sudden warmth. This was a treasured moment, one that allowed the President to shed any vestige of self-doubt.

The morning sky over West Texas was calm, but an air of electric anticipation soon gathered on the horizon. An imposing 747 jumbo jet glided in over the city, announcing its arrival at El Paso International Airport with the deafening roar of four GE Turbofan engines reversing thrust. Air Force One taxied off Runway 4/22 and onto a secure portion of the tarmac, adjacent to a perimeter fence. Within minutes, a 60-passenger articulated bus and a large refueling truck assumed positions astride the craft. Tamara Sheldon met with the three dozen media representatives in the rear seating area, informing them that, as a precaution, Air Force One had landed to check a potential mechanical malfunction. They were assured the on-ground delay would not exceed 60 to 90 minutes. Secret Service agents escorted the Press out the rear hatch of the plane and onto the awaiting bus for transport to the terminal.

The head of the President's traveling security detail was Agent Frank Delucci, a 22 year veteran of the United States Secret Service. Being a serious, by-the-book type, he had already expressed his concerns regarding Webber's secret rendezvous. The individuals she intended to meet had not been subjected to background checks nor had they been questioned in advance. In his opinion, this constituted an unacceptable security risk. He sought once more to change her mind, but could not overcome Webber's iron resolve. The encounter would take place as planned.

A car approached. The vehicle came parallel with the jet and parked beside the retractable stairway leading to the rear hatch. Two Secret Service agents escorted four individuals aboard, all of whom were received mid-deck. Although the visitors had already been thoroughly searched, Delucci ordered his men to repeat the process. Once cleared, they were led down a narrow hallway along the portside of the craft and ushered inside a surprisingly large conference room. The four were about to seat themselves when the President entered through a side door. Introductions were made. C.J., Kevin, Moses and Major Osborne, the family's designated representatives, were welcomed warmly and offered beverages of their choice. Black coffee was selected in a landslide vote. Having been awake for the better part of two days, they were unable to hide the physical effects of their sleep deprivation.

"Are you all right?" Webber asked, peering into C.J.'s hopelessly red eyes.

"Nothing a long night in dreamland won't cure." He smiled at her evident unease. "That's a joke, Madam President."

She was a good sport, honoring his refusal to directly address the subject. They were assuming their seats at the conference table when Kevin leaned over in awkward apology. "Oh, uh, Madam President...about that unfortunate vibrator talk we had last night. Maybe we could just, you know, forget that it ever happened?"

She nodded in amusement. "It'll be our little secret."

"Good," he blurted in relief. "Glad to hear it."

Their discussion began in earnest, with Webber taking the lead. "First, I want to offer my condolences on the loss of your mother. She was a remarkable woman. I'm saddened that I didn't have the chance to meet her."

The brothers remained silent, holding their tongues out of respect for the office she held. However, Major Osborne felt no such restraint. "I doubt she'd have wanted to do that, Madam President…seeing that the Government was trying to kill her for the past 60 years. Most people don't take too kindly to those who wish them dead."

"Gentlemen, I can assure you I had nothing to do with that," quickly setting the record straight. "The decision to target her and her family was made by a secret group in the Government, known as the MAJIK-12. I was made aware of their existence only three months ago…after they murdered President Petersen."

Webber stopped, closing somber eyes in the wake of her announcement. The world knew the facts of Petersen's heart attack late last year, but not the truth. Audible gasps were heard from her assembled staff and security detail. It was clear the cat was now out of the bag…and running like hell down the street. The President made a decision to disclose the rest of the story. "The MAJIK-12 tried to kill me, too. I took into my confidence Secret Service Agent Steven Yeager, who was the individual that shared information with you. Richard Stern, my National Security Advisor and a member of the MAJIK-12, threatened my life at gunpoint. In my defense, Agent Yeager shot and killed Mr. Stern in his White House office. He and Agent Glenn Marrero were disposing of the body when both went missing." She paused for a wave of emotion to pass. "It's my belief the MAJIK-12 had something to do with their disappearance. I don't know where they are. I wish I did."

Webber's final comment betrayed her true feelings, revealing a hidden agenda. C.J. was alert enough to realize that this situation had become exceedingly personal for her. "Did you confront the MAJIK-12 with your suspicions?"

The contentious altercation was still fresh in her mind. "I did so the other day and they denied involvement. But, the good news is they'll no longer be a threat to anyone else."

"What does that mean?" asked Moses, perplexed.

"The Attorney General, who's also a member of the MAJIK-12,

has agreed to testify against the others. The Justice Department will be prosecuting all of them to the fullest extent of the law," visibly delighted at the prospect of their fate. "In light of this development, I demanded their immediate resignations. Soon, the MAJIK-12 will be nothing more than an insidious footnote in history."

Major Osborne perceived her as being a bit too naive in regard to who she was dealing with. "Madam President, can you confirm that members of the Joint Chiefs and CIA are still part of the MAJIK-12?"

"They are indeed."

He expelled a sigh of dramatic length, hoping to impress her with appropriate concern. "These are serious people, Madam President. They don't respect our laws or freedoms. They don't have to. The only thing they care about is survival. These are men drunk with power and they'll do anything to keep it. Now, you've backed them into a corner. Do you really think they'll just bend over, so you and the Attorney General can have your way with them?"

She smirked at the mental image. "I don't think I'd put it quite that way, Major. However, I do appreciate your candor. This isn't about power. It's about justice. Justice for Mary Ellen Hart and the hundreds of others who've been terrorized or killed by the MAJIK-12. It's got to end...and with God's help, it will."

Agent Delucci was stationed in the hallway just outside the conference room door. From his position, he noted four individuals descending the spiral staircase from the flight deck. The military pilot and co-pilot, flight engineer and communications officer assigned to Air Force One were now leaving their posts in apparent haste.

"Hey! Where do you think you're going?"

They did not respond, completing their march to the hatch and egress from the jet. Delucci peered out a side window, watching the four enter a military Humvee which had been driven up within feet of the craft, without authorization. The vehicle swiftly departed, soon leaving his sight.

Another agent dashed through the hallway, approaching from the aft section of the jet. The news he imparted sent collective chills through the assembled security detail. "The running back's gone."

It was their designation for the military aide who carried the football, the briefcase that contained attack codes in the event the President was forced to launch a full-scale nuclear response. His job was simple. His orders inviolable. He was to stay with the President at all times...and at all cost.

"Are you certain?" asked Delucci in disbelief.

"Sir, I've checked everywhere. He's not on board."

Those in the conference room had turned to the topic of disclosure. How and when the President planned to tell the American people what actually happened in Roswell. She was in favor of holding a joint news conference, inviting Mary Ellen's children to be present. It was a wonderful idea. An idea which would never be allowed to materialize.

The Major looked out a side portal and took note of several military vehicles now approaching Air Force One. The Army jeeps and half-tracks broke formation, assuming stationary positions at various points along the runway and aircraft taxiways. Their intent was clear. The jet would not be allowed to take-off.

Osborne bolted from his seat without apology. He strode into the hallway, grabbing a surprised Delucci by the arm. "Take a look at this."

They returned to the conference room, squatting down beside the nearest window. The military activity outside was evident and undeniable. At first, Delucci wanted to dismiss it as nothing more than an Army contingent protecting the Presidential aircraft. But, the swarm of heavily-armed soldiers and the strategic positions in which they were currently deployed left him quaking with anxiety. Osborne did nothing to allay his fears, whispering ominous words. "This has all the makings of a coup."

Their eyes met in common horror. It was a scene right out of some third-world military dictatorship. Agent Delucci tried to grasp the meaning of it all. *This can't be happening. Not here. Not in the United States of America. Who the hell ordered this? What in God's name are they planning?*

An answer to his quandary soon presented itself. A flare of concentrated light, aimed directly at the jet, captured Osborne's attention. The beam originated on a hilltop overlooking the airport, spanning a distance of approximately a mile and a half. He now understood why the soldiers had not approached the craft. It was an intuitive moment, a revelation that made his voice tremble with urgency. "That's a laser target designator. We're getting lit! Trust me, we're about to have a very bad day."

Moses responded at once, jumping up to join the Major. Agent Delucci sprung to action, physically lifting Webber from her chair. "I'm sorry, Madam President. We have an emergency situation. You must leave Air Force One immediately."

"What's going on?" Kevin barked.

Shrieks of panic now echoed through the cabin. Two other agents converged on Webber, shoving her down the hallway toward the aft section of the jet. Trusted aides and administration personnel were forcibly cast aside, cleared from the President's fevered path. For the Secret Service, the only thing that mattered was getting the Client to safety.

Osborne dashed from the room, motioning Moses to follow. "Let's take the cockpit!"

"What's up, Major?" wondered C.J., receiving no answer.

Now alone, Kevin looked at his brother in dismay. "Ever get the feeling they know something we don't?"

Trying to focus through the flurry of activity, the President remained incredulous. *How could I have been so stupid? As long as they're alive, they'll never quit.* She knew this despicable plot would stain the nation forever. Webber did not fear for her life, but for her country. If she were killed, the truth would almost certainly die with her. *I have to tell the people. They have to know. They have to know now...*

Her security cordon arrived at the rear hatch. Beyond them lay the retractable service stairway, 36 steel steps separating them from the tarmac. Parked feet from its base was the car that had delivered Mary Ellen's children to Air Force One. The keys were still inside. Though tantalizingly close, the required distance to shepherd the President to safety made Delucci cringe. Army sharpshooters had taken up positions outside the craft. By the time they could escort her to the vehicle, Webber and her security detail would be shredded by gunfire. One agent volunteered to go alone. He would attempt to get the car into a tactical defilade position, blocking the shooters' line-of-sight and thereby increase their chance of survival. The desperate attempt was fraught with peril, but there seemed no other choice. Delucci made the difficult decision, wishing his subordinate luck. Summoning reserve courage, the agent heaved a breath and vaulted down the steps. A hail of bullets greeted him midway, forcing a retreat. The agent's legs collapsed, receiving fire from different angles. President Webber was spun down onto the deck as Delucci laid his body over hers in a textbook defensive display. Left incapacitated on the stairway, the agent screeched forth with unrelenting anguish. Two of his comrades ignored the danger and swooped to his aid. Cradling his blood-soaked flesh, the three ascended the steps and re-entered the jet in breathless terror. They sprawled him upon the floor, his body convulsing in agony. Six high-powered rounds had passed through his lower extremities, one of which had severed his femoral artery just above the right knee. The others quickly tore their shirt sleeves to use as tourniquets while blood pooled about their feet. Delucci, still smothering the President, gasped at the scene.

"How is he?"

"Bad!" an attending agent responded. "He's losing a lot of blood. Could be going into shock!"

"Try and stabilize him," Delucci ordered. "We'll get him to a hospital as soon as we can."

A third agent cried out in confusion. "What the fuck is going on? Those are our guys out there! U.S. Army soldiers! They could've killed us!"

"Containment fire," surmised Delucci. "They're trying to keep us from leaving the plane."

"What the hell for?"

The answer was too terrible to contemplate. High above them, at an altitude of 16,000 feet, an F-117A Nighthawk had just released a 2,000 pound, laser guided bomb. The GBU-15 fell through the morning sky, locking onto the laser energy received from the hilltop ground source. Guidance canards attached to the front of the warhead acted as flight control surfaces, allowing the weapon to maintain its deadly track. The target was Air Force One. Those aboard were now trapped inside a military gauntlet, with two chances to die and none to live.

As Delucci braced for the inevitable, he detected a mystifying aural whine. The jet's massive engines began rousing from their slumber. He had seen the pilots leave and was at a loss to explain the activation.

"Who's at the controls?"

The turbines powered up, slowly at first, finally intensifying to a definitive roar. Air Force One suddenly lurched forward, dragging the retractable stairway along the tarmac. A shower of sparks flew as steel greeted asphalt. The generated noise was shrill, leaving every ear in distress. However, this would be a minor annoyance in comparison to the spectacle about to transpire.

The hilltop target designator had been locked on target, lasing the 747's hull. When Air Force One moved out of the way, the refueling truck flanking the jet was unintentionally lit. Before Army spotters could redirect the beam, the GBU-15 made a last-second adjustment and deftly split the truck in two.

An orgy of sight and sound now terrorized their senses. The generated fireball bloomed wide, claiming an area 300 feet in diameter and elevation. Yards of tarmac heaved upward, producing a crater of indeterminate depth and filling the sky with jagged chunks of debris. A sonic concussion of ear-shattering force accompanied the explosion, felling everyone in a half-mile radius. Remains of the fuel truck, which had catapulted skyward, rained down upon the jet in a torrent of burning shards. Secret Service agents ducked their heads as bursts of flaming gas climbed the stairway and channeled through the open hatch. Secondary fires ignited within the cabin, scorching seats and window curtains. Nearby extinguishers were quickly secured. The President remained motionless underneath Delucci, his body seemingly fused to hers. Both of them were awed by the attack, lost in a squall of incomprehension. As particulate matter continued to strike the hull, the clatter of automatic weapons fire began peppering the aircraft. As a safety precaution, Air Force One had been designed with thin plates of Kevlar insulation, making the jet bulletproof. This engineering foresight was never more appreciated than now.

Delucci staggered to his feet, depressing the switch that would close the hatch and retract the stairway into the plane. The mechanisms were undamaged, functioning as normal. He returned to his charge, this time lying prone next to her. "Madam President, are you all right?" She nodded, still in shock over the attempt on her life. "Stay down," stressing the importance with a firm hand on her back. "We're not out of this yet."

Seated inside the cockpit, Osborne and Moses assessed the situation. The runways were blocked. Smoke and debris continued a slow separation from the air around them. Army sharpshooters scattered for cover, not having anticipated this operational scenario. One particularly pesky soldier stood in front of the moving jet, firing his handgun as if he alone could stop them. The Major knew this type. A junior officer thinking he'd impress his superiors with a misguided Rambo-like mentality.

Moses remained dumbfounded by the idiot. "Want me to shoot him?"

"No, I'll handle this..." Osborne throttled up, significantly increasing their forward speed. The jet's nosewheel cleared the obstruction, rocking them briefly.

"Ooooh," groaned Moses. "That'll leave a mark."

The 747 had little room to maneuver. Trying to plow through the Army fortifications could damage the craft to the point it would no longer be capable of flight. Still, something had to be done. Osborne noted a squad of soldiers preparing to fire a barrage of Rocket Propelled Grenades at the jet.

"We've got incoming RPG's at our 8 o'clock!" the Major announced. "This thing's equipped with countermeasures. Find them and deploy!"

Moses frantically searched the controls before him, spun from his seat, and at last located the countermeasure release above the Flight Engineer's console. With decoy flares and clouds of chaff now dispersed in their wake, Osborne made the only decision possible. He leaned forth on the throttle assembly, bringing the engines to full power. Air Force One swung hard right, heading straight for the airport's perimeter fence.

"Oh, shit," Moses sputtered, bracing for collision.

The Major sighed. "I always wanted to see El Paso."

What had become a surreal scene soon escalated into a major hallucinogenic event. The jumbo jet hurtled a five foot berm and crashed through the metal barrier with hardly a scratch. Motorists along Airport Road, the street separating El Paso International from Fort Bliss, ditched their cars into grassy culverts, shaking in awe as the craft's massive wings roared over them.

The first salvo of RPGs took flight, blossoming in explosive hues. Some detonated within the airborne chaff, others chased flares twisting harmlessly across the tarmac. A second wave was launched. They left trails of arcing tailfire as the weapons gained elevation and distance. Passing the countermeasures, the RPGs entered the 747's turbulent jetstream, the engine backblast forcing them to veer off into surrounding road signs and structures. When the craft adjusted its course down Airport Road, the angle of attack became less difficult for the shooters to target. A third volley was ordered. The RPGs raced through the sky, desperate to stop the fleeing jet. Most fell short, some detonating near cars parked along the roadway. But, two missiles found their mark.

One, a glancing blow on the outer port engine nacelle, did not cause appreciable damage. The other hit with devastating impact, breeching the rear flight deck where the craft's communications network was housed.

An explosive concussion shook the cockpit, caving in the access door. Moses, still standing at the Flight Engineer's station, was propelled violently into the console and collapsed in a semi-conscious state. A wall of fire swept through the flight deck, causing Osborne to shrink further in his seat. Outside air funneled through a gaping 38-inch hole in the cupola, fanning the conflagration to an even greater degree. In seconds, the communications area behind the cockpit was fully involved in flame. Osborne slid open the side windows, allowing acrid smoke to vent. The Major did not have time to fight the fire. He kept his hand firmly on the throttle, aware that every second placed more distance between them and a military execution.

Half a continent away, the remaining members of the MAJIK-12 were watching the events unfold in El Paso. High definition digital images, taken from a satellite in geosynchronous orbit, were displayed on the central screen. General Stevenson had ordered subordinates at the National Reconnaissance Office to re-task the satellite, placing it 22,300 miles above the city, allowing them to obtain visual confirmation of Webber's demise. General Connolly had briefed Colonel Gregory Wright, the Fort Bliss Field Commander, on the situation. He informed him that a heavily armed group of Al-Qaeda terrorists had commandeered Air Force One and planned to crash the jet into the White House after refueling in El Paso. General Connolly cautioned Wright that the President was most likely dead and the aircraft could not be allowed to leave the ground. The Colonel cooperated fully with his superiors, directing the Army response. Never once did he question such a lame cover story. Never did he wonder why these orders were coming directly from the Joint Chiefs and not through the normal chain of command. He could have recognized the plot for what it was, but was blinded by duty. The MAJIK-12 could not have found a more perfect and willing stooge.

As they watched the bomb miss its intended target, their prideful arrogance morphed into full-scale panic. Obscenities and epithets poured forth. But once Air Force One left the airport and began roaming the streets of El Paso, their mood could only be described as one of wrathful incomprehension.

"Jesus Christ! The plane's left the field!" Admiral Holliman screamed. "Who do you have in charge down there, Colonel Klink?"

General Connolly had a headset on, holding up his hand in a bid for calm. "I have Colonel Wright on the line. He says he's handling it."

"From where I'm sitting, he's not handling shit!" railed General Stevenson.

"This is a nightmare," mumbled Secretary Roth under his breath.

CIA Director Langlois pointed helplessly at the screen, watching in horror as the jet lumbered through a major El Paso intersection. The jaw-dropping imagery rendered him incapable of verbalizing his dismay. NASA Administrator Leonetti and Professor Blau sat at a table across from each other, eyeing their instruments of suicide, wondering who would opt for the first bullet.

The conversation continued between General Connolly and the Field Commander. "We're looking at it right now, Colonel…Yes, we have real-time visual…" A lengthy pause. "You were ordered to keep Air Force One from leaving the airport…What difference should that make?...It did take off, right down the street...What do you mean I wasn't clear?"

Langlois went ballistic, physically snatching the headset from Connolly. "Now you listen to me, Colonel Fuckhead! We've had enough of your shit! Destroy that plane right now or I'll shove a grenade up your ass, along with your wife's, your son's, your daughter's…and your little dog, too!" Breathless from his tirade, he flung the headset across the room in full-foaming rage. "Holy fuck! Why does every moron in the world end up working for the U.S. Government?"

The flames were getting uncomfortably close to the cockpit. Excessive heat and smoke sapped Osborne's strength, making it difficult to breathe. Air Force One escaped further attack, now safely beyond range of the Army RPGs. Whatever danger remained, apart from the raging fire on the flight deck, was limited to the innumerable utility poles being claimed by the craft's nearly 200 foot wingspan. Oncoming traffic proved to be no obstacle as every vehicle yielded to the jumbo jet's unquestioned dominance of the roadway.

Having compromised his safety by remaining in the cockpit, the Major's actions helped ensure the survival of everyone aboard. His courage was rewarded when he heard fire extinguishers creating a commotion beyond.

"Hurry up! It's getting toasty in here!"

A few more extended blasts of compressed gas and the flames faded from view. Appearing behind him were an incredulous C.J. and Kevin.

The relief in Osborne's voice was genuine. "Glad you could join the party."

"I don't remember getting invited," retorted C.J.

Kevin appeared disoriented by the maze of strip malls and fast food joints slipping past the window. "Where the hell are we?"

"That's a damn good question," the Major admitted. He pointed to their brother on the floor. "Wake him up. I need directions."

Moses was welcomed to reality by the icy breath of a fire extinguisher. He roused quickly, with Kevin helping him to his feet. "You know the rules. If we can't sleep, neither can you."

Gaining his bearings, he winced in pain from a welt rising beneath his scalp. He staggered forward and expressed shock. "We're still moving?"

Osborne reiterated their need. "Look, you know this town. Which way to the border?"

Peering out the windshield, Moses assessed their position. They were on Montana Avenue, fast approaching the junction with East Paisano Drive. "Hang a left here."

The Major responded quickly, but the 747 took longer. The craft went wide in the turn, taking out a city bus enclosure, two park benches, an information kiosk and four separate traffic signals. Vehicles scattered wildly, seeking salvation at any cost. A police officer witnessed the mayhem but did not pursue, perhaps believing the President had the right of way.

Reality began to crystallize when Moses spotted a highway overpass looming ahead. Interstate 10 snaked its way through El Paso on an elevated roadway, effectively bisecting the city. Travel between the airport to the north and southern border crossings required passage underneath the highway. At no point along this route were clearances sufficient to accommodate a 747. Moses knew something had to give. "I'm afraid we've got a problem."

Kevin snorted in sarcasm. "About damn time. Been close to 15 seconds since the last one."

Their dilemma was clarified. Osborne forced a breath of resignation, once more reaching for the throttle. "Well, since we can't go under it..." If the Major said anything else, it became lost in the aural signature of full engine thrust.

"I'm not sure I like this," C.J. mumbled, preparing for the added mayhem.

Air Force One accelerated into a looping right turn. The intersection of East Paisano and Gateway Blvd. bloomed with chaos as the craft bounded over a concrete sidewalk and entered the outer third of a service station parking lot. The right wing took out an 80 foot signage post along with a main support stanchion, caving in the roof over the fuel pumps. Cars willingly careened into each other, appearing to huddle in fright. Two unlucky vehicles were captured within the engine backblast, briefly taking flight into the side of a semi.

Making a slight course correction, Air Force One cleared the I-10 ramp abutment, shredding its landing gear tires on the starboard side, and began to ascend the elevated portion of the Interstate. The massive left wing was now pinned underneath the overpass deck, 60 feet of which was sheared off upon its engagement with a concrete pier support. Twisted debris rained down onto the roadway below, cascading into stalled traffic. A small fire ignited along the truncated edge of the wing assembly, but was extinguished when Osborne shut off the fuel injectors to the missing engine. The crippled jet forced three slower vehicles from its path and, at last, entered the Interstate. A spontaneous ballet of cars and trucks commenced, their brake lights lit in panic. A pair of semis jackknifed then rolled onto their sides, two steel whales beaching themselves on the asphalt. Oncoming traffic was snarled behind, reducing congestion along the highway. The Major fought with the wounded craft, having to compensate for the extensive damage. An exit for the I-110 spur was ahead.

"Take this," Moses suggested. "It'll bring us to the Cordova Port of Entry."

As the 747 merged onto a flyover ramp, Agent Delucci entered the cockpit, gun in hand. "All right, you maniac. Stop this plane now! You're destroying Government property!"

His intent was clear. He was merely trying to reclaim the tattered remnants of his authority, but Moses would have none of it. The Army Ranger reached back, easily appropriating Delucci's sidearm with a slick martial arts maneuver. "This maniac just saved your sorry ass! Next time, show a little more respect."

The agent, now stripped of his weapon as well as his pride, slinked away in awkward silence. Moses kept the gun, planning to present it to Osborne as a treasured memento.

They soon arrived at their destination. The highway spur terminated at the international border, just yards in front of the Cordova foot bridge into Juarez. Air Force One rolled to a stop, its remaining engines powering down in a blissful chorus of relief. The four vacated the flight deck, meeting up with the others in the rear cabin.

Osborne shook Webber's hand, noting the lost expression on

her face. "It's been a real pleasure, Madam President. Sorry about the plane."

He brushed past her, activating the retractable stairway and fleeing to the ground below. Moses and Kevin followed swiftly, the latter offering a word of encouragement. "You got my vote, lady."

C.J. paused for a more serious thought. "For what it's worth, Madam President, I believe you. I just hope you live long enough to do what you've promised."

Her eyes came to his, showing firm resolve. "Mr. Hightower, you have my solemn vow that the American people will be told the truth."

They shook hands and C.J. departed. Delucci sent his men to flag down a vehicle, so they could rush the wounded agent to a local hospital. Tamara Sheldon approached Webber, placing arms around her aunt in a loving hug. They soon separated, in deference to their sense of professionalism.

"What would you like me to do now?" her Press Secretary asked.

"Contact the nearest TV affiliate. Tell them I wish to make an emergency address to the nation."

The President had reached a decision, but so had the MAJIK-12. They would stop at nothing to prevent her from making such a disclosure. The Joint Chiefs were already plotting another response, one that would bring the full force of the United States Military to bear…and quash the truth from becoming known to all.

CHAPTER THIRTY-ONE

*A*fter crossing the border, they hailed the nearest taxi. Nothing was said during their return to the mission, as each allowed their pounding heart to speak for them. The four knew all hell was about to break loose. What they didn't know was how swiftly it would be upon them.

They arrived to witness a scene of frenetic activity. The mission grounds had become a theatrical stage with their family part of a supporting cast. Shannon had the role of lead actress, portraying her angst with a series of awkward gestures, spinning about in hysterics.

The men sprang from the cab, injecting themselves into the melodrama.

"What is it?" C.J. bellowed.

Fighting for composure, his sister flung angry tears from her face. "She's gone!"

"Who's gone?"

Shannon gasped for breath. "Hope! The baby…she's gone!"

Incredulous, C.J. fell tongued-tied, stumbling through a series of painfully obvious questions. "Gone? How? When? Who took her?"

"Roberta!" she sputtered forth. "It was Roberta!" Her distress once again intensified. "Why, God? Why?"

The others, less despondent than their sister, shared what little they knew. Barbara had advised Roberta to take a short nap after seeing her nearly collapse down a flight of steps. The girl agreed, but only if they'd lock the door to her room, so she wouldn't be in a position to bring harm to the baby. An hour later, they discovered the broken latch. Roberta had apparently slipped into Shannon's bedroom and snatched Hope from her arms while she and the infant slept. The girl's clothes and suitcase were missing. A baby stroller had been taken from the orphanage. Connecting the dots became a relatively simple task.

The abduction caused C.J. to shudder in fear. He knew all too well the strength of Lucifer's manipulative dreams. How incredibly potent the nightmares could be. The virgin mind of a 14 year old would provide a fertile landscape to harvest His malevolent intent. Lucifer was forcing Roberta to do His bidding, compelling her into actions which she'd normally never contemplate. *Would she be able to fight His subliminal suggestions? Could she prevent herself from harming her baby sister?* C.J. shut his eyes, unable to find mental solace. The situation was grim. Every second counted. They had to stop her before the inevitable occurred.

Shannon and C.J. embraced one another, lost in collective concern. "Try not to worry," he comforted her. "We'll do whatever it takes to get them back."

The Major questioned Captain Tejada and Garza. They had seen Roberta with the baby, but had never been ordered to prevent those already inside the mission from leaving. Osborne silently cursed his oversight, probing their recollection of her departure.

"It was about 20 minutes ago," Tejada explained. "She walked out with the stroller. I didn't think much of it until I saw her get in the cab."

"What cab?"

"About three blocks down," pointing south of their position. "She took the baby from the carriage and jumped into the taxi with a small suitcase. That's when I informed the Padre."

As the family trudged back inside, the Major eyed the mission's bell tower. "Captain Garza, I need you to take up position in the belfry. Monitor the border crossings. If you spot anything out of the ordinary, any kind of military presence, contact me immediately. Understood?"

"Yes, sir." He scampered off to assume his post.

"Captain Tejada, watch the skies. Be on alert for any kind of aerial reconnaissance or military overflight. I want to know as soon as possible."

The officer acknowledged his orders, responding with a query of his own. "Expecting trouble, Major?"

Osborne set his steely gaze on the border. The distance seemed to shrink before his eyes, now appearing closer than ever before. "Captain, I think you can damn well count on it."

Inside the mission, further investigation was yielding other clues to Roberta's plans. Sister Lupe searched the girl's bedroom, noting that the money she'd been saving for a trip to the Pan Am Games was missing.

"It was the only thing she cared about," explained the nun. "We were certain she'd medal in gymnastics. The church even sponsored a bake sale to help raise funds."

"How much had she collected for the trip?" inquired Kimberly, wondering about the extent of her resources.

"Over 10,000 pesos," Lupe revealed. "About the equivalent of a thousand U.S. dollars."

Sister Victoria steeped some green tea, presenting a cup to Shannon in the hopes of soothing her raw emotions. She was sick with worry and left to ponder her own inaction. By not locking the door to her bedroom, Shannon had no one to blame but herself, suffering endless self-incrimination.

"It's my fault," gasping in anguish. "I knew there was a risk. But, I never believed it would come to this."

C.J. sat beside her at the kitchen table, tenderly holding her hand. It was a side of him she hadn't seen before. A comforting, paternal behavior that calmed her nerves, making it easier to think things through. "There's no sense in beating yourself up over this," he counseled. "Roberta could've done this at any time, day or night. It wouldn't have mattered whether you were asleep or not."

She sighed bitterly at the thought. "Mother asked me to take care of the baby. With her dying breath, she entrusted that life to me..." Her voice caved, consumed in sorrow. "What would she think of me now?"

C.J.'s smile bloomed from the heart. "She'd think just what she did before. That no one in this world would love her child more than you."

His words restored Shannon's spirit. "Thanks, C.J. That was something I really needed to hear."

"Did Roberta say anything to you before this? Anything that might have triggered her to act?"

"No. But, I did speak with her."

"What about?"

"Carlos Ayala. The boy she had dinner with in Las Vegas." His vacant expression made her realize that further information was required. "I told her he was a hero. How he saved us just before the quake. Then, I gave her his phone number. I promised Carlos I would."

"Did she call him after that?"

"I don't know."

Casey entered the kitchen, brandishing a sheet of paper. He'd just completed a routine check of the Padre's office computer which Roberta had been known to use. During his investigation, he'd come across several tell-tale cookies, an internal list of websites recently visited online. He handed the printout to C.J., convinced this was the smoking gun. "Take a look."

His brother scanned the list. "Amtrak?"

Casey nodded, pointing to a particular entry. "Specifically, the westbound timetable for The Sunset Limited...El Paso to L.A."

Another cookie further piqued C.J.'s interest. "She searched for sleeper accommodations. The kind you get for overnight travel."

Shannon managed to verbalize her concern. "She's going to California?"

"Where does this Carlos kid live?" probed C.J., acting on a hunch.

"East L.A." Shannon's eyes lit with comprehension, matching those of her brothers. "Oh, my God. Casey, when does that train leave?"

He checked his watch. "Should be pulling out of the station about now."

"Damn." C.J.'s frustration mounted. "I guess we'll have to try and stop it." His gaze fell back on Shannon. "We better contact Carlos. Do you remember his number?"

Their sister had a photographic memory, reciting the digits with ease. As Casey copied down the information, an ominous sound reverberated throughout the mission. It shook the walls and rattled their souls. The old iron bell atop the church now rang with urgency, a portent of imminent danger, bringing everyone to their feet.

Osborne was already at a dead run, bounding up the ancient wooden staircase leading to the belfry. Upon his arrival, he found Captain Garza in a state of uncommon agitation, eager to relinquish his binoculars.

"Check this out, Major."

He set his sights on the nearest border crossing. What he beheld was a vision exceeding his darkest fears. An impressive array of U.S. Army vehicles had just smashed through the security checkpoint, entering sovereign Mexican soil. The invading force was comprised of three M1A2 Abrams Tanks, Four M2/M3 Bradley Fighting Vehicles, more than a dozen half-tracks and Humvees, as well as an AH-1W Cobra attack helicopter to provide the motorized equipment with strategic air cover. They moved with speed and purpose, advancing at will. The low-flying chopper churned dust and debris in their wake, ensuring that Mexican border officials mounted no counterattack. Tourists and civilians alike screamed in terror, stampeding for their lives down side streets and alleyways. Pandemonium cascaded through the adjacent shopping plaza, forcing everyone to seek immediate shelter. Street vendors bolted from open-air tables, leaving their merchandise unguarded, not knowing when they could return. Abandoned cars caught in the Army's path were simply flattened underneath the treads of their tanks. Innocent children scattered for cover, some fighting back with a barrage of stones. It was clear that nothing would stop the military from reaching their objective. The Guadalupe Mission and everyone inside were about to be claimed as casualties of war.

"Let's get out of here," Osborne ordered, a command with which Captain Garza was more than willing to comply. They descended the staircase in record time, never feeling the steps beneath their feet.

Emerging from the bell tower, they were confronted by a gaggle of concerned guests and inhabitants. Osborne didn't see the need to sugarcoat the situation. "Well, I could lie to you...but we don't even have time for that."

The ugly truth was made known. Assuming authority, the Padre instructed the Sisters to immediately shepherd the orphanage children through the catacombs to the adjoining mission in El Paso. Existence of the underground passage was news to the visitors, with Moses taking a moment to brief them about the secret escape route. The Padre pushed open the fireplace façade, allowing a gush of rank air to assault their senses. Captain Tejada located a box of glow sticks in his satchel, handing out the luminescent rods to every adult present. An orderly procession took form, as the Sisters led each child down into the hellish tomb. To their surprise, none of the youngsters complained about the incredible, unrelenting stench to which they were now subjected. Three of the children, still too young to walk, were carried by Sisters Carmen and Raquel. The single file column at last disappeared within the earthen bowels, following the narrow-gauge hand car rails to safety.

After informing the El Paso mission of their emergency, the Padre ran to join his flock. He was intercepted by C.J. at the tunnel entrance, apologizing for the disruption. "I'm sorry that we brought this upon you and your people, Father. Please forgive us."

The Padre smiled. "Whatever happens is God's will. How can I be upset with that?"

C.J. reciprocated with a grin of his own. "Good luck, Father."

"Do not tarry, my son," the Padre warned, clutching his arm for emphasis. The priest noted that some of C.J.'s family had gone to gather their belongings. "The children of Maria Elena were brought to Earth for a holy cause. Nothing in this church is worth your lives. Follow me at once." He then slipped off into the darkened labyrinth.

The Major hugged Kimberly, urging her to depart. "You go on. I'll catch up with you later."

"Can't you come now?"

"This is a military operation," he explained. "Moses and I are going to set a few traps. I'll be right behind you." Osborne kissed her in apparent haste, motioning to Casey who was standing nearby. "Take care of her."

"Come on, Kim. Let's get going," said her brother, extending a hand.

After initial hesitation, she surrendered to his logic and followed Casey into the putrescent void.

The Major turned to address the Israeli nationals who'd remained at the mission overnight. "You two are on your own. You can stay here and get killed, or take your chances down in this stinkhole."

Ariel remained resolute in his devotion to the family. "As I said last night, I am here to serve the Archangels of Elohim. For me, there is no higher calling and no greater good."

Osborne cast a bemused look at C.J. and Kevin. "He's all yours." The Major and Moses snuck off with a satchel full of explosives, plotting guerilla warfare tactics against the enemy.

Kevin looked around the room with concern. "Where is he?"

"Who?" asked his brother.

"Who do ya think?" he snapped. "The boil on my balls. The pain in my ass. Where'd the little numnut get to?"

Barbara and Shannon now joined the others, each toting a change of clothes and a small makeup kit. Kevin was left stunned by the timing of their vanity. "Have either of you seen Ben?"

"He was in his room a few minutes ago," claimed Barbara. "Didn't he leave with the other children?"

"No. I'll take care of it." Kevin huffed, dashing down the hallway.

C.J. gained the attention of those present. "Captain Tejada? Captain Garza? I'd appreciate it if you'd escort the ladies through the tunnel. We'll be right behind you."

They acknowledged with courtesy, guiding the women as they descended into the subterranean crypt. Afterward, C.J. motioned the Israelis to the portal. "Let's go." The two went willingly, proceeding down steps of stone into the oppressive netherworld. Only a few feet behind, C.J. suddenly stopped, chiding himself due to a critical oversight. "Oh, shit! I forgot the CDs!" He waved them onward. "Follow the others. I'll join you in a minute."

After positioning several explosive boobytraps throughout the mission, Moses and the Major were at the main entrance, rigging the final charge. Their manic motions left no doubt the military engagement was about to commence. They could hear the squall of humanity outside, screaming and cursing the invading force, but remaining powerless to stop them. With each breathless moment, the distinctive aural signature of oncoming tanks grew more intense. The advancing armament arrived at the mission gate, revving their engines in anticipation of the primary assault. Circling overhead, the Cobra helicopter scattered remaining bystanders with a warning barrage from its triple-barreled, 20mm cannon. The perimeter fence surrounding the church was now breached, with the trio of tanks coming to rest in a triangular formation around the mission. Having assumed tactical enfilade positions, each armored vehicle began to de-elevate their 120mm smoothbore main gun in preparation for the order to fire.

Kevin found Benjamin in his room, caught in the act of downloading songs from one iPod to another. From his reaction, it was clear ownership of these devices had been a well-kept secret.

"Don't tell the Sisters," he begged. "They'd take 'em from me."

"Kid, do I look like a snitch? Come on! We gotta get outta here!"

The tyke shook his head in defiance. "Just a couple more minutes."

"There's no time for that!"

C.J. ran into the Padre's office, unlocking a desk drawer. He removed the Dreamland CDs from their hiding place, mere seconds before the onslaught.

The sound and the fury arrived at once. A frightening cannonade erupted as three high explosive rounds detonated simultaneously, spreading instant devastation the length and breadth of the mission. The entire structure shook to its foundation, propelling fragments of adobe brick through interior walls and collapsing large portions of the roof. Massive ceiling joists dislodged from the rafters, tumbling down amidst billowing clouds of dust. Kevin covered his younger brother, trying to protect him from the falling debris. C.J. collapsed behind the Padre's desk, pinned underneath by the sudden weight of a 12x12 wooden crossbeam. Coughing repeatedly in the squalid air, he looked up through a dense haze to witness Moishe Gerhin standing over him. At first, C.J. thought he was there to lend a hand, but soon realized his true intent.

"You're a fortunate man, Mr. Hightower," said the Mossad agent, grabbing the coveted CDs. "This saves me from having to kill you later."

Gerhin bolted from the room, leaving C.J. to spout an obscenity-laden tirade in his wake. Desperate to free himself, he was finally able to slide his legs out from under the beam. C.J. hobbled to his feet, suffering the effects of a painful thigh bruise.

Deep underground, the catacombs were rocked by the assault above. The roof of the main tunnel was compromised by the tremulous effects, precipitating a cave in of rock and mud into the void. Casey and Kimberly were ahead of the earthen collapse, scurrying forth to escape a wave of acrid dust. Captain Tejada saw the tunnel buckle in front of him, pivoting back upon Barbara and Shannon to shield them from the crushing debris. A cloud of particulate matter engulfed them all, triggering lengthy bouts of respiratory distress. An oppressive atmosphere had quickly become intolerable. Captain Garza helped the others to their feet, recognizing Tejada had twisted an ankle during his awkward pirouette from danger.

"I can make it," he assured them through clenched teeth. The four knew it was too risky to head back, choosing an alternate tunnel which branched off to their immediate right. They were now on an uncharted path, in search of yet another way to the surface.

With the CDs in hand, Gerhin swiftly descended into the tomb, passing his fellow Israeli without a word. The agent fled into a tunnel running perpendicular to the main, using the ebony camouflage to full advantage.

Above, C.J. cried out in alarm. "Moses! Moses!"

His brother was with Major Osborne, lying in wait to ambush ground forces when they stormed the mission. Hearing C.J.'s voice, he scampered through a copious amount of interior debris, arriving back at the catacomb entrance to find him limping up an adjacent hallway.

"What happened?"

"Gerhin stole the CDs!"

Brandishing a semiautomatic 9mm Beretta, Moses bolted

down the stone steps receiving directional guidance from Ariel. "He went into that tunnel."

The handgun was waved in his face, a none-too-subtle warning about the penalty for disinformation. "You better be right."

Moses sprinted into the darkness. C.J. came down the steps at a slower pace, but with similar urgency. He eyed Ariel with contempt. "This is how you intend to serve us? With betrayal?"

"I do not know his heart," he confessed. "I only know my own. You should not judge me based on the actions of another, but for deeds which I alone bear responsibility."

Not in the mood for a philosophical debate, C.J. shook his head in disgust, lurching forth to join the pursuit.

The tank loaders had replaced the spent casings with new armament and propellant charges. Tank gunners redirected their main guns 10 degrees in an east-west azimuth, so as to penetrate additional areas inside. The Company Commander again issued the order to fire. Generating iridescent clouds of flame, the tanks sent another deafening salvo of high explosive rounds into the mission at speeds in excess of 1400 meters per second.

Kevin was carrying his brother through the great hallway when the second wave announced itself with a vengeance. Thrown to the floor by the shockwave, the thick adobe walls were vaporized above the level of the intersecting munition tracks. The lower portion leaned over them at a 45 degree angle, providing a measure of protection from the cascading ceiling debris. Dozens of wooden crossbeams crashed down, shearing off into razor-sharp airborne flechettes. Plaster, tar, metal sheeting and other roofing materials rained upon them, eventually exposing the midday sky. A dust cloud of improbable density coated the area in a thick blanket of grit. Once certain that nothing more could fall, Kevin looked up to survey the devastation. His wheezing relief at being alive was tempered by the prospect of another military barrage. He checked on Benjamin, who was busy ensuring that his iPods were still in working order. Kevin staggered to his feet and scooped the tyke in his arms. They bounded through a maze of rubble, at last arriving at the catacomb entrance. It was there they met up with the Major, who was carrying a bottle of propane gas from the kitchen.

"Why are you still here?" Osborne gasped.

Kevin felt truth was stranger than fiction. "Oh, we've been busy downloading some tunes."

"Very funny," dismissing the comment as sarcasm.

"What's that for?" pointing to the propane.

"Another present for our friends out there. Let's go."

The three entered the catacombs, spotting Ariel at the base of the steps. "Has everyone come through?" asked the Major.

"Yes, they have."

Osborne closed the façade behind him and snap activated his glow stick. He negotiated the remaining steps, finally joining the others. The boneyard was now bathed in an eerie green light, making their ghoulish surroundings seem all the more macabre. Kevin tried to breathe only when necessary, desperate to find relief from the hideous stench.

"Whew! I thought it was bad upstairs! What the hell's causing this stank? A 300 year-old turd?"

The Major was more intrigued by what they couldn't smell. The intricate network of catacombs extended over a wide area, housing the earthly remains of more than 130 departed souls. Each had been laid to rest in sealed crypts, decomposing slowly over time, clustered within a poorly-vented underground chamber.

For Osborne, the conditions couldn't have been more perfect. "There must be a ton of methane gas in these tunnels. This place is a bomb waiting to blow."

His words left Kevin in a quandary. "So, that's what's making us gag?"

"You can't smell methane," Osborne lectured. "But, I know it's in here. We might be able to set off an explosion."

Ariel was quick to disagree, shaking his head with conviction. "It won't work. You've got to have just the right percentage of methane to oxygen. Five to fifteen percent, if I'm not mistaken. Also, temperature and pressure have to be taken into consideration. There are too many variables to ensure success."

Osborne smiled at his encyclopedic knowledge. "Well, we won't know who's right until we try. Let's pop the lids on these crypts. We'll need the full effect of the gas."

"No way!" Kevin objected in childlike fright. "This nasty ass tomb's creepy enough without having to look at a bunch of skeletons."

"Skeletons!" squealed an excited Benjamin. "Oh, yeah! Let's do it!" He raced over to the first ossuary, working in tandem with Ariel to remove the stone covering. Upon seeing the human remains within, the youngster knew exactly where he wanted this year's Halloween party to be held.

The Major walked past the visibly spooked former football star. "Come on, you big baby. Let's get this done."

Outside the mission, three separate assault teams were preparing to invade the sanctuary. They approached with caution, fanning out in standard two-by-two formations. Storming the main entrance with a fusillade of automatic weapons fire, one team kicked in the door, triggering a block of C-4 to detonate above the transom. The explosion instantly claimed the soldiers, sending a torrential wall of debris into the courtyard. Another team was attempting entrance into the kitchen when one of the men brushed a trip wire with his boot. The base of the adjacent bell tower was destroyed by a series of daisy-chained RDX-based explosives, toppling the entire three story structure upon the astonished commandos.

These guerilla tactics enraged the Company Commander, quickly recalling his surviving ground troops. He instructed each of his tank crews to load an M1028 anti-personnel cartridge and prepare to engage. The lethal ordnance was essentially a 120mm shotgun shell, propelling 1150 tungsten steel balls to impale anyone within 500 meters of the blast. Within seconds, the crews signaled they were ready. The order to fire was given.

A thunderous discharge of metal now savaged the mission, the death knell echoing long after impact. Thousands of holes were bored through solid brick, a lasting testament to the pernicious attack. The sanctuary began to crumble, audibly groaning from its wounds, a victim of structural evisceration.

Infantry units again approached the church, safe in the knowledge that nothing inside could have survived. They entered the structure and an exhaustive room by room search was conducted. Mountains of debris lay before them, all of which had to be checked for any trace of the suspected Al-Qaeda terrorists that had captured Air Force One and kidnapped President Webber. The MAJIK-12's cover story was clearly working, justifying this extreme military response.

A block and a half away, the cover over a storm drain was forced open. Emerging from the underground funk was Moishe Gerhin, having navigated a maze of rat-invested tunnels. His clothes were disheveled, smeared with a malodorous substance not previously thought to exist. In spite of his ordeal, the Dreamland CDs remained in his possession.

The Mossad agent ran back toward the mission, using a series of trees and store fronts to avoid being spotted by the Army helicopter still circling overhead. Approaching several parked Humvees, he brazenly entered the last in the queue and started the engine. The Cobra's sonic backwash prevented the lone sentry from detecting the vehicle's departure until too late. Gerhin spun the Humvee in a tight arc, accelerating rapidly toward the U.S. border. Firing several shots, the military guard was unable to stop the elusive thief.

Moses' head popped out from the storm drain. He was about to extricate himself when he witnessed Gerhin's Humvee bearing down on him with lethal intent. Retracting into the void, the vehicle's tires rolled over the opening as Moses barely escaped decapitation. Gasping for breath, he vaulted out of the storm drain and cursed his fleeing prey. Moses knew there was no sense wasting ammunition. The Humvee was heavily protected with armor plating. It would take a vehicle of far greater size to bring Gerhin down.

Now sprinting with resolve, Moses proceeded due west, each impulsive step bringing him closer to the mission grounds. The military guard attempted to intercept him, his rifle at the ready.

"Where do you think you're going?"

Without breaking stride, he exposed his sidearm, shooting the soldier in the left foot. Moses left him sprawled in agony, continuing his daring advance under a canopy of trees which lined the street. Scaling what remained of the mission fence, he snuck up behind one of the tanks and mounted the hull from the blind side. The tank commander had his head out the open hatch, taking a drag from a cigarette. Moses refused to hesitate. With the stealth of a cat he crept up onto the turret, placing his Beretta to the man's right temple.

"You've got three seconds to order your men out."

He radioed his command in less than two. "Hatches up, gentlemen. Exit the vehicle."

The gunner, loader and driver began their egress from the tank, unaware of the highjack attempt in progress. When they recognized the threat, two members of the crew went for their sidearms.

"Try it and I'll blow his head off," warned Moses. "Weapons down...feet on the ground."

The officer swallowed hard, knowing he was one false move from oblivion. "Do it," instructing his men.

They complied, dropping their guns and abandoning the hull for the turf. The commander was then motioned from the hatch. "Let's go."

As he made his exit, Moses climbed inside, completing the hostile takeover. However, the transfer had taken far too long. The Cobra pilot witnessed the incident, bringing the helicopter around for a strafing run with its 20mm cannon. Scattering for cover, the tank crew dashed for their lives alerting other unit commanders to the danger. Moses buttoned up the commander's hatch, hearing the Cobra's high powered rounds nearly pierce the armor. He took over the gunner's position, locating the fire control system for the 7.62mm coaxial machine gun which worked in tandem with the main gun. Looking through the Gunner's Primary Sight, he observed the helicopter as it banked right preparing for another strafing run. Moses aligned the reticule over the oncoming silhouette, while the Laser Rangefinder fed distance-to-target data into the computer. He heard the gun elevating in anticipation of engagement. Before the Cobra could strike again, Moses executed the order to fire.

The weapon was deadly accurate. In a declaration of superiority, the gun howled to life, filling the sky with hundreds of depleted uranium rounds. The cockpit was devastated, physically split in two before a midair explosion downed the craft. Crashing ungainly into the mission courtyard, the fiery debris sent a message to every soldier present. The enemy was amongst them.

Through the periscope vision blocks, Moses saw the other two tanks begin to rotate their turrets in his direction. Although the M1 was designed for its survivability under attack, it would not withstand a direct hit from an Abrams 120mm main gun. He was a sitting duck and mere seconds remained. During his training as an Army Ranger, he'd been given a modest amount of instruction on M1 Tank systems and capabilities. Recalling this information would be the only chance Moses had to survive.

He located the countermeasures by the commander's digital display console. Two six-barreled smoke grenade launchers activated, obscuring the tank from view. Contained in the plume of smoke was a phosphorous compound which helped mask the heat signature of the vehicle. Moses dropped down into the hull, assuming the driver's reclined position. Fortunately, the 1500 horsepower engine was still idling. He grasped hold of the steering handles, trying to place the tank in reverse. Nothing happened. The vehicle wouldn't budge. His mind searched frantically for an answer. *What am I forgetting? Is there a parking brake? Shit, I'm out of time...*

At the final moment, his eyes found what his brain had lost. He twisted the handlegrip throttle towards him and the metallic beast lurched backward. A brilliant flash of light now consumed his peripheral vision followed by an intense acoustic wave. A high explosive anti-tank round had been fired, just missing its mark between the hull and the elevated main gun. The hypersonic shell traveled onward, detonating within a four-story building across the street, collapsing the structure in an orgy of flame.

Continuing to reverse course, Moses' tank departed the mission grounds, crushing two Humvees on its way into the street. The M1 that fired upon him would need a few seconds to reload. The other was fully occluded with no clear shot, blocked from engagement by its sister tank. Not wanting to fight a major battle in the streets of Juarez, Moses decided that Moishe Gerhin had to remain his top priority.

Twisting the handlegrip forward, his tank changed direction, now moving briskly for the border. The nearest M1 reversed gear, trying to paint the fleeing target and obtain a firing solution. Before they could zero in, Moses activated the smoke generator. By injecting some diesel fuel into the exhaust manifold, a billowing black cloud obstructed their view, separating his tank from the others. The Company Commander ordered both M1s to remain at the mission, contacting headquarters about the renegade tank and awaiting further instructions.

C.J. had just freed himself from the storm drain. The normally bustling avenue was deserted as fearful faces watched from nearby storefronts and apartments. He witnessed the people's desperation and understood their concern. An M1 Tank approached, symbol of an imperious government that respected no territorial sovereignty or international law. His initial thought was to run and hide, but C.J. decided to make a statement. This would be a Tiananmen Square-type confrontation with flesh and blood bravely staring down armor. It was an opportunity to either live or die, one he was not about to forsake. He strode to the middle of the street and stopped. C.J. was determined not to move. The tank came ever closer. Bracing for the inevitable, he heard the vehicle begin to brake. To his infinite relief, the M1 stopped less than ten feet in front of him. Rejoicing in triumph, C.J.'s mood soon morphed to one of utter astonishment. The driver's hatch popped open, revealing his brother in a reclined pose.

"Don't just stand there," he chided. "We've got a Mossad agent to catch."

Moses buttoned back up, waiting for C.J. to embrace the bizarre situation. This was not the defining moment he'd expected. Forcing a bewildered sigh, he mounted the tank, gaining access through the still open loader's hatch. The M1 surged forth, now in a renewed pursuit of Moishe Gerhin.

Five blocks to the south, another storm drain cover slid open. Captain Garza pulled himself up through the hole, greeted by two stray cats in an abandoned alleyway. He bent down and began assisting others to the surface. First Barbara, then her sister Shannon, were hoisted by their arms out of the pit. Deadlifting Captain Tejada would prove more difficult. Due to his severe ankle strain, he was unable to place much weight on his left foot. The three helped bring him to daylight, each expressing impassioned relief at their deliverance. Shannon guided Tejada to some nearby steps, finally able to inspect his injury. He winced in pain as she probed for bone or ligament damage.

"It's not broken, but he could use a splint."

"There's no time for that," his voice driven by urgency. "We've got to keep moving."

But, that begged the question. *Where to now?* The family had been scattered by circumstance, forced from their native home in a modern-day diaspora. The when and where of their reunion was yet to be determined. An attempt to contact the others by cell phone was rendered impossible due to signal gridlock. The Army incursion into Juarez had overloaded the system with anxious relatives phoning loved ones in the city. Barbara suggested they proceed to the airport to inquire about next-available flights and wait for the others to join them. It seemed like a logical course of action. They hailed a cab and were soon on their way to Gonzalez International, about a 15 minute drive to the southeast.

Casey, Kimberly and the rest of the church refugees arrived safely at the Nuestra Senora del Carmen Mission in El Paso. Their passage under the Rio Grande had been relatively free from underground seepage, due in large part to a month-long drought in the area. While the Sisters tended to the children's needs, Casey and Kimberly tried to reach their family by cell phone. Neither could obtain an available signal. With their anxiety exacerbated by the cave in, they took comfort in the fact that there had to be other ways to the surface.

"There were a lot of tunnels down there. They could be anywhere," Casey explained, remaining positive for his sister's benefit. "Don't worry. I'm sure they'll be all right."

Kimberly exhibited confidence. "If anyone can get them out of there, it's Robert."

With the cell lines jammed, Casey used the mission's landline to call the Amtrak station in El Paso. He was told the Sunset Limited had left for Los Angeles approximately ten minutes ago. The next stop was in Deming, New Mexico in just over an hour. Armed with this information, they both agreed to go after Roberta and Hope.

Leaving the mission in haste, Casey led his sister on a half-mile jog to a highway overpass. Climbing the embankment, they came to a concrete K-rail separating them from the westbound lanes of Interstate 10. The two entered the right service lane and attempted to flag down a passing vehicle. Casey's plan was simple. Get someone to drive them to Deming and board the train there. But, the execution of his plan needed work.

With his thumb stuck in the path of traffic, Kimberly's geeky brother was a comic sight to behold. It was painfully obvious he'd never done anything like this before. Car after car whizzed by his cartoonish pose, some leaning on their horns in anger. The novice hitchhiker kept the faith, thinking at any moment their ride would materialize. She wanted to laugh, but that would've been cruel. His intentions were too pure to make fun of. Still, the futility they were suffering had to end.

Kimberly stepped back behind Casey, waiting for just the right moment. An 18-wheel semi was fast approaching them in the nearest lane. The woman, never a fan of bras, suddenly yanked up her shirt exposing her most stunning assets. The truck's air brakes were tested like never before, lost in a thick plume of smoke, rubber and noise. Fighting a severe fishtail effect, the semi remained upright, coming to rest along the side of the road. Before Casey could turn around his sister had already covered herself.

"Hey, I got us one!" visibly pleased with his effort.

The two scrambled to the truck, its cab door already opened in welcome. Inside, they found the epitome of a southern characture. The driver was male, mid-30's, sporting a Stetson hat, denim shirt, blue jeans and a chaw of Skoal planted in his right cheek. A radio blaring country music was also a nice touch. His horndog smile refused to fade, leering at Kimberly with all the testosterone he could muster. "Oh, Miss Boobie...you is one purdy filly," drooling over her lasting image. "I saw 'em. Oh lordy, I saw 'em good. They gotta be the finest set of puppies in all of Texas. Yes, in damn deedy. Worth a thousand miles of bad road to see them Double D darlin's. You sure 'nuff know how to make a trucker's day."

Casey interrupted, paying no mind to the man's lustful rantings. "Excuse me. Can you take us to Deming?"

An awkward silence ensued. The driver looked to Kimberly for guidance. "Boyfriend?"

She shook her head with resolve. "Brother."

"OK, Miss Boobie," his smile now restored. "Deming it is. Hop on in here and slide them blouse bunnies next to me."

They climbed inside the cab. Kimberly assumed the center seat, blithely allowing the man to rub up against the side of her chest. Casey remained oblivious to what was going on. "It's real nice of you to do this."

"The pleasure's all mine, brother. All mine." He accelerated back into traffic, looking once more at the objects of his erection. "Oh, yeah," he whispered happily. "I saw 'em real good."

After opening more than 75 crypts, Osborne felt confident that enough methane gas had been released. They'd worked efficiently at the thankless task, keeping their complaints to a minimum. Kevin was still creeped out by what he'd been forced to do, never once looking inside the exposed vaults. It was a successful strategy, a classic example of mind over decomposing matter.

The four made their way through the same escape tunnel used by Moishe Gerhin. Benjamin ran on ahead, eager to report his findings as often as possible due to the resident echo. The others trudged a few yards behind, wondering if their unpleasant labors would soon be rewarded.

After a long and lamentable trek, they ascended to the surface. All eyes were now fixed on the mission. No one moved. A pervasive silence held firm, denying them the opportunity to verbalize their thoughts. Osborne checked his watch. Too much time had elapsed. It seemed inconceivable that the soldiers hadn't located the access to the catacombs. *I should've made it easier for them. I should've left the façade open just a crack. That was a damn stupid move…*

They continued to wait, anticipation swelling through their pores. However, it wasn't long before reality reared its ugly head, dashing hope their trap would be sprung.

"I knew it wouldn't work," Ariel crowed in retrospect. "The conditions had to be perfect."

Osborne's spirit flared with anger, but his tongue remained calm. Deep down, he knew Ariel's words rang true. The Major had always been a pragmatic man. However, he'd counted on something else entering the mix. A dash of divine intervention that would have ensured success, bringing everything into alignment. He couldn't understand why it hadn't happened. *Come on…Come on!*

Nothing was heard but the heartbeat of fear still gripping the city. The Major sighed philosophically, at last abandoning his faith. "I suppose you're right. Too bad we all can't be as smart as..."

His breath was taken by the blast. Deep underground, an explosion of immense size and power convulsed the earth, sending each of them to their knees. A gargantuan fireball rose out of the mission, setting the sky ablaze in brilliant hues of orange and red. Bursts of flame channeled up through cracks in the surface, causing secondary fires to spread across an ever widening area. The mission grounds began rolling like a tempestuous sea, cresting and falling in concentric waves. Without warning the 70 ton tanks flipped over, crashing onto their turrets, the sight reminiscent of two turtles left helpless on their backs. The ruins of the church now collapsed within a 30 foot deep, block-wide sinkhole, burying the commandos under a mountain of compressed debris. As the inferno burned itself out, a final burp of incendiary gas exited the storm drain. A dust cloud of thickening density began its inevitable march across downtown Juarez. The earth went silent...and then the city erupted. People came running into the streets in wild celebration, screaming for joy and pumping their fists in victory.

The soldiers had indeed found the catacombs. Osborne left the propane bottle against the façade, knowing the commandos would fire through the wall before entering. A single bullet ignited the pressured tank and the mission's honored dead took care of the rest.

As the city's revelry continued, an incredulous Kevin spoke for them all. "Whoa! Don't underestimate the power of baked beans."

Ariel was in shock, trying to comprehend the event. "I don't believe it. There's no way..." He shook his head, absorbing a much needed gulp of air. Osborne thought an apology might be forthcoming, but Ariel couldn't yet bring himself to admit he was wrong. "It must have been the propane."

"Propane?" the Major chortled. "Ever see a little tank of propane set off an explosion like that?"

His disbelief lingered. "Then, what was it?"

Osborne couldn't help but smile, watching Ariel take his first bitter taste of humble pie. "Just chalk it up to the will of Elohim."

The TV stations in El Paso had never experienced such a breaking news avalanche. Morning shows were yanked from the air, so that area viewers could be informed in real-time of the events affecting their city. Local reporters were dispatched to a multitude of sites, doing live cut-ins as they gathered eyewitness accounts. Affiliated broadcast networks and national cable news outlets were picking up the El Paso feed over satellite, breaking away from their continuous coverage of the Las Vegas earthquake disaster. The attack on Air Force One and its subsequent travels through the city, as well as the U.S. military incursion into Juarez, was now being beamed to an international audience. Television newsrooms were in a state of what could only be described as controlled chaos. Limited resources of manpower and equipment were spread so thin that normal work activities were curtailed. Even the stations' incessantly ringing phones had to be left unanswered.

This breakdown in communications was frustrating the efforts of Tamara Sheldon. The Press Secretary had been tasked by President Webber to obtain TV air time for her emergency address to the nation. Unable to reach anyone in authority with the local media, Tamara called in a favor from a producer at CBS in New York. She was given the private cell number of Brenda Hoffman, General Manager at KDBC-TV, which was the CBS network affiliate in El Paso. After three attempts, the two were finally able to speak. Told of the President's intentions, and that she would have an exclusive on the most sensational story of our times, Hoffman excitedly invited the President and her entourage to the station. Tamara assured her they would be there soon.

Before departing the emergency room at Providence Memorial Hospital, Susan Webber insisted on getting an update regarding the condition of her wounded Secret Service agent. She was told he'd recover, but would have to remain at the facility for about a week. Satisfied with his prognosis, the President was ready to leave. Her security detail had arranged for the El Paso police to escort them to the TV station, a little over a mile distant. The official motorcade consisted of four patrol cars, two police vans, six motorcycle officers and a SWAT team helicopter escorting them overhead.

Safely ensconced inside one of the vans, Tamara had a moment to address the President. "Would you like me to draft a speech?"

Webber's eyes were intently focused. "No. There's no script for this," her voice hardened by recent events. "Today, I speak from the heart. The people are going to hear the truth whether they want to or not."

High above the earth, a spy satellite tracked the caravan as it snaked its way through downtown El Paso. For seven individuals hunkered down at Fort Meade, the mere sight of this procession signaled professional failure on a grand scale. The MAJIK-12 had tried to kill the President of the United States, but in spite of their efforts, Susan Webber remained alive. With their sinister plans exposed, everything they valued was hanging in the balance... including their lives, their fortunes and their sacred dishonor.

CIA Director Langlois had assumed de facto control of the group, aware their next decision could be their last. He squinted at the central monitor as the Presidential motorcade came to a stop. "Tighten on that image, General. I want to see where she's going."

Stevenson deftly manipulated the controls, increasing magnification and clarity on screen. Now apparent in greater detail was a two-story structure occupying a city block. It was located next to Interstate 10, directly across from the expansive Southern Pacific rail yards. Upon closer examination, Langlois was able to count up to ten separate dish antennas used for satellite uplinks, closely arrayed across the building's roof. Suddenly, his worst fears were confirmed.

"It's a TV station. She's going live," whispering only to himself.

His voice then thundered, repeating his admonition with rage. "It's a goddamn TV station! The fucking bitch is going live!" He turned to face the others, the percussion of his heart loud enough for all to hear. "This is it, gentlemen! The end of the line! If we don't do something right now, we might as well start eating bullets!"

"We could cut the power in El Paso," suggested Professor Blau. "Keep the station from broadcasting."

"Don't they have generators?" Secretary Roth challenged.

"Fuck that!" roared Langlois, dismissing their comments with venom. "General Stevenson, this is an emergency! Get on the line with your people. Find out what they've got in the air, ready to go."

Contact was made with the Commander at Holloman Air Force Base outside Alamogordo, New Mexico; approximately 90 miles from El Paso. The information General Stevenson was given made him freeze, not knowing exactly how to respond. He placed a hand over his headset mouthpiece, clearing an apprehensive throat. "There's an MC-130 Hercules on special maneuvers over White Sands. They're about to drop a new weapon. The BLU-82C. An enhanced Daisy Cutter with a fuel-air detonator."

The room went silent. They understood the ramifications of using such a device, the reality of which chilled even these cold-blooded creatures.

"No way," General Connolly argued, his breath taken by the thought. "An explosion like that would destroy half the city. We need a surgical strike, one without a lot of collateral damage."

"We tried that General," Langlois reminded him, clearly warming to the idea. "Desperate times call for desperate measures. I'd say this qualifies."

Connolly disagreed. "The Daisy Cutter's the most powerful conventional weapon in our arsenal. And, this one's been mated with a fuel-air explosive. The loss of life would be beyond belief. Do you really want that on your conscience?"

Langlois became lost in reflection, feeling the stark emptiness of his soul. "At this point, my conscience is the least of my

concerns. All I know is something has to be done…and done now."
His attention fell back to Stevenson. "General, how soon can they
arrive over target?"

"About 20 minutes."

He acknowledged with a limp nod. "Send 'em in," three
small words that belied the horror behind them. Langlois now
beseeched the others. "Unless I hear any other objections?" Their
mute response came as expected. "No," murmuring in solitude. "I
didn't think so."

Stevenson again addressed the Base Commander. "Patch me
through to the Hercules. Have them stand by to receive new orders
from Brass Hat."

Communications were re-routed so that the General could
speak directly with the crew. After explaining the nature of the
emergency and what the Joint Chiefs were directing them to do,
the Hercules pilot, Major William Pace, conveyed his deep and
overwhelming dismay. Stevenson tried to alleviate his concern
with a raft of lies.

"I understand your reluctance, Major. But, military intelligence
indicates that Al-Qaeda agents have entered El Paso and are about
to set off a biological weapon. One that could wipe out everyone
in a 200 mile radius. The heat generated from the explosion will
kill the organism and eliminate the threat."

"But, we're dropping this thing on a U.S. city," Pace related
in shock. "Sir, I just want to go on record as being completely
opposed to this course of action."

"So noted, Major. Now, you have your orders. Proceed to
target at once."

Pace was only four months from retirement and had no desire
to jeopardize his hard-earned pension. "Yes, sir," gasping in
disbelief. "We'll be over El Paso in 15 minutes."

President Webber entered the offices of KDBC with her
entourage and was greeted by General Manager Hoffman. She was
shown to a ready room where stylists worked on sprucing up her

hair and makeup. Tamara Sheldon walked in, her face rendered pale with dread. A piece of paper was handed to the President. It was a bulletin from the Associated Press which read:

A U.S. Government aircraft crashed shortly after take-off this morning from Reagan National Airport in Washington D.C. Aboard the jet were United States Attorney General Sharon Ortiz-Bennett and Secretary of Homeland Security Malcolm Tressler, along with a flight crew of four. There were no survivors. The aircraft's flight plan listed...

Webber closed her eyes before reaching the end of the statement, crumpling the paper in hand. She remained speechless, allowing her an opportunity to fully absorb the news. The MAJIK-12 had struck again, this time forever silencing a key witness. Though she'd never be able to fathom the depth of their iniquity, she was no longer shocked by their actions. She forced a lengthy sigh, drawing renewed strength for battle. "It's showtime, Tamara."

The President was escorted onto a soundproofed stage located in the center of the complex. She assumed a seat before the cameras and was fitted with a concealed microphone. As technicians tested the lighting and sound levels, Tamara left the room, content to watch her aunt on the closed circuit monitors in the reception area.

The Hercules aircraft flew into El Paso airspace at a level altitude of 9,000 feet. Coordinates for the drop had been provided by General Stevenson. As the rear cargo door began to open, a sense of abhorrence and shame constricted the crew. Their innate morality told them not to do this, but the men were career military officers. As such, they were not about to countermand direct orders from the Joint Chiefs.

The time had come. The decision was made. Issuing a prayer for the unfortunate souls below, the 16,000 pound BLU-82C was pushed out the back of the plane on a palletized trolley.

The massive munition cleared the craft. As the Hercules began its banking maneuver to escape the oncoming shockwave, a static release line deployed a bomb stabilization parachute which would deliver the device to target. The updated weapon consisted of a 17 foot long cylinder filled with a watery mixture of ammonium nitrate, aluminum powder and polystyrene, otherwise known as GSX slurry. Mated on both sides were two BLU-95's, each a 500 pound fuel air explosive that sprayed a concentrated aerosol cloud of ethylene oxide prior to detonation. By combining these armaments into one, the military could harness the strength and brisance of a small nuclear explosion without incurring the radioactive fallout. Now falling at a rate of 340 feet per second, this instrument of annihilation was about to make its debut.

A television stage director cued the President and she began her unscripted address to the nation. "My fellow Americans," her tone made somber by circumstances. "I'm speaking with you today on a matter of incredible national security interest. It involves elements of murder, treachery and deceit at the highest levels of this Government, all directly attributable to a secret group known as the MAJIK-12. This organization, formed after the 1947 UFO crash in Roswell, New Mexico, has killed or terrorized hundreds of law-abiding citizens, whose only crime was to inadvertently cross their insidious path..."

Tamara heard the Hercules aircraft banking over them at high speed. She walked toward the floor-to-ceiling windows along the perimeter of the building, joined by the President's Secret Service detail and members of the El Paso police force. They were unable to see the plane due to a fine, clear mist which began to coat the outside of the glass. The BLU-82C finally became visible, a sudden breeze causing it to drift over the adjacent rail yards. None of them were able to react. There wasn't enough time. During the first millisecond of detonation, Tamara's optic nerve beheld a radiant spark as it emerged through the bomb casing. She never knew that she was staring into the pilot light of Hell.

They instantly departed this world, victims of thermodynamic immolation. The initial charge torched the sky, converting air into fire. A wall of flame engulfed the building, propelled with hurricane force through ducts and vents. Those inside could no longer breathe as oxygen was extracted from their lungs, replaced with globules of burning fuel that cauterized internal organs.

Television viewers witnessed only a moment of the carnage before the signal was lost. They saw the President open her mouth, unable to scream. Her eyes flew wide, feeling the superheated air begin to singe her flesh.

The glass walls would have melted had it not been for the overpressure wake which struck the building. Shards of glass sliced through them, cleaving their bodies open. The roof and walls were obliterated, exposing what was left to the raging firestorm. Once the shockwave passed, a vacuum was created, sucking everything not nailed down back into the explosive core. At this point, the GSX slurry ignited in a blast so prodigious, it generated an atmospheric pressure greater than 1,000 pounds per square inch. Multi-ton rail cars were swept from their tracks, taking flight through the conflagration, twisting and spinning like discarded toys. One locomotive impaled an office tower with such force it exited the structure three stories higher than the floor it entered. An empty boxcar crashed inside the TV station, landing in an inverted position amidst the flaming debris. Others sheared through elevated portions of the Interstate, destroying concrete piers, metal girders and ramp abutments. With the highway severed, cars fell into the open chasm, exploding on impact. Vehicles caught within the focused detonation wave were scooped airborne and deposited into buildings, trees and rooftops. The inferno surged through downtown streets, setting fire to dozens of panic-stricken pedestrians. They spun wildly into store fronts and moving cars, desperate to extinguish their clothing. Trucks and buses were upended, their tires and undercarriages left ablaze. Every window in a mile radius burst from the severe harmonics that reverberated between high-rise buildings. Older structures simply collapsed from the intense sonic concussion. A slew of cascading debris fell from the sky, burying people alive within the thermal flash zone. The city was immersed in flame well after the initial blast as secondary fires were spawned from ruptured gas lines and leaking fuel tanks.

Back at Fort Meade, the MAJIK-12 watched the calamitous event unfold before their eyes. Langlois looked upon the scene with a perverse veneration, his body shaking in near orgasmic glee. "We got her! Die, bitch, die!"

It took a few minutes before fire and ferocity began to wane. Atmospheric pressures returned to normal. The acoustic onslaught abated. What had been a pyromaniac's wet dream was now transformed into smoldering debris, smoke and ash. Acres of nondescript rubble concealed the dead and dying. Survivors began to moan in a loathsome chorus of pain. These unlucky souls had been physically brutalized by the devastation. Blood seeped from blinded eyes and deafened ears. Broken bones and open wounds were too numerous to count. Convulsions and trauma were common. Bladders and bowels had long since emptied. Soon, the fevered cries of rescue workers were heard, searching for those in need of medical attention. Police and fire units responded, their sirens giving hope to those still trapped in cars, buses and elevators. Downtown hospitals opened triage centers, awaiting the multitude of injured.

It wasn't long before the military responded with much needed supplies for the relief effort. They were also there to search for bodies. One in particular. Locating the remains of the President had been deemed a top priority by the Joint Chiefs, a grisly effort upon which no expense would be spared. After sifting through the detritus, a female corpse was discovered. Barely more than a decapitated torso, its flesh had been charred to the bone. However, the personal effects were of greater significance. Underneath the body was Susan Webber's private cell phone. Her engagement ring was residing on the bony finger of a severed hand. The President's diamond Rolex was a few feet away. Although a wider, more concentrated search was ordered, the head was never found. With no possibility of dental record identification, the corpse was taken to Fort Bliss for DNA testing. Cell samples from internal organs were compared with hair follicles found in the President's private quarters aboard Air Force One. The results were a match.

Due to the grievous condition of the body, the Presidential casket would remain sealed. Full military honors were conveyed, placing the remains on a C-5 transport to Andrews Air Force Base outside Washington D.C. Not looking to prolong the agony, the Department of Defense issued an announcement to the media. It was official. The United States of America had lost its queen.

CHAPTER THIRTY-TWO

"The President of the United States is dead…" Those eight words left Steven Yeager agitated. The mournful news that flowed from the bedside radio deflated his heart and crippled his soul. He received the announcement with profound sorrow, trying to comprehend why it affected him so deeply.

Yeager no longer remembered his professional responsibility to Susan Webber nor their secret relationship. His impaired condition was a direct result of a psychotropic cocktail of liquid Ketamine and OxyContin being administered to him via a steady, intravenous drip. He forced open watery eyes to perceive the blurred images of his hospital room. Non-descript objects melded together in a ghostly palette of silver and white. Yeager had fought his way through a swirl of hallucinations to arrive at this semi-lucid moment, but temporal and spatial orientation remained elusive. He had no idea where he was or how long he'd been here. The Secret Service Agent could not even recall his own identity. That information was trapped inside a mind now seized by narcotics. He remained prone in his bed, listening to the radio.

Concentrating on the broadcast, Yeager attempted to focus upon each spoken syllable. The news anchor paused for a ten-second break at the top of the hour to announce the station's call letters. "This is WTOP...Washington D.C." He slowly absorbed the data. Though suffering the effects of drug-induced amnesia, his location within this city seemed subconsciously appropriate. He channeled a labored sigh, angered by his memory loss and inability to move.

A door creaked open. Through an optic haze Yeager witnessed five figures enter the room, each wearing dark-colored robes. Three remained silent while the others snickered at his distress. Their faces were indecipherable, rendered obscure by a combination of distance and sensory confusion. But, not all his faculties had failed. He detected the smell of body odor apparently coming from the group as a whole. A tell-tale sign of those lacking in personal hygiene, showing no appreciation for their physical state.

Unable to express his dismay, Yeager reduced air intake to a minimum. He wondered who these odious visitors were and why they'd taken him captive. What sounded like a heated conversation commenced between the five. It was terse and unintelligible. He assumed the drugs were masking his aural comprehension, but it was more than that. They were speaking a language only they themselves understood.

Soon one approached, appearing inches from his face. Yeager's clouded vision yielded to a distinct image, that of a forty-something female. Her angular cheekbones extended beyond slit-like eyes. A long, sloping nose pointed the way toward a pair of cracked lips. Matted black hair nested above a near unibrow. He suddenly reasoned that no amount of drugs would improve her appearance.

She brushed a cold hand over his forehead, whispering to him in soothing tones. "There. There. You've been through quite an ordeal. You must rest."

The radio newscaster once more repeated the startling announcement. His eyes darted toward the sound, making her aware of his angst. "There's nothing you can do for her now," she declared, breaking into a smile. Her final words were enigmatic, leaving him gasping in alarm. "Don't worry. The Master's plan has yet to unfold. When the time comes, you'll be freed. Only then will you understand His magnificence and His divine glory." She rolled him onto his side. "Sleep well. It's for your own good."

As his perception changed, he noticed the intravenous drip extending from an elevated pouch into his wrist. With what little will he could muster, he placed his elbow over the plastic tube in an effort to restrict the flow. Fatigued by the encounter, his mind quickly faded, casting him into another psychedelic realm.

A swarm of reporters filled the Pentagon Press Room, waiting impatiently for the news conference to begin. Recent events demanded answers and the assembled media were determined to uncover the truth. Military Brass were known to be experts at disinformation, but no amount of deception would deter those present. The crowd was hostile. The room intense. It was destined to be a meeting like no other, televised to a worldwide audience of more than one billion people.

Now entering through a side door was Secretary of Defense Phillip Roth along with the Joint Chiefs of Staff, fresh from their recent stay in the Fort Meade bunker. They each stood in rapt attention, allowing the Secretary to assume his place at the podium.

"Ladies and Gentlemen, we'll take your questions after I've read the following Defense Department statement." He cleared his throat to proceed, holding the official cover story on two sheets of paper. "Today, the United States Military, with our deepest sadness and regret, is forced to announce the death of our Commander in Chief, Susan Webber. This terrible tragedy is directly attributable to an active and ongoing engagement with suspected Al-Qaeda forces in the El Paso, Texas and Juarez, Mexico area. At approximately 0630 hours Pacific Daylight Time this morning, six terrorists, posing as aircraft maintenance personnel, boarded Air Force One at Reno-Tahoe Airport. After killing two military officers, they concealed themselves in the lower galley until the Presidential jet left Nevada for Andrews Air Force Base, Maryland at 0647 hours. The six stormed the cockpit in flight and assumed control of the aircraft, but not before a coded hijack signal was sent by the flight crew to the U.S. Northern Command at Peterson Air Force Base in Colorado. A squadron of F-16's shadowed Air Force One as it was diverted by the terrorists to El Paso International Airport. At approximately 0935 hours Mountain Daylight Time, other Al-Qaeda operatives boarded the jet after coming across the border from Mexico. Military intelligence indicated that they were transporting a biological weapon, a deadly mixture of anthrax and tularemia, which they planned to detonate over Washington D.C. using Air Force One as a delivery mechanism." Roth paused for a sip of water, noting the icy stares of his audience. "U.S. Army units at Fort Bliss were dispatched to the airport, preventing the Presidential jet from taking flight. After a failed attempt to disable the aircraft, the terrorists responded by piloting the jet through the streets of El Paso to the international border. There they kidnapped President Webber, holding her hostage inside a Catholic Mission in Juarez. U.S. Army forces responded and engaged the enemy, prior to the terrorists destroying the church with high explosives. It was later discovered that the Al-Qaeda operatives had escaped, using a hidden network of underground catacombs. With their plans now exposed, the terrorists re-entered the United States planning to release the biological weapon, thereby threatening the entire population of the El Paso - Juarez area. It was at this point, the Joint Chiefs felt there was no other option. A Daisy Cutter with fuel-air detonator was dropped on their position, killing the Al-Qaeda members and incinerating the deadly pathogen within the generated inferno. Although our actions saved the lives of millions, President Webber became a victim of this engagement. She will go down in history as an unfortunate casualty in our country's continuing war on terror." He folded the statement, placing the papers in his coat pocket. "On a personal note, I've known President Webber for more than 40 years and it was my privilege to call her friend. I cannot adequately express the emotional pain this has caused me. I'm sure that feeling is reflected throughout the entire military establishment. Susan Webber died a national hero and she will be honored as such. Her state funeral will be a shining testament that the United States Government will do whatever it takes, bear any burden, suffer any price, until the scourge of terrorism is forever purged from this world." He took another sip of water, girding himself for the impending media onslaught. "We'll now take a few of your questions."

The feeding frenzy commenced with a strident vocal eruption as every reporter shouted in full throat. Roth held forth his hands, attempting to elicit order from the chaos. "Please! Please! One at a time!" he cried, pointing to a long-time network correspondent. "We'll start with you and work our way to the back." The others fell into their seats, reluctantly yielding to their senior colleague. His caustic tone left no doubt this would be a contentious exchange.

"Mr. Secretary, I want to focus specifically on the President's televised speech, what she considered, and I quote, '...a matter of incredible national security interest...' But, before she could finish, the United States Military dropped a 16,000 pound bomb outside the television station from which she was broadcasting. Do you really expect the American people to believe this was just a coincidence and not assassination on a grand scale?"

"I resent those remarks," Roth snapped, clearly shaking with more fear than ire. "The men and women of the Armed Forces are not assassins. They are true patriots, each blessed with the highest moral character. To even imply that this was done deliberately is a despicable thought and I will not address it further," deflecting the incendiary question. He motioned to another journalist seated behind the first. "Yes?"

Roth was again confronted by a slew of vitriolic words. "Did you or any of the Joint Chiefs know the President was in harm's way? And if not, why not?"

"That's a stupid insinuation," momentarily losing his cool. "Of course, we didn't know. It was an extremely fluid situation and decisions had to be made. Millions of lives were at stake. Unfortunately, not every military operation goes as planned.

Losing the President was a horrible tragedy, but there was no conspiracy. No deliberate attempt to harm her in any way." He sighed, expelling the lie from his lungs before singling out a different reporter. "Next question."

The media's verbal wrath continued. "So far, the death toll in El Paso has exceeded 1,500 innocent lives. Another 7,000 have reportedly been injured or crippled by the blast. In retrospect, wasn't this an incredibly flawed decision, one made in haste without any appreciation for the consequences?"

"That isn't true," he contended icily. "We weighed several options, none of which would have neutralized the threat. I'm sorry anyone had to lose their lives. But, when you realize we were seconds away from an attack that would've dwarfed September 11th, I'd make the same decision without any reservation."

Another correspondent stood upon being acknowledged. "Perhaps the military can explain why a Daisy Cutter, a bomb of immense destructive force, had to be used in this circumstance. Wasn't there any other weapon that could have been deployed without causing such massive collateral damage?"

"I think I'll let General Stevenson speak to that," Roth answered, backing away from the podium.

The officer approached the microphone. "Our decision was made due to time constraints. I contacted Holloman Air Force Base, the nearest installation to El Paso. The only device they had in the air and ready for engagement was the BLU-82C. Another weapon might have taken upwards of 30 minutes to deploy. Minutes we simply didn't have." He surrendered the podium to Roth who now scanned a sea of raised hands, selecting a female reporter in the third row.

"Before her death, the President spoke of an organization called the MAJIK-12. Are you familiar with this group? Have you or anyone you know been a member of this secret society?"

His response was less defiant, embracing the topic with additional subterfuge. "There is no MAJIK-12. We honestly don't know what she was talking about. You have to remember, the President was under extreme duress. The terrorists were just off camera. It's possible she was trying to send us some coded message. Our cryptologists are reviewing the broadcast as we speak. Hopefully, we'll have more to report later on."

Two rival correspondents leapt to their feet with simultaneous questions. The vocal overlap became incomprehensible as neither would concede the floor to the other. Roth lost his patience, bringing an end to this rather embarrassing display. "Enough! Either act like professionals or leave! One at a time..." He gave a nod to the nearest, while the scowling loser refused to take a seat.

"The President made mention of the 1947 UFO crash in Roswell, New Mexico, speaking as though the event actually happened. This is the first time such a high-ranking Government official has acknowledged the incident as fact. Why would Al-Qaeda terrorists, who clearly have their own agenda, force the President to talk about what happened in Roswell over 60 years ago?"

Roth paused noticeably, thinking through his response. "First, let me assure you, the U.S. Government never recovered an Unidentified Flying Object in Roswell, New Mexico. That is the exclusive paranoia of science fiction writers. As I said before, she may have been sending us some sort of code. Perhaps, she was drugged. But, as things stand right now, we simply don't know." He pointed to the man's sparring partner. "And what was your question?"

"You stated the military tried to 'disable' Air Force One. Our El Paso affiliate reports that you dropped a 2,000 pound laser-guided bomb which barely missed the aircraft. The President was on board, her life again being jeopardized by your actions. Is the military normally this reckless when it comes to the safety of their Commander in Chief?"

The Defense Secretary looked to his left, asking General Connolly to assume the podium. He cleared his throat three separate times before issuing a less than convincing rebuttal. "Only the right wing of the aircraft was targeted, not the fuselage.

As for the safety of the President, the true status of her condition was unknown at the time. We had unconfirmed reports that she might have already been killed. If we hadn't cared about her well being, we would've just stormed the plane. The actions we took gave us the best chance of getting her out alive." He abandoned the lectern before being asked anything else.

Another journalist spoke. "You said earlier that military intelligence had provided information about Al-Qaeda's biological weapon. If you had such detailed knowledge of their plans and method of attack, why didn't you act sooner to prevent this scenario from occurring?"

"We knew they had assembled the components of such a weapon," Roth admitted. "But, we didn't know how they planned to deliver it, nor were we sure about the timing of an attack. Those assessments we had to make on the fly." He then sought a different query.

The chosen reporter stood, hurling his inflammatory question with the force of a Molotov cocktail. "What gives the U.S. military the right to invade another country?"

Admiral Holliman, never accused of being discrete, lashed out at the man without need of a microphone. "They took our Commander in Chief hostage! We're not going to wait for a diplomatic solution while she's being tortured and raped…stupid jerk!"

Hoping to move past the awkward moment, Roth hurriedly selected another individual seated in the last row. "Go ahead."

The young man was a novice reporter, covering events in the nation's capital for a politically liberal newspaper based in Northern California. His nature was always to question authority, regardless of situation or consequence. "Now, let me get this straight," theatrically rubbing his forehead prior to an extended soliloquy. "In the past few weeks, the U.S. Government has accused Al-Qaeda of bombing the United Nations; the downing of Flight 242; destroying the Lloyd George Federal Building; blowing up a Justice Department jet; as well as being responsible for today's hijacking of Air Force One, taking the President hostage and nearly wiping out half of the Eastern Seaboard with a biological pathogen." He paused while a smattering of laughter cascaded through the room. His insolence then crested. "Don't you think they might be guilty of other crimes, as well? I mean, how do we know they didn't cause the earthquake in Las Vegas? Or, maybe the flash flood at the Hoover Dam? How about the nuclear blast that destroyed your secret base in Nevada? You know, the one you always said never existed? Would you or the Joint Chiefs care to comment?"

The young reporter was an obvious pain in the ass, but he had deftly exposed the MAJIK-12 to its feculent core. Roth was stunned by the cynicism, wanting to respond but unsure exactly how. Instead of lending further credence to his assertions, the Defense Secretary ignored him entirely, taking a question from a more seasoned correspondent.

"Can you tell us the whereabouts of the Vice President and if he's assumed the oath of office?"

The inquiry had been anticipated. Roth sighed, bracing himself for their subsequent reaction. "Due to the events in El Paso, Vice President Jacobs, along with several key members of Congress, were escorted to a secure location for their protection. He will not be sworn in as President until the Joint Chiefs have determined that the threat from Al-Qaeda has passed. Pending that decision, this Government will remain under military control."

The initial silence in the room was replaced by a squall of verbal disbelief and outrage. Reporters came to their feet in shock, murmuring amongst themselves and abandoning professional decorum. Even the most senior newsmen, who'd covered Washington politics for decades, could not recall such a blatant grab for power. Our democracy was at a tipping point. A Constitutional crisis unlike any this country had known.

Roth begged for order, receiving an intense barrage of questions. He attempted to shout over the escalating cacophony. "Ladies and Gentlemen, please! Let me explain! Please listen!"

The commotion began to wane as anxious journalists waited for their turn to pounce. "This is just a temporary measure, one which we feel is prudent. Once we're convinced the danger has passed, the reigns of Government will be ceded back to civilian control."

An anonymous voice blared forth. "You can't do this! It's unconstitutional!"

Admiral Holliman snapped in rage. "Don't lecture us! We'll decide what's constitutional and what isn't!"

"That's the job of the Supreme Court!" another yelled.

The press briefing was about to degenerate into a histrionic shouting match. Mindful of the worldwide television audience, Roth once more made a desperate plea for calm. "I assure you, this is merely a precaution. We have to be certain the Al-Qaeda threat was neutralized. There could be other terrorist cells waiting to strike, planning an even more deadly attack. Do not jump to the wrong conclusion. Our nation is strong and will endure this challenge. Have faith."

The correspondents weren't fooled. The stench of this plot was greater than a 20 mile fish kill, but these media professionals were now at a loss for words. In their minds, they were still trying to process the enormity of the news, coming to grips with the endless political and global ramifications. It was left to the youthful reporter in back to succinctly encapsulate their feelings.

"Since you're obviously jerking us off here, the least you could do is provide us with towels!"

A chorus of nervous laughter echoed through the room, infuriating the Admiral. As a career military officer, the thing that angered him most was impertinence. Their authority was being mocked and he was not about to watch these proceedings collapse into indignity. He surged past Roth, nearly choking the microphone in hand. "This meeting is over!"

As he stormed from the podium, he came upon one of his aides still standing at attention. "What the hell are you waiting for?" he snarled, pointing back at the cocky scribe. "Go put a bullet in that fuck!"

The Defense Secretary walked out with the others, sarcastically assessing his performance. "I'd say that went about as well as expected."

The moment of levity was short lived. It was clear to each of the MAJIK-12 conspirators that they had exceeded their ability to manage this situation. Events were now spiraling out of control, taking on a life of their own. What had been placed in motion, could no longer be stopped.

CHAPTER THIRTY-THREE

CARLSBAD CAVERNS, NM — MAY 9ᵗʰ — 12:43 PM MDT

$\mathscr{T}$he rearview mirror held no further fascination for Moishe Gerhin. Watching an empty ribbon of road for the better part of two hours had caused his attention to wane. There was no visible threat approaching from behind. The career agent for the Israeli Mossad knew that whatever danger he now faced lay directly ahead.

Gerhin's cell phone had remained in continuous use since his escape from Juarez. The recipient of this frantic communication was Viktor Sabarov, a highly-feared member of the Russian underworld and someone with whom Gerhin had dealt with on numerous occasions, using the intermediary to purchase high-tech weaponry for Israel on the Black Market. They were not friends. The words 'mutual trust' resided in neither man's vocabulary. The two tolerated each other's existence merely for professional convenience and financial gain. But, with the Dreamland CDs safely in Gerhin's possession, the stakes were far greater this time. Upon hearing news of the successful acquisition, the scheming Sabarov informed Gerhin that he too was in the El Paso area and urgently requested a rendezvous. The Mossad agent was nobody's fool, silently cursing the situation. No one hated to be spied upon more than a spy. Despite Gerhin's escalating concern, it was clear their proximity would help facilitate a more rapid sale of the merchandise. Seeking a discrete area, he suggested they meet inside Carlsbad Caverns located along the extreme southern border of New Mexico. Sabarov thought his El Paso Airport hotel suite would make for a more practical locale, but the Israeli was resolute. He knew that the miles of solid rock would make impossible any wireless transmission of the secret data to an outside source.

The men agreed upon the site. Sabarov and two of his aides chartered a flight to Cavern City Air Terminal in Carlsbad, New Mexico and awaited Gerhin's arrival at the National Park's visitor center. While there, word spread of the devastating blast in El Paso and of President Webber's possible fate. Park officials huddled in private, wondering whether they should close the caverns for the remainder of the day. Calls were made to the National Park Service in Washington, D.C. for guidance in the matter. They were told to remain open until further notice.

The stolen Humvee entered the visitor's parking area, coming to rest in front of the cavern's massive bat flight amphitheater. Gerhin emerged from the vehicle clutching the coveted box of CDs. As he strode toward the visitor center, a steady stream of humanity passed by all displaying various degrees of shock, sadness and raw emotion. The news from El Paso was now inescapable. He paused near the main entrance, taking time to absorb the information and wondering just how his theft of the discs might have compelled the military to overreact. For the first time, the magnitude of this situation began to crystallize in his mind becoming a force greater than he envisioned. Events had reached a critical mass, without any hope of containment. Suddenly, this cold blooded warrior found himself seized with fear.

Upon entering the lobby, the men made eye contact in an almost subliminal manner with no overt movements or gestures. Gerhin noted the throngs of tourists congregating near a bank of television monitors, hoping to gain additional insight about the explosion in El Paso. With most of the visitors' attention diverted, the waiting line for the next elevator remained noticeably short.

The Russians walked toward the queue, casually merging into a single file formation with Gerhin. They said nothing, nor did they acknowledge each other's presence. Sabarov was impeccably dressed, his $3,000 Gucci suit standing out amidst the blur of typical tourist apparel. His heavy-set frame was bedecked in excess bling, desperately wanting the world to know he was a man of considerable means. In sartorial contrast, Gerhin was still wearing the clothes he escaped with from the Juarez sewer. His rank condition caused him no embarrassment. All that mattered was the box tucked firmly under his arm.

The elevator doors opened. Soon, they were inside the cab riding with 10 others into the heart of the caverns. Gerhin stole a furtive peek at the other men. He knew neither, but had already guessed their designated responsibility. The smaller of the two was the techno-geek, who was carrying a laptop computer in a shoulder bag. The other possessed a formidable physique and was undoubtedly Sabarov's bodyguard-assassin. Although the Russian mobster had strength in numbers and was not above the occasional double-cross, Gerhin had prepared for any eventuality. As a man with 30 years experience in the Israeli Secret Service, he approached every encounter with the skill of a chess master, always remaining five moves ahead of his opponent. But this time, he wondered if he'd outsmarted himself. The Mossad agent was secretly making this deal for his own financial gain, without the knowledge or approval of his Government. He had been a loyal and trusted soldier for the state of Israel all his life. But, facing mandatory retirement with a meager pension, he knew this was his best and final chance to cash in. It was a calculated risk, one he hoped to survive.

With their descent complete, the elevator doors opened allowing them access to an underground concession and rest area. A Park Ranger led the tour group down a stone corridor and into a surreal world of wonder, the monolithic magnificence of the subterranean vault known as the Big Room. It was here that dramatically lit calcite deposits formed awe-inspiring displays of stalactites, stalagmites, cave pearls, draperies, lily pads and rimstone dams, all spread across an expanse greater in breadth than a dozen football fields. As the astonished visitors continued to marvel at God's impressive creation, Gerhin veered down a damp concrete path with his Russian entourage. Carlsbad National Park was an interlaced network of approximately 80 different caverns, each with its own unique structure, size and difficulty of access. It wasn't long before they found their way inside another cave directly adjacent to the Big Room. Now assured of privacy, the men began their negotiations.

"What's with the mutant?" asked the Israeli, pointing at Sabarov's larger than life bodyguard. "I thought we agreed to meet alone."

"Calm yourself, Moishe," the mobster implored. "It would be most unwise for a man in my position to travel alone. I don't like taking risks."

Gerhin snorted at the irony. "Well, you're taking a big one now. Do you know what's in this box?" Sabarov glared at the object in question, his eyes filled with greed. "It's the beating heart of the U.S. Government." The Mossad agent paused to open the case, allowing the room light to reflect off a CD in his hand. "Don't tell me to be calm. We're leaping into Hell together, my Russian friend. Just the two of us."

After experiencing a momentary loss for words, Sabarov resumed his broken English. "First, we must verify the merchandise." He motioned to the man with the laptop. The aide placed the computer atop a truncated stone column, readying the device with surprising speed. Gerhin surrendered the CD for analysis of its contents. While the technician took time to scroll through the data, an extended delay morphed into torturous anticipation. They suffered the anxiety in silence, each awaiting the verdict with tenuous breath. The man had finally seen enough. He looked upon Sabarov, nodding his head in official confirmation.

Gerhin had little time to celebrate. In fluid motion, the Russian mobster turned to his bodyguard with a subtle cue. A loaded handgun emerged. Sabarov jumped back as though protecting his suit from the shower of blood certain to follow.

"I don't think so!" shouted the Israeli.

The assassin never fired, his finger frozen on the trigger. Wondering why things had not proceeded as planned, Sabarov spun around taking note of the live grenade now lodged in Gerhin's hand.

"Listen to me, Viktor," stated the Mossad agent, his voice laden with venom. "Unless you want to get swept up with a wetvac, tell your steroid freak to take that gun and jam it up his ass as far as it'll go. Have him do it right now."

An incredibly tense moment yielded when Sabarov addressed his bodyguard in Russian, hoping to eliminate any possibility of a lethal misunderstanding. With seeming reluctance, the man replaced the safety catch on his weapon and tossed it onto the limestone bedrock. A glacial interlude was broken only by a few drops of water falling from the ceiling above.

"I knew you'd be too stupid to play this straight," Gerhin huffed. "So, from here out we're doing this my way. On my terms. And, if you try anything else...I'll bury you in that precious suit of yours."

Visitors to the National Park scattered in fear as an M1 Tank rolled into the parking area, eventually coming to rest directly behind the stolen Humvee. Their pursuit of Moishe Gerhin had been accomplished with surprising ease. Moses was familiar with the electronic capabilities of the tank, in particular the Inter-Vehicle Information System known as IVIS. All military vehicles incorporated this GPS position/navigation equipment, allowing other units to pinpoint the location of friendly forces on the battlefield. The exact coordinates, speed and direction of travel was displayed on a graphical interface map over the Commander's Console Monitor. Unbeknownst to the Mossad agent, Moses and C.J. had secretly tracked his escape route for the past two hours and were now closing in on their quarry.

They emerged through separate hatches with each jumping to the ground. On their way to the visitor center, Moses eyed an incredulous man seated outside his Winnebago.

"Hey buddy, can you watch our tank?" pointing back at the armored vehicle. "I don't want anyone denting it with a car door."

The man said nothing, still in shock from their unorthodox arrival. Upon entering the lobby, the two were exposed to the devastating news from El Paso. They approached a nearby television with wide-eyed incomprehension, unable to formulate the most basic word or thought. Surrounded by the visitors' anguished gasps and sobs, Moses and C.J. looked upon each other in disbelief. They knew the truth. They knew why it happened. The MAJIK-12 had killed the President in their unrelenting effort to shroud decades of tyranny and wanton murder. C.J. wished he could tell the people, explaining the reality that had been cruelly withheld from them. But, without substantive proof his claims would ring hollow and be forever disavowed by the Government and media. Their mission now took on even greater urgency. A recurrent theme began to echo through his mind. *We have to get those CDs...*

Renewing their quest, the brothers marched toward the elevator and joined a short queue. In less than a minute, another cab was available. They descended with eleven others for nearly a quarter-mile in a shaft bored through solid rock. Soon, the limestone cavity began to widen announcing their arrival within the eviscerated bowels of Earth. As they filed out, a thorough check of the underground concession and rest area failed to provide any clue as to Gerhin's whereabouts. The two now entered the Big Room, stopping briefly to revel in its unparalleled majesty. Neither had ever been to Carlsbad Caverns. The colossal formations and otherworldly sights filled them with abiding wonder. Moses stepped to one side, absorbing the atmospherics of the cave and listening for any ambient sounds. Acting more on a hunch than suspicion, he led C.J. down the concrete path that Gerhin and the others had previously trod.

Their search continued in earnest. Temperatures within this subterranean realm never varied, remaining at a constant 56 degrees. What had been an initial relief from the heat above was now becoming somewhat chilly, causing C.J. to lament not having warmer clothing. Twice more Moses stopped, hoping to get a bearing on the Israeli's location. He suddenly detected a rogue noise that caused him to quicken his pace down an alternate path. C.J. followed, trying to keep up while matching the stealth of his brother. It wasn't long before they heard Gerhin's voice echoing from an adjacent cave, discussing the terms of a business arrangement.

"I want 100 million in U.S. dollars deposited to my Swiss bank account no later than the 15ᵗʰ of this month. Don't tell me you need more time, because you won't get it. If there are any delays, you lose the deal and I go to another source. The CDs stay in my possession until the money's wired. Understood?"

As additional words were exchanged, Moses and C.J. crouched low assuming a defensive position behind several stalagmites. At last, they could see Gerhin and the three Russians standing about fifteen yards distant. It was clear the time had come to arm themselves. Moses opened his weapon satchel and removed two handguns, presenting one to his brother. Hopefully, the men would surrender the CDs without bloodshed. That lovely thought, however, was tragically short-lived.

The top of C.J.'s head inadvertently bobbed into sight, precipitating what would become a vicious, chaotic melee. Sabarov's bodyguard alerted the others with a torrent of Russian obscenities, grasping his gun from the ground. Gerhin bolted into the furthest recesses of the cave in an effort to find an alternate exit. The engagement commenced with a few stray rounds, escalating significantly when Sabarov's computer geek unleashed a barrage from a concealed Kalashnikov AK-47. The brothers were pinned down behind the stalagmites, compressed into fetal positions to escape the sudden hail of bullets.

"Oh, man!" C.J. gasped. "We're in a shit storm now!"

They waited for their chance to return fire, but the initial salvo never seemed to end. Moses fired randomly over the rocks, letting the enemy know they were armed as well. The Russians assumed cover behind a wall of stone and began digging in for an extended battle. Continuous gunfire raged over them, assaulting their ears with acoustic misery. Surrounding rock was soon targeted in the chance a wayward round would somehow ricochet into them. As the onslaught refused to yield, it became evident that handguns were no match for automatic weapons. A decision was reluctantly made. Moses dug down into his satchel and pulled the safety pin from a Hyper-grav grenade. After judging the required distance, he lofted the ordnance over his head but with a greater degree of arc than anticipated. The device prematurely detonated in midair, directly above their Russian foes. An indescribable sonic cascade shook the cavern, ending with what sounded like a deep squelching noise. The gunfire immediately ceased. Welcoming the silence, Moses and C.J. shared a common concern. They had already witnessed the pernicious effects of a Hyper-grav at Dreamland and neither looked forward to greeting the scene beyond. Girding themselves for the thankless task, they stood with their handguns at the ready. The two bolted forth, aiming their weapons in cover formation. What they found left them bewildered. There were no bodies. No crater in the ground. Nothing indicative of an extreme gravitational explosion.

"Where the hell did they go?" C.J. asked in near reverence.

Moses declined to speculate, noting the lack of spent shell casings in the engagement area.

"You think they could've...vaporized?"

The Army Ranger shook his head. "I've seen a lot of strange shit, but nothing like this. It's like they were never here."

C.J. shrugged in disbelief. "Well, that's not so bad."

Before his eyes, Moses watched the falling subterranean water droplets morph in color from crystal clear to blood red. He then tilted his head toward the cave ceiling. "Oh, yes it is..."

In a scene of horror evoking Vlad Dracula's 'Forest of the

Impaled', the Russian trio had ascended into the cavern, gored to death on razor-sharp stalactites. So rapid was their demise they had no time to register astonishment, instantly transformed into a hanging garden of flesh.

The searing image left them chilled and nauseous. Several anguished seconds elapsed before C.J. was able to vocalize his thoughts. "It's a good thing we skipped lunch."

Moses refocused on their mission. "Gerhin ran that way with the CDs."

Their pursuit continued. Dashing through a maze-like landscape of soda straw formations, the two bounded over a series of fissures in the cavern floor and around the edge of a deep green pool of water, owing its color to a lustrous base of pure malachite. About 30 yards further the cave walls started to narrow significantly. The last of the overhead lights were now behind them, providing a stark reminder that what lay beyond was shrouded in unfathomable darkness. They arrived at an opening in the rock not much larger than a typical dog door, known to cavern explorers as a spider hole.

"He's got to be in there," Moses reasoned. "There's no other way out."

C.J. accepted the logic, but overcoming a multitude of fears took longer. "Okay. You first."

Showing little hesitation, Moses snap activated a glow stick from his satchel and proceeded to slither into the void. A pungent smell of ammonia greeted his senses. The tunnel walls and floor were damp with a yellow-white substance which he recognized as guano. Due to the freshness and volume of the excrement, there was little doubt they were entering a cave which housed a very active colony of Mexican Freetail bats.

Further on, the spider hole emptied into a large chamber filled with jagged rock columns and stalagmites. The sound of dripping water was pronounced. Moses came to his feet, casting the eerie light in a wide arc. There was no sign of Gerhin. However, human footprints were clearly visible across the guano-laden floor, leading toward a larger cave in the distance. C.J. followed soon after, grumbling at the indignity of their entrance. Suddenly, three gunshots echoed through the chamber, the muzzle flash briefly lighting the threshold to the anterior cavern. Moses yelped in pain, tumbling to the ground after taking a round in the leg. He slid quickly behind a column for cover. After dropping to the deck, C.J. crawled furiously toward his brother to assess his condition.

"Are you hit?"

"Yeah," enduring another wave of torment. "Just below the left knee."

"What can I do?"

"Nothing," he confirmed. "Let's get this prick." Moses shut his eyes and spat forth a potent expletive. The anguish he felt was mainly to his pride. This was not the first time the Army Ranger had been shot, but it was certainly the most preventable. The glow stick had rendered him far too easy a target. He channeled an extended breath, trying to place mind over agony.

C.J. shouted into the darkness. "Give it up, Gerhin! There's no way out!" A dense silence prevailed. He once again tried to reason with the thief. "We just want the CDs! Hand 'em over and we'll let you go!"

This time, a voice was heard coming from the cavern beyond. "That's quite an offer. Fortunately, I have a much better one waiting for me in Zurich."

"Only if you make it out of here...and that ain't happening!"

Gerhin took time to weigh his diminished options. "Any chance I could interest you in a bribe?"

"This isn't about money!" flared the indignant reply. "It's about the truth!"

"Wrong answer," declared the Israeli, conscious of what he now had to do. "I thought you'd be smarter than that."

From his reclined position, Moses found a crevice in the limestone column large enough to safely fire his weapon. However, the target had to be illuminated if only for a second or two. After fishing another glow stick from his satchel, he tossed the object at the cavern entrance with such force it fractured the glass vial within. The instant luminescence was all the Army Ranger needed. Now frozen in the soft green light was Gerhin, his arm raised to lob the live grenade he was holding. Four shots rang out, two of which shattered his wrist. As the explosive fell, it began to bounce across the uneven bedrock. The Mossad agent was shrieking in pain, desperately trying to kick the metal orb into the chamber. His manic attempts failed as the device lodged itself at the base of the entrance. He ran for his life, executing a full somersault over a nearby ledge. Moses and C.J. braced themselves, covering their heads in anticipation of the blast.

The weapon detonated, filling the cave with a brilliant flash and tremulous, lingering echoes. High velocity fragmentation weakened the surrounding rock causing a partial cave in. Thousands of bats suspended on the cavern ceiling were rudely awakened from their slumber, sending them into a massive, disoriented swarm. They dove toward the entrance, escaping along the only route they knew. Moishe Gerhin came to his feet at the worst possible moment. Standing directly in their path, the bats engulfed the man in a spiraling cloud of confusion. The winged rodents were everywhere, pressed firmly against his body, their combined force momentarily lifting him in midair. With his delirium cresting past human endurance, the squealing agent began to hyperventilate. He lost his footing and then his life, tumbling headfirst into a 400 foot crevasse. The brothers heard Gerhin's endless, receding scream into the abyss and shared the dismay that in his possession were the Dreamland CDs...swallowed whole within Earth's yawning throat.

Funneling through the chamber, the bats found their way down the open spider hole. They flew in a swirling mass not unlike a horizontal tornado, indistinguishable from one to the next. Using sonar echolocation, they exited the cave with a peculiar buzzing sound leaving Moses and C.J. clutching their ears in terror. The swarm's sheer volume further weakened the entrance which suddenly began to collapse inside an avalanche of immutable stone. A shrill vibration shook the chamber, making them feel the entire void was about to disintegrate. Rocky dust choked the air nearly obscuring the glow stick in Moses' hand. Amidst their respiratory distress, they heard the fluttering of bats ascending into the recesses above. The two waited patiently for the tremors to subside, trusting their subterranean womb would convulse no further. At last, C.J. rose to his feet employing the use of another glow stick to survey the damage. What he discovered chilled him more than the low cavern temperature.

"Oh, shit. I can't find the way out."

Moses demanded an explanation. "What happened to the spider hole?"

"It must've caved in," his voice spiked with panic. "I think we're trapped."

The unwelcome news was rife with consequence. C.J. would be unable to seek help for his wounded brother. The miles of surrounding rock left their cell phones useless. They were imprisoned in a cave with no ventilation and limited air. And, worst of all, no one knew they were there.

Moses, still grimacing in pain, inspected his injury for the first time. The bleeding was light but continuous, saturating his pant leg and pooling on the guano-splattered floor. He applied an emergency tourniquet just above the knee, the fabric torn from the tail of his shirt. The soldier elevated his leg, experiencing additional misery from the sudden motion. The bullet had definitely struck bone. In this condition, he'd be of little benefit to his brother who was attempting to clear several large boulders blocking their means of escape.

C.J.'s efforts were strenuous and unrewarding. He swore under his breath, frustrated with his inability to note any progress. The tumbling debris had camouflaged the spider hole to such an extent he wasn't sure if the opening remained intact nor was he even aware of its location. Exhausted from his labor, he sat on the floor and closed his eyes in fatigue. The two knew the situation was dire, but chose to address the topic with an exchange of gallows humor.

"So, what's the verdict?" asked Moses.

C.J. sighed heavily. "The jury says we're fucked on all counts."

"That figures," he snickered. "How do they plan to execute us?"

"Death by asphyxiation...death by impalement...death by hypothermia..."

"Hey, you forgot death by hemorrhage."

"Let's just hope we don't end up like Gerhin...flying like a bat into Hell."

From the darkest part of the chamber, came words that were equally foreboding. "Believe me, Michael, there are worse things than Hell."

Caught in a web of awe, the brothers remained motionless wondering if the other had experienced the same auditory hallucination. Before they could react, a hooded figure entered their sight through the pale green glow. On instinct, Moses bolted to his feet only to fall backward in excruciating pain. C.J. failed to move, left bewildered by the sudden apparition. He soon recognized this ghostly visitor as one of the Capuchin Monks that had accompanied the Pope to the mission. Though mired in astonishment, he somehow managed to ask a coherent question.

"Who the hell are you?"

The monk removed his hood, revealing a forty-something male with dirty blond hair and a thick crop of facial stubble. Probing C.J. with reflective, cat-like eyes, a discolored smile greeted him without warmth.

"You know me, Michael," his voice reverberating through the murky grotto. "You've known me for countless millennia."

He began to advance uncomfortably close, forcing Moses to level his weapon. "Back off, asshole! Right now!"

The man stopped, peering over at the gun-wielding soldier. "This doesn't concern you, Azrael," abruptly altering his tone. "I know you've never been the brightest bulb in the store, but even you should know when to mind your own business. This is between Michael...and me."

C.J. waved Moses off, peppering the monk with a rapid fire interrogation. "Who are you? What do you want? How did you get in here?"

The arctic smile returned. "What happened to the spirit I've come to loathe and detest? Those questions are for the fearful and I don't remember you being afraid of anything." Continuing his approach, he squatted down beside C.J. scanning his body with visible distain. "I've dreamt of this moment for as long as I can remember, hoping to greet you here in this realm. But, I never believed it would be quite like this. Seeing the great archangel Michael, lying before me in a pile of fecal matter. I love karma, don't you?"

The smell of bat guano did not fully mask the odor of the man himself, a fact that C.J. was compelled to discover. "I don't know who you are. I've never seen you before in my life."

A tinge of frustration began to swell in his voice. "You have to think beyond the physical. This body is merely a disguise." He began pulling at the skin on his arm with a look of genuine contempt. "It was created for me in a laboratory. Conceived by an IBE and borne of a woman who the authorities later killed. I forced myself into this fucking bag of flesh, just so I could be here with you now. Doesn't that give you a clue as to who I am...and what you really mean to me?"

C.J. remembered the discussion with Ariel regarding the hybrid humans raised under the Government's evil eye. How they'd been trained to develop special powers and how each had gone insane. "I don't remember anything about you," he groaned. "Just tell me what this is about."

"It's about justice!" his voice howled. "It's about honor and respect. Concepts of which you know absolutely nothing. This isn't some petty grudge. I'm not here because you keyed my car or banged my wife. I'm here because you condemned my soul to eternal damnation. I'm here, Michael...to avenge myself upon you."

The discussion had become overtly spiritual. It reminded C.J. of their captivity at Dreamland. How desperately Lucifer had wanted them to join with His archangels, the minions of the Devil. A mystic vibration transported him back to another place at another time, releasing him from any corporeal thought. In a leap of faith, he reached deep into his immortal essence and correctly greeted their guest. "Mammon," oozed the breathless response. "Member of the Grigori."

The man sealed his eyes with near orgasmic relief. "Ahhh, Michael. I knew you'd eventually remember. I didn't want you to die without being fully aware of who killed you."

C.J. recalled a previous encounter. "You...you were at my house once. The day of the fire. You were one of the firefighters."

"Oh, I've been much more than that," admitted the fallen archangel. "I've been watching you for quite some time. I was the teacher who gave you your only failing grade in math. I was the reporter who broke the story of your wife's infidelity when you were Mayor. I was the chef who gave you that horrible case of botulism sixteen years ago. I was your aunt's little Pekinese who pissed all over your shoes."

C.J. summoned the memory of each event. "And now you're in this body...still watching."

"That's right," he stated with contentment. "I'm here to watch you die."

"But, why now? You could've killed me before."

The man nodded at his logic. "True. But, you wouldn't have known why... and what would be the fun in that?"

After a dramatic sigh, C.J. looked over at Moses who'd been listening so intently to their encounter that he was no longer showing any outward signs of distress. "So, what exactly did I do to deserve this fate?" he continued.

Left incredulous by the query, Mammon began to expound on his various sins. "Once we were kindred spirits, you and I. Then you severed that bond, all because the Grigori challenged the word of Jehovah. Because we saw a better way. A more evolved way to exist through Lucifer's teachings. Were we heard? Would the archangels listen to reason? No. Jehovah sought to destroy us and used you as the method of His vengeance. And, when the war in Heaven was over…after you claimed victory by turning two of our own against us…we begged for mercy. But, there was no love in Jehovah's heart. He decided to cast us out, treating us as inferiors, unworthy of His compassion. I pleaded for you to intercede on our behalf, but you remained mute. I saw you sitting at the throne of the Almighty, mocking the Grigori as we were stripped of our divinity. In our moment of greatest need, you mocked us…YOU MOCKED US!"

Mammon clutched C.J. by the shoulders, grappling with him for leverage, his body now pulsing with rage. "You kept us from our rightful place in Heaven. You blocked the path of our souls to enlightenment. Did you think we'd forget? Show you the forgiveness you failed to show us? Did you honestly believe that we would EVER give you up?" He released C.J. with a shove, causing him to bang his head against the adjacent rock wall. Mammon rose to his feet, backing away from his ancient foe.

"So, what are we supposed to do? Fight to the death?" asked C.J., overly animated from their tussle.

Mammon assured him otherwise. "In a few hours the lack of oxygen will claim you. But, don't despair. I'll return before your final breath."

"Return?" eyeing him in confusion. "How are you getting out?"

His specious grin resurfaced. "The same way I came in, Michael. Through the open door…"

It happened in an instant and it was like nothing they'd ever seen. A dark crack seemed to appear before them in three-dimensional space, defying every known physical law. It was opaque with no light able to escape the void. The fissure suddenly bloomed wide, revealing a hidden portal into another domain. Then, in a surreal flourish, the body of Mammon slipped into the rift, sucked inside with the force of a pneumatic tube. The spatial cavity closed, leaving nothing behind but a pair of distended mouths and several moments of near total hysteria.

CHAPTER THIRTY-FOUR

*T*he Sunset Limited had arrived in the town of Deming and was now preparing to depart. A few blocks east of the station, the semi carrying Casey and Kimberly barreled down an I-10 exit ramp and onto a side road running parallel with the tracks. They hadn't expected the timing to be this close. The truck had been delayed at a U.S. Border Patrol checkpoint west of Las Cruces, singled out for a random inspection of its contents.

Executing a wide turn into the parking area, the 18-wheeler bounded over a curb and decelerated to a stop next to the concrete platform. Having already declined Casey's offer of payment, the trucker had but one request of Kimberly. "Miss Boobie, if I could get me a last peek at them purdy puppies, I'd be very much obliged."

She saw the rail cars begin to lurch forward. "Move your ass, Casey! The train's leaving!"

Her brother bolted from the cab, allowing her a private moment to reward the man for his courtesy. She then dashed across the platform, leaving the trucker to express his infinite thanks. "Oh, lordy! I saw 'em real good that time! Yes, in damn deedy! Makes me wanna git on my knees and beg for mercy!"

Kimberly followed Casey onto the train, arriving breathless in the entry port of a double-decker coach car. A conductor helped her inside, reaching for the door to seal it shut. He turned, looking at the two with a jaundiced eye. This Amtrak employee of 22 years had seen his fair share of last second boardings, but none until now without any luggage whatsoever. It seemed sensible to ask the frenzied pair if they'd forgotten something even more important.

"Tickets?"

"Oh, we're traveling with Roberta de la Cruz," Casey explained, hoping to avoid being charged. "She has a sleeper unit."

The conductor reached inside his coat pocket and scanned the passenger manifest. "You're going to L.A. with her?"

He answered with a particularly clumsy response. "Yeah, unless we get off first."

"Well, you still have to purchase tickets."

"But, we didn't have time at the station," Kimberly interjected.

"You can buy them from me," the conductor assured her. Two pieces of yellow paper were double punched before they could stall him with another excuse. "That'll be $99 each."

Admitting defeat, Casey unfurled his wallet handing the man a crisp pair of hundred dollar bills. He waited patiently for the meager amount in return which never materialized. "I don't carry change," informed the conductor.

A breath of exasperation followed. "Can you tell us where to find Roberta's compartment?"

"She's in car 8020, unit number 9. It's seven cars forward, past the diner."

Armed with the information, Casey felt the lost two bucks was money well spent. They each pocketed their tickets and began to ascend a narrow staircase to the coach car above. The two marched down the aisle, rocking side to side from the train's lateral movement on the tracks. Most of the seats were occupied. They screened the passengers as they went by, so as not to miss their sister by accident. A majority of the riders appeared somber, some whispering amongst themselves, others shedding quiet tears. Small groups clustered around those with radios, seeking whatever information was available. After traversing two additional coach cars, stray words and snippets of conversation teased them with an insidious buzz. However, it wasn't until they entered the lounge car that the magnitude of the El Paso carnage was fully conveyed. Here they stopped, listening to the inebriated and overly verbose speculate on what happened. Dueling radios were set on maximum volume, affecting every ear in range. Brother and sister exchanged a look of horror, aware the military had deliberately silenced its Commander in Chief. Once more, Kimberly tried to contact Major Osborne on her cell. The lines were hopelessly jammed. Casey assured her their loved ones were safe. The catacomb cave-in would have prevented any of the others from being in downtown El Paso at the fateful moment. His logic was inescapable and brought her renewed comfort.

Forging through the shock, they next entered the crowded dining car. The lunch hour patrons were unusually boisterous, seated at tables across from one another. A young Latina mother and her newborn drew particular interest, until closer inspection proved their suspicions wrong. They sidled past the busy wait staff and into the first of the sleeper cars. The compartments consisted of ten small roomettes and five larger bedrooms, all of which were draped for privacy. Arriving at the threshold to the adjacent car, Casey spotted the number 8020 imprinted on the outer portal. They were now mere steps from their sister. The two hoped to surprise Roberta, cornering her so she'd have no chance to flee. As the hatch slid open, Casey and Kimberly bracketed the entrance to unit number 9 on their immediate left. The roomette's sliding door was left ajar and the privacy drape cast aside. No one was within. They entered to find their sister's satchel resting on one of the seats, alongside her iPhone and headset.

"She's aboard alright," proclaimed Kimberly. "Probably in one of the bathrooms."

Casey concurred. "Let's check it out."

As they left the compartment, the pair froze mid-step. Coming through the gangway between cars was Roberta and their infant sister, Hope. Once the inner door slid open, the teen shrieked at the sight of her siblings.

"What are you doing here? You guys followed me?"

Kimberly sought to calm her fears. "We were worried, Robbie...about you and the baby. We're a family and we need to stick together. Come back with us."

She shook her head, issuing a decisive "No."

The automatic door began to slide shut. Casey lunged forth, blocking the portal with his foot. Misinterpreting his advance, Roberta backed away and callously placed her infant sister in jeopardy. She pushed the baby past a seam in the articulated wall, threatening to drop her between the speeding rail cars. "Don't make me do it!" the girl shouted over a gust of wind. "I will if you come any closer!"

No one moved, left speechless by the unfolding scenario. Although convinced that Roberta was incapable of such a heinous act, Casey had no intention of provoking her further. Hope commenced a rueful cry, buffeted by the onrushing air and generated noise. The conflicted youth was quivering in panic, her legs visibly wobbling atop the flexible metal bridge. Roberta's bright eyes were sunken by fatigue and a face typically full of joy had become gaunt with angst. Striving to defuse the situation, Kimberly made repeated attempts to reason with her.

"I know you're tired, Robbie. I'm tired, too. We all need sleep. But, you can't give in to this. Don't take it out on the baby."

"She's evil."

"No, she's not. That's Lucifer making you believe that. Don't you remember what we went through at Dreamland? All the things he did to trick us. Trust your heart, Robbie, not your head."

A stray tear stalled their conversation. "I don't know what to think. When I close my eyes, I see Hope talking to me. She says the most awful things. Like how mother didn't know she was giving birth to the Devil." The girl paused, blubbering for breath. "That voice...I just don't want to hear it anymore."

"It's a dream," Kimberly assured her. "We've all had that dream. But, it's not real. Don't fall into Lucifer's trap. He wants you to harm her. We can't let Him win. Not after all we've been through."

Roberta shut her eyes, struggling for the truth. Casey, who'd remained silent until now, brought an end to her doubt.

"If mother was here with us, would you trust her? Completely believe what she'd say?"

His sister appeared wounded by the question. "Of course, I would."

"Then, listen to her words," he pleaded, attempting to channel the Madre's spirit. "Do not destroy that which God has created... for she is destined to be the savior of humanity."

It was her brother's voice, but she was certain her mother's soul had spoken. Overcome with emotion, Roberta slowly brought the infant to her breast, hating herself for what she'd almost done. In a gush of tears, she handed Hope into Casey's gentle grasp. Two elderly passengers suddenly entered the gangway, allowing Roberta to dash off into the adjacent car. Kimberly tried to follow, but was impeded by the slow moving pair. She eventually left in pursuit, leaving Casey to comfort his newborn sister inside Roberta's compartment.

This was the first time he'd been alone with Hope and the two seemed to bond quickly. He tried to style her windblown hair, but soon discovered that it was naturally unruly. She cooed at the silly sounds he made and burped for him on cue. As Casey strummed her lips with his finger, Kimberly returned to the sleeper car alone.

"I can't find her. There's a million places she could hide."

"She'll show up. All her things are here." He again took note of the babe in his arms. "Hey, look. Hope's smiling at me."

"She's too young to smile. It's probably gas."

Unwilling to accept her pediatric insight, Casey returned the gesture with an exaggerated grin of his own. He took a moment to scan the compartment, as well as Roberta's satchel. "I don't see any formula. She'll have to have some."

"I could check Robbie's luggage. Maybe she's got a bottle or two in there."

He endorsed the logic. "Okay. I'll ask in the diner. They might have some on board."

While his sister departed for the baggage area downstairs, Casey trekked to the dining car cradling the newborn. Disclosing his need, a member of the wait staff directed him to the lounge car with word that infant formula was sold at the snack bar on the lower level. He walked onward, transitioning through the double door gangway and onto an enigmatic stage.

The lounge car was empty. Arrayed lengthwise in front of wrap-around windows, 48 swivel seats awaited their next occupant. A newly released DVD played on the monitors to a phantom audience. Even the aisle was devoid of life. Before him were a wealth of mixed drinks waiting to be consumed, still resting in numerous cup holders. Snack bags were left open, their contents untouched. Casey blinked in disbelief, wondering the odds of such a mystifying occurrence. *This place was packed with people not 10 minutes ago. Could all of them have left at once? Where did everyone go?*

Moving cautiously, he arrived at the center of the car and descended the narrow staircase to the snack bar below. What Casey now faced was no less cryptic, entering a nearly deserted room with a lone patron seated at a card table. The man was in his mid to late 40's, displaying an average build no heavier than 180 pounds. His countenance reflected a peculiar mixture of boredom and satisfaction, two steel-grey eyes held captive by a video monitor on the near wall. Patches of adult acne circumnavigated the elongated face, framed by wiry brown hair that covered his ears like an aviator's helmet. A box of Drake's Devil Dogs was perched on the table before him. He held one cream-filled chocolate cake in each hand, alternating bites from each. As the man continued to feast, bits of the confection tumbled down the length of his robe, a vestment that confirmed his identity as one of the Capuchin Monks from the Pope's visit.

At first Casey said nothing, opting to walk over to the concession area. With each step a fetid odor increased in strength, affecting his senses as none he'd ever experienced. A hint of smoke permeated the air as though something had cooked far too long. His curiosity now piqued, Casey addressed the esoteric figure.

"Where's the lounge car attendant?"

The incessant munching ceased. "Oh, him? He didn't like me very much, but that's okay 'cause I didn't care for him either. I told him to leave, but he stayed and made a complete ash of himself."

With ample trepidation, Casey peered over the service counter. An indistinguishable mass of bone and blood lay fused to the floor, encased in the charred remnants of an Amtrak uniform. The attendant had been burned beyond recognition, a grisly victim of spontaneous combustion. Casey shut his eyes, fending off a sudden attack of nausea.

The monk finished his Devil Dogs and began tearing the cellophane wrapper from another. "I've never appreciated the presence of humans," he explained in a cursory tone. "I'm not a fan of physical beings. That's why I made the others leave. I didn't want any of those disgusting creatures to ruin my enjoyment of these delicious snacks." He directed another to his mouth, smacking his lips in evident bliss. "I've experimented with drugs and sex, but nothing gratifies me quite like a sugar rush."

After a few anxious moments, Casey's queasiness abated. Ensnared in this sanctum of horror, he struggled to make sense of it all. "Who are you?" Almost immediately, he revised the question. "What are you?"

Still licking chocolate cake from his fingers, the monk indulged his inquisitive nature. "My friends call me Belial. Everyone else calls me trouble."

Casey summoned the memory of his research. "You're part of the Grigori. One of the fallen archangels."

Belial chose not to respond, concentrating his attention on

the video monitor's remote control now in hand. The channel was switched from a recent Hollywood release to a chaotic scene of mayhem and carnage. Although Casey had not been a witness to this particular event, he recognized it immediately. Somehow he was watching a recorded replay of the Las Vegas earthquake as the seismic catastrophe actually occurred.

"I prefer reality programming over scripted material, don't you?"

Casey's slack-jawed reaction refused to subside, absorbing the on-screen pandemonium with an insatiable thirst. "How the hell did you get this?"

"Oh, I was there," he confessed with pride. "Me and my digital camcorder. This was a one-of-a-kind, planetary extravaganza. I wouldn't have missed it for all the assholes in Heaven." The ground-level perspective was taken alongside Las Vegas Boulevard, panning back and forth to capture the full range of human tribulation. Belial smiled at the vast tableaux of hysteria. "Look at these spiritual retards. At this point, they know they're toast. They should be preparing their souls for the transition. But they just run around and scream, desperate to remain jammed inside these ridiculous, blood-filled cocoons." As the devastation escalated, Belial began to chortle at the horrific imagery. "Some say I'm depraved, but I'd like to think of myself as tragically misunderstood." His derisive laughter resumed.

A timer rang out behind Casey. "What was that?"

"The microwave," he explained. "I took the liberty of heating up the baby's formula." A glacial interlude followed. "Well, that's why you came down here, isn't it? To find her some formula?"

Stunned by Belial's insight, Casey strode to the kitchen and popped open the microwave door. There before him was an eight ounce baby bottle, filled to the nipple with a whitish liquid. He looked back at the crazed archangel with a justified lack of trust. "How did you know what I was after?"

The question was conspicuously ignored. "Go ahead," Belial insisted. "Give her the formula. She needs her nourishment."

Casey removed the bottle, squirting a small amount of liquid onto the back of his hand. It was the perfect temperature for consumption. He brought a drop to his lips as a taste test, detecting nothing out of the ordinary. The two persisted in their quiet resolve, probing one another with palpable anxiety.

Belial once more issued the instruction. "Give her...the formula."

This time, Casey remained motionless. He was intent on letting this situation play out until the other side blinked. His patience was soon rewarded.

"Give that goddamn bitch the fucking formula!"

Casey threw the bottle across the room, striking Belial in the chest. "You made it. You drink it."

Displaying an openly malevolent demeanor, the man rose from his seat, securing the bottle in hand. "Now, you're just pissing me off."

The spiritual foes prepared for physical battle. Casey laid Hope down on an Amtrak blanket that he spread across the kitchen countertop. Turning to confront the enemy, he assumed a defensive posture waiting for Belial to make the initial move.

"I wasn't trying to poison her," he contended. "I've got much better plans."

"Like what?"

"I thought about snapping her neck, but that would be a little too quick. Intense suffering is what I'm after. So, I decided to dismember her with a meat cleaver. Pretty cool, huh?"

"You'll have to get past me first."

Without notice, Belial deftly unscrewed the cap on the baby bottle. "Oh, I think that's a given..." His left hand flew forth, splashing the formula into Casey's eyes. With his opponent temporarily blinded, Belial lifted his foot and punted Casey backward into a metal refrigeration unit. He grabbed the meat cleaver from a secure location, sighting a clear path to the baby. As he dove toward Hope, his legs buckled from Casey's tackle, the sharpened blade missing the infant's arm by a mere two inches.

Falling face first to the deck, Belial swung the weapon behind him in a random search for flesh. As the two staggered to their feet, Casey jumped back as the meat cleaver made another errant pass. Belial then spun anew toward Hope. Her brother jumped the man from behind, seizing his right arm which was poised for a lethal chop. While attempting to transfer the blade to his free hand, Casey demonstrated his martial arts dexterity by elevating his foot into Belial's neck. In a squall of anguish, the pair lost balance, once again caving to the floor. Hoisting the man above him, Casey used his knees to send his adversary into an awkward somersault, giving him a moment to regain his footing. Charging in haste, he was abruptly greeted by the steel refrigerator door which Belial had deliberately swung open. His forehead struck the appliance, causing him to collapse upon the kitchen tile. It was now Belial's turn to advance, clutching the meat cleaver with manic intent. Casey grabbed a nearby stool, blocking four separate thrusts of the blade. On the fifth attempt Casey marshaled his strength, using the padded seat to catapult Belial over the service counter. Dazed by his ungainly gymnastics, it took the rebel archangel a few seconds to recover. He stood in time to receive a series of rapid-fire kicks from Casey, the blows tenderizing him from head to groin. At last, the meat cleaver flew out of his hand, landing across the room. Leveraging his weight against him, Casey used a classic judo flip maneuver to send Belial crashing into the card table from whence he came. As the battered man wobbled to his feet, it appeared much of the fight had been taken out of him.

"That was stimulating," he declared, wiping some stray blood from his mouth. "I love pain. It's the most interesting of all the physical sensations."

The sound of footsteps could be heard coming from the stairwell. Kimberly arrived, bewildered at the scene. "What's going on here? Who's he?"

Belial protested immediately. "This isn't fair. Two against one? How am I supposed to beat both of you? You wouldn't want me to fight dirty, would ya?" Without warning, he propelled himself into Casey's sister, dropkicking her squarely in the face. Kimberly pirouetted violently into a bulkhead, collapsing to the deck from severe trauma.

Left livid by the attack, Casey's ire was fueled by the man's appalling lack of chivalry. "You can't do that to a woman!"

"Sorry," flashing a malicious grin. "Guess I didn't get the memo."

Casey lunged at him in rage. Jumping atop the card table, Belial tore the fluorescent light box from the ceiling. Debris rained down, disorienting Casey long enough for the man to roll a 500 pound ice cream freezer into his legs. After pinning his foe against a wall, Belial began to dash for the baby. Vaulting over the service counter, Casey caught the man flush on the side of his head, slamming his face into the microwave. The two tumbled to the floor, rolling over and under each other. Belial foamed from the mouth like a rabid animal, trying to sink his teeth into Casey's neck. Well-placed elbows and knees scored points for both, but after wrestling for several minutes neither was able to claim victory.

A rough patch of track caused the train to rock excessively. The lateral motion helped arouse Kimberly who began to focus on the men fighting beyond. Regaining her faculties, she came to her feet and grabbed the abandoned meat cleaver which was lying nearby. The woman ran toward her attacker, intending to bury the blade in his back. Belial noted her approach and prepared his exit strategy. Just as she swung the weapon, he disappeared into the same spatial rift that Mammon used inside the cave, the fissure closing as fast as it opened. Kimberly gasped at the supernatural departure, her eyes and mouth dilated in shock. Casey experienced an unusual draft of cold air followed by a powerful suction that instantly swept Belial from his grasp. He now joined his sister in mutual astonishment.

"Did you see that?" her words quavering in awe.

"I did," mumbled Casey, unable to say anything more.

After cleaning up the area, they returned to Roberta's

compartment. Kimberly stayed with Hope, while Casey had the unenviable task of alerting the conductor to the lounge car attendant's demise. The Sunset Limited arrived in Lordsburg, New Mexico which was the next scheduled stop. They remained at the station for more than five hours while police questioned witnesses and the county coroner examined the remains. During the lengthy investigation, Casey stayed on the platform watching to see if Roberta would leave the train, but his sister never appeared. With no evidence of homicide or theft, the authorities allowed the Sunset Limited to continue on its night-long journey to Los Angeles.

Casey and Kimberly waited patiently for Roberta to return to the compartment. As the sun fell over the horizon, the desert landscape became obscured behind a lush ebony veil. Maybe it was the darkness or the train's gentle rocking motion. Perhaps it was boredom or the fact they'd been awake for more than 60 hours. Whatever the reason, the two eventually closed their eyes and were soon back in dreamland...with Hope nestled by their side.

CHAPTER THIRTY-FIVE

JUAREZ & WESTERN TEXAS — MAY 9ᵗʰ — 12:48 PM MDT

$\mathcal{I}$n the space of an hour, Gonzales International Airport had morphed from a rather mundane facility into a scene of incredible tumult. Panic began to escalate after the U.S. military attack on the Juarez mission, but reached a fever's pitch when the terminal windows shook from the El Paso blast eight miles away. Frantic residents flocked to ticket counters purchasing available seats on any scheduled aircraft, regardless of destination. The wealthiest competed for private charter flights, offering up to ten times the asking price. Security personnel increased their vigilance, screening every passenger with obligatory suspicion. Lines snaked through the terminal as people engaged in reciprocal bouts of pushing and shouting. News of the devastation in El Paso only exacerbated the chaos, leaving an anxious multitude to pray for their lives and those of their loved ones.

Trapped within the fray were Barbara and Shannon, accompanied by Captain Garza and the still gimpy Captain Tejada. By now they'd hoped to establish contact with the rest of their family, but cell phone communication remained impossible. Barbara thought it best to depart immediately for the United Nations, alerting the General Assembly to the truth about Roswell and how the MAJIK-12 had covered up this fact with the blood of innocent thousands. She had secured a ticket on a jet bound for Mexico City, but was frustrated to learn that the flight had been cancelled. Soon, other possible connections through Cancun, Monterrey and Guadalajara were also grounded. The Mexican authorities had no clue what was happening across the border and out of an abundance of caution decided to suspend airport operations until further notice. A collective groan echoed through the terminal as departure boards flashed the unwelcome news.

"That's just great," sighed Barbara in dismay. "Looks like we're stuck."

"We could rent a car and drive," proposed Garza. "But, Mexico City's 24 hours from here."

Shannon shook her head with resolve. "I've got to get back to the States."

"Every border crossing's sealed tight," Tejada announced. "Once you show your ID, they'll arrest you on the spot. God knows what would happen to you then."

"I've got to stop Roberta," she argued, her angst intensifying. "She's got Hope on that train. The baby's my responsibility. I promised mother I'd take care of her." She brushed away a disobedient tear. "Please, you've got to help me."

Although the military officers had been hired by Major Osborne, he'd made it quite clear that the members of Mary Ellen's family were in their charge and to assist them in any way possible. The two considered their options and finally reached a consensus. "I suppose we could try an incursion," disclosed Tejada.

Shannon sought clarification. "What's that mean?"

A pair of sly grins bloomed before her. "We're Mexicans. If we can't get over the border, who can?"

They left the terminal, hailing the first cab in the taxi queue. Captain Tejada engaged in a discussion with the driver, the nature of which was lost in a brief exchange of Street Spanish. Once their conversation concluded, Shannon had a request of her own.

"Primero, llevenos a una clinica medica." Her pronunciation

was comical, but the message was received nonetheless. The Mexican officers swiveled their heads in surprise, waiting for an explanation. "I did my residency at an L.A. hospital. You're bound to pick up a few words."

As she requested, the taxi stopped at a nearby medical center. Captain Tejada was examined by a physician who soon concurred with Shannon's diagnosis. An attending nurse heavily taped the ankle and immobilized the damaged joint in a splint. He was provided a prescription for pain medication and, much to his chagrin, a pair of wooden crutches. Embarrassed by these symbols of debilitation, the prideful soldier had to be coerced into using them before leaving the clinic.

Their taxi now headed south. As they left the outskirts of Juarez, the landscape transformed into a vast expanse of parched earth, wind-whipped dust and tumbleweeds. The road slowly began to curve, initiating a course correction due east. Ahead in the distance were ramshackle farm buildings, graced with an occasional herd of cattle. After several miles, the road again veered south paralleling a continuous bank of saltcedar and tornillo trees. The presence of vegetation signaled their proximity to the only source of water in this region. The Rio Grande glistened in the sunlight, beckoning them across its shallow waist. Texas lay beyond, tantalizingly close. The cab left the main highway, maneuvering carefully over an undulating dirt road replete with massive ruts and holes. Their furtive approach was aided by a thick overgrowth of mesquite and saltbush, camouflaging the taxi from view. The driver appeared undaunted by the terrain, proving to the jostled passengers that he'd been down this road before. They mercifully came to a stop in front of a dense shroud of wetland grasses. Captain Tejada once more addressed the man in conversation, thanking him for his courtesy and discretion. As the four exited, Shannon paid the driver handsomely in American currency. They watched as the taxi reversed direction, leaving the area in a dusty wake.

"He said the river's only a foot or so deep at this point," explained Tejada. "I guess we'll find out in a hurry."

Barbara expressed a different concern. "But, where are we? Once we get across, where do we go?"

"The town of Fabens is about four miles east. They have a small airport. We should be able to rent a car there."

"Four miles?" squawked Shannon, eyeing his ankle. "Can you make that?"

He snorted with defiance. "Just watch me."

The four ventured onward, scaling a grass embankment and proceeding to the river's edge. They found the conditions to be precisely those forecasted by the taxi driver. The river bottom was lined with flat stone providing them with an excellent fording opportunity. Barbara and Shannon removed their shoes and hiked up their jeans before wading in. Captain Garza helped Tejada maintain balance on the crutches, clearing any potential obstacle from his path. Although the water temperature was comfortable, he kept his ankle elevated so as not to submerge the splint. The women seemed to enjoy the experience with Barbara splashing her sister from behind in a playful manner. Shannon returned the favor, sprinting to the other side to avoid certain retaliation. Each arrived on American soil in a breathless giggle. While waiting for the men to join them, the two wiped themselves dry and returned shoes to feet. Tejada cursed his condition, having underestimated the effort required and realizing he was now more of a liability than an asset. After negotiating a muddy portion of the riverbed, the soldiers arrived on shore with Tejada rendered crimson in frustration. Confronting them was a rusty, six-foot high metal fence extending as far as they could see in both directions. In light of the Captain's infirmity, scaling the barrier was not an option. Locating a wire cutter in his satchel, Garza began the laborious process of snipping the steel mesh filaments from top to ground. With time, he was able to push a section of the fence back allowing the others to walk through. Having successfully traversed the border, the four emerged from the veil of vegetation and continued their trek across the rolling west Texas countryside.

Their exuberance was quickly shattered by the sound of

gunfire. A warning shot streaked over their heads, fired from a white Land Rover LR3 speeding towards them. Captain Garza acted immediately, snaring the women in each arm and forcing them to dive for cover behind an earthen berm. Slithering up beside them was Tejada after abandoning his crutches in the field beyond. He unholstered his handgun, peeking through a gap in the rocks at the approaching vehicle which was clearly marked U.S. BORDER PATROL. A second shot missed a few yards to their left. With their positions compromised and lacking reciprocal firepower, Tejada knew the situation was dire. He reached into a pocket for his cell phone, speed dialing the Major's number. This time, a connection was made.

As his call was answered, he could clearly discern the sonic wash of Osborne's helicopter in flight. "Major, this is Tejada. We could sure use your help."

"What's going on, Captain? Where are you?"

"We're pinned down, receiving fire by U.S. Border Patrol agents. I'd say we're about six and a half klicks west-northwest from the town of Fabens, in a cotton field just east of the Rio Grande."

Osborne hesitated. "Understood...Who's with you?"

"Captain Garza and I are escorting Ms. Pinder and Dr. Hewson." A much longer pause ensued. "Are you in the area, Major?"

"'Fraid not," came the disheartening news. "But, I've just hired three ex-SEALS to give us more guns. Let me try and reach 'em...Hold on."

Tejada was incredulous. *Hold on? Hold on yourself, you crazy Gringo.*

The Land Rover thundered to a stop about 30 yards from their position, kicking up a passel of dust. Two uniformed agents exited the vehicle brandishing rifles, along with a plain-clothed office type who appeared to be unarmed. Due to the deference they were showing the man, it was reasonable to assume that he was their immediate superior. The agents' demeanor was surprisingly jocular, chortling as they approached. Initially, Tejada thought they might be intoxicated, but soon discovered the men were there to taunt them with a slew of racial epithets.

"Come on out, you friggin' beaners!" one of them commanded. "Git outta that trench before I cap your stinkin' asses!"

His partner chimed in. "Hey, chili shitters! We're talkin' to you! What's a matter, you don't spic English?"

They laughed with a maliciousness that was hard to fathom. The Mexican officers looked at each other, sharing a bitter indignation. Shannon, the only American of the four, was left disgusted by her countrymen's actions. Another rifle fired, the bullet grazing the top of the berm.

One of the agents began goading them further, making the sound of a clucking chicken. "Pollo! Pollo! We're gonna cook ya, pollo!" The other men howled in protracted merriment.

Barbara felt compelled to break her silence. "You know, I've never really been a fan of U.S. immigration policy."

"What the hell are those idiots doing?" wondered Shannon.

"They're just being pricks," Tejada assured her. "They'll keep toying with us as long as we don't represent a threat."

Captain Garza lifted his sidearm. "Well, maybe we should."

Although lusting for retribution, Tejada knew a firefight would turn deadly. "Not yet. I'm still waiting for the Major to get back…"

Osborne's voice blared over his cell. "Captain, are you still there?"

"Yes, sir."

"I just got off the phone with Captain Roberts. He told me he and his SEAL team are in the area. I informed him of your location and situation. Don't ask me how, but he said he'll be there in under five minutes."

Tejada cringed in cynicism. There was no way they could arrive that quickly, and even if they could, the Border Patrol agents would spot them and radio for reinforcements. "OK, Major," the soldier sighed. "If we're alive in six, I'll get back with you."

"Roger that."

As he pocketed his cell, another bullet whizzed over his head. "Get out of that dirt, you stupid taco eaters!"

At last, Shannon's ire came to a boil. "I'm an American, you bigoted jerks!"

The Border Patrol agents began hooting in a sexually derisive manner. "Ooooh! Boys, sounds like we got us a wetback bitch! Better git ready, 'cause we gonna have us some fun with a Mexi-ho!"

Her wrath crested full. "I'm not a ho, you fucking limp dicks! Now get outta here before we shoot you in the nuts!"

Tejada and Garza broke into involuntary laughter, clearly enjoying her rebuke. The agents were less amused, their voices turning caustic. "You gotta big mouth, chocha! Now, git your ass up before we smash you like a piñata!"

The rifle fire resumed in a continuous barrage. Captain Tejada nodded to his partner, letting him know the time had come to engage the enemy. Before they could assume offensive positions, Captain Garza spotted three black dots in the sky free-falling toward them at terminal velocity. In an instant, the objects became men. Their suicide plunge ended at a mere 700 feet, blossoming into a trio of ram-air parachutes. The HALO jumpers had just four seconds to adjust their angle of attack, crushing each of the Border Patrol agents as they landed. Two of the men tumbled to their knees after the collision, but one stood proudly upon his kill. With their dramatic insertion at an end, they released their canopies into a light breeze.

The man standing removed his oxygen mask and officially introduced himself. "Captain Manley J. Roberts, reporting as ordered."

In a vocal mélange of shock and excitement, the Mexican officers rose from the ditch, buoyant at their deliverance. They trotted over to the SEAL team, with Captain Tejada scarcely feeling his injury.

"Holy shit!" Garza yammered. "That was incredible!"

"Wasn't it though?" Captain Roberts crowed, his chest puffed at the sudden accolade. "We started as BASE jumpers, but we've been doing HALOs for almost five years now."

"That has to be the ballsiest thing I've ever seen!" declared Tejada. "Didn't it hurt when you hit this guy?"

"Yeah," the man admitted, smiling through his pain. "It did actually. Quite a bit." The other members of his team clustered nearby. "This is Lieutenant Hawkins and Lieutenant Murphy." Greetings were exchanged all around. The soldiers bonded, discussing the intricate aerodynamics of the feat while neglecting their female audience. The sisters glanced at one another, wondering who would take the lead in ending this testosterone lovefest.

"Excuse me!" Shannon exclaimed. "Before this goes any further, shouldn't you guys get a room?"

Lieutenant Hawkins took immediate umbrage with her remark. "That's very rude! Insulting us after we just saved your ass?" He started to advance toward her, but was motioned back by Captain Roberts. "It was just a joke. Chill."

Apologizing for their oversight, the Mexican officers included the women in belated introductions. As the SEAL team shed their jump gear, Barbara expressed concern over the Border Patrol agents. "What do we do with them?"

Hawkins failed to understand the question. "What do you want us to do, lady? Glue their spines back together?"

"They're dead?"

"Well, let's just say they won't be breathing for the rest of their lives."

After collecting some scattered belongings, the seven entered the Land Rover and sped their way onto Interstate 10. They found the westbound lanes closed, a decision by state and county authorities to restrict the amount of traffic entering the devastation in El Paso.

Shannon's frustration bubbled forth. "But, I've got to go this way. Roberta's train is headed to L.A."

"Looks like you'll have to go east first," Captain Roberts

explained. "There's an airport in Midland. It should take us about four hours to get there."

As they set out on their eastbound journey, Tejada called Major Osborne with a status report. The sisters maintained a speechless communion, visually scrutinizing each of the newcomers. Captain Roberts was an overly handsome 30 year old, sporting a cut physique. His coifed blond locks and surfer tan created the perfect frame for a pair of glacier blue eyes. Although somewhat younger, Lieutenant Hawkins was no pretty boy. His most prominent features were a lengthy scar running from chin to ear, along with thin brown hair pulled back into a four-inch ponytail. It was difficult to discern the color of his eyes, due to a perpetual squint that reinforced his grim countenance. Lieutenant Murphy, the third member of the team, was a total enigma. Barbara estimated his age at anywhere between 25 and 50. The man hadn't spoken a single word since they arrived nor would he look directly at anyone. His brown eyes seemed to be glazed over, peering inward instead of out. With a field of stubble on his head and an unhinged mouth as centerpiece, this guy looked like your typical, garden-variety lobotomy patient.

As Captain Tejada finished his conversation with Major Osborne, Shannon extended her hand for the phone. "Hold on. I believe Dr. Hewson wants a word with you." He surrendered the device.

She clutched the phone tightly to her ear, speaking into the cupped mouthpiece at a low whisper. "Who are these guys you hired?"

"They're a former SEAL commando team."

"Why do you say 'former'?"

Osborne sighed. "Because, the Navy bounced them out of the service."

Her interest was now piqued. "And, the reason for this?"

"I heard they did a lot of crazy things."

"Like what?"

"Jumping into live volcanoes, fighting with their superiors…

harmless stuff." There was a lengthy pause, as she digested the information. "Shannon, have these guys done anything to make you feel you're in danger?"

"No," she confessed. "It's just that they're very weird."

"Hey!" Lieutenant Hawkins barked. "We're sitting right here, you know! That's more rudeness...unbelievable."

Chagrined, Shannon resigned herself to the situation. "I'll get back to you."

The trip across western Texas remained uneventful, despite using their official vehicle to speed through a Border Patrol checkpoint. An hour later, they stopped at a convenience store in the town of Van Horn for a much needed pit stop. Barbara agreed to buy the snacks and drinks they'd need for the rest of their journey. She waited for each of the soldiers to place their items on the service counter. Lieutenant Murphy was the last to do so, sheepishly adding a single stick of butter to the pile.

"Don't you want anything else?"

The man thought a moment. He returned to the display cooler and retrieved an additional stick. His bizarre selection left Barbara mystified and she remained so in light of his explanation.

"It makes me go."

Outside the store, Shannon sidled up to the SEAL Team Captain as he pumped gas into their vehicle. "Manley J. Roberts... sounds like the name of a porn star."

"Well, I certainly have the hose for it."

She eyed him in shock until noting the fuel line in his hand. "Oh, right," amused by the man's nimble wit. "What's the deal with Lieutenant Hawkins? He always seems to be itching for a fight."

"I think he was dropped on his head as a baby," kidded Roberts. "He just doesn't like people telling him what to do. The military told him to cut his hair, but he refused. A drill instructor caught him napping one day and decided to do a Sampson on him. That's how he got the scar. He lost a lot of blood that day, but the drill instructor lost more."

"So, what happened?"

"They put him in a military prison for awhile. Of course, they had to let him out 'cuz all the guards were scared shitless. They didn't know him like I do. He's really quite a tame…most of the time."

Shannon saw Lieutenant Murphy walking back to the Land Rover, sucking on a stick of butter. "And, what's his story?"

"It's a sad one," he admitted. "The North Koreans captured him on a secret recon mission back in '03. Held him for years in a little sweat box. He didn't like taking his dumps in there and developed a severe case of constipation. After his release, he discovered that butter was the only thing that works for him."

The tank was now full. As Roberts replaced the hose and secured the gas cap, he encountered her final question. "What about you?"

"Oh, me? I'm completely normal. No idiosyncrasies. No problems of any kind," he volunteered. "Unless you think pure narcissism is a bad thing." He reached for the car door. "Let's get going."

Prior to their arrival in Midland, Major Osborne relayed some welcome news. Casey had called after finding Roberta on the Sunset Limited. Their infant sister was alive and well. Shannon released hours of mental anguish with an extended, heartfelt sigh. Grateful that her brother had accomplished what she could not, she sent forth a prayer asking for her mother's forgiveness. Soon, the woman felt an aura of serenity embrace her, like the caress of an unexpected breeze. Intuitively, she knew the Madre had heard her plea and would never allow feelings of guilt to come between them.

With Shannon no longer compelled to travel west, placing Barbara on a flight to New York was their top priority. Arriving at Midland International Airport, the sisters entered the terminal and engaged in discussion with an airline ticket agent. There were few open flights, the best of which would require waiting three hours in Midland and almost six in Houston. It was suggested she could be placed on a wait list in case a seat became available or drive to Dallas-Fort Worth Airport where she could catch any number of flights. The women returned to the Land Rover and conferred with the soldiers. Their decision was unanimous. They would travel the five extra hours to Dallas.

As the sun began to set, the vehicle cast an ever-lengthening shadow upon the road ahead. Barbara was on her phone, talking with members of the United Nations and support staff of the Bahamian delegation. She was busy laying the groundwork for the world organization to expose the Roswell incident and surrounding cover-up, including the U.S. military's complicity in the death of the President. After candidly sharing these issues with the U.N. Secretary General, the soldiers understood the magnitude of this event and why they'd been hired. They were in the eye of the storm, on a mission as important as any they could have imagined.

Shannon's face was pressed to the window, watching as Interstate 20 extended its reach to the dusky horizon. With Hope's safety no longer a concern, she started to daydream about another special person. One who'd touched her heart. One that had been forcibly taken from her life.

Oh, Troy...What have they done to you?...I wish I could hold you and tell you what you mean to me...This should never have happened...I dragged you into this mess...It's my fault...It's all my fault...

Her doleful tears trickled down the glass, prompting Lieutenant Hawkins to question the woman's condition. "What's with the waterworks?"

She snapped to reality, dabbing the wetness from her eyes. "It's nothing."

He pointed to the streaked window. "If you ask me, that's a whole lot of nothing."

Embarrassed, Shannon wiped the glass with a tissue. "I'm

sorry. I was thinking about someone. Someone I'm not sure I'll ever see again."

"And, why's that?"

She hesitated, not wanting to confide in a stranger. At last, her emotions proved too strong to withhold. "The Government arrested him for trying to help me. He's being held in a military prison…in Quantico, Virginia."

Hawkins snorted in disbelief. "Jesus. The Marine Corps brig?"

"You've been there?"

"Oh, yeah. I was a guest of theirs for a few weeks. It's a real shithole."

Shannon grew excited, now having a glimpse into Troy's world. "They told me he was being sent there for re-education. Do you have an idea where they'd be holding him?"

"Probably in Special Quarters 2…Solitary confinement."

"What would they do to him?" she asked, fearing the answer.

"Same things they tried with me. Psychedelic drugs. Shock therapy. Whatever they think will work."

His words caused her soul to ache. She flopped her head back, purging whatever air she had left in her lungs. Remaining lifeless, she heard the voice of Captain Roberts snatch her spirit from the depths of despair. "Want us to get him out of there?"

Shannon's heart jumped, sending her body rigid. "You could do that?"

The man smiled. "Lady, you've got yourself a team of commandos. You can do anything you want."

Looking at the soldiers, she marveled at the circumstances that had brought them together at this place and time. For her, it was a moment of divine revelation. An opportunity that might never come again and one she had no intention of forsaking. "I suppose we could," Shannon stammered in humility. "That is, if you guys are willing to try." They each assured her they would.

Upon arrival at Dallas-Forth Worth Airport, Barbara booked a flight to New York City that was scheduled to depart in less than an hour. Certain that TSA officials would not appreciate a stash of weapons being carried through security, the soldiers' journey to Virginia would continue in the Land Rover. Shannon made the decision to accompany them on the 18 hour trip to Quantico. The sisters hugged goodbye and parted ways.

A few miles outside of Dallas, Shannon fell asleep dreaming she was back in Troy's arms. Two hours later, she awoke with a start. Surrounded by five men she barely knew, the woman internalized, checking herself for any paw prints on her clothing. She was unmolested and chastened by her thoughts. In spite of their quirks, these were men of honor, sent to her by God. They were here to do something totally outrageous. They were here to save the man she loved.

Shannon closed her eyes, soon returning to a blissful sleep. After initial misgivings, she was now one of the boys.

CHAPTER THIRTY-SIX

Major Osborne sat at the controls of his Huey, once more executing the dangerous nap-of-the-earth maneuvers which helped cloak his craft from radar. His trio of passengers remained buckled in, left speechless by the precision aerodynamics. Flying 50 feet over the contoured landscape, the chopper banked and veered past numerous terrestrial obstacles, never deviating from its fevered pace. After enduring nearly ten minutes of sinuous aviation tactics, they crossed the international border and entered U.S. airspace. Osborne soon lofted the craft to a safer altitude, allowing those onboard to give prayerful thanks for retaining their lives, as well as their lunch.

They were approaching Fort Huachuca, where the Major had begun his journey. Before leaving Juarez, Ariel informed the others of his 14 year residency at this remote Army base. It was here that he'd experimented with specialized signal equipment, communicating with the future human race. It was here that he'd developed his genetic gifts as the child of an IBE. Inside this compound lay the hidden secrets of Project Destiny.

Kevin registered annoyance with Benjamin as the youngster perched over his left shoulder. "Stay in your seat, kid."

"I can't see back there."

"Strap yourself in before you get hurt."

"There's no turbulence."

"Who said anything about turbulence?" Benjamin remained, leaving Kevin to wonder whether his sarcasm had been too subtle. He finally heaved a gasp of exasperation. "Why don't you listen to some music? I know you've got those stupid iPods."

"They're not stupid," his little brother contended. "Each one stores 15,000 songs, 128 video games, accesses satellite radio and lets you text message your friends. Bet you wish you had one."

Kevin surrendered to his curiosity. "Let me see." Benjamin obliged, placing one of the devices in his open palm. "This is what almost got me killed?" He inspected the unit with deliberation. "How did you get this? Don't these things cost like 500 bucks?"

The tyke huffed, amazed at his brother's naiveté. "Nobody pays retail in Juarez."

Minutes later, the helicopter landed upon a cracked slab of concrete within the main fueling depot at Fort Huachuca. As they disembarked, they were greeted by Osborne's friend, Captain Parnell, whom the Major had phoned mid-flight.

"Looks like they blew the hell out of El Paso," he announced, reporting the latest news. "You weren't involved in that shit, were you Oz?"

He confirmed the man's suspicions. "Right smack in the ass of it."

After being introduced to the others, Parnell escorted the four across the compound to Fort Huachuca base headquarters. Once inside his rather austere corner office, the Major briefed him on what had transpired over the last few hours. Their conversation was informative, devoid of evasion or subterfuge. Osborne explained the underlying reasons for the military response, revealing the truth of Roswell. In fact, he was surprised at his own candor, relating the top secret specifics without any mental reservation.

Parnell absorbed the news with lingering skepticism. "It's

incredible," he whispered, more to himself than those around him. "You really expect me to believe all this?"

"The President believed it and now she's dead," Osborne bristled. "They murdered her before she could tell the nation."

Hours earlier, Parnell had watched Webber's address and remembered his shock at the moment of detonation. He saw her face turn ashen while vaporous fire filled her lungs. It was a searing image, destined to be etched forever upon the American psyche. The Captain drew a breath of outrage and accepted Osborne's word. "So, what do you want from me?"

Ariel announced their goal. "Building 23, room 7"

"That area's off limits," explained Parnell. "It's been sealed ever since I've been here." He paused, allowing his inquisitive mind to roam. "What's so special about it?"

"Years ago, I was part of a Government program called Project Destiny. It was in that room where most of the experiments were conducted."

"We're looking for additional evidence," Osborne added. "Anything that can help prove the conspiracy."

Before Parnell could respond, the Major's cell phone rang. It was Casey, finally able to achieve a connection after multiple attempts. "Kimberly and I found Roberta on the Sunset Limited," he reported, his voice laden with fatigue. "We have the baby. She's fine."

Osborne paused to relay the message to the others. "That's awesome. Shannon's gonna shit daisies for a week. Where are you now?"

"At the Amtrak station in Lordsburg, New Mexico."

"We're a few miles southwest of there," the Major declared. "I could come pick you up."

Casey explained their dilemma. "Not yet. Roberta ran off and we haven't found her. I can't just leave her on the train."

"Roger that. Let me know if the situation changes."

A weary sigh ensued. "There's something else, Major. Remember those monks at the mission? A few minutes ago, I had to fight it out with one of them. Something happened...I can't really explain. It was beyond anything I've ever seen in my life."

"Wait a minute," Osborne interrupted. "Ariel's here. I'm gonna put you on the speaker." He pressed a button and asked him to start again. "Go ahead."

"I think I just had a run in with one of your IBE pals," Casey informed the Israeli. "He told me his name was Belial. A member of the Grigori."

The disclosure clearly caught Ariel by surprise, shedding new light on a situation that had vexed him for years. He'd always known that some malevolent entity had tried to hijack his body, but until now the incident had seemed more paranoia than fact. He urged Casey to continue. "What happened?"

"The fight was pretty intense," he divulged. "We were on the floor and I had him in a firm grasp. Kimberly came after him with a meat cleaver. Then, right in front of us, he just...vanished before our eyes."

Ariel swiftly discerned the cause of the phenomenon. "Did you see the wormhole? The spatial rift I spoke of last night?"

His delayed response was noteworthy. "I sure as hell saw something. Whatever it was, he went through it like a greased pig."

"That's the gateway," the Israeli acknowledged. "At least that's what we always called it."

Osborne strove for clarification. "Well, what is this thing? Is it alive or..."

"No!" interrupted Ariel, exhibiting rare impatience. "It's a portal into an alternate realm, allowing instant transit to another place or time. And, it's DNA specific. The gateway can only be accessed by those with an enhanced chromosome structure."

The Major breathlessly completed the thought. "The children of an IBE."

Ariel nodded in affirmation. He turned, addressing Kevin with a passionate appeal. "This is why I came. To help you and your family find your spiritual path. The gateway is but one of many divine tools at your disposal. Allow me to show you your destiny."

"I can't even think straight," he whined, enervated by hours of sleeplessness. "Try your mumbo-jumbo on Ben. He's in better shape than I am."

Ariel faced the youngster. "Would you be ready to take that next step?"

"Sure!" he proclaimed, unable to contain his excitement. "That'd be cool!"

The Major deciphered a significant threat to their security. "If these guys can vanish without a trace, couldn't they also appear before us without any warning at all?"

"Conceivably, yes."

"So, what does this gateway look like?"

Determining that a visual aid would increase their comprehension, Ariel stepped back, separating himself from the others. "It looks quite a bit like…this."

Erupting from the heart of alternate world, the rift materialized before them mimicking the crude shape of a thunderbolt. Space itself was now ripped open into a jet-black chasm, stupefying their senses and challenging lifelong perceptions of reality.

Captain Parnell recoiled in shock, desperately fumbling for his handgun. "Holy fuck! What in the name of God is that?"

The others remained slack-jawed, leaving them incapable of comment. Kevin forced his eyes to blink, wondering if what he beheld was some kind of insomnious apparition. The always enthusiastic Benjamin was rendered mute, his body pressed to the back of his chair in uncharacteristic fear.

Ariel held forth his hand in an obvious request for calm. "Gentlemen, I present to you the gateway."

The Major picked up the phone, maintaining his gaze upon the anomaly. "Casey…" his voice trembled, "I'll call you back."

He pocketed the device and began to inch toward the paranormal manifestation. As Osborne came within range, he experienced an indefinable displacement of air emanating from the void with atmospheric pressure and temperature in a constant state of flux. It seemed to be generating a vacuum effect, but one that produced no discernable suction. The cavity hovered in midair, its ebony core pulsing with mystic intent. He slowly circumnavigated the opening, proving it had no measurable depth. Osborne summoned the courage to probe its vacant interior, his hand emerging from the opposite side as though nothing was present to impede his movement.

The Major looked upon Ariel in stark confusion. "It doesn't exist."

"Yes, it does," corrected the Israeli. "But, it exists solely for me. I'm the only one who can use it."

"And, it takes you where?"

"Any place you wish to go. A location that you've visited before or any other you can visualize in your mind. The transport is instantaneous."

Kevin failed to restrain his sardonic nature. "Forget frequent flyer miles. This is gonna run the airlines right out of business."

"How do you open it?" wondered the Major.

"It's a series of tonal cues in the mind. Once learned, you never forget."

A moment later, the gateway disappeared and the demonstration was officially over. Osborne felt goose bumps surge the length of his flesh, trying to assimilate the knowledge they'd been granted. Each witness was left humbled by the surreal encounter.

"You can teach that to them?" the Major asked.

Ariel nodded. "I can. That's why we require access to building 23, room 7."

All eyes now shifted toward Captain Parnell. The officer shrugged his shoulders during a prolonged sigh of resignation. "I guess I'll grab the keys."

As the door jarred open, the musty air of years past created an indelible imprint upon their senses. They were aware that their every breath was now steeped in history. Arrayed before them were several folding tables, each of which supported various items of electronic equipment shrouded beneath opaque dust covers. Cockroaches scurried across the wooden floor, slipping behind cracks in discolored walls. Intricate spider webs were hung at acute angles, their gossamer filaments unbroken by time. It was obvious to all that room 7 had been devoid of human contact for the better part of almost two decades.

Ariel hesitated, issuing a subconscious gasp which confirmed his emotional recognition. Slipping past the Israeli, Major Osborne walked over to an adjacent window, peeling back a thin sheet of black mylar from the glass pane. A beam of harsh sunlight now pierced the room, exposing a slew of particulate matter suspended in the air about them. Captain Parnell approached one of the tables, running his fingers through a visible layer of dust.

"I'll have the orderlies fix this place up," he stated in apology.

"I'm afraid that wouldn't be wise, Captain," Ariel insisted. "The less people who see this room the better."

The Major concurred. "We'll clean it ourselves. How long can we keep what we're doing here a secret?"

Parnell wobbled his head in doubt. "The Garrison Commander's due back at 0900 Thursday. Whatever you've got planned, it's got to be done by then."

"That doesn't leave you much time," Osborne reasoned, directing his attention to Ariel. "Can you teach Ben what he needs to know on a deadline?"

He embraced the challenge with one condition. "It all depends on how willing the boy is to learn."

Benjamin looked up at the men, failing to understand their procrastination. "What are you guys waiting for?" complained the youngster. "Let's shake some butts!"

The five procured cleaning materials from a nearby closet and in short order had the room sanitized. After unveiling the electronic equipment, Kevin stared at the devices in amazement. *How is this antiquated junk going to help?* Before him were a set of signal and waveform generators wired in series, along with a bank of oscilloscopes and several plot graph printers. Experiencing more fatigue than curiosity, he remained silent, satisfied that ignorance was bliss. Benjamin, who did not share his brother's indifference, eagerly sat down and began powering up the equipment. Ariel joined the child hoping to shepherd his unbridled enthusiasm. Realizing that their continued presence might be a distraction, the others excused themselves and soon returned to Parnell's office.

The Major placed a courtesy call to Shannon, informing her that Hope had been rescued safely. Gratified to hear the woman's impassioned relief, he then phoned Casey as promised. "Any sign of Roberta?"

"Nothing yet," came the response. "I've been trying to reach C.J. and Moses, but I keep getting their voice mail. Have you had any luck?"

Osborne sighed, admitting his efforts had also been for naught. He pondered upon the implications of their silence. "If they don't recover those CDs, we're going to need other evidence."

"Like what?"

"A witness. Someone who knows everything about the MAJIK-12."

Casey recalled the list of names from his previous review of the data. "Most of them were top military or agency types."

"They'll never talk," contended the Major. "They've got no reason to."

"There was one civilian," tapping his memory further. "He's the head of GG&E...the Dreamland contractor."

Osborne's interest began to percolate. With the secret complex destroyed, and the MAJIK-12 desperate to tie up loose ends, this guy should now have the life expectancy of a mayfly. In order to save his skin, he would make the ideal witness. "Do you remember his name?"

"I think it was LeClerke. Pierre LeClerke."

"We gotta grab this clown before they wipe him off the Earth," asserted the Major. "Thanks, Casey. Get back with us if you hear anything else."

"Roger that." It was a parting phrase that he'd been itching to use.

Parnell's office computer allowed them to conduct their due diligence on GG&E's top corporate officer. The company website displayed a photograph of LeClerke along with a lengthy bio. After digesting the information, they began to speculate with a common focus.

"This guy's a player," Osborne announced. "Got his engineering degree at Stanford, his masters and PhD at Cal Tech. He's been the company's CEO since 1997 and a significant shareholder longer than that."

Kevin appeared confused. "Which means?"

"He was hand picked by the Government. This man has no business background, yet he's been running this 284 billion dollar corporation for years."

"An independent company isn't going to control a top secret military base," Parnell added. "GG&E has to be a front. The DoD awards them contracts then recycles the funds for black programs. That way the GAO can't track the money."

"But, why him? What makes this dude so special?"

"The Government routinely keeps track of exceptional students," explained the Major. "Especially those without the finances for college. They provide them with full scholarships, as well as lucrative jobs when they graduate. But, it has nothing to do with benevolence. When the time comes, they expect to collect on their investment."

A call to GG&E headquarters in La Jolla, California was placed. Osborne asked to speak with LeClerke or his personal secretary and was told that neither were available. After sweet-talking the receptionist for the better part of five minutes, he was informed the CEO was on vacation and not due back for two weeks. Additional prodding yielded nothing further. He thanked his reluctant source and hung up. The situation was frustrating, but also fortuitous. LeClerke's elusive status would make him a difficult target for any potential assassin.

Captain Parnell examined GG&E's corporate history and discovered an interesting bit of trivia. "Their headquarters were based in downtown San Diego for over half a century before they moved to La Jolla in 1997. That's the same year LeClerke became CEO."

"Sounds like he didn't want to commute," deduced Kevin.

Osborne nodded in agreement. "He didn't want to go to the company. He made the company to come to him. LeClerke lives in La Jolla."

"But, where?" wondered Parnell. "That's still a big community."

From the depths of exhaustion, Kevin provided an answer. "Torrey Pines."

The soldiers eyed him curiously, anxious to hear his logic. "He's got money and his bio states he's an avid golfer. It's Torrey Pines."

Now concentrating upon the swank country club estates perched atop the La Jolla cliffs, they utilized various search engines in an effort to pinpoint LeClerke's residence. After numerous phone calls and cyberspace dead ends, the website for the San Diego County property tax assessor listed a parcel in Torrey Pines for Pierre K. and Sylvia M. LeClerke. His address on Crown Crest Lane was now theirs.

Although the home phone was unlisted, Osborne was able to cross reference the data to obtain numbers for two of his neighbors on the exclusive cul-de-sac. The first call went unanswered, but the other quickly bore fruit. Introducing himself as a representative from the law firm of Osborne, Parnell and Reese, the Major informed the lady of the house that Dr. LeClerke's aunt had just passed away and designated him as executor of her estate.

"We understand he's on vacation, but we need to speak with him as soon as possible," he explained. "Do you happen to know where he is?"

The neighbor was most accommodating. "Why, yes I do. Pierre and Sylvia are on an Alaskan cruise. They're treating it like a second honeymoon. He so seldom gets time off."

"A cruise?" his voice peaking in mild surprise. "Did they tell you which ocean liner they're booked on? We could contact him by ship-to-shore radio."

"I believe it's the Lord of the Seas…out of Vancouver."

He exhaled in triumph. "Ma'am, thank you so much for your help."

"I'm sorry about Pierre's aunt," the lady continued. "How old was she?"

The Major picked a number. "103."

"Oh, my goodness! What did the poor dear die of?"

Caught off guard, Osborne responded with as little thought as possible. "Blowing out too many birthday candles." He decided to end the call before he could say anything more absurd. "Thanks again."

A quick search of the web revealed the Lord of the Seas was due to dock at the Port of Valdez in the morning. Leaving Benjamin and Ariel in Captain Parnell's care, Kevin and the Major agreed to endure a night-long flight to Alaska. There they'd find Pierre LeClerke, the only witness left alive who could expose the MAJIK-12. But first, they'd have to save him from near certain assassination.

CHAPTER THIRTY-SEVEN

WASHINGTON, D.C. — MAY 9ᵗʰ — 11:02 PM EDT

$\mathcal{A}$t the end of an incredible day, a somber nation gasped for breath. It was one of those indelible moments in history when all of humanity froze, transcending time and place. The streets of Washington were lined with thousands of mourners, most grieving openly, others simply there out of respect. They stood in a misting rain, their faces vacant, as the hearse carrying the President's casket made its way down Pennsylvania Avenue to the east front of the Capitol building.

Bathed in the chilled night air, the illumination from swarms of television camera crews captured the lasting images of America's spiritual anguish. The effect of this tragedy would be felt long after the flame of liberty was but a dying ember. It incapacitated the mind and confounded the soul. Questions abounded without answer. How could this have happened? What were the chances that two youthful Presidents would die in office six months apart? Was this a military coup or another terrorist attack? How could this country survive such an obvious Constitutional crisis? Conspiracy theorists were already in full throat, making the rounds on cable news broadcasts and saturating the internet with their spin. For most, it was too much to absorb. The only thing that mattered was the sight of President Webber's two teenage daughters weeping uncontrollably over their mother's flag-draped coffin and having no one there to comfort them.

The official State ceremonies commenced. A joint service color guard began their march up the steps of the Capitol, while a military drum and bugle corps received their cue to play. Upon the first ruffle and flourish of 'Hail to the Chief', cannon fire erupted on the grounds in a 21 gun salute to the fallen leader. An elite detail of eight men were tasked as pallbearers. They deftly removed the heavy maple casket from the rear of the hearse, rotated 90 degrees and began to slowly ascend the concrete steps leading toward the east portico. Ushered ahead of the procession were Webber's immediate family, close friends, members of her cabinet, as well as select White House staffers. The rain became more persistent, prompting one TV network correspondent to label the downpour "Tears from Heaven." At any other time such maudlin sentimentality would have been deemed unprofessional, but on this night it felt oddly appropriate.

Members of Congress waited patiently behind velvet rope barriers in the Capitol rotunda. The imposing circular room remained the iconic centerpiece of the building, consisting of an ornate orchestration of architecture, sculpture and frescoes. Although the polished marble floor and overhead canopy tended to reflect sound like an echo chamber, nothing was heard from the assembled throng other than an occasional cough or sniffle. Moments later the procession arrived, entering the rotunda through the National Statuary Hall. The pallbearers carried the casket to the center of the room and placed it gently upon a large, draped catafalque. In choreographed precision, the soldiers filed out and were immediately replaced by the ceremonial Guard of Honor, consisting of five servicemen representing the Army, Navy, Air Force, Marines and Coast Guard. Attired in formal dress uniforms, the quintet assumed positions around the casket acting as a protective cordon for the deceased. Then, in a display of respect that swelled the emotions of many, the five saluted their slain Commander in

Chief. The tribute was executed flawlessly, as each raised their arms in unison and finally lowered them in measured deliberation. Every 30 minutes a new Guard of Honor would relieve those on post while the casket remained in the rotunda. The itinerary called for the President's body to lie in repose during the next two days, allowing the public a chance to file past. Afterward, an official State funeral would be held with the entire Congress, Supreme Court, diplomatic corps and Presidential cabinet in attendance, before the remains were flown to her family's home in Ohio for burial.

Once Webber's close friends and associates had a chance to lay flowers at the foot of the bier, the rotunda was opened to the American people. The visitation queue was soon measured in terms of a five-hour wait, stretching in serpentine fashion onto the adjacent National Mall. The masses stood reverently with their umbrellas opened, waiting in the rain for a fleeting glimpse at the closed casket. There they would issue a silent prayer, not only for the soul of a courageous leader, but for the fate of their beloved country.

Several hours later, the Chief of the Capitol Hill Police received an urgent communiqué. A 757 jet airliner scheduled to land at Reagan National Airport had veered from its designated flight path and was now circling the city without authorization. Ever since the terrorist attacks of September 11, 2001, any incursion of airspace over Washington D.C. was treated as an emergency breach of security. The decision was made to evacuate the Capitol at once.

Radio squawk boxes throughout the complex broke the news to every on-duty officer. Within seconds, Congressman and staffers were being herded out of the building in waves. Shouts and screams from those in the rotunda sabotaged the solemnity of the proceedings. Panic cascaded down the length of the viewing line, causing mourners to bolt from the queue, dashing across the grounds in bedlam. The feed from the TV network cameras was cut in an effort to contain widespread chaos.

The Chief of Police ran over to the Joint Forces Commandant and explained the situation. "We have to evacuate! Get your men out!"

He made it clear that abandoning the casket was not an option. "The honor guard stays! They're not leaving their posts!"

A look of resignation came over the Chief, nodding at the logic. "Okay! Everyone else out...right now!"

Amidst the tumult, the five soldiers dutifully remained. They bestowed another salute, as if letting the President know they would not leave her side. This time, the gesture had been rendered without witness. The Capital rotunda was suddenly vacant.

Fifteen minutes expired before the 'all clear' was given. The jetliner did not represent a threat, having strayed off course inadvertently. Capitol Hill Police allowed the mourners to return and no further incidents were reported.

When word of the honor guard's allegiance to duty reached the media, the soldiers were universally lauded for their heroism. The Joint Forces Commandant maintained they were merely doing what was required. At a time when distrust of the Armed Forces was at record levels, this simple act of integrity became just what the military needed to mend their tattered public relations.

CHAPTER THIRTY-EIGHT

C.J. awoke with a start, his labored breath forcing him to consciousness. The cold sweat that dampened his brow was a tangible reminder that death was near. Entombed by a million tons of cubic earth, the amount of air left inside their chamber was now all but exhausted. Drifting in and out of reality for the past several hours, he found it difficult to think, his mind made sluggish due to oxygen deprivation.

The last of the glowsticks remained by his side, its luminescence fading from view. C.J. spotted his sedentary brother in the pale green light and began to question whether he was still alive. "You okay, Moses?"

Although bemused by the inquiry, the wounded soldier lacked a witty response. "Tell me you're kidding."

"I suppose I am," he sighed at length. "How long have we been in here?"

"Almost 17 hours."

Resigned to their fate, C.J.'s voice turned hollow. "It won't be much longer…will it?"

Moses shut his eyes, frustrated by his inability to do anything about their situation. "I sure hope not." The pain from his wound had lessened somewhat as had the bleeding. What had intensified was his self-incrimination, holding himself accountable for their reckless entrance into the cave. He offered an apology before it became too late. "I'm sorry, C.J. I never thought it would go down like this. I should've waited for Gerhin to come out on his own."

His brother sputtered in laughter. "I've been sitting here for the last hour trying to remember how we got in this place."

"It was my stupidity."

Mammon emerged from the darkness beyond, swiftly placing an end to their banter. "You're only human, Azrael," expressing satisfaction at the thought. "At least for a few more minutes."

This time, the sudden arrival was met with less consternation as both had anticipated his return. C.J. gazed upon him, noting his appearance. It might have been the lighting, or perhaps his diminished eyesight, but the man now looked clean shaven and his blond hair slicked back with gel.

Before anything else was said, Mammon tossed a bottle of aspirin toward Moses, snickering at his expense. "I figured you might need some of these. No sense dying in misery."

The anguished soldier grasped the container, hurling it back in a fit of rage. "Shove 'em up your ass, fuckhead!"

"Oooooh," came the retort. "Your balls just keep getting bigger all the time, don't they? Give it a rest, Azrael. Hormones won't save you from this."

C.J. issued a plea. "Just let us die in peace. Is that too much to ask?"

Mammon settled beside him, closing within a few inches of his face. "No, I can't do that, Michael. This is something I have to witness."

"An eternity's a long time to hold a grudge."

The man concurred. "That may be. But, isn't it fascinating how it's the only thing that truly endures?" He scanned the body sprawled before him. "Tell me. What does it feel like to die?"

"Why don't you find out for yourself?"

Mammon flashed a smirk. "Well, that's one experience I intend to live vicariously." He paused in thought. "Are you prepared, Michael? Do you believe your life has had meaning?"

A delayed response belied his words. "I'm content with what I've done."

"Really?" he challenged. "What about the plight of poverty in the world? It's a cause you've talked about most of your life. But, what have you actually accomplished? Oh sure, you wrote about it…sitting in your big ass house, on your big fat ass. How many children could've been fed with the money you dropped on that lakefront estate? Two million? Maybe, three? You say you're such a spiritual person, but all you do is collect wealth, ensuring your comfort at the expense of others. What kind of person gets rich by discussing the needs of humanity and then gives nothing in return? You're just a material whore."

The tears pooling in C.J.'s eyes gratified Mammon, aware he'd struck a soulful nerve. Silence prevailed, as the effect of the message was absorbed.

"Don't listen to him," Moses admonished. "The bastard's just trying to yank your chain. He's full of shit."

His brother's head began swaying in denial. "No, he's not. All these years, I've been a hypocrite. I could've done so much more."

As C.J. contemplated the deficiencies of a life laid bare, Mammon continued his verbal assault. "And, what did you do for your brothers and sisters in Africa? The multitude of black babies born with AIDS? Did you ever visit them? Behold with your own eyes their untold misery? No, you thought more about your own well being. You chose not to expose yourself to disease or wade in their filth. How many could have been saved with your precious money? Hundreds of them are now dying as we speak… from cholera…dysentery…ebola. At night, when you're safe in bed and the dreams come, can't you hear their souls crying out? See the mounds of bloated, fly-ridden corpses? Don't you realize their blood is on your hands?"

"That's enough!" bellowed Moses. "Shut the hell up!"

"No, you shut up!" C.J. yelled, surprising his brother with unexpected scorn. "I know you're just trying to help, but don't. Everything he said is the truth. Let me confront my own demons... including this one."

Moses retreated into silence, left bitter by the rebuke. Their verbal sparring emboldened Mammon, pleased he was filling their final moments with distress. "You're dying bravely, Michael. Of course, I'd expect nothing less from you. A great soul such as your own always selects the proper place and time to perish. After all, the measure of one's life is determined by the way they die."

"Who made you the expert?" challenged C.J.

"I'm a member of the Grigori," Mammon reminded his long time enemy. "We've been watching generations of humanity come and go for thousands of years. I think that should qualify me to speak on the subject."

Trying to fashion a rebuttal, C.J. found his thoughts mired in disorientation, unable to communicate in a coherent manner. The lack of breathable oxygen was becoming critical. He opted to hold his tongue rather than embarrass himself with a spate of mindless babble.

Mammon continued. "Do you know the meaning of life, Michael? Philosophers and theologians have debated that question for centuries. But, it's quite simple actually. Souls are imprisoned inside these bodies to learn. That's it. The world around us is nothing more than a great big schoolyard. If you can see the bigger picture...comprehend higher reality surrounded by crude physical matter...then you graduate. You become the teacher's pet and receive a diploma, just like you and I. But, most never learn and end up being treated like spiritual delinquents. They're forced to do the course over and over again until they get it right. For them, it's just an endless cycle of birth and death." Mammon briefly halted the lecture to take hold of C.J.'s wrist, checking on his erratic pulse. He noted the chest was heaving with greater frequency, working harder to capture air. Satisfied with his foe's progression toward death, he resumed his insightful monologue.

"Ever wonder why God keeps people in the dark about the

afterlife? Think about it. If the students knew what they were missing, they'd start cutting class and that wouldn't please the principal at all. That kind of knowledge would trigger suicide parties…mass slayings…rituals of demise that would overwhelm society. Everyone would leave this world as fast as they could. There'd be a whole slew of wannabe Kevorkians helping to usher humanity through the door. Nobody would stay inside these sacks of flesh if they knew what awaited them. God's grand experiment would be a total failure." He paused for a moment of reflection. "They say there's no greater crime than murder. But, do the killers understand they're simply sending their enemies to a better existence? If they did, the homicide rate would drop 80% overnight. And then, there's karma. Once the spirit is released, it can assume any form it wants. A rabid dog…a malignant tumor…even a stray bolt of lightning. You just never know how it'll come back to bite you on the ass. Sometimes, it's best to leave the person alone. Keeping them in their skin is often a far greater punishment."

C.J.'s voice gurgled with spite. "So says the Devil."

His tormentor smiled, chiding him for his naiveté. "Do you know there are other civilizations in this universe that consider your God the evil force and honor mine as the Almighty? Humanity's never heard both sides of the story. They only get their news from one source. Most of them don't even know Lucifer's Ten Commandments."

A flash of curiosity lit C.J.'s face, prompting Mammon to action. "You've never been exposed to the Holy truths? Oh, I have to share them before you pass on." He came to his feet and assumed a theatrical pose. What C.J. beheld was beyond his experience and he questioned whether it was real or simply a mind-induced hallucination. Mammon rotated his arms around each other in a circular manner, creating what appeared to be a brilliant ball of flame suspended in midair. C.J. cringed, realizing he was now witness to a dramatic reenactment of the 'Fire of God' scene from the movie *The Ten Commandments*.

As Mammon clasped the burning sphere in hand, he mimicked

the windup of a major league pitcher, hurling the object at the adjacent rock. His booming voice echoed through the chamber, taking pride in announcing the Devil's Top Ten list.

"THOU SHALT NOT SHOW WEAKNESS!"

With the searing heat of a branding iron, the orb struck the wall and etched the corresponding message in stone using letters from the ancient Hebrew alphabet. A shower of sparks tumbled to the bedrock beside C.J., his eyes glazed in awe. Mammon prepared to throw another strike.

"THOU SHALT NOT BEAR ANOTHER'S BURDEN!"

Again, the edict was inscribed by fire. A third was cast, this time with a casual sidearm delivery.

"THOU SHALT NOT HONOR AUTHORITY!"

Mammon was thoroughly enjoying his flamboyant presentation, showing no further concern over C.J.'s rapidly declining status. He lobbed a fourth over his shoulder.

"THOU SHALT NOT SIN IN VAIN!"

His melodramatic performance became absurd, at one point actually bending over to hike a fireball between his legs.

"THOU SHALT NOT BE STUPID!"

Other precepts came in quick succession, each engraved in flame.

"THOU SHALT NOT SNITCH!"

"THOU SHALT NOT WHINE!"

"THOU SHALT NOT COVET CRAP!"

Mammon's over-the-top histrionics were mercifully nearing an end. The ninth law was recorded after bounce passing the blazing spheroid as though it were a Jai-Alai pelota.

"THOU SHALT NOT HANG WITH LOSERS!"

The final commandment was executed with athletic flourish, launching the flare skyward like a last-second buzzer shot.

"THOU SHALT NOT FUCK ANYONE UGLIER THAN THEE!"

The effusive pyrotechnics ceased. Still aglow from the intense heat, Lucifer's Decalogue now resided on two stone tablets, suitable for display. Mammon inhaled deeply, competing with the others for scant traces of oxygen. Although dizzy with fatigue, he felt the spiritual enrichment one normally derives from proselytizing their faith.

"Now those are words to live by," stating his case in a winded tone. "Why can't they teach that in Sunday School?"

His breathless elation was squelched upon sight of the inanimate body before him. Fearing he'd missed the moment of death, he dashed to C.J.'s side, checking for any flicker of life. Mammon was rewarded by the faintest sound of respiration.

"That was close," he professed. "I didn't want you to die without an audience."

C.J. tried to respond, his parched lips fluttering with purpose. Mammon's curiosity took hold, positioning an ear to detect his final message. What he heard sent a wave of trepidation coursing through his soul.

"Release me."

Suddenly, the implications of C.J.'s death became too terrible for Mammon to contemplate, leaving him conflicted by the paradox. He was desperate to witness the physical death of his enemy, but Michael's awesome spirit was immortal. Now that C.J. desired freedom from the constraints of his body, what kind of wrathful forces would be manifested by his incorporeal state? Mammon knew all too well about the vengeance that an archangel could wreak. Could he take the chance of letting C.J. die and risk a number of far worse scenarios?

"Release me," he again moaned.

The man shook with fury over a choice he was now compelled to make. "No, I don't think so! You're staying with me! You'll stay until I say otherwise."

Aware that little time remained, C.J. once more tweaked his foe. "Release me." It was a shrewd manipulation on his part, knowing Mammon would be reluctant to let him die once he'd stated his yearning to do so. He was counting upon the man's maniacal hatred to save his life and that of his brother's.

Precious seconds expired while Mammon remained lost in debate. He grabbed C.J. by the arms, lifting him off the bedrock. "That's what you want, isn't it? That's been your plan all along. This aging body you're in is all used up. You want something new... something more powerful you can use against us," he conjectured. "Or, you could be trying to trick me. Maybe you actually want to stay inside this disgusting carcass. Maybe it's the only way you can think of to get me to save your sorry ass." He clutched the sides of C.J.'s head, peering into his vacant eyes. "I want the truth! Answer me, you miserable bastard! Which is it? Which is it?"

"Release me..."

He attempted another breath, but found nothing left to inhale. His body went limp, falling backward against the rock. As the life he knew faded to black, he forced Mammon into the most difficult decision he'd ever had to face.

Hours later, C.J. opened his eyes to a world of light and color. Squinting at the open spider hole, he raised his head and luxuriated in the longest breath ever drawn. In slow but steady increments, he worked his way into a standing position and with a wobbly gait, soon arrived at his brother's side. Moses was still alive, his bloodied legs compressed against his chest. Once fully roused, the men shared a long and impassioned hug, grateful for their deliverance and mindful of how it had been granted.

CHAPTER THIRTY-NINE

LOS ANGELES, CA — MAY 10th — 8:11 AM PDT

Casey and Kimberly shared a common dream, confined in an uncommon space. Exhausted from their encounter with Belial, they yielded to their need for sleep, disregarding their own admonition to remain awake. Each experienced the nightmare they feared as their baby sister spoke the Devil's own words and tried to convince them of her malevolence. At first they fought the image, but it persisted for hours. There seemed to be no refuge from the subliminal onslaught. The generated illusion affected them on a primal level, filling their subconscious minds with anxiety and murderous rage. Once these impulses were at a fever's pitch, they were thrust to reality, ready to act upon their most savage instincts.

Brother and sister awoke face to face, their arms and legs intertwined like a human pretzel. Regaining their faculties, they promptly separated amidst the icky reaction typical of such intimacy. It wasn't said, but this moment of revulsion helped subdue their barbarous inclinations, providing them needed time to recover from the trauma. Both knew they could not afford to fall asleep again.

After recognizing their surroundings, a wave of panic struck the pair. They frantically searched the compartment and the corridor beyond, but there was no trace of their sister. Hope had vanished.

"I had her in my arms when I drifted to sleep," Casey explained.

Kimberly deduced the obvious. "It must've been Roberta. Maybe she's still on the train."

They exited the compartment in search of answers. A sleeper car porter was making his rounds when approached by the two.

"Excuse me," she asked. "Have you seen a teenage girl with a baby?"

He nodded in regret. "Sure 'nuff did. Kids havin' kids. Breaks my heart to think about it."

Kimberly saw no reason to set the record straight. "Do you know where she is now?"

"Got off an hour ago in Pomona."

Issuing a silent curse, logic dictated her final question. "Where's the next stop?"

"End of the line...Los Angeles. We'll be at Union Station in a few minutes."

They thanked the man, returning to the compartment in dismay. Aware of Roberta's 800 mile quest to meet Carlos Ayala, Casey located the young man's contact information previously provided by Shannon. He called the number on his cell, soon hearing the voice of a Latina youngster.

"Hola?"

For some reason, he hadn't expected to encounter a language barrier. "Okay...uh, habla Ingles?"

"Yes..."

Casey sighed with relief. "Is Carlos Ayala there?"

Assured that he was, the little girl ran off to summon him to the phone. After considerable delay, the young man answered. "Yeah?"

"Carlos? This is Casey...one of Roberta's brothers. We met at the Hilton in Las Vegas."

His response was hesitant. "Sure. What's goin' on?"

"We think Roberta might be on her way to see you. She's got our baby sister with her."

"Oh, I got that package this morning," came his cryptic reply. It was clear that Carlos had no chance to speak freely.

"She's there?"

"That's what I said."

"Look, Roberta's in a bad state of mind. Just keep her company 'til we can get there. What's your address?"

"Send the bill to 1538 South 7th Street…in Montebello."

Casey thanked him for his discretion and hung up.

Carlos heaved a sigh of concern before returning to the living room. Before him was Roberta, sitting on the couch with the newborn nestled comfortably in her lap. He was delighted to see her again, but baffled by the unexpected visit. Seeking privacy, he sent his kid sister to their aunt's house two blocks away. As Roberta dabbed a tear from her eye, he sat beside her, engaging the girl in an emotional conversation that shifted frequently between Spanish and English.

"You okay?"

She thought about her response. "I don't know."

"Did you tell your family you were coming here?"

Roberta shook her head. "No."

"Are you in some sort of trouble?"

She shrugged slightly, refusing to answer. He was becoming frustrated with her evasiveness, deciding to probe the girl's motivations without allowing her the opportunity for an easy reply.

"What are you doing here, Robbie?"

His words were met with a burst of tears that seemed to flow without end. "I miss my mom," she blubbered, gasping for breath. Carlos folded her in his arms, doing what he could to help soothe her anguish. Deep down, Roberta knew this cathartic release was necessary. She'd not been able to adequately purge her grief over the Madre's death, but now that the floodgates had opened, she had no intention of holding back. Carlos now understood why she was there and was saddened that she'd had to come so far just to find a shoulder to cry upon. He caressed her hair, using the same gentle stroke her mother had used when Roberta was a child. Theirs was a relationship that transcended sexual chemistry. The two shared a spiritual bond, one which would endure long after youth and flesh had vanished. It was nothing less than a communion of souls.

"Shannon told me what you did in Las Vegas," the girl disclosed, mopping her face with a tissue. "She said you were a hero. How you saved Hope's life and her own."

Carlos shivered at the memory. "Shannon saved me," he admitted. "She made me leave the city just before the quake. I barely made it out of there. It was like nothing…" His voice faltered from the gruesome mental imagery. "That night, I heard the screams of a million people and there was nothing I could do but run." He lowered his head in solemnity, closing with a final thought. "I'll never doubt the wrath of God again."

The two cautiously brought their lips together and kissed in mutual solace. Their conversation became more insightful as Roberta discussed how she and her family had been held captive at Dreamland. Carlos was mesmerized by the account, never doubting a word no matter how bizarre. She told him of her dreams. The nightmarish specter of evil embodied in her baby sister and why she was being coerced into harming her. He could feel the girl's inner torment and attempted to rationalize the situation.

"You need sleep. I'll watch Hope while you take a nap."

Roberta declined the offer. "I can't be trusted. Nobody can. That's why I took her from my brother and sister this morning."

His eyes darted to a clock. It had been nearly an hour since Casey's call and their impending arrival was foremost on his mind. Carlos was conflicted, wondering whether he should let her know. From what he'd been told, her older siblings could represent as much danger to the infant as Roberta. He decided to remain silent, hoping for a resolution to the thorny matter. It finally occurred to him things might work out better if he had possession of the child.

"Can I hold her awhile?"

"Sure."

With Hope safely in his arms, he began tickling her to the point of laughter.

Roberta smiled, impressed with his paternal nature. "You look like you've done this before."

"I have," he admitted. "I practically raised my kid sister on…"

His mouth fell at the sight of Belial entering the room beyond. "Isn't that sweet? I like seeing a gangbanger in touch with his feminine side."

Stunned by the intrusion, Carlos shouted in territorial alarm. "Who the fuck are you?"

"Give me the baby," demanded the psychopath. "You can keep the bitch."

With his protective instincts fully aroused, he unleashed a barrage of expletives, taking time to hand Roberta the threatened infant. "I don't know who you are man, but you're gonna die!"

Before he could turn to face his foe, the fight was on as Belial smashed a six-foot metal floor lamp across his back. Roberta squealed in terror, vaulting to her feet to safeguard the child. Lunging from the floor, Carlos engaged the enemy with an array of kicks and blows, most of which were reciprocated with equal ferocity. Shattered tables and chairs were used as weapons while several wall hangings crashed to the floor. The viciousness with which they fought astounded Roberta, repelled by the sight of blood oozing onto their clothes. Their extended brawl continued in the wake of breathless howls and obscenities. She screamed for them to stop, but neither was willing to concede. As the two tumbled the length of room, Roberta fled to the kitchen locating a knife from a butcher's block. Returning to the melee, she was taken by surprise when Belial sprang forth, snatching Hope from her loving embrace. The baby now cried in fright, her body squeezed within the demon's hands. Carlos jumped him from behind, locking arms around his in an upright tackle. Incensed by the abduction, Roberta didn't hesitate. She swung the knife back in preparation for the lethal thrust. What occurred next happened in an instant, but its bitter consequence would last far longer. In a surge of motion that challenged their senses, Belial escaped through the gateway, sucked from Carlos' grasp with the force of an in-flight decompression. Hope twisted in midair, finding sanctuary within the crook of Roberta's left arm. But the girl's right hand continued onward...plunging the nine-inch blade into the one she loved.

Casey and Kimberly had just emerged from their cab. Approaching the Ayala family's modest home, they heard their sister's high-pitched wail of grief blaring forth with the prolonged intensity of an air raid siren. Charging to the door, they broke inside to confront a scene of genuine horror. Carlos had fallen to his knees, the knife still lodged in his belly. Roberta stood over him, her eyes and mouth swollen in delirium. As blood began to pool across the carpet in an ever expanding circle of red, they were prompted to immediate action. Kimberly grabbed the baby from her sister and dashed outside, stopping the taxi driver from pulling away. They decided to leave the knife where it was, so as not to exacerbate the injury. Draping a towel around the boy's midsection, Casey led him gingerly to the cab which then rushed them to the nearest hospital.

The waiting room soon overflowed with the friends and family of Carlos Ayala. During his surgery to repair the abdominal wound, Roberta made an effort to approach each of his loved ones and beg their forgiveness. Everyone knew it had been an accident, but that didn't ease her feelings of guilt. As time progressed, the others began consoling her, making Roberta understand that she was not at fault. After a three hour operation, word of his condition reached anxious ears. Carlos was stable and would fully recover. Amidst the relief felt by all, Casey and Kimberly had even more reason to celebrate. This brush with disaster had seemingly strengthened Roberta's spirit, transforming her back to the sweet-natured girl they'd come to know and love.

Immediately thereafter, a group of streetwise Latinos entered the waiting room sporting typical biker attire, their bodies replete with studs and tattoos. The eight men milled about, inspecting everyone in attendance with a cynical eye. They were members of Carlos' gang. One of them approached a member of the Ayala clan and addressed him in Spanish.

Casey leaned over to his sister. "What are they saying?"

Roberta listened intently before translating. "His uncle just told him that we're close friends of Carlos and we can be trusted."

The gang then talked amongst themselves, soon forming a line in front of the three siblings. Unsure what to expect, Casey bit his lip in apprehension. Any concerns were quickly dispelled when the leader held out his clenched hand, fist bumping the trio in silent greeting. The others followed suit until each of them had received their gesture of respect.

Later, Kimberly took Hope to the ladies' room for a much needed change. Sprawling the baby onto a folding table, she deftly wiped the mess and secured the infant in a clean diaper. Leaving her sister for just a moment, she tossed the offensive matter in the trash and proceeded to wash her hands. Once finished, she turned to confront an empty table and heard a man's voice paying her tribute.

"You know something?" Belial smiled, baby in hand. "I just love your tits."

Before she could react, he shoved a nearby cart full of cleaning supplies into her legs. Kimberly fought her way through the scattered obstructions, sprinting into the corridor after him.

A squall of panic was heard in the waiting room, marshalling everyone to attention. Kimberly appeared in the foyer, breathless. "He's got the baby! We've got to stop him!"

Casey and Roberta joined their sister, bolting down the hallway after the deranged archangel. A member of the Ayala family related the news to the others in their native language. The eight gang members took off in pursuit, willing to do whatever was required to save the infant.

After negotiating a maze of hospital corridors, Belial emerged through a rear service door and spotted a means of escape. An oversized, front-loading garbage truck was idling next to a row of dumpsters which had just been emptied. He ran to the open hatch and, without remorse, tossed the newborn into the accumulated bed of trash. Dashing to the truck's cab, Belial ejected the driver and assumed his position behind the wheel.

The fleet footed Roberta arrived on the loading dock ahead of the others, hearing Hope's baleful cry for help. She saw the truck lurch forth and quickly gave chase, jumping onto the vehicle before it achieved cruising speed. Casey and Kimberly witnessed their sister's leap onto the massive rig, but were too late to join her. The gang members appeared in haste and motioned the two to follow. Their motorcycles were parked in an adjacent lot. The men mounted their Harley-Davidson Dyna Wide Glides and kick started each with urgency. Brother and sister assumed pillion seats behind two of the riders, bracing themselves for the trip. With the bikes screaming to life, they opened their throttles, soon closing the distance between them and the speeding truck. What ensued thereafter was destined to be the most incredible case of road rage in Southern California history.

The front-loader swerved onto an entrance ramp for Highway 60, a major arterial route running into downtown Los Angeles from the east. Accelerating onto the thoroughfare, the truck cut in front of several vehicles on a mostly lateral path into the diamond lane. A chorus of car horns blared as angered motorists registered their displeasure. Inside the cab, Belial finally located the activation switch for the trash compactor mechanism.

Roberta was jostled about in the hopper, desperately trying to rescue Hope who was being continually covered by moving garbage. At last, she detected a tiny hand rising above the debris.

She dove to the area, expeditiously bringing the baby to the surface. Spontaneous hugs of relief ended once the compactor blades started to move. A deafening whine echoed through the chamber, announcing their imminent death from hydraulic compression. Roberta squealed in terror as the trash piled around her legs began restricting her movement. She could tell they were sinking further into the waste as though mired in quicksand. The girl thrashed her body from side-to-side, corkscrewing her lower half free. Rolling across the odious surface, she fought her way up an ever increasing angle and grasped hold of a metal flange leading to the rear portal of the hopper. A large plate of steel was coming down on top of them, preparing to block their exit. Being an expert gymnast, Roberta was confident she could spin her body around and vault backward through the hatch, but not with the child in her arms. In a decision rife with peril, she released the newborn and prepared for the daring maneuver. As if performing a routine on a pommel horse, Roberta windmilled her legs through the air and executed an inverted dismount, propelling herself clear of the advancing blades. With only seconds to spare, she reached back inside the hopper and plucked the baby safely to her breast.

Seizing a breath of victory, the girl staggered to the open rear gate, holding onto a thin metal cable running along the truck's interior wall. She estimated the vehicle's speed at more than 80mph, due to the number of cars they were passing on the roadway. Roberta spotted a group of eight motorcycles closing in from behind. She recognized one of the riders as her brother Casey, his arm outstretched in a frantic wave. The girl responded in kind, lofting the child into view to let him know Hope was all right. Aware of the situation on board, two of the cyclists raced ahead in an attempt to force the vehicle to stop.

The motorcycle cordon was soon tested as Belial began using the multi-lane slab of concrete as his own personal test track. Negotiating a series of high speed S-curves, the imposing vehicle asserted its superiority on the road, keeping those in pursuit guessing as to its next move. Roberta swayed ungainly from the serpentine motion, but was determined to remain on her feet. Once Belial had clipped two cars and sent a third into a retaining wall, they knew this would not end without a fight. The truck suddenly accelerated, ramming its front grill squarely into the Harleys. Realizing they were about to become fatality statistics, the men surged forth then throttled back to rejoin the others.

The gang's most experienced cyclist decided to engage in a daring act of heroism. He came parallel with the truck's rear hatch in an effort to pull Roberta and Hope onto his bike. Casey's sister seemed willing to try the ballsy scheme, motioning him to come closer. Witnessing the operation in his rearview mirror, Belial forced the vehicle into a K-rail running the length of the center median. The cyclist was barely able to brake in time as a shower of generated sparks engulfed the riders.

Downtown Los Angeles loomed ahead. They entered a major confluence of freeways where Highways 60 and 101 and Interstates 5 and 10 all meet in a jumble of elevated cloverleaves. Traffic was notoriously slow in this canyon of concrete and today was no exception. Belial refused to reduce speed, heading into a scrum of slower vehicles ahead. The bikers prepared themselves for a clash of metal and were rewarded for their foresight.

The truck sideswiped a line of cars backed up on an exit ramp, spraying the road with shards of glass and twisted metal. Several automobiles went airborne from the force of impact. Others, some costing hundreds of thousands, were instantly turned to scrap. Roberta fell to the deck in a howl of anguish, banging her head on the hopper. She scrambled back to her feet, holding onto the metal cable with all her might. The trailing motorcycles deftly avoided the debris, maneuvering between cars that were now strewn in diverse tangents across the highway.

The truck continued to barrel forth, clearing vehicles from its path like a gigantic scythe. Cars merging onto the road from another highway pulled into the breakdown lane to avoid contact. In the space of five minutes, the Los Angeles Police Department and California Highway Patrol received over 350 calls from angered and injured motorists, all demanding action from the authorities. Units were urgently dispatched to intercept and arrest the perpetrator.

Now proceeding west on Interstate 10, the truck encountered less traffic and was able to resume a speed well in excess of the posted limit. The gang remained in pursuit, wondering what could possibly happen next. Two police cruisers zoomed past with their lights flashing. They took up positions ahead of the vehicle in a textbook blocking maneuver designed to impede its forward progress.

Belial was amused by their interference, leaning his head out the side window. "Get out of my way, you doughnut-eating pricks! Didn't ya hear? There's a wild man on the loose!"

One of the patrol cars positioned itself directly in front of the onrushing front-loader, providing Belial with an idea for additional mayhem. He lowered into position two eight-foot steel prongs used for lifting dumpster waste into the top of the truck. Reminiscent of a charging bull elephant, the beast then surged into the car, spearing the rear windshield with its metal tusks. The officer inside was hysterical with fear, searching frantically for a means of escape. Suddenly, the main hydraulic system activated, hoisting the cruiser off the road. Implementing its designated function, the mechanism elevated the vehicle above the cab and tried to release the load into the hopper. Too large for the opening, the police car bounced off the truck's roof, crashing to the highway in a surreal scene of destruction. Roberta shrieked in awe as she witnessed the vehicle flip a half dozen times, sending fragments of metal and glass the breadth of the Interstate. The motorcycles were trapped in the storm of debris, navigating wildly through the wreckage. Two of the gang members wiped out on their bikes, surfing the asphalt for hundreds of feet.

Laughing derisively, Belial engaged the other police cruiser, impaling this one as well. The vehicle suffered a similar fate, performing a high speed demolition dance across the highway. The cyclists had learned their lesson, maintaining a more discrete distance from the back of the truck. Soon, six other vehicles joined the cavalcade of carnage, somersaulting over the front-loader in a massive orgy of broken bodies, metallic discharge and fire ravaged chassis.

Drunk with malevolence, Belial found an oldies station on the radio, now singing karaoke to a classic Stevie Wonder tune. "Very superstitious, nothin' more to say…Very superstitious, the Devil's on His way…Thirteen month old baby, broke the lookin' glass… Seven years of bad luck, good things in your past…"

TV station helicopters began hovering above, televising the unfolding devastation live to a stupefied audience. California Highway Patrol vehicles had blocked the access ramps to and from Interstate 405, further reducing traffic and forcing the wayward garbage carrier into the city of Santa Monica. Police units cleared the highway ahead, laying down a series of spike strips to puncture the truck's tires. Belial drove directly into the gauntlet without deviation. Leaving the area in a haze of smoke and rubber, the speeding behemoth started to fishtail then adjusted its course up a nearby exit ramp. The motorcycles drove into the far left median to avoid the spikes and maintain their pursuit.

Pedestrians dashed for safety upon sighting the truck's reckless entrance onto local streets. Smashing its way through three lanes of vehicular gridlock, the truck careened to the left and looked like it was about to tip over before regaining its balance onto Colorado Avenue. Shredded bits of overheated rubber flew in all directions, spraying diners in front of ritzy, open-air restaurants. The screams of thousands could not compete with the beast as its exposed wheel rims clattered noisily across the pavement. Another busy intersection was transformed into a glorified salvage yard after no less than 17 cars were totaled from their encounter with the ocean-bound transport.

Shattering a heavy chain separating them from the famed Santa Monica Pier, the truck entered the pedestrian-only boardwalk, gouging the heavy wooden planks with its metal footprint. People scattered wildly, some jumping into the water below. Terrified parents snatched their children into adjacent storefronts. Carnival riders were left aghast at the scene as were those on the beach.

With less than 300 feet of pier remaining, Casey and Kimberly knew the truck would never stop. They could only pray that Roberta and the baby would be spared a watery grave. The cyclists followed them to the end, watching helplessly as the 25 ton vehicle broke through the final barrier and executed a dramatic plunge into the sun-drenched Pacific surf.

Casey was an excellent swimmer and dove off the pier without hesitation. Kimberly and the gang assembled at the edge, hoping for the best. The truck lay fallow upon the surface, but quickly took on water. Roberta managed to extricate herself from the sinking vehicle, bobbing her head above the waves. To her infinite relief, Kimberly noticed a tiny head perched in her sister's arm. Casey swam to the pair and aided their rescue to shore. With the exception of some cuts and bruising, his kid sisters remained alive and well.

It wasn't long before the police were there asking a multitude of questions. Dive teams scanned the underwater wreckage, but found no trace of the driver. After a thorough investigation, the authorities remained baffled by the disappearance…wondering how the man could have vanished into thin air.

CHAPTER FORTY

*A*fter a marathon journey of over 3,000 miles, their night-long quest was nearing an end. Captain Parnell had called ahead, enlisting the aid of several Army National Guard bases strategically located in Arizona, Utah, Idaho and Washington to provide fuel for Major Osborne's Huey. Their last stop was at a commercial aviation depot in Sitka, on the southeastern Alaska coast. Directly ahead lay the cobalt blue majesty of Prince William Sound and the port city of Valdez, now becoming visible in the pale dawn light.

Kevin had slept fitfully between their repeated stops to refuel. Conversation remained infrequent as neither wanted to discuss the series of vocal outbursts caused by his recurring nightmares. He soon began stirring in his seat, squinting at the ill-timed break of day.

"How can the sun be rising? It's 3:30 in the morning."

"We're getting close to the Arctic Circle," explained Osborne. "They have short nights this time of year."

Kevin huffed in exasperation, aware that any further sleep would remain elusive. He shook the cobwebs from his mind, taking note of the approaching coastline. It was then he spotted a large vessel at the mouth of the sound, headed toward Valdez harbor.

"Is that it?"

"Looks like it could be. I'll swoop down to check her out."

The Huey began to descend over a series of narrowing ocean breakers and isolated spits of land. They skimmed the surface at 200 feet, approaching the vessel on an intersecting tangent from astern. The ship's running lights were still illuminated in the icy haze, making identification of the craft more difficult. Once the helicopter came parallel with the bow, they were finally able to ascertain the vessel's designation emblazoned on its side. The 1,100 foot long, 16 deck Lord of the Seas was before them, churning water at 21 knots for its scheduled 5:00 am arrival in Valdez.

With their target acquired, Osborne called the harbor master on his cell phone, asking to talk with the ship's Captain on an emergency channel. After being patched through via ship-to-shore radio, he was placed in contact with the Lord of the Seas' Executive Officer on the bridge.

"The Captain's currently in his quarters. With whom am I speaking?"

"XO, this is Major Robert Osborne, U.S. Army Ranger Corps. I'm piloting the UH-1 helicopter hovering off your port bow."

"What can we do for you, Major?"

"You have a passenger aboard by the name of Pierre LeClerke. I have orders from the Pentagon to escort him to Elmendorf Air Force Base where he's to fly to Washington this morning on a matter of extreme national security."

The Executive Officer paused, searching the ship's passenger manifest. Pierre LeClerke and his wife were indeed on board.

"Major, can't this wait until we dock in Valdez?"

"I'm afraid not, XO. His presence is required by the Joint Chiefs of Staff."

"How do you plan to transfer him?"

"I'm requesting immediate clearance to land on your vessel."

A moment of hesitation arose. "That's a decision I can't make on my own. Hold on..."

The Executive Officer phoned the Captain's Quarters, alerting his superior to the unorthodox situation. In less than a minute, the ship's commander was on the bridge. Osborne's discussion with the Captain echoed the one previously held. The man peered out at the Army helicopter, his eyes riveted on the main gun and eight heat seeking missiles arrayed underneath. Convinced of the Major's official status and intent, he granted their request. The Huey circled into position, directed to land upon an open-air sports deck just aft of the forecastle. This area normally hosted volleyball tournaments, but had been used in the past to remove sick passengers onto emergency rescue choppers. Skillfully lowering the craft to the deck, Osborne executed procedures to power down and emerged from the cockpit. He and Kevin, each attired in Army fatigues, strode over to the ship's Security Officer who greeted both with a handshake.

"The LeClerke's are in our Royal Suite on deck 14, aftmost portion of the ship," he revealed. "I dispatched one of our stewards to bring him here."

"Very good," the Major stated tersely. Both he and Kevin were exhibiting crisp military comportment, spurning the officer's blatant attempts to gain further information. They knew this charade was a risk, but it seemed the most logical way to get LeClerke to accompany them without question.

It wasn't long before Pierre emerged onto the sports deck, led to those awaiting him by the Chief Cabin Steward. Osborne recalled seeing his photograph on GG&E's corporate website and knew immediately they'd found their man.

The Security Officer wasted no time with introductions. "I apologize for the intrusion, Dr. LeClerke. These Army officers are under orders to take you to Elmendorf Air Force Base for a flight to Washington."

The bleary-eyed CEO looked upon the men with a hint of insight, but decided to remain silent until he was provided additional clarification. Noting his caution, the Major spoke with appropriate urgency. "Dr. LeClerke, my orders come directly from General

Kenneth Connolly, Army Chief of Staff. He told me to inform you this is an emergency situation…a MAJIK-12 directive."

LeClerke snapped to attention, feeling the gravity of his words. The man nodded in compliance, requiring no further explanation. "Give me ten minutes," he implored. "I have to grab my suitcase and let my wife know I'm leaving."

"We'll give you eight," announced Kevin, clearly embracing his role as a military tough guy.

The CEO bounded to the elevator and returned to his suite in haste. On his way, he used his satellite BlackBerry to text message General Connolly regarding the nature of the emergency. His transmission told the MAJIK-12 all they needed to know about their rogue member, including his current location and circumstance. What LeClerke received in response was totally unexpected, leaving him in fear for his life.

Kevin and the Major stood stoically, waiting for the man to return. During the delay, they continued to engage the Security Officer with innocuous banter relating to his abbreviated stint in the Marine Corps. Time elapsed in ever widening increments, forcing both to check their watches in dismay. The imposed deadline had expired and still there was no sign of LeClerke. Anxious seconds passed while sighs of frustration mounted. Osborne chided himself, upset that he hadn't escorted him to his suite. *Where the hell is this guy?*

The Security Officer's radio squawked to life. It was one of his lieutenants, reporting an incident aboard ship. "Sir, there's been a disturbance in Dr. LeClerke's stateroom. I think you'd better come at once."

Leaving the helicopter unguarded, the three broke formation, dashing down a flight of steps that led to the promenade deck. They scurried through a lengthy corridor and descended another large stairway to the grand ballroom and the ship's luxury suites beyond.

Inside the Royal Suite, Sylvia LeClerke was reporting her ordeal to a member of the security staff when the trio arrived in breathless consternation. The woman was sitting on her bed, blubbering forth in a near sob. She was clutching her left arm in pain, the result of a fall during a recent altercation.

"What happened here?" the Security Officer barked.

His subordinate briefed him. "Dr. LeClerke's been abducted. His wife was injured after a scuffle with the man."

"Who was it?" directing the question to both. "A member of the crew?"

"I never saw him before," she sniveled. "He was a ghastly character, full of spite…laughing like a fiend. He slapped my face and threw me to the floor. Pierre wrestled with him…before he put a knife to his throat. I don't know which way they went."

"What did this guy look like?" he continued to probe.

She paused, allowing her memory to gel. "He was about 45 and a little over 6 foot tall. Probably 200 pounds. Black hair, cut close. And, he had the strangest eyes…just dark as night."

Upon hearing her account, the Major felt an involuntary chill surge through his soul. The man's description was reminiscent of the monk he'd exposed at the mission. He could never forget his piercing eyes, black and lifeless like those of a doll. Osborne reflected upon the haunting image then motioned Kevin to follow. They left the suite with quick, decisive strides, executing a fevered return to the chopper.

"Sounds like they got him," Kevin theorized.

"I doubt it. A professional assassin wouldn't leave a witness alive."

"So, who are we dealing with?"

Osborne shuddered at the thought. "I'm almost afraid to say."

As the pair approached the stairwell leading up to the sports deck, the Major's worst fears were realized. He heard the distinctive aural signature of a helicopter's engine revving at full power, preparing for takeoff. There was no need to search for an explanation or motive. Both of them knew the Huey had been commandeered and was leaving without them.

Emerging topside, they stood in shock while the craft elevated skyward, kicking up an icy blast of air in its wake. Seated in the cockpit was Pierre LeClerke, his manic contortions representative of a man scared shitless. Beside him at the controls was his black-eyed captor, another member of the Grigori. The archangel Azazel was now amongst them and prepared to wreak havoc on an unprecedented scale.

Osborne grasped his sidearm, aiming at the man's legs through the glass canopy. Azazel returned the favor, activating the turret on the M134 minigun and painting them with its laser sight. Recognizing the threat, the Major yanked Kevin behind a metal bulkhead just prior to the onslaught. 500 rounds of high velocity ammunition screeched down from above, testing the integrity of the steel plating and deflecting rounds in all directions. They slid to the deck, retracting their arms and legs in mortal terror. Shrill acoustics savaged their ears, the pernicious effects lasting longer than the fusillade itself. The assault ended as abruptly as it came, leaving the pair to wonder if they'd survived the encounter unscathed. Peering around the bulkhead, Osborne was witness to more devastation as the chopper loosed an additional barrage into the ship's bridge, wounding every officer present. The Major knew the firepower Azazel had at his disposal and cringed at the thought of its use. In desperation, he fired three rounds at the Huey hoping to disable the craft. The Army helicopter yawed right, strafing the vessel indiscriminately from bow to stern.

"Holy shit!" yelped Kevin. "What a mess this turned out to be!"

Osborne winced. "It's liable to get a lot worse. Once he figures out how to fire those heat seekers…" He stopped short, aware his premonition of doom was about to become reality.

The chopper lofted to a greater height and adjusted its downward pitch, hovering a few hundred yards off the vessel's port side. In an eruption of tailfire, a rack-mounted Stinger missile was fired, detonating amidships with a thunderous concussion just below the waterline. An emergency siren began to peal, awakening all 2,800 souls aboard. Watertight hatches closed automatically, sealing off flooded areas so the Lord of the Seas could remain buoyant. The Security Officer's voice was heard over the ship-wide PA system, urging everyone to remain calm. Cabin stewards handed out inflatable life vests to the startled passengers, assuring each that it was merely a safety precaution.

Still not satisfied at the extent of damage, Azazel maneuvered the Huey to the vessel's starboard side and readied another missile to fire. This time, the lower engineering section was targeted. The Stinger pierced the ship's outer casing and ruptured one of four ancillary boilers, causing a massive explosion that blew a hole through seven decks. The entire vessel convulsed from the blast, triggering widespread chaos among passengers and crew alike. A veritable stampede of humanity surged into corridors and stairwells, dismissing previous muster drills to the contrary. The central atrium was soon choked with panicked voyagers, all attempting to proceed topside. Efforts to regain order went unheeded, lost in a squall of tumultuous alarm.

The Huey broke off the attack and initiated a turn to the northeast, now on a direct course for the Port of Valdez. Forced to pursue, Kevin joined the Major inside a service elevator which began to descend into the bowels of the cruise liner. He wasted little time expressing his dismay.

"Everyone's going up and we're headed down?"

"It's the fastest way off the ship," Osborne explained. "We gotta get to the docking bay where they keep the tender boats… Trust me."

At that moment, the Lord of the Seas' main generators failed, shutting off electrical systems throughout the vessel and plunging the elevator into darkness. For Kevin, the timing couldn't have been more perfect. "I'm sorry. What was that you said?"

A few seconds transpired before emergency power was restored. After resuming their descent, Osborne answered his snarky comrade. "Trust me."

Arriving on Deck 3, the two sprinted down a smoky corridor

following signs which led them to the Tender Docking Bay. Once inside, they cornered several crewmembers who were busy winching one of the boats into position for possible passenger evacuation.

"We're Army Rangers on official military business," the Major declared. "We have to stop that chopper."

The Dock Master shook his head in dissent. "The fastest thing we've got is that Zodiac," pointing to an inflatable raft equipped with outboard motor. "But, we can't let you have that."

"Well, Captain Beretta says you can," insisted Osborne, swiftly exposing his handgun. "Drag it onto the gangway…right now!"

The crew complied with his demand, placing the high speed tender on a hydraulic platform. The men were lowered into the water then scrambled inside the boat. Once the outboard roared to life, they soon began skipping across Prince William Sound in excess of 50 knots.

Leaving the Lord of the Seas behind in an effusion of sea spray, the Zodiac performed a series of evasive maneuvers, zipping past small islands and jetties under Osborne's deft command. The turbulent motion made their quest more difficult, scanning the azure horizon in search of the stolen Huey. Kevin could barely keep his eyes open as the ice cold air whipped against his flesh. He detected a small speck in the sky ahead, losing sight of the object before reacquiring the target seconds later.

"Is that it?" thrusting a finger toward the rising sun.

Osborne acknowledged the discovery. "Looks to be! They've probably got about five miles on us."

Kevin retained his skeptical nature. "How are we gonna catch a helicopter with a boat?"

It was an excellent question, one the Major had already posed to himself. Even if they managed to catch up, the Huey's firepower would propel them instantly to Davy Jones' Locker. In order to save LeClerke's life, they'd need to secure a vehicle of equivalent size and capability. *But, how…and from where?* As they entered the mouth of Valdez harbor, their plight was resolved. A few hundred yards off their starboard bow was a United States Coast Guard air base, already at max alert due to a distress call from The Lord of the Seas. A half dozen rescue choppers were arrayed on the tarmac being prepped for takeoff, their main rotors spinning with anticipation.

Unable to ignore such a fortuitous circumstance, they glided the Zodiac to shore and bounded across a rocky seawall before approaching a yet-to-be-manned HH-65C Dolphin. After opening the hatch, the Major witnessed a Coast Guard pilot racing over to intercept them.

"Hey! What the fuck's the deal?"

Osborne leveled his weapon, stopping the officer cold. "I'm taking her for a spin. Any objection?"

"Man, you're gonna get about 5,000 years in jail for this," he admonished. "I hope you know what you're doing."

Kevin sauntered past the man. "That makes two of us, pal."

They entered the craft and buttoned up for flight. The Coast Guard pilot dashed back to base headquarters, alerting three MPs who were too late to prevent the brazen theft.

Once airborne, the Major took a few moments to familiarize himself with the controls then proceeded to track down their foe. The Dolphin helicopter was larger and faster than the Huey, but because it was built for rescue at sea it had no need for armament. Any aerial engagement would be a one-sided affair, but Osborne was an excellent pilot and his intimate knowledge of the UH-1 would undoubtedly work to their advantage.

A thin layer of clouds mitigated the sun's glare, allowing them to gain an accurate fix on their quarry. The Huey was approximately a mile and a half due east, hovering aloft at 2,000 feet. Osborne failed to understand why they were maintaining a stationary position, granting precious time for the Dolphin to play catch up. *Are they turning to fight? Baiting us into a confrontation we can't possibly win?* The Major mulled through a number of tactical scenarios before gaining insight into the mind of a demon.

"Oh, my God…"

Below them lay the sprawling oil depot of Valdez. Three supertankers were currently docked, filling their cargo holds with crude petroleum, pumped here from Prudhoe Bay through the 800 mile long Alaska Pipeline. Clustered beside the harbor were 18 immense storage tanks, laden with over nine million barrels of unrefined oil. The complex was undefended and completely oblivious to the threat from above. Six heat seekers remained, now primed and ready for launch. Frozen by the coming horror, the two assumed front row seats to witness the greatest ecological disaster in modern world history.

The missiles sped free of the craft, each leaving behind a thick trail of propellant fumes. Detonation bursts unleashed an ever-expanding canopy of fire which blanketed the site within seconds. An array of mushroom clouds now sprouted atop thousand foot pillars of boiling flame. Fragments of metal rode skyward on thermal updrafts, returning to the streets of Valdez in a deluge of shrapnel. Sonic concussions shook the chopper, while superheated air created near catastrophic turbulence. Secondary explosions began to blossom as other storage tanks ignited within the chain reaction inferno. Oil booms loading the ships with Alaskan crude caught fire, channeling the blaze directly into their cargo holds. In an incandescent convulsion of flame, the supertankers splayed open in three prodigious blasts as the gates of Hell yawned wide. The generated shockwave was so intense that Osborne clutched the cyclic with both hands, certain the helicopter's safety glass would crack. Dense smoke billowed into the windless dawn, soon casting a black veil over the sun. The pyrotechnics raged onward, engulfing the valley floor in a conflagration without end. Viscous rivers of burning oil poured into the harbor, glowing in a red-hot mass like that of a lava flow. The petroleum was destined to spread throughout Prince William Sound, destroying animal habitats, fisheries and estuaries on an unprecedented scale. Emergency sirens blared forth in a mournful chorus while damage control personnel used a combination of water, foam, carbon dioxide and HALON to battle the firestorm.

The devastation at the Valdez marine terminal turned into a full blown cataclysm once a series of explosions began to erupt northward, transforming the Alaskan Pipeline into a gigantic lit fuse. Over a million barrels of combustible fuel pushed the blaze up precipitous Thompson Pass and into the heart of the Chugach Mountains. Wildfires spread on both sides of the ravaged tube, consuming hundreds of acres of pristine forest. The Alyeska Pipeline Service Company, an ownership consortium of seven oil corporations, was able to sever the flow of crude at Pumping Station 12, a few miles from the harbor. Fortunately, the explosive incident was contained, thereby sparing the vast majority of Alaskan wilderness from harm. The company would now begin the laborious process of rebuilding their infrastructure and restoring the environment in the wake of a trillion dollar disaster.

Azazel laughed maniacally at the devastation he alone had wrought. His reluctant passenger was whimpering like an abused child, tears of irrepressible fright cascading down his face. The archangel finally addressed his captive.

"Awww, what's a matter? Did you pee yourself?" he asked in a mischievous tone. "Come on, you pudgy little shit. I want you to laugh with me...Laugh!" He reached over, grabbing LeClerke's cheek in an abortive attempt to force a smile. His own amusement ended when Osborne buzzed past the Huey mere feet from their windshield. With his wrath restored, Azazel banked the chopper in pursuit, firing a lengthy burst from the M134 minigun. The Dolphin helicopter dove for cover behind a thick curtain of black smoke, avoiding the deadly barrage. After making another surprise run at the Huey, the Major caused Azazel to deplete his ammunition further.

Safely shrouded in a plume of smoke, Osborne assessed the situation. "That should just about to it. One more pass and he'll be done."

Kevin, clutching his seat harness, agreed. "Yeah, and maybe so will we."

The Dolphin emerged from the murky cloud on a different tangent, drawing the last of the Huey's fire. With his weapons now exhausted, Azazel left the engagement area, flying at max speed toward the majestic peaks of the Chugach mountain range.

The Dolphin gave chase, quickly closing the distance between the two aircraft. For more than 20 minutes, they parried in frenzied pursuit, eluding terrestrial obstacles in their path without any margin for error. The helicopters climbed into rarified air, lofting past peaks in excess of 10,000 feet. A thick carpet of white spread across the landscape for miles, its awesome beauty lost on those dueling above. In fact, this remote area of Alaska annually received the most snowfall of any in the Western Hemisphere.

As they continued on a weaving, high speed course amidst towering trees and calving glaciers, Osborne bestowed grudging respect on his adversary. Even seasoned pilots would've had trouble maintaining this sort of hair-raising flight path. Whether it was his skills as an aviator or nothing more than sheer luck, Azazel had proven to be a formidable opponent.

"He's gonna run out of gas soon," predicted the Major. "It was three quarters empty when we landed on the ship."

Kevin questioned their options. "So, what do we do? Just let 'em crash?"

He proposed a daring plan. "Get the cargo winch ready."

"Huh?"

"The cargo winch," he instructed, pointing to a motorized hoist system by the main hatch. "If we get close enough, maybe we can snare one of her landing skids and set her on the ground."

"Excuse me?" voicing his apprehension. "Are you trying to prove that brain cells die in cold weather?"

"You have any better ideas?"

Kevin unbuckled his seat, taking a reluctant stroll to the cargo area. He read the specifications stamped on the industrial winch motor. "It says the maximum weight load is 6,000 pounds. How heavy is a Huey?"

Osborne's response did little to allay his fears. "10,500

fully loaded. But, she's running light. There's only two aboard and they've got no fuel or ammo." He paused to calculate their chances. "She's still probably half a ton more than we can handle." The Major vented a breath of defeat, cursing the situation.

In a surprising reversal of character, Kevin abandoned his cynical nature to recall a televised news story. "You know, I once saw one of these things haul a full grown whale back out to sea. I'll bet that pilot had second thoughts, too."

The decision was made. Osborne maneuvered in as tightly as he dared, placing the Dolphin a few feet above and to the right of the Huey while matching the craft's forward speed and banking angle. Kevin attached himself to a safety harness before sliding open the main hatch and extending the steel winch cable. On the end was a metal grasping hook about 30 inches in size which was lowered alongside the smaller craft. After encountering sudden turbulence, he came to realize how difficult this task would be.

"The cable's swaying all over the place!" he yelled. "It's gonna get chopped up in their rotors!"

At that moment, the Major detected a loss of power aboard the Huey. Turbine speed was reducing rapidly, causing the helicopter to lose forward thrust and pitch. The vehicle appeared to shudder in midair as though knowing its life was at an end. What they'd previously feared had come to pass. The doomed craft was now out of fuel.

"Hook that thing up now!" bellowed Osborne in panic. "We won't get another chance!"

Over the sonic wash of the Dolphin, Kevin could hear the Huey's death knell as the final drops of petrol were sucked dry. Both main and rear rotors were spinning slower by the second, becoming visible to the naked eye. The grasping hook was positioned between the chopper's hull and its skids, searching for the right gust of wind to achieve a connection. An errant miss. Then another. A third also failed. Desperation swelled as time expired. With a final sputter, the helicopter rolled over and began its plunge to earth.

Once the pull of gravity intervened, the grasping hook snared the traverse support member to the landing skids and the laws of physics took hold. The winch motor assembly issued a high pitched squeal of distress, straining to hold the sudden weight. The Dolphin lost its aerodynamic balance, wobbling in all three axes of flight. Osborne tried to compensate, but the excessive load factor was exerting too much force. They were rapidly losing altitude and seemed destined to be joining the Huey inside an immutable tomb of snow and ice.

As Kevin looked down the length of the cable, he saw Pierre LeClerke force open his hatch, screaming in delirium. The man was hanging upside down, inverted in his chair and unable to release his seat harness. Azazel had left him to die, escaping through the gateway to safety. With the hoist mechanism still retracting the winch cable, the distance between the two craft had closed significantly. Kevin was compelled to action, unable to watch the man perish. He impulsively slid down the steel tether, reaching inside the Huey to assist in LeClerke's rescue. The seat restraint finally snapped free, allowing him to extract Pierre through the open hatch. Performing an awkward pirouette, the portly CEO lost his footing and pulled Kevin off the cable.

Freefalling for more than 60 feet, the two plummeted into a cushioned bed of newly fallen snow. Quickly assessing his condition, Kevin exhaled in relief, euphoric at his survival. LeClerke was alive as well, bruised and sore from a graceless landing. In that instant of blissful solace, neither man thought of anything but himself. It was a purely existential moment, soon lost in a thunderous crash of metal not far away.

Oh, my God...The Major...

Kevin scrambled to his feet, poking his head above the wall of fresh powder. He sighted the mangled wreckage approximately 150 yards distant, burrowed into a cluster of trees and churned snowpack. Flailing his arms and legs in a manic dash to the scene, he arrived exhausted, the thin air having taken its toll. The Huey lay decimated, its hull crushed from the impact. The Dolphin appeared relatively intact, although its main rotor had been sheared off from the fuselage. His chief concern was the potential for an explosion, but the thick bed of snow made that scenario extremely remote. He surged through piles of jagged debris, finally reaching the cockpit. Kevin found the Major slumped over the instrument panel with the cyclic buried in his abdomen. Clearing the area of obstructions, he forced open the hatch and pulled the battered body into a reclined position. Osborne wheezed for air, coughing up a frothy stream of blood. The two achieved eye contact and the silent communion they shared transcended words.

"Oh, Major," Kevin gasped in a rare show of emotion. "You were right awhile back. Things did get worse, didn't they?"

Osborne acknowledged with a gentle nod, the torment etched on his face. "Yeah...I'm afraid they have."

CHAPTER FORTY-ONE

CARLSBAD, NEW MEXICO — MAY 10th — 4:13 PM MDT

Seated in the waiting room at Carlsbad Medical Center, C.J. closed his eyes, reflecting upon the past few hours in his mind. After assisting his wounded brother from the caverns, the two were able to exit the crowded visitor's center without drawing undue attention. The M1 Tank they'd arrived in was gone, towed away to be examined by the authorities. They approached the driver of an empty school bus, bribing him with $500 to take them into town while a group of third graders he was waiting for were on a guided tour. Moses was admitted to the emergency room where he was treated for his injury. The doctor on call informed C.J. that his brother had come through surgery with flying colors and was listed in good condition. He'd be able to see him as soon as the anesthesia wore off. Although grateful for the news, his joy was subdued at the thought of how the incident had occurred. The Dreamland CDs were gone forever, smashed to bits within the Earth's darkened core. He blamed himself for the loss and was keenly aware of the implications. *Without those discs, no one's going to believe a word we say. What the hell are we going to do now?*

Venting a breath of dejection, C.J. used the available time

to contact his siblings for updates. Barbara was in New York, organizing a meeting of the United Nations General Assembly which was scheduled for tomorrow afternoon. On the agenda was the U. S. Government's complicity in the Roswell cover-up, its exploitation of recovered technology and the systematic elimination of all those who'd tried to expose the truth…including the assassinations of former Presidents Kennedy, Petersen and Webber. The delegates in attendance, along with a worldwide television audience, would be presented the evidence obtained from Dreamland. C.J. hung his head, not knowing what to say. To have this kind of opportunity was a godsend, but to squander it would be devastating. Even if they provided their own eyewitness accounts, the court of public opinion would demand proof. He decided not to tell Barbara what happened until after he'd spoken with the others.

Casey informed him of Hope's rescue and their continuing battles with Belial. He and his sisters were flying to San Francisco where his grandparents resided, hoping the elderly pair could provide a safe haven for the baby. Shannon was on the road a few miles east of Nashville, Tennessee, on the way to Quantico with her escort of hired commandos.

This left Kevin and Benjamin as the only members of his family unaccounted for. He tried calling his brother's cell three separate times, but reached his voice mail on each occasion. Major Osborne's phone also rang without answer. Frustrated by the persistent lack of response, C.J. followed his instincts and placed a call to Kevin's home in Scottsdale. He was soon speaking with Lynda Knight, the young woman they'd met prior to leaving for Juarez.

"My God!" she cried, her voice burdened with fear. "I was hoping it was Kevin. I'm really getting worried."

"Why? What's going on?"

Lynda told him what she knew. "Kevin and the Major stopped here last night. He said they were heading to Alaska to find some guy on a cruise ship. Then, an hour ago I saw the news on TV."

He tried to make sense of her story. "What news?"

"The fires in Valdez!" she squawked. "They said a helicopter blew up three oil tankers and a petroleum storage facility. The whole harbor's in flames! I just know he's involved in this."

C.J. probed the woman for further details. After calming her nerves, she recalled Kevin saying they'd left Benjamin with one of the Major's Army buddies at Fort Huachuca. Relieved his kid brother was out of harm's way, he responded to an obvious question from Lynda.

"We're in Carlsbad, New Mexico. Someone stole the CDs we had," he sighed, growing fatigued at the memory. "Moses and I followed him here, but we ended up losing them. It was my fault. I suppose it wasn't meant to be."

"Oh, don't worry about that, C.J.," she chirped. "I made a copy."

He froze in disbelief, wondering if he'd heard her correctly. His lips trembled, attempting to phrase a reply. "What did you say?"

"The morning you were here, while you guys were trying to sleep, I made a copy of those CDs," Lynda acknowledged. "They looked important, so I thought I'd make another set." She paused, wondering if she'd done the right thing. "I guess I should've told you…Sorry."

Rendered speechless by her disclosure, C.J. experienced a wealth of emotion unlike any he'd felt before. He was amazed at how despair could turn to triumph in so short a time. This woman entered their lives in such seemingly random fashion, but had been tasked with a purpose greater than they could have foreseen.

He thanked her for restoring his spirit. "Lynda, you're an angel…and I mean that literally."

Graciously accepting his praise, her thoughts turned somber. "I'd give anything to hear Kevin say that," she blubbered. "I just want to know he's okay."

"He'll be back," professed C.J. "He'd be a fool not to see you again."

She burst into a nervous giggle. "What do you need me to do?"

He instructed her to download the secret data onto Kevin's hard drive then make three more sets of CDs. The two agreed she would place one copy in a safety deposit box at her bank; bury another in Kevin's backyard, while the third Lynda would take to an investigative reporter at the _Arizona Republic_ newspaper.

"What about the original copy?" she asked.

"I know it's asking a lot, but could you bring it here to New Mexico? I'll reimburse you for the flight."

She checked the internet for possible connections to Carlsbad. Nothing was available. However, there was one flight she could catch that would allow her to land just 70 miles to the north. "There's a Mesa Airlines flight that'll get me in at 9:10 tonight. Can you meet me in Roswell?"

After a reverent pause, he assured her they would. With their conversation at an end, C.J. smiled at God's remarkable sense of irony. Due to this stunning twist of fate, they were being lead back to where it all began.

CHAPTER FORTY-TWO

Casey and his sisters arrived in the city by the bay, exhausted from their morning travail. Not only was it becoming more difficult for them to stay alert, but having to remain on guard for the crafty Belial was sapping their spiritual strength. With Hope's safety compromised by their escalating fatigue, they required assistance from people they could trust. Casey addressed the problem logically. Who better to help them than his beloved grandparents, Stanley Chou and Mimi Kwan?

The rental car pulled up to a two-story Victorian residence, located in the Marina District just off Divisadero Street. The multimillion abode was a gift from their wealthy grandson, which boasted superlative views of the Golden Gate Bridge, Alcatraz and the city of Sausalito to the north. As Casey and Kimberly exited the vehicle with their infant sister, Roberta opted to stay inside and finish her phone conversation with Carlos Ayala. Although she'd spent over two hours in the hospital with him before leaving L.A., the girl couldn't get enough of the dashing youth, now using up her cell minutes at an alarming rate.

Casey had called ahead, informing his grandparents of their

planned visit. He rang the bell and instantly heard the yelp of a ferocious canine, barking and snarling on the opposite side of the door. Several seconds elapsed, but no one answered. Another ring triggered further hysteria from the crazed animal, sounding as if it were about to chew its way through the surrounding drywall.

Kimberly expressed concern, cradling Hope tighter in her arms. "You didn't tell me they had a dog?"

"I didn't know," Casey confessed. "Must be a recent addition."

"It doesn't seem too friendly."

He shrugged. "Probably just needs to go to the bathroom."

Mimi finally opened the door, exposing them to the feral beast. Weighing about 50 pounds, the handsome brown and black Shepherd-Chow mix sniffed each of them on the leg. Convinced of their benign intent, he then returned to his favorite couch without so much as a whimper.

Casey hugged the woman with genuine affection. "Grand-mother Kwan, how are you?"

"I'm fine," declaring her love by rubbing his back. The elderly female looked over his shoulder at Kimberly and the babe in her arms. "Oh, dear," she moaned, quickly pushing him to arms length. "I can't believe this! You've had a child out of wedlock?"

He smiled at the misunderstanding. "No, that's not what happened."

"You got married?" her voice peaking in glee. "Well, why didn't you tell us? Stanley, get out here! Our grandson's hitched! He's already got a kid and a really hot wife!"

"No!" he protested. "Kimberly's my sister. The baby's also my sister." Roberta then joined them at the door. "And, this girl's my sister, too."

Mimi eyed him cynically. "Don't try to con an old lady. They've got laws against that in this state...Come on in girls. Make yourselves at home."

They all entered and official introductions commenced.

Stanley approached, feeling his way along a nearby wall. Casey embraced the optically challenged man in greeting.

"Grandfather Chou, it's great to see you again."

"Yes, yes. Forget that drivel," he groused openly. "What's this nonsense about getting married?"

"That's just what it is...nonsense."

Stanley leaned over to whisper a word of warning. "Easy, kid. She's standing right there. It's a little soon to be pissing off the old ball and chain." Through his myopic gaze, he bade official welcome to an adjacent hat stand. "Whoa. You're just a little wisp of a thing, aren't you? You really need to put some meat on those bones."

"No, grandfather," stated Casey, guiding him to his left. "She's over here."

As he spun around, his outstretched hand came into contact with Kimberly's ample breast. "Ooooh, there you are. Glad to make your acquaintance young lady."

Forgiving his intrusion, she shook his hand cordially. "It's nice to meet you, Mr. Chou."

"It's too early for dinner," Mimi stressed. "I thought we'd eat about 7:00."

"No, grandmother," Casey corrected. "She wasn't asking for food."

Once Kimberly and Roberta understood the nature of their infirmities, it was far easier to attempt communication with the elderly pair. In fact, the girls were now enjoying their visit, finding the couple endearing and immensely likeable.

They adjourned to the living room where a magnificent panorama of the bay awaited them. "Wow!" gasped Roberta. "What a view!"

"I suppose its okay," Stanley huffed. "It'd be better if I could see it. Casey could've jammed us in a cardboard box and I wouldn't be able to tell the difference."

Kimberly made friends with the dog, stroking his luxuriant fur. "He's really a sweetheart. What's his name?" Receiving no response, she raised the decibel level to repeat her question.

"Oh, that's Smacky," Mimi declared, formally introducing their pet. "We've had him about a month now. Stanley and I picked him out at the animal shelter downtown."

"Why did you name him Smacky?" wondered Roberta.

"Because this mutt smacks his lips all night long," complained the elder Chou. "Mimi doesn't hear a damn thing, but I sure do. Can't get any sleep at all with that flea bag around."

Kimberly rubbed the dog's belly, addressing him in baby speak. "Aww. Don't listen to him. You're a good puppy, aren't you?"

Indeed, their pet was a perfect angel, bonding with the entire family. He appeared especially attracted to Hope, even licking the infant's hand in affection.

"Tonight's our bingo night," explained Mimi. "We go to the rec center down the street."

Roberta spoke slowly, trying to clearly enunciate her words. "Oh, do you like playing that game?"

"I'm sorry, sweetie. I don't remember your name."

"No, grandmother," interjected Casey. "She asked if you liked the game?"

"What game?"

"Bingo, you twit!" her husband roared. "And, no we don't like it. Haven't won a game in three years. I can't see the damn card and she can't hear the number when it's called. The whole thing's frustrating as hell."

Kimberly appeared perplexed. "So, why do you keep going?"

"I like their snacks," he admitted. "They've got great egg rolls and these little bitty weenies. They're really small, but succulent. Sometimes they're so juicy they just spurt in your mouth." The suggestive mental image was too much for Kimberly, causing her to gag in amusement. "What's the matter?" he asked innocently. "Don't you girls like little weenies?"

She burst into a disconcerting cackle, forcing Casey to answer. "I guess we'll take that as a 'no'."

"Would you like to come with us?" wondered Mimi.

Their grandson squelched the idea. "Sounds like a lot of fun, but I think we'd rather get some rest." He proposed an alternate plan. "Why don't the two of you take Hope? Maybe she'll bring you luck." The elderly duo promptly accepted the offer.

After Casey's grandparents left, the exhausted siblings entered a spare room containing two twin beds and a trundle daybed. They extinguished the lights, performing a trio of face-first dives into respective mattresses. Their eyelids grew heavy, soon lowering a blissful curtain upon the world. A feeling of serenity was theirs, knowing that no matter how potent the nightmare they would not be in a position to harm the baby. Releasing themselves from their worldly cares, the three surrendered to the mystic enchantment of dreamland.

The dog crept into their quarters, acting upon his protective instincts. He curled into a ball on the floor and issued a contented sigh. It wasn't long before the animal provided aural confirmation of his presence. A slight sound resonated, lasting no longer than one or two seconds. Casey recognized it as the result of saliva sticking to the black, fleshy protuberances surrounding the canine's mouth. Silence once more graced the room. The brief disruption had nearly faded from his conscious mind when a similar noise emanated from the creature. An indeterminate amount of drool was sucked back into the dog's mouth, triggering another acoustic disturbance. Instead of drifting back to sleep, Casey found himself waiting for the next audible incident. It occurred like clockwork, lasting an equivalent length of time as the others. In fact, the periods of silence between each episode of slobber were nearly identical. The generated sound wasn't objectionable. It was the frequency and persistence of the act that made him cringe. He was soon empathizing with his grandfather, mindful of the name bestowed upon the pet. *Unbelievable...This dog really does smack its lips!*

His sisters were exhibiting displeasure as well, fitfully tossing pillows about their heads. The incessant jowl flapping was keeping them awake, provoking Casey to reprimand the pooch.

"Knock it off, Smacky."

A period of welcome silence soon ended with another bout of slaver.

"We've had enough of that," he snapped. "Shut it."

As expected, the dog refused to listen. Roberta slammed her arms on the bed in restless disbelief. "Oh, this is so not happening."

"Get him out of here," cried Kimberly, still buried underneath her pillow.

Their brother came to his feet, ushering the animal from the room. Once the door closed, they heard the same caterwaul of protest encountered upon their arrival. The rambunctious barking immediately ceased after the dog gained re-entry, sprawling back onto the carpet as though nothing had happened.

Casey admonished the canine against further intrusion. "This is your last chance. Keep those lips shut. Understood?"

He rolled back to bed, convinced he'd have to take additional action. However, peace prevailed, allowing them to drift into a euphoric slumber. Just as they were nearing the land of nod, a familiar sound wrenched them to reality.

"Jesus!" blurted Kimberly in wide-eyed exasperation. "I can't take this shit! Somebody get me a gun!"

"Let's move into different rooms," Roberta suggested. "He can't be in three places at once."

Clearly, Smacky would be the biggest nightmare they'd face tonight.

The bingo hall was packed with octogenarians who resided at the adjoining senior care center. These were Stanley and Mimi's friends, a curious collection of race, gender and creed that had unified amidst their contempt for a world which treated them as second class citizens. They were societal castoffs, some never even receiving a visit from family members too busy to be bothered. The tight-knit clique had dedicated the rest of their lives to each another, trying to spread some cheer in an otherwise dreary existence.

Therefore, quite a commotion befell the crowd when Mimi walked in holding her 'great-granddaughter' Hope. The infant beamed for the fawning onlookers, all of whom expressed their joy in being this close to a life so young. After the obligatory 'ooohs' and 'aaahs', they assumed their seats for the much anticipated bingo match. Mimi grouped their chips into an orderly pile and perused the ten printed cards they'd been provided. Stanley was already munching on his little weenies when the first bingo ball was announced.

"B7", repeating the selection so that Mimi could hear. Another call was made. "N44," he spat. Then, a third was revealed. "O71..."

Mimi jumped from her seat. "Bingo!"

Stanley choked on his meat, nearly dropping an F-bomb. "What did you say, woman?"

She grinned, pointing excitedly at the table. "Bingo!"

"Me-ass!" He grabbed the card, placing it in front of his glasses. This was an amazing occurrence. After three years of futility, they'd finally won a game. The group politely applauded their victory and the next round began. Four picks later, Mimi's voice again pealed in triumph. "Bingo!"

Stanley's half-eaten weenie landed three tables distant. "What in Heaven's name is going on here?"

Hope rocked forth, gurgling in amusement. A tone had been set for the evening as Casey's grandparents won game after game, defying statistical odds in the trillions and leaving numerous players green with envy. After their incredible run of good fortune, the rec center's management team wanted to take photos of the lucky pair for the local newspaper. Mimi handed Hope to her closest friend, Gertrude Swenson, during the hullabaloo surrounding their publicity shoot.

Gertie was a kind old lady, but tended to be absent minded, even when it came to the most important things. She decided to give the newborn a present, a lovely bassinet that she'd had for many years. Returning to her private room, she laid the sleeping infant on her bed and removed the oblong basket from the closet. Inside was her daughter's first doll, a treasured toy from over 60 years ago. She meticulously rearranged the bedding and the cushioned liner, helping to ensure the child's comfort. Then, without checking on her precious cargo, the addled woman tucked the doll back inside the bassinet and closed the door to her room.

Minutes later, Gertie presented her friends with the unexpected gift. It was a much appreciated gesture, one that Casey's grandparents thanked her for many times over. They took the bassinet in hand and peeked under the hood.

"Aww," Mimi gushed. "She looks just like a little doll."

"Ssshh," cautioned Gertie. "The baby's sound asleep."

"Thanks again," she whispered.

The two left the rec center, stopping inside a neighborhood store to buy Hope some other gifts. Stanley set the bassinet down while they selected a doll, two plush toys and a rattle. They hurried to make their purchase since the store was about to close.

Upon their return home, Mimi fumbled for the front door keys. During her frenzied search, she accidentally knocked the bassinet from Stanley's hand, watching in abject horror as it crashed down a series of concrete steps. The woman cried out in shock, swooping down to inspect the child for injury. What she discovered left her at a loss for words. Mimi thrashed through their shopping bags in search of the missing infant. To her infinite dismay, she realized they now had two dolls...and no baby.

Casey, Kimberly and Roberta had given up any thought of obtaining sleep that evening. Smacky had earned his moniker well. The three were seated in front of the television when his grandparents entered, their faces left vacant from incomprehension.

"We've got bad news, boy," sighed Stanley.

"Let me guess," Casey teased. "Somebody ate all your little weenies?"

"No. That's not it."

"Did you lose at Bingo again?" wondered Roberta.

"Nope. We won 10 games in a row."

"That's fantastic!" Kimberly squawked. "You should be really happy."

"Well…we should be, but we're not."

Casey knew his grandparents as well as anyone and their current demeanor was troubling. He rose from the couch and approached the pair with due concern. "What's happened?"

Mimi's countenance swelled with emotion, thrusting the doll into view. "This is what we came back with!"

"What the hell?" cried their grandson. "Where's Hope?"

Stanley begged for mercy. "Don't blame us! We're old!"

Once Casey grasped the urgency of the situation, his voice jumped a full octave. "Holy shit!"

Amidst a spate of escalating panic, the five dashed out the door leaving Smacky alone in the house. Scrambling for the rental car, they retraced their steps, returning to the toy store in the thought they'd somehow left her inside.

The bingo hall had closed and the participants were shuffling back to their housing quarters at the senior care center. Many of them now congregated in the large meeting area where they could watch television and socialize with their neighbors. Gertie had not yet retired for the evening, comforting a sick friend who sat slumped in her wheelchair. Although a ventilator was providing the aged woman with pure oxygen, her breath was labored and representative of her internal distress. Emerging from a side door, the archangel Belial approached to offer his spiritual insight.

"Don't despair," he informed the ailing female. "In three days time you'll be shedding this body. You won't remember any of this."

"Why would you say such a terrible thing?" Gertie cried in outrage. "Who are you anyway?"

He smiled with evident malice. "Just call me an observer of souls."

"Who's to say how long she has to live? How would you know that?"

"It's written all over her shriveled face," he contended. "She's got three days left...and you've got 512." Belial spun around, pointing to other interested onlookers. "She has 459 days...this one 738...that one 1,146...and here's the grand prize winner, clocking in at 1,603." He smirked, displaying supreme hubris. "Don't question me. I know more than all of you combined."

"I don't want to be told when my time's up," snarled an elderly man. "None of us do."

"Don't feel bad for her," Belial counseled. "She's coming back as an heiress to an oil fortune. You all have predetermined destinies. In the next life, she'll be a famous author...he'll be a Chinese rice farmer...this one going to die during the fourth World War...and believe it or not, you'll be a Haitian prostitute involved in a sensational murder case."

Another man chuckled. "A Haitian prostitute. That's a good one."

"I don't know what you're laughing at," chided Belial. "You're coming back as a fly on a horse's ass. Enjoy your next incarnation." The loathsome archangel now clapped his hands for attention. "All right, listen up you incontinent geezers! I want the little bitch baby you were drooling over tonight and if you don't hand her over, I'm gonna yank out all your nose hairs! Now where is she?"

Gertie addressed the demon with rancor. "She's not here, you despicable, pock-faced maggot! Get lost!"

At the most inopportune moment possible, the elderly group heard a sound resonating down the hall. It was the wail of a newborn baby, expressing her displeasure over a soiled diaper that had yet to be changed. Belial grinned at the auspicious timing, turning away from the others. "I'll just follow the stench."

He soon located the appropriate room. Finding the door locked, he broke the latch with a well placed kick. There on the bed lay his long sought prey, defenseless and alone. He scooped the infant into his arms and was rendered jubilant by the find. His pupils swelled, eyeing the prize with an insatiable blood lust. At long last, the child was his.

Belial knew he could not escape through the gateway with the baby. The wormhole would only function for its DNA specific user. Forced to make a physical exit, he approached the door, only to be greeted by a gaggle of seniors blocking his way out. They stood angered and resolute, prepared to defend the infant by whatever means necessary.

Belial was undeterred. "Get out of my way, you fucking fossils."

He began pushing his way through the gauntlet and was quick to receive their wrath. In a parade of punishment that could only be described as 'old school', the aged warriors pummeled the fiend the length and breadth of his body. Canes and walking sticks were used to strike, gouge and spear him in sensitive areas. Wheelchairs became battering rams, buckling his knees and crushing his feet. One woman used her metal walker to indelicately probe his rear. Belial staggered from their relentless kicks and blows, losing his balance in the midst of the elderly mob. Snatching the infant from his grasp, a man handed the child to Gertie, still in shock that she'd left Hope in her room.

"Get the baby out of here!" he commanded. "We'll handle this!"

The woman bolted from the scene, leaving the senior care center to hail an available taxi. Belial was now pinned to the floor, having been beaten with objects as diverse as enema bags, bedpans and oxygen tanks. He cried out from the ceaseless torment. "Pain...I love it!"

Before the seniors could call the police or extract further retribution, Belial fled through the gateway, leaving the traumatized elders to question their mental faculties.

Casey had phoned an emergency number, requesting an answering service to page the night manager of the toy store.

After waiting impatiently for his arrival, they were finally granted entrance into the building, searching every aisle in vain. Hope was not inside. They apologized to the man for the intrusion and decided to proceed to the senior care center.

The taxi rolled to a stop in front of Stanley and Mimi's house. Gertie exited the vehicle with the baby and instructed the driver to wait for her. Spotting the abandoned bassinet on the ground, she placed Hope inside and prepared to voice her heartfelt regret. Activation of the doorbell sent Smacky into another manic outburst. As he gnawed the wood from the surrounding door jamb, the dog detected another noise that brought him to silence.

Belial appeared, accosting the woman with a vicious slap across her face. Gertie fell to the grass and began whimpering in shock. The bassinet flew from her hand, bouncing across a concrete walkway before landing a few feet distant. Mustering a mournful wail, Hope cried in terror, alerting the entire neighborhood to her impending abduction.

The dog's instincts were fully aroused, parting the drapes with his snout to peer out the front window. He was in time to witness Belial snare the screaming infant and eject the driver from his cab. The vehicle spun wildly, executing a reverse turn prior to accelerating from the scene. Twirling in agitation, the protective canine retreated to the kitchen then finally charged forth, smashing through the window like an errant cannonball. Shards of glass sprayed across the lawn, but inflicted no injuries. The dog bounded to his feet and began racing down the middle of Divisadero Street, completely ignoring its own safety. Car horns blared in dismay as traffic swerved to avoid the animal, now pursuing the taxi with the homing sense of a guided missile.

After receiving eyewitness accounts of what occurred at the senior care center, Casey and his family were headed home, waiting for a traffic light to change. Once the light turned green, several cars were forced to brake as a taxicab roared through the intersection, followed in close proximity by what appeared to be some sort of deranged creature. Casey blinked, wondering if his eyes were deceiving him. The blur of fur appeared to be a dog, one he'd become quite familiar with.

He shot a glance at Kimberly who was seated beside him. "Is that?..."

"I think it is!" she confirmed.

Casey hung his head out the window. "Smacky!" The hightailing pooch was not about to break off pursuit, causing consternation among those left in his wake.

"Follow him!" Roberta implored.

The car surged into the intersection, narrowly avoiding two vehicles that happened to turn the same way. Casey stood on the accelerator, trying not to lose sight of the fleet footed canine. The animal was maintaining a blistering pace with no wasted motion, its powerful back legs actually gripping the road ahead of its body.

Mimi eyed their pet in awe. "Look at that dog haul ass!"

The cab spun left onto Marina Boulevard, passing the Palace of Fine Arts and merging onto Route 101 on the grounds of the Presidio. At this point, the highway began a steady incline which led vehicular traffic toward Marin County across the famed Golden Gate Bridge. Belial's insidious plan was about to be realized. He wanted to kill the infant in the most sensational manner possible... dropping her from mid-span into the turbulent waters of San Francisco Bay.

A previous accident involving four cars and a pickup truck had yet to be cleared from the entrance to the south approach viaduct. As a result, northbound traffic was inching past in the far left lane, creating a cascade effect of automotive gridlock extending more than half a mile. The stolen taxi hurtled toward the trailing edge of the obstruction, noisily eroding its brake pads to avoid impact. Cursing the situation, Belial jumped out of the cab, paying attention to a teenager approaching on a Vespa LX50 motor scooter. He clotheslined the unsuspecting youth with an extended arm, sprawling him to the pavement. With bassinet in hand, he commandeered the slender vehicle and began weaving a path through the congested traffic.

Smacky was encountering fatigue, his forward progress inhibited due to his ascent up the roadway. Still he had yet to falter, his spirit heartened by Belial's recent transfer to a much slower conveyance. The faithful canine pressed onward, sprinting past stalled cars and clouds of exhaust fumes to close the distance between he and the threatened infant.

At last, Kimberly caught sight of their nemesis on the road ahead. "It's Belial! He's got Hope in the bassinet!"

Although Casey was not one to make rash decisions, he nonetheless did, slamming on the brakes and reversing around oncoming vehicles, transforming the road behind them into a high speed slalom course. His passengers rocked side to side, wondering why they were risking their lives only to head in the wrong direction.

"What are you doing?" cried Kimberly. "He's getting away!"

"The northbound's closed…" he explained during the car's squealing descent down a nearby entrance ramp. Decelerating to a full stop, Casey switched gears, propelling them across a grass embankment and underneath the divided highway. "So, we're gonna use the southbound lanes." The car executed a sharp right turn and proceeded to climb the exit ramp on the opposite side of Route 101. Those with him were now thrust into a catatonic state, left incapable of voicing complaint or alarm. They stared straight ahead, counting the vast number of headlights flaring through the windshield, wondering how they could possibly miss them all.

Belial surged past the accident scene and was finally on three lanes of unobstructed highway. With a top speed of just over 30mph, the motor scooter was not the ideal getaway vehicle, a fact he realized upon spotting Smacky in his rear view mirror. Making the final turn from the south pier onto the elevated deck, the iconic symbol of San Francisco loomed before them. With its entire 8,900 foot span illuminated in the dark windswept sky, the architectural marvel known as the Golden Gate Bridge awaited their arrival. The magnitude and splendor of the reddish-orange structure was of no consequence to Belial. For him, this edifice of man was nothing more than an elaborate platform from which to hurl the baby to her death.

Casey managed to successfully navigate around the onrushing flow of traffic and guided their rental car through an open lane of the southbound toll plaza. He swerved in front of two tractor trailers, sideswiped a construction barricade and rumbled over a bed of exposed rebar before bounding onto the northbound bridge deck.

Directly ahead was their tiring canine and Belial's motor scooter a few yards in front. Flooring the vehicle, Casey zoomed past the dog and came to an angled stop in front of the Vespa. The blocking maneuver forced Belial to slow significantly, allowing Smacky time to cover the remaining distance. Emitting a triumphant yelp, the animal lunged, sinking his fangs into the man's right thigh. Screeching in anguish, Belial tried desperately to shake the dog loose, but Smacky was not about to let go. The scooter slipped around the car and continued for another fifty yards prior to toppling over onto the pavement. Unleashing his full fury, the dog circled the man, biting him on the legs, rear and groin.

As Belial's blood flowed freely, he once more expressed his fondness for the sensation he was experiencing. "Pain...I love it!"

Casey and his sisters dashed from the car, running toward the crazed archangel who was now kicking the exhausted creature. One particularly vicious blow sent the canine reeling backward, disoriented from the assault. Taking note of their rapid approach, Belial made his decision. He wanted to drop the baby from the center of the bridge, but the elevation at this point would be just as lethal. Scooping the bassinet in hand, he ran on a diagonal tangent toward the pedestrian railing and the open expanse beyond. There was no way they could reach him in time. Hope's life now hung in the balance. The siblings cried out in terror, seeing the infant's angelic face peering out from the hooded basket. Kimberly thought she saw the child's eyes close as if resigning herself to her fate. However, none of them could have imagined what would happen next.

In an eruption of land and sea, the forces of nature were brought to bear. Seven miles to the west, the San Andreas Fault began to convulse, a slippage of the tectonic plates caused by subterranean pressure from the Las Vegas earthquake four days ago. The seismic jolt was localized but intense, generating waves of increasing energy that shook the structure to its bedrock foundation. Mimi and Stanley scrambled free of the car, taking stock of their precarious situation. The others ended the chase mid-stride, frozen in fear while contemplating their own ephemeral hold on life.

Retrofitted to withstand an 8.3 temblor, the bridge was now put to the test. The road deck started to sway and heave, creating an endless web of fissures across fractured pavement. Escalating stress upon the lateral steel bracing soon exceeded its certified torsion strength. Load factors began to increase. Gusset plates buckled. Reinforced concrete shear walls broke apart, plunging into the bay. The entire span writhed in metallic fatigue, producing a woeful cry evocative of some tortured prehistoric beast. Seismic isolation bearings failed to function as designed. Rivets separated, spraying the area with high velocity fragmentation. At this point, a number of the vertical truss members underneath them collapsed, sending a large section of the deck into a 12 degree decline. Their rental car became jammed into an open breach on the roadway, snared within the traverse floor system chords. Stanley and Mimi fell against the car, preventing their tumble into the churning waters below. Smacky was alert enough to jump to safety, landing upon the intact southbound portion of the roadway. Another vicious lurch caved the slab further, increasing the slope to nearly 20 degrees. Casey and his sisters tried to hold on, but the paved surface would not provide them an adequate grasp. The three lost their footing, each eventually halting their slide against the trapped vehicle.

Belial was still elevated atop the truncated portion of the deck, clutching an expansion joint with one hand while holding the bassinet in the other. As loosened bolts continued to ping across the structure, a 175 foot long vertical suspension cable snapped free, instantly severing his arm at the elbow. Amidst the archangel's thunderous squeal of excruciation, alternate shrieks of panic arose from below. Hope's bassinet was now plunging toward them. There was no chance to speak and even less time to react. The basket twisted during its descent, placing it on a path just to the right of the car. Stanley was the closest and the only one who could prevent the infant's demise. To the amazement of all, the visually challenged senior swooped down and snatched the bassinet with a deft lunge. Hope was safe, cooing with gratitude as the seismic event waned. There was little doubt they'd just been witness to a miracle.

"I saw her," declared Stanley, his voice quavering in reverence. "I saw her as clear as day."

With his plans thwarted, Belial escaped through the gateway, leaving behind his dismembered lower arm. The earth grew silent and a gentle calm came upon the seas. Fog horns sounded the length of the bridge, their deep baritone alerting ships in the bay to the possibility of more falling debris. Emergency evacuations occurred as human and canine survivors were airlifted by rescue helicopters to the shore. Casey's family counted its blessings, still visibly shaken in the quake's aftermath.

The siblings made arrangements to fly to New York City in the morning so they could attend the United Nations' open forum on the Roswell incident. This left them a few more hours to rest in San Francisco prior to departure.

"Take our room," Mimi informed them. "We'll watch the baby."

Casey looked down at the dog which was already salivating at the prospect of a long night with their guests. "If it's all the same to you," their insightful grandson countered, "I think we'll just get a hotel."

CHAPTER FORTY-THREE

SIERRA VISTA, ARIZONA — MAY 10th — 6:49 PM MST

$\mathcal{A}$riel remained frustrated, failing to understand the reason for his pupil's reluctance. From the start of their sessions together, Benjamin had shown remarkable aptitude and skill, as well as a genuine thirst for knowledge. He was attentive and seemed eager to please. Over the past day, the youngster's analytical mind had allowed him to make great strides forward in his comprehension of the subject matter. It was therefore puzzling as to why the boy refused to take the next logical step in his training.

Captain Parnell had ordered the base MPs not to disturb the two and had granted them access to the mess hall and barracks. But since their arrival at Fort Huachuca, neither had expressed interest in doing anything other than continue the esoteric instruction which Ariel was willing to impart.

The Israeli had commenced his lecture using a globe to illustrate his point. "Let's say you're here in the United States," pointing at the circular map. "And, you want to go to Israel, which is all the way over here. You could take a plane or boat and travel the physical surface of the Earth," running his hand along the sphere, "As all other people do...or you could briefly leave this three dimensional world and instantly arrive at your destination," dropping his finger down for emphasis. "That's what the gateway allows you to do. It's a portal that takes you out of this realm and places you back into it…whenever and wherever you wish. It frees you from the constraints of time and space."

"And, I can go anywhere I want?" the boy asked, seeking confirmation. "Even to places I've never been?"

"That's right. It could be a place you've visited many times or one that you've seen in a photograph. As long as you have a mental image of the location in your mind, the gateway can transport you there."

"What do I have to do to open it?"

"You access it with a specific set of tones that you can either hum or just recall in your mind. They're specific in that they're unique to you alone. Think of it as a private combination lock that only you know…and only you can open."

"How do I find out what tones are mine?"

"Well, that's why we need this equipment," he responded, directing his attention to one of the oscilloscopes. "We'll be able to determine that on this display screen. Have you ever heard the term 'psychokinesis'?"

Benjamin paused in thought. "Isn't that what they call it when somebody bends a spoon with their mind?"

"Yes, that's part of it. Psychokinesis has to do with the mind's influence over matter, time, space and energy. What we're going to do is to test your ability to manipulate electrical and magnetic fields with nothing more than your thoughts. Once you learn how to do that, you'll be able to open the gateway and a whole new world will be yours to explore."

He started by positioning Benjamin in front of an electronic screen which displayed numeric digits from a random number generator. Small, unobtrusive electrodes were positioned on his head and fingers to collect biometric data which would be relayed to a printing device for Ariel's review. A separate scatter plot would show how successful his young student would be at precognition of the generated numbers to a statistical mean. After 30 minutes of testing, Benjamin had proven his prescient skills by announcing each number before it was revealed. The printer was trying to plot coordinates that were off its track, leaving a clean sheet of graph paper for analysis.

"Okay," Ariel sighed, stunned by the child's perfect score. "How did you know what every digit would be before it was shown?"

"Oh, that was easy," he confessed. "I just kept thinking of my friends' phone numbers."

"Phone numbers? That's what we've been seeing for the past half hour?"

"Sure. I didn't want to guess at a number I didn't know."

The Israeli was astounded. Benjamin had not only aced his precognition test, but had manipulated the random number generator to display the exact digits he had in mind. Ariel made the wise decision to bypass further fundamental training and proceed directly to more complex tasks.

The child was then tested on the oscilloscope. On the display was an AC sine waveform with curved crests and troughs. His instructions were simple. "Flatten the wave so it can no longer be seen."

He stared at the screen for several minutes, unsure of just how to accomplish what was being asked of him. "I don't get it," Benjamin conceded. "Is there a secret to this?"

Ariel mentored him through the process. "It's an electric current with a constant frequency. Your brainwave patterns work on a similar principle. Use the impulses from your mind to influence what you see here." His student remained discouraged, forcing the Israeli to change his approach. "I understand you're a musician."

Benjamin perked up immediately. "Yeah, keyboards mostly."

"Have you ever played a wind instrument, like a clarinet or oboe?"

"Sure."

"Well, when you blow into an instrument, the sound it makes

is at a certain frequency. And, if you want to alter that frequency, you do that by varying the vibration."

The boy suddenly grasped the concept. "So, I just need to figure out the harmonic and use my mind to adjust the pitch. Okay, I know how to do this."

Amused by the child's chutzpah, Ariel left their sanctum for a few minutes to take a bathroom break and purchase a couple of cans of soda from the base PX. Upon his return, he found Benjamin staring at what appeared to be a blank screen. "Did the power go off?"

The preoccupied youngster responded tersely. "Nope."

He set the drinks on an adjacent table, examining the device from a closer perspective. "Did you mess with the controls?"

"I didn't touch anything," the boy assured him.

"Then, what happened to the wave?"

The squiggly form suddenly became visible. "Its right there... See?"

Benjamin had adjusted the sine wave's amplitude along with its intensity, reducing its strength so that it barely registered on the oscilloscope.

"Are you kidding me?' his instructor gasped. "That takes weeks to..." Ariel knew that additional words would be superfluous. Over the years, the Israeli had been exposed to paranormal phenomena that defied the accepted laws of science, but what Benjamin had accomplished in so short a time was truly impressive. It was every teacher's dream to tutor a pupil this gifted. Aware he'd only scratched the surface of the child's potential, Ariel took a leap of faith and removed the electrodes from the boy's head. "Okay. Let's see what you can do without the training wheels."

"Huh?"

"This will be a lot harder, because you're no longer connected to the equipment. Try and do exactly what you did before. Don't get frustrated. Just relax and concentrate on the screen."

Benjamin did as instructed, staring relentlessly at the stubborn wave. His concentration never wavered and remained potent long after most people would have surrendered to the tedium. After several minutes of abject futility, the two observed the beginnings of a slight fluctuation. Almost imperceptibly, the wave's deep crests and troughs started to moderate, softening their amplitude. The progress was much slower than before, measured at times by nothing more than the width of a photon. Refusing to quit, Benjamin began to visualize the wave in his mind, collapsing further until it morphed into a flat line. Soon, perception became reality as the oscilloscope registered a thin streak bisecting the screen.

"Good," Ariel declared breathlessly. "Very, very good."

Using a mathematical formula, they were able to input the given frequency of the sine wave and the known amount of amplitude deflection, to determine which of the youngster's brainwave harmonics had the greatest effect on the electromagnetic field.

"Your optimal frequencies are in the high beta state, between 29.38 and 31.42 cycles per second," explained Ariel. "I've plotted eight separate intervals in time when you experienced the most influence manipulating the wave. Once we isolate these exact harmonics, we can use the signal generator to convert them into aural tones." Benjamin was one step closer to being given his own set of 'keys' to open the gateway.

After cross-referencing the data, eight tonal cues had been identified and produced. The youngster donned a headset, detecting the audible sounds and placing each to memory. It wasn't musical in the traditional sense, but more akin to the buzzing of a bee, changing ever so slightly in pitch and timbre.

"It isn't very melodic," his pupil whined.

"Were you expecting the 1812 Overture?"

Benjamin grinned, now hearing the tones repeat. "How long do I have to listen to this?"

"Until you know it like you know yourself."

"I've got it," assured the boy.

Ariel expressed doubt, recalling how long it had taken him to memorize his own set of cues. "Are you sure? You've only heard it twice?"

"I can see music in my head," boasted the child. "I'm sure."

His instructor shrugged, turning off the equipment. If it had been anyone other than Benjamin, he would've dismissed this break in training as a clever ploy to dupe him into granting some downtime. Although Ariel found it hard to believe that his student could have processed what he needed to know so quickly, there was one sure way to find out.

"Okay. Show me what you've learned."

The boy finished a gulp of soda, seemingly stalling for time. "What do you want me to do?"

"Repeat the tones in your mind and open the gateway."

"I can do that now?"

Ariel nodded. "If you've mastered the aural cues like you say you have."

His reluctance became obvious, testing the patience of his mentor. "I'm really tired. Maybe we could do it later on."

The man's voice was brusque and resolute. "Just try it, Ben... right now."

A sense of unease drifted upon his face. The boy's demeanor was no longer that of a cheerful and confident youth, but of someone encountering a great deal of emotional stress. He sighed with deliberation, closing his eyes to concentrate on the eight tones that would part an invisible electromagnetic curtain into another world. His palms had become damp and his heart rate high. Benjamin's lungs heaved for air, his body nearly hyperventilating. The cues rang forth in his mind...over and over...faster and faster. At last he heard Ariel cry out in jubilation.

"You did it!"

His eyes opened to a small but clearly defined spatial breach, bobbing like a buoy on an angry sea. The ink black interior throbbed with mystery, an enigmatic void seemingly alive but lifeless, beckoning him to enter. He felt its intangible force cradle him with vaporous hands, ready to snatch him to the bosom of the unknown. Benjamin squirmed in his chair, grasping the edge of a table and knew instinctively he was not prepared. Suddenly, as though caught in the rush of God's breath, the ethereal specter vanished.

Ariel was ecstatic, reaching over to hug the child. "That was amazing! With as little time as we've spent together…you're an incredibly gifted young lad. I'm so proud of you, I can hardly contain myself."

His pupil was less enthralled with the accomplishment, visibly exhibiting equal amounts of shock and dismay. "Did I really do that?"

"Yes!" the Israeli exclaimed. "It was you…all you! You've broken through to a whole new level of reality. One that you'll never forget or return from. This is a defining moment in your life. You should be thrilled by what you've achieved."

"I'm not sure how I feel," he mumbled truthfully. "Is the training over?"

"No, we've barely begun. There's an entire universe to explore and I can't wait to show it to you."

The boy forced a meek smile, thinking he should show the man some gratitude for his effort. "Thanks for helping me and my family. You didn't have to do this."

"You're wrong," proclaimed Ariel. "My devotion to Elohim left me no other choice."

As their conversation stalled, Benjamin's gaze fell upon the door. "Are we done for today?"

"Let's try one more thing," proposed his instructor. "Can you open the gateway again?"

The child shrugged his shoulders, involuntarily gulping at the thought. He once more ran through the tonal cues in his mind and watched as the portal blossomed before him in ebony splendor.

Ariel lauded his performance. "Well done, Ben! Well done." He looked at the boy with a near twinkle in his eye. "Would you like to go through it? Just to know what it feels like?"

The question had been anticipated, but his response proved difficult. "No, I don't think so."

"It doesn't have to be far," his teacher suggested. "You

could go from here to the other side of the room." The silence he received was troubling. Ariel looked at the youngster, finally sensing the reason for his hesitation. He was pressed into his chair, clutching the side armrests with vice-like hands. The child's legs and feet were hyperactive, behaving as if compelled to walk a tightrope. His eyes were dilated and jaw clenched. Benjamin had previously shown such enthusiasm and bravado that Ariel never suspected he'd be affected like this. His heretofore fearless pupil was currently in the throes of an anxiety attack.

He sought to ease his trepidation. "There's nothing to be afraid of, Ben."

"I'm not afraid." The uneven pitch in his voice betrayed him.

"I remember how I felt the first time. It was a little scary, but I got over it."

The boy shook his head with resolve. "I told you I'm not scared."

"It's always difficult when we face the unknown," Ariel continued. "We're taught from birth what to expect in this world and the things we perceive become real for us. If we're exposed to anything that threatens our core beliefs, it can be really tough to face. But to achieve spiritual enlightenment, we have to get past what we don't understand."

"I don't think I want to hear this," Benjamin huffed.

His mentor refused to give in, convinced he needed to help the youngster overcome his apprehension. "It's like jumping into a pool of water. It doesn't hurt and once you've done it, you'll never think about it again. Just relax. Let your body go and…"

The child's voice crested full. "I'm not doing it!"

Like a flower folding its pedals at the end of the day, the gateway closed and their session was officially over. Ariel sighed in regret. "Okay…okay. I didn't mean to force you. Let's call it a night."

The Israeli met with Captain Parnell in his office, informing him of the progress Benjamin had made. In the Army officer's hand was a printout of an email he'd recently received.

"The Garrison Commander's returning early from leave. He should be here sometime tomorrow afternoon. How much longer are you going to need with the kid?"

"I'd like another day."

"You don't have it," insisted Parnell. "Once the GC arrives, he'll be briefed by the Provost Marshal. He's in charge of the base MPs. When he finds out that I countermanded a direct order by letting you in that room, all hell's gonna break loose."

Ariel reflected on the news, realizing the Captain had made a career decision that could end up costing him dearly. "We appreciate the courtesy you've shown us. But, we never intended to place you in this kind of situation."

Parnell dismissed his concern. "You didn't. The actions I took were mine alone. My main concern is for the boy's safety. When can you leave?"

"I'd like to run him through a few more tests in the morning. He's made great strides, but he needs to put aside his fears." He paused, aware that he had yet to answer the Captain. "How about noon tomorrow?"

The officer nodded his approval. "Agreed...1200 hours."

At the Israeli's suggestion, Captain Parnell instructed the base orderlies to establish sleeping quarters for Ariel and Benjamin inside Building 23, just down the hall from their work area. This way, if teacher and student wanted to resume their tests in the middle of the night they'd disturb no one.

They sprawled out on their bunks, located on opposite sides of the room. The only illumination was through a lone window from a sodium vapor light on the compound beyond. Bathed within its pale yellow glow, Ariel observed the youngster roll onto his side, keeping his face hidden. He hadn't said a word since his outburst in the lab and his mentor worried about his commitment to continue.

"Good night, Ben."

There was no reply. Convinced that further communication

would be unlikely, Ariel closed his eyes and attempted to purge his mind of stressful thoughts. Minutes passed as he began to feel a much welcome sense of serenity. Nearing the gentle embrace of slumber, he detected a timid voice beseeching his counsel.

"What's it like?"

The man stirred. "I'm sorry…what?"

"What's it like to go through the gateway?"

He stole a composing breath, deciding he shouldn't lie to the child. "It's difficult to describe. There's a feeling of extraction, like being yanked into a wind tunnel. All light and air vanish. Just for the briefest period of time, you experience a disconnection from your body. Almost like a split-second taste of death. Then the light and air flow back around you…and you arrive in a surge of force as if being expelled from a womb. The entire transition takes only a moment or two, but its one helluva rush." Ariel feared he might have said too much, quashing any chance of getting the youngster to make the attempt.

Benjamin appeared grateful for the man's candor. "Does anybody really know what happens when you go through?"

He shook his head. "Government scientists tried to conduct tests, but they weren't able to reach any conclusions. You've got to remember, there's only a handful of us that have this ability. We're special, Ben. Our fathers bequeathed us a great gift."

"Does the gateway always work?" asked the boy, posing another thoughtful query. "Is there a chance you could go in, but never come out?"

"As far as I've heard, no one's ever been lost. However, it does have its limitations. When the Government investigated the Roswell incident, they determined the reason for the ship's crash was due to the violent lightning storm it was traveling through that night. Apparently, the gateway can't function around intense electric fields. Those same fields also disrupted the metallurgic integrity of the ship. It's strange to say, but you and I wouldn't even exist if it hadn't been for some nasty weather."

Benjamin looked up at the ceiling, contemplating the event

that defined his mother's life and wondered why things happened the way they had. He focused on an earlier conversation with his mentor. About how psychokinesis could manipulate space and time. Reflecting upon the possibilities, he questioned if he might now have the ability to traverse time as well. "Will I be able to go back into the past? It'd be great if I could see the Madre again."

A pronounced delay followed. "That wouldn't be wise, Ben. It would require a lot more training and discipline on your part... and it's very, very risky. The actions that you take in the past could cascade into something far worse in the future. Anything you say to your mother might cause her to react differently, changing our present, perhaps threatening the lives of your family or even your own. Too many things could go wrong."

"But, if I went back to Roswell...before the crash...I could warn her."

"Even if it meant your life?"

The boy hesitated, mindful of the consequence. "Wouldn't it be worth it?"

"Perhaps," he mused. "But, that's not going to happen. You can't go back."

Benjamin's disposition turned cross. "Why not? You just said I could if I had more training."

"You can't go back to Roswell," Ariel explained. "None of us can. You can only travel to an era that you've previously experienced during your lifetime. We need to have those memories. That sensory recall in our minds. Without it, the gateway is useless."

"Oh," he blurted, acknowledging the disclosure. The youngster channeled a sigh of frustration, crestfallen that his plans had been for naught. His inquisitive nature refused to rest. "How old are you, Ariel?"

The man was amused by the brash question. "I'll be 46 next month."

"How far into the past have you gone?"

"Quite a few years," the Israeli admitted. "But, I didn't

do it for personal reasons. I went under the strict orders of my Government."

Benjamin became intrigued. "What did they have you do?"

"I was sent on a number of covert operations…most so secret that I can't discuss them," he revealed, rubbing his eyes in remembrance. "All I can tell you is that some extreme terrorist events have occurred in Israel. Events you've never heard about because I went back in time and stopped them from happening." The man paused, allowing his emotions to swell. "I'm a faithful soldier of Elohim, but I'm also proud of my Jewish heritage. If I can use my gifts to save my country from the hatred and hostility of others, then that's what I'm going to do. I won't let another holocaust befall my people."

The youngster intuitively felt the man's pain, hearing the tortured throb of his soul. "It sounds like you've been through a lot."

He peered at the boy, amazed at his spiritual insight. "You're very perceptive, Ben. Very perceptive." Ariel checked his watch and loosed a pensive breath. "Let's get some rest. We've got a busy morning ahead of us."

Not ready for sleep, his precocious pupil decided to listen to some music. He reached under the bunk, fumbling through his duffel bag. As time passed, his search became more frantic, forcing him to his feet to turn on the overhead light.

"What is it?" asked Ariel, chagrined.

"My other iPod. It's not here!" Benjamin suddenly remembered where he'd left his prized possession. "Ohhhh! It's on the helicopter. I was showing it to Kevin before we landed."

"Don't worry. I'm sure he'll bring it back to you." He rolled over on his side. "Turn out the light."

The sulking child complied, quickly returning to his bunk. With his earphones in place, Benjamin allowed the tunes to soothe his rampant annoyance. What he could not have known, but would soon discover, was that his loss would turn out to be Kevin's gain.

CHAPTER FORTY-FOUR

CHUGACH MTS., ALASKA — MAY 10th — 7:51 PM AKDT

The three men huddled inside the wreckage, contemplating the vagaries of fate. None of them knew what the future held nor what past actions might come back to haunt them. All they could think about was the present. Osborne lay bleeding before them, suffering from internal injuries sustained during the crash. Kevin was not a physician, but he could tell that the Major's prognosis was poor. They were marooned in the heart of the Alaskan wilderness, miles from civilization and aid. Their cell phones were unable to locate a signal. Soon, the men would be concealed behind the shroud of night and any possibility of rescue would become even more remote.

Salvaging what he could from the devastated Huey, Kevin made an assessment of their provisions. He'd been able to recover their weapons satchel, containing the secret ordnance they'd taken from Dreamland. Aboard the Dolphin was an array of arctic survival gear such as parkas, gloves, boots, a flare gun and supplies of potable water and food. Ancillary personal items were also found, including Benjamin's prized iPod. A rather extensive first aid kit was of little use to the Major, other than a half used bottle of ibuprofen. The man required immediate medical attention or his chances of survival were slim. For hours they'd waited, but help had not arrived. Remaining at the crash site was no longer an option. Osborne would not be alive by morning. Kevin knew the only way to save the Major's life was to trek across the inhospitable Alaskan terrain.

Pierre LeClerke sat in a corner of the cabin, his head bowed in despair. Although grateful for their heroic efforts, he knew he was more captive than guest. For the better part of the day he'd remained silent, still recuperating from his harrowing ordeal. He still did not have an understanding of either man's identity or intent, wondering how they became privy to the existence of the MAJIK-12. Even if he could escape, there was nowhere to go. He was as much a prisoner of circumstance as the others.

The Major rested upon several layers of blankets, wrapped around his body in an attempt to keep him from going into shock. He was running a slight fever, rocking his head fitfully in distress. Every so often he'd cough up a spittle of blood into a towel. Kevin was anguished by his plight and knew he had to do something. He motioned for LeClerke to accompany him outside. The two met a few yards from the damaged fuselage so Osborne could be spared the grim news.

"He's not gonna make it unless we get him to a hospital," Kevin declared. "We've got to find our way back to civilization."

LeClerke shook in protest. "That's insane. It's probably miles to the nearest village. We could freeze to death before we're half way there. Our best chance is to stay here until somebody finds us."

"How long do you think he's got? I'm not gonna sit around and watch him die. He's already sacrificed too much to save your sorry ass. I'll be damned if I let him lose his life over a worthless putz like you."

"Who are you anyway? How do you know about the MAJIK-12?"

"Oh, I think you know me," snarled Kevin. "We just haven't been formally introduced. That's because you and your butt buddies in Washington were too busy sending hit teams after us."

LeClerke froze in recognition. "My God," he gasped. "You're one of the Roswell kids. Mary Ellen Hart's child."

"That's right...and tomorrow the MAJIK-12 will be history. We were at Dreamland, pal. We've got the CDs, the secret weapons... even a star witness."

"Who's that?"

Kevin chortled. "You my flatulent friend. You're coming to New York to tell the United Nations everything you know."

The man shook his head in denial. "I'm not going anywhere."

"The hell you aren't, dick!" he spat with venom. "We haven't gone through all this to have you weasel out. You're gonna sing in front of the whole world... and I'll be squeezing your nuts to make sure you hit all the high notes."

"You can't speak to me like that!" shouted the indignant LeClerke. "I'm a very important person with more connections than you could possibly imagine."

Grabbing the man with his fist, Kevin swiftly intimidated the powerful Washington insider. "Let me give you the scoop, Jack. Just because you're some big shot CEO with tons of people lining up to kiss your ass doesn't mean squat to me. Do you think you're better than that man in there? That you're somehow entitled to his respect? The only thing you're entitled to is the heel of my boot! To me, you're nothing but an insignificant turd swirling in the bowl. You either cooperate...or you'll get flushed down the drain. It's up to you."

He released the man, certain that he'd adequately conveyed his contempt. LeClerke remained mute, expending no discernable effort to collect his tattered shreds of dignity. Once the combatants parted, an uneasy truce was called. Both of them knew they'd need each other's help in order to survive.

Kevin trudged up a steady slope for about 50 yards to a clearing in the trees. He surveyed the area, looking in all directions for the optimal escape route. Continuing west into the path of the setting sun, he came to a halt, scanning beyond the apex of what appeared to be a 10,000 foot peak. Looking down the declivitous slope,

Kevin witnessed almost two miles of undisturbed white powder, winding its way toward the distant valley floor. Thick stands of spruce bracketed the lane of snow, with only a sporadic cluster of trees dotting the landscape in between. It occurred to him that this arboreal formation was framing the world's most perfect natural ski run.

He returned to LeClerke to discuss his find. "There's a long, open slope over that rise. We might be able to slide down the face of the mountain."

"Slide down?" the man asked, perplexed. "How?"

"Maybe, we can find something to use as a sled," proposed Kevin, as he began to sift through the wreckage. "Anyway, it's worth a shot. I don't know how else we're gonna get the Major out of here."

After probing through the debris field, an object of unique size and shape caught LeClerke's eye. "What about this?"

He was pointing to the starboard side hatch of the now devastated Huey. It was a seamless piece of metal and shatterproof glass, five feet long by seven feet wide and curving upward on all edges. There appeared to be enough room for three men to lay astride one another and steer the makeshift sled with their overhanging feet. The shallow parabolic shape and smooth convex surface underneath seemed to satisfy all their design parameters.

Kevin dashed inside the Dolphin to check on Osborne's condition. He disclosed their plan and asked the Major if he felt well enough to endure such an excursion. The wounded officer fought for air, gurgling forth a plea which left his audience distressed.

"Leave me here. I'm done…"

"No, I can't do that. I'd never be able to face my sister again."

He grabbed Kevin's arm to stress an important point. "If you see Kimberly, tell her I love her and ask her not to grieve for me. I'm just not worth it."

"You can tell her yourself," he asserted. "I'm going to get you to a hospital, and you will be alive when I get you there. Do you understand me, soldier?"

Osborne answered with an impaired laugh, tormented by the swelling in his chest. He managed to ask a pertinent question. "Which way are we headed?"

"Due west. Isn't Anchorage that direction?"

He coerced his head to nod. "Roughly…Probably more west-southwest."

With the Major unable to walk any appreciable distance, two ropes were tied to the Huey's inverted hatch in preparation to pull him to the summit beyond. LeClerke helped Kevin lift the injured man into the center of the sled while placing their emergency provisions on both sides of him. The arduous part of the journey was about to commence. Marching up the steep incline with their tethered cargo proved to be more strenuous than anticipated, with both men straining under the load. As the thin air took its toll, their forward progress became less evident, at times drifting more laterally than desired. The task sapped their strength, requiring them to use increased energy just to lift their feet from the deep snow pack. After 40 yards of pure struggle, LeClerke refused to budge, suffering from a spate of respiratory distress.

"I can't do this. I've got to rest."

"Come on," Kevin whined. "We're nearly there."

The portly man shook in protest, his lungs heaving for oxygen. "I'm not in as good a shape as you."

Spurning the chance to debate the obvious, he took hold of LeClerke's rope and draped both over his shoulders. Pressing onward, the former football star continued the burdensome climb, doing his best imitation of an ox strapped to its yoke. He dismissed his body's internal warning signals, aware he too was exceeding the limits of his endurance. Kevin's motivation wasn't pride. It was urgency. He was determined to get Osborne the medical attention he so desperately needed. Huffing and snorting all the way to the summit, the triumphant athlete fell to the snow, granting himself some precious time to recover.

LeClerke eventually joined the others, now positioned atop the pinnacle. The Major's eyes widened when he saw the expanse unfurl before him, momentarily ignoring his own travail.

"Holy shit!" he cried. "We're going down this? Are you serious?"

The breathless CEO, an engineer by trade, also expressed his doubts. "This is a severe slope. We're going to obtain a high rate of speed and we've got no way to steer this thing mechanically."

"I thought we could use the ropes to do that?"

"Well, think again," ridiculing his design strategy. "They're not tied symmetrically to the vertical axis. You yank on those ropes and we'll start spinning out of control."

"So, do you have any better ideas?"

Before LeClerke could answer, he detected the unique aural signature of a low flying aircraft. Searching the sky, he spotted the vehicle silhouetted on the wisps of thin, evanescent clouds. "Oh, my God. It's an MQ-1."

"What the hell's that?"

"Predator drone," responded Osborne in anguish. "They've found us."

"Who's found us?"

"The military," LeClerke acknowledged, expressing shock. An aura of resignation consumed the man's face, mindful of the fact that this unmanned, fully armed platform was used primarily to carry out seek and destroy missions in remote territory. It was clear this was no rescue operation.

Kevin solicited further clarification. "How could the military know where we are?"

"I might have tipped them off," the CEO confessed, gulping at the thought. I sent a BlackBerry message to General Connolly before I left the ship." He peered to his left, watching his captor turn purple with rage.

"You stupid twerp! I outta kick your butt all the way to

Anchorage! We came here to save your sorry ass before they could find you! Then, you go tell them? What a jackoff you turned out to be!"

LeClerke fumed at the blistering rebuke. "How was I supposed to know what was going on? I didn't tell anybody I was on that ship! Why shouldn't I question two guys trying to take me away in the middle of the night. I've been a loyal member of the MAJIK-12 for years. Why would they want to kill me now?"

Kevin rocked his head in disbelief. "In case you missed the latest pal, Dreamland went up in a mushroom cloud three days ago. That makes you Mr. Expendable." He paused upon sighting the man's traumatized look of horror. "Yeah, you heard right. Your company just found themselves an 800 billion dollar tax deduction. I'm sure your stockholders will be thrilled."

The Predator swooped down for another surveillance run, making its presence known from the generated buzz of a 4 cylinder, 101 horsepower engine. Visually acquiring the three men within the scan of its color nose camera, a remote pilot operating the craft at Elmendorf Air Force Base contacted his superiors for engagement orders. Two heat seeking missiles were mounted underneath, awaiting clearance to fire. They watched the drone begin to execute another banking maneuver, its 48 foot wingspan going vertical into the turn.

Osborne knew time was of the essence. "He's gonna blow us to hell on the next pass! We've got to get going!"

LeClerke quickly assumed a prone position to the right of the Major. Kevin dropped to his knees inside the metal saucer, eliciting stares from the others.

"You've got to push!" explained the CEO. "Haven't you ever gone sledding before?"

"I grew up in Texas!" he barked. "I'm not used to this white stuff!"

"Get our momentum going then jump inside."

In a blur of frozen spray, Kevin churned his legs, soon feeling the massive plate of steel start to move on its own. He jumped aboard with an awkward belly flop, nearly ejecting his fellow passengers. Regaining a tenuous balance, the three were now surging down a windswept path toward the valley floor, accelerating at an alarming rate. Minute particles of ice pelted their faces, restricting forward visibility. Numbing cold greeted exposed skin. Onrushing air became almost impossible to breathe. The ungroomed surface of the snow created less than optimal slope conditions, resulting in an incessantly bumpy ride. At some points the sled would go airborne, returning to earth with jarring impact. There was no relief from the endless vibrations, intensifying Osborne's misery and provoking him to bellow out in pain.

"This isn't doing me any good!"

The Predator glided in behind them, maintaining speed and distance above the precipitous landscape. Its multi-spectral targeting system was brought to bear, incorporating the most technologically advanced electro-optical sensor package in the military's arsenal. The word had been given. The drone was now cleared to fire. Two AGM-114 Hellfire missiles were primed and ready for release. Back at flight headquarters, the remote pilot zeroed in on the elusive mark and loosed the first weapon.

A last second deviation in their course spared them from certain death. The missile detonated a few yards to their left, incinerating a large swath of ice and snow within a searing ball of flame. Sparing nothing in its path, the blast wave engulfed the trio, launching them skyward into a full 360 degree uncontrolled spin. Landing amidst a squall of obscenities, the makeshift sled caromed across the glacial surface, still rotating to the lament of those aboard. They dropped their feet into the semi-frozen crust and eventually established a modicum of rudder control. The men's headlong speed had increased since the attack, now exceeding a velocity that alarmed them to a greater degree than the threat from above. Tremulous echoes dispersed through the area, triggering a number of small avalanches at higher elevations.

The second Hellfire rocketed forth. A sudden depression in the sled's path caused the weapon to overshoot its target, exploding within a thick stand of trees. Flames erupted into the sky, transforming a large portion of this idyllic countryside into raging inferno. Once more the collateral shockwave sent them into a spontaneous gyration, spinning helplessly until they could employ their feet as low tech control devices. The three maintained their speed and descent, expressing silent gratitude that the aircraft had no further missiles to fire. It was therefore with considerable trepidation that Osborne observed two more Predator drones closing in on their position. The Air Force routinely utilized three to four Predators per operational mission. What was unusual was the lack of stealth and the determination being used to wipe them out.

The other drones broke formation, initiating their attack from divergent tangents. Entering an area of moderately scattered trees, the sled meandered in and out of view, obscured at times by the heavy foliage. With target acquirement achieved, two more missiles were fired, their exhaust plumes converging directly overhead. Just prior to a devastating rendezvous, a protective cordon of white spruce intercepted the projectiles and absorbed their explosive wrath. A pair of rolling fireballs merged into a red hot thermal canopy, consuming the air and providing mere inches of clearance for the men. As they were showered with disgorged splinters of ice and wood, the sonic concussion savaged their ears and sent them into another tumultuous whirl. The massive trees began to fall over them as they passed, their lacerated trunks snapping under the strain. Crashing to the snow laden tundra, rivulets of flame burst in all directions, converting yards of timber into an incandescent pyre.

Other obstacles loomed ahead. Calculating their trajectory, LeClerke was certain they were about to strike the third tree in an upcoming cluster unless evasive action was immediately taken. He yelled out, sending a frantic message to his sledmates. "Lean left!"

The weight of the men fell against Kevin as he fought to hang on. By redistributing their center of gravity, the speeding object began to deviate from its intended path, avoiding a potential head on impact. They then shifted their mass in the opposite direction, overcorrecting their course and propelling them into a wide, right handed curve. Regaining some semblance of balance, the threesome finally angled themselves onto a more advantageous track.

The drones remained in pursuit, attempting to gain a laser fix on the sled which was made all the more difficult by its serpentine motion. Another Hellfire missile was released, homing in with lethal resolve. As it bore down from above, their maneuverings to avoid a much larger tree shunted them onto the route necessary to avoid disaster. The heat seeking weapon became ensnared in the tree's branches, detonating above ground like an errant fireworks shell. An eruption of flame scorched the sky, followed by a percussive blast that disoriented their senses, blanketing them with a thick sheath of hoarfrost falling from decimated tree limbs. They executed a wobbly pirouette, landing backwards and plunging down the mountain feet first. The panicked trio began rocking to one side in a desperate struggle to turn the sled around. From this new perspective, Osborne was able to glance at the third Predator and confirm what he suspected.

"There's one missile left," he announced, coughing up a smattering of blood. "They won't use it unless they've got a clean shot."

LeClerke looked behind them, eyeing yet another obstacle rooted in their path. "Lean right!"

The others obeyed, their faces frozen in shock as they barely missed an imposing tree trunk. Frantic to reclaim a head on view, they paddled their feet through the snow, eventually sluing back into a more favorable position. The trio had successfully descended over a mile of virgin mountainside, but was unable to estimate the remaining distance having lost sight of the valley floor beyond.

LeClerke yammered in fright. "Is this ever going to end?"

"Not until they fire that last rocket!" Kevin squealed.

The sled increased its forward speed to near 70 mph as the

terrain declination became more severe. Entering a long, sloping curve, the three leaned over to compensate, buffered by a towering snow bank that resembled the polished contour of a halfpipe. They were now facing the setting sun, its brilliant orange glow making them far too easy a target. The Predator closed to within a few hundred meters, painting the trio with its laser sight. At the instant the missile was unleashed, the sled slipped over the edge of a glacial mound, casting the screaming passengers eight feet in midair and down another slick embankment. The heat seeker sailed over their heads, locking onto the solar glare and harmlessly detonated about a half mile away.

After recovering from their drop over the precipice, the valley floor was no longer a distant sight. The inclined slope began to moderate as a mostly vertical journey soon assumed a more horizontal aspect. They were still moving at a torrid pace, unable to restrict their forward momentum. Breathing was somewhat easier, a combination of the lower altitude along with the thought that they just might survive this hair-brained scheme. With their descent nearly complete, they realized the large open area their sled was destined for was actually a sizeable frozen lake about a half mile across. Dropping their feet over the edge did nothing to stop their approach onto the massive sheet of ice, which now provided a smooth and comfortable ride for the final leg of this trip. With friction no longer a factor, they continued to coast onward, eventually coming to rest near the opposite shore.

Immense relief was tempered by an understanding of their current location. It was difficult to gauge the thickness of the ice or whether it would be able to support their combined weight. None of them appeared overly anxious to test the integrity of the surface, remaining motionless for an extended period of time. After numerous breaths of deliverance, Kevin finally vocalized the feelings which they all shared.

"I think I just put a load in my pants."

"My God," murmured LeClerke. "It's a miracle we're still alive."

The Major declined comment, not wanting to discuss the exacerbation of his injuries. Kevin peered over his shoulder, witnessing a group of fires burning the length of the mountainside and shaking in amazement at the path they'd blazed. Circling above them was one of the Predator drones, forced into reconnaissance duty due to its lack of armament. Not one to miss an opportunity, Kevin greeted the aircraft with an extended middle finger salute, informing the military that their attempts had failed. The drone left the area and was not seen again.

Surveying the desolate surroundings, LeClerke asked a most pertinent question. "So, what do we do now?"

"You think we could walk across the ice?"

"I don't know," he responded. "If you want to try, be my guest."

The three refused to act impulsively, deciding to best utilize their energy to think through the dilemma. A possible solution soon appeared. LeClerke nudged the others, calling their attention to a large animal now present on the shore.

"Look...a moose!"

Their eyes beheld the 1,500 pound mammal, located approximately 10 yards in front of them, poised along the bank of a small cove. It was a male bull standing six foot tall, adorned with early spring antlers, munching away on some young shoots and tree bark. Unfastening the sled's tether ropes, LeClerke knotted the two together, forming a lengthy line that looked as if it might just reach the boreal creature.

Kevin became intrigued. "What are you doing?"

"I'm going to toss this over. Maybe he'll grab it and pull us to shore."

"That's the most ridiculous thing I've ever heard. Do you actually get paid to come up with ideas like this?"

"It's worth a try." He coiled the rope in hand and hurled it toward the stationary animal. The end fell a foot or so short of its mark. Reeling it back in, the man attempted another throw, this one with far better results. With the rope resting inches from the mammal's left hoof, LeClerke began his earnest pleadings with their potential savior. "Come on...Come on...I know you can do it. Just pick it up and pull us over. There it is. It's right there. Come on big boy. I've got a treat for you. Just pull us over and I'll give it to you. Yes, I will...Come on..."

The moose paid no attention to the rope, continuing to chow down on the nearby vegetation. LeClerke's childish talk was grating on Kevin's soul like so many fingernails on a blackboard. His tolerance was soon exhausted, losing his patience with the animal in a thunderous ultimatum.

"Pick up the rope, you big stupid idiot!"

Expressing immediate displeasure, the moose reared back, slamming its front hooves into the surrounding ice. The frozen surface began to crack and buckle, casting a web of fissures all the way to the front of their sled. Kevin took note of the chain reaction fracture, silently chiding himself for his outburst. With its peace disturbed, the creature bolted from view, now leaving the men to their own devices.

LeClerke was livid. "You called the moose a stupid idiot? Do you want to get out of here or not? If you'd kept your mouth shut another minute, he might've pulled us to shore! Now look what kind of mess we're in!"

Kevin was equally irate. "Oh, please! How can you breathe with that head jammed so far up your ass? If you thought Bullwinkle was gonna save us, then you're smoking some really primo shit!"

Continuing a verbal exchange that nearly brought them to blows, the Major issued his demand for a truce. "All right, that's enough! Thanks to the two of you, I'm leaving this world with a friggin' migraine. Focus on the problem, not each other."

Kevin sighed in frustration, searching the sled for anything that might be used to secure their rescue. He spied the weapons satchel by his feet and feverishly inspected its contents. "Maybe, we've got something in here..."

Upon sighting the secret armament appropriated from Dreamland, the CEO voiced his indignation. "What the hell? Where did you get those? That stuff belongs to the U.S. Government, possession of which incurs a mandatory life sentence. You're on your way to a Federal penitentiary."

Answering with a smirk, Kevin schooled him in the fine points of law. "Oh yeah, and what's the charge? You guys always claimed the base didn't exist, so I guess these don't either…do they?" The sight of an anti-grav mine soon provided Kevin some inspiration. "Would this thing work? Maybe we could point it at the ice and get ourselves out of here."

The others agreed it was worth the risk. Holding the device over the edge of their sled, he sent forth a silent prayer and activated the unit. The three sped backward almost immediately, impelled by a force greater than they'd imagined. The slick surface caused them to pinwheel across the frozen lake, sending the trio into an ever widening, directionless circle. As the dizzying performance entered its fourth revolution, LeClerke sought to end their misery. "Turn it off!"

Kevin complied and their futile transit slowed, coming to a rest after executing a long, ungainly spiral. Finding themselves further from shore than ever, the resident engineer made a suggestion. "What we need are short, directional bursts. Turn it on, then turn it off…repeating as necessary, until we can glide off the ice. Got it?"

Nodding in comprehension, Kevin did as asked, propelling the sled on a more or less straight course toward the nearest spit of land. Their speed remained moderate and controlled, bringing renewed hope that their innovative plan would at last succeed. Once he felt they were close enough, Kevin turned off the device, letting momentum carry them to their destination. They arrived ashore with a short bump and were soon overcome in a wave of spiritual solace.

The snow was only an inch or two thick around the lakefront, providing optimal conditions to drag the sled while affording Osborne the chance to lay prone during their trek. Darkness was beginning to fall over the Alaskan countryside. A moonless night would not be conducive to further travel. As they contemplated their meager options, LeClerke took note of a structure ahead, barely visible in the dusky shadows.

"It looks like a logger's cabin," he theorized. "Do you think anyone's inside?"

"Who gives a rat's ass?" Kevin snapped. "We're bustin' our way in whether they like it or not!"

After two polite knocks on the door, a persuasive foot broke the lock and allowed the men to enter. They fumbled in vain for a light switch before realizing the dwelling had no electricity. Striking a match, LeClerke lit a nearby oil lamp which furnished the visitors with initial illumination. The one bedroom cabin was about 800 square feet, sporting a cramped kitchen and indoor bathroom. A quick check of the living quarters assured them that the structure was empty. They lifted the Major from the sled and laid him gingerly onto a tattered couch, placing an adjacent throw pillow under his head. Blankets were located in a storage closet and wrapped around the wounded soldier, granting him some measure of comfort. Kevin brought their supplies and weapons inside, closing the door to block out the chilled night air. It was time to make an assessment of their surroundings, finding whatever they could use to assist in their rescue.

An electric generator was discovered on the back deck, bestowing power to the cabin upon activation. Plundering through the kitchen drawers, they came across a passel of official documentation from the Alaska Department of Natural Resources. This dwelling was the summer residence of the Park Ranger during a four month period of time when the lake was officially open to the public. There were no phones present, nor any other means of communicating with the outside world.

"There's no cell service," lamented Kevin. "The Ranger must use a satellite phone. Wish I still had mine." He paused in quiet deliberation. "Didn't you tell me you sent a BlackBerry message? Where the hell did that end up?"

"Ask the maniac who kidnapped me. I'll probably never see it again."

"That's just great," he fumed. "We keep surviving, we keep beating the odds, but we still can't send a message. Unbelievable."

"At least we have some food and shelter."

"What good is that gonna do him?" Kevin asked, lowering his voice in respect for the Major. "I told you, he won't make it through the night."

LeClerke loosed a ponderous sigh. "The cabin has a TV dish. It's possible I could rewire the thing to send a signal instead of receive one. But, it wouldn't be voice communication…more like Morse code. Of course, there's no guarantee anyone would hear it or know what it was."

Kevin believed the plan had merit. "Might as well try. I'll check out back and see if there's anything we missed."

Appropriating a flashlight from under the sink, he walked out the back door and began scanning the area with the beam. His search continued in a slow, deliberate motion, illuminating nothing more than tree trunks and oversized rocks. Just as Kevin was about to return inside, he spotted the roof of another structure that was mostly obscured due to a drop in elevation. He proceeded with diligence, lighting his path over fallen twigs and branches. Before him was what appeared to be a workshed, about half the size of the neighboring cabin. A well maintained dirt road led away from the building, extending without end into the veil of night. As he approached the barnlike door, he noted the imposing padlock in place and knew it would resist his attempts at entry. Instead of wasting time trying to force his way in, Kevin walked back to the cabin, convinced that a short burst from the Dreamland sonic gun would eliminate the problem.

Upon his return, he found a gleeful LeClerke busily inspecting Ben's cherished property. "I was going through the satchel looking for some tools and I came across this. Do you know what it is?"

"Yeah, it's an iPod."

"Not just any iPod," the man contended. "This one has all the bells and whistles, including text messaging between friends."

Kevin rolled his eyes in disbelief. "Okay, put that thing down. You're starting to sound like my kid brother."

He paused for effect. "Satellite text messaging."

Suddenly, the reason for LeClerke's excitement became clear. "Are you shitting me? It can't be that simple."

"We can contact anyone with an iPod as long as we have their address. There's one here loaded into memory. It just says... Ben."

"Oh, no!" placing hand over face. "That little munchkin will never let me live this down." He took a few moments to think the issue through. "You send it."

"There's not a lot of capacity. It'll have to be short."

The men worked together to compose their urgent communiqué. It read: AT LAKESIDE CABIN IN MTS. EAST OF ANCHORAGE AK...MAJOR BADLY INJURED...EMERGENCY...SEND HELP ASAP. Once satisfied with the brevity and content of their message, a button was pressed and the data transmitted.

"How long before we get an answer?"

LeClerke shrugged. "Hard to tell. It should show up on his iPod in a few seconds. But if he doesn't have it on, we might not hear for hours."

"Oh, don't worry about that," amused by the remote possibility. "If I know Ben, he's probably had the off switch surgically removed." After a composing breath, Kevin recalled his previous objective. "There's a shed out back. We need to check it out."

Leaving the Major alone to rest, they headed toward the adjacent structure, brandishing the appropriate tool to grant them entry. A one second, hypersonic burst disintegrated the lock and surrounding wood, leaving no further impediment to their search. As the doors slid back, LeClerke probed the nebulous interior with a flashlight beam. Occupying nearly all available space within was a 1991 LMC 1500 snowcat, an enclosed 5 passenger, caterpillar track vehicle, used for plowing late season snow and mud from the access road leading to the lake. It was in excellent condition and after trying the keys found inside, the men joyously set about preparing the Major for transport.

Prior to their departure, the iPod's tiny message screen flashed the words: HELP ON THE WAY. Ben's abbreviated reply did not sit well with his brother, wondering why he couldn't have provided a bit more information.

"What does that mean?" growled Kevin. "Help from where? From who?"

LeClerke debated the implications of leaving. "We might miss our one chance to get him to a hospital. Maybe we should stay."

"Hell no," came the immediate retort. "If they can find the cabin, they can find us on the road heading out of here. Let's send another message."

Their electronic response was: FOUND SNOWCAT…ON THE MOVE VIA LAKE ACCESS ROAD…HURRY.

The men made a bed for the Major on the rear bench seat, placing him inside as humanely possible. His condition seemed to be worsening by the hour, drifting in and out of consciousness. While Kevin was loading up their gear, LeClerke discovered a road map which had been yellowed with time.

"We're about 70 miles from the village of Chickaloon," he reported. "If I can find their longitude and latitude, I might be able to estimate ours."

Bringing the metal beast to life, Kevin made a logical suggestion. "Send that information to Ben. See if he can get somebody to send a MedEvac chopper to that town." LeClerke sent an updated message as the three began to rumble down the isolated dirt road.

Achieving a top speed of 25 mph, the snowcat was unquestionably the fastest vehicle on the road. It was also the only one. Almost two hours of darkened terrain passed and they had yet to come across a living soul. Kevin watched the odometer as it slowly counted out each grueling tenth of a mile. He consoled himself with the knowledge that no matter how gradual the progress, it was progress nonetheless.

The Major was entering a stage where he was barely lucid, vocalizing his distress in an endless series of guttural moans. His suffering had become unbearable, both for the victim as well as his caregivers. Kevin stopped the vehicle so he could look after their patient.

"Take the wheel," he ordered. "I'll do what I can for him."

LeClerke slid over and assumed the role of driver. After dabbing some water on Osborne's blood stained lips, there was little doubt that death was near. His lungs labored for air. His face was listless. Kevin propped his head up with a pillow and placed a cold cloth on his forehead. Retreating to the passenger seat, he checked the iPod for any text update from Benjamin. The screen remained blank. Cursing the situation, he sent another message to his brother. WHERE'S THE MEDEVAC CHOPPER? He kept waiting for a response, hoping the device would soon provide a positive word. Anxious minutes passed and still nothing was received. The delay became excruciating as had the circumstance. He shut his eyes and felt the enormous weight of his soul. Kevin had done all he could, but it appeared his heroic efforts to save the Major's life would not be nearly enough.

LeClerke blinked, almost dismissing an aberration in the heavens. He turned his head, peering out at a brilliant star on the horizon. It moved toward them, gaining volume and intensity. He suddenly realized that it was the search beam of an approaching helicopter.

"Oh, my God," he gasped. "Look! They found us. They found us!"

Kevin swirled in his seat, lunging for the flare gun they'd taken from the Dolphin. In near rapture, he fired skyward out the side window and rejoiced as the craft began to circle down. Their shouts of joy continued as the MedEvac chopper landed in a swoop of white powder about 50 yards ahead. A blissful aura of deliverance buoyed their spirits. However, it wasn't long before

Kevin tempered his euphoria, taking note of the crew's curious lack of response.

LeClerke noted his sudden change in mood. "What is it?"

"I don't know," he admitted. "It seems strange they're not running over here. We're the ones with the emergency." He reached into the weapons satchel and took hold of a magnetron rifle. "Better to be safe than sorry."

Kevin exited the vehicle, dashing underneath the helicopter's whirling blades toward an open cargo hatch. He engaged in a quick introduction with the three crew members aboard and was soon placed at ease. The doctor, an African-American male in his mid 40's, greeted him cordially.

"We had a helluva time finding you!" he yelled over the rotor noise. "Where's the injured man?"

"In the snowcat! I'm pretty sure he's got some internal bleeding! He's not going to make it much longer!"

The physician grabbed his equipment bag, jumping to the ground while motioning the pilot to join him. Kevin stole a peek at the female nurse remaining in the craft, but immediately wished he hadn't. Featuring an angular face teeming with acne and weeping pustules, the woman's ghastly image was nearly akin to the legendary Medusa. Before turning to stone, Kevin managed to look away and followed the men to the snowcat.

Sighting their approach, LeClerke abandoned the cab, yielding access for the medical professionals. In a flurry of activity, Osborne's vital signs were checked, the results of which caused the first responders considerable consternation.

"He seems to be in a postictal state," declared the doctor. "Did he have a recent seizure or convulsion?"

"No," Kevin assured him. "I think we would've noticed that."

After taking further bioreadings, the man left the patient's side to join the others. "Your friend's in grave condition," telling them what they already knew. "He has massive internal bleeding along with evidence of liver and renal failure. It's going to be tough getting him out of there without injuring him further. We've got a gurney in the chopper. Want to give me a hand?"

Kevin nodded, scampering back to the helicopter with the physician. Strolling to the opposite side of the snowcat, LeClerke came up behind the pilot who was still wearing his flight helmet. As the man reached inside the vehicle, an electronic device fell from his jacket prompting Pierre to assist in its recovery. "Hold on. You just dropped something."

As he glimpsed the device, there was an instant of recognition that sent goose bumps the length of his flesh. It was LeClerke's stolen BlackBerry. He had just enough time to look up and watch the man's clenched fist send him into unconsciousness.

Halfway to the chopper, the iPod suddenly vibrated in Kevin's pocket. He stopped midstride in order to view Ben's latest message. It read: NO MEDEVAC AVAILABLE...ALL IN USE FOR BURN VICTIMS OF VALDEZ OIL FIRE...C.J. SAYS HELP IS ON THE WAY...

Kevin froze, listening to the percussion of a jackhammer heart in his ears. A quivering finger slowly began to coil itself around the magnetron's trigger. "I forgot something," he told the paramedic. "I'll be right back."

The pilot once more leaned into the snowcat and grabbed hold of their weapons satchel. Eyeing the man with concern, Osborne rolled to one side and willed his voice to life. "Do I know you?" the Major gasped.

Azazel removed his helmet, exposing his signature black eyes. "Yesss," he hissed. "I think you do."

Having returned to the vehicle, Kevin leveled his weapon at the demon. "Drop the bag asshole!" The psychopath loosed a smile of pure malevolence, protracting the moment by his torpid response. "I won't ask again," he insisted. "Put it down...right now!"

The satchel was lowered back in place while Azazel raised his hands in mock surrender. As the psychopath began his measured withdrawal from the vehicle, he swept his arms under Osborne's body and wrenched him erect, using the injured soldier as a human shield. The Major's agonized scream was strident and uncontained, the sound of which left Kevin nauseous.

"Drop the gun, asshole!" Azazel shrieked, enjoying the role reversal with his foe. "I won't ask again!"

Through his tribulation, Osborne beseeched Kevin to ignore the order. "Shoot," he gurgled forth. "I'm dead anyway. Just do it...do it now."

Kevin was further distracted by the chopper beyond. The other members of the Grigori lifted the craft into the air, aware their identities had been surmised. They hovered above, circling with menace over the scene. Osborne continued to writhe in pain, suffering additional hemorrhage and trauma. Knowing he could not allow the satchel to be taken, Kevin made his decision, convinced he would relive this horrific moment for the rest of his life.

"Forgive me Major..."

Suddenly, a revived LeClerke sprung upon Azazel from behind, separating his hold on Osborne. They tumbled to the ground, wrestling one another as the Major collapsed to the floor in torment. Kevin rushed to his aid, helping the anguished officer sprawl onto the bench. With no further hope of securing the Dreamland weapons, the airborne Grigori slipped through the gateway, sending the abandoned helicopter into a chaotic dive. Azazel kicked himself free of LeClerke, coming to his feet as the chopper crashed to the ground. The resulting explosion set the area ablaze. Shards of metal were propelled with hurricane force. The main rotor sheared off, impaling the radiator and engine block of the snowcat. Drenched with expelled aviation fuel, Azazel stumbled through the fire laden debris field, his black eyes unable to focus. Kevin rose up, spotting the deranged archangel through the vehicle's shattered windshield. He gave chase, arriving alongside the man at point blank range. Finally discerning an enemy presence, Azazel fought through his disorientation and opened the gateway to escape. Kevin refused to hesitate. He fired the magnetron, instantly igniting the demon's petrol soaked clothing. As Azazel went through the portal in flames, they could hear his savage screech of travail echoing through the firmament, transcending time and space.

LeClerke was unharmed, struggling to his feet and expressing shock at the scene. The blaze raged on, as flying embers set fire to several nearby trees. A large amount of engine coolant was now pooling around the front of their vehicle, signaling the end of what little hope they had of getting the Major to a hospital. Their journey was over and despair soon became a most unwelcome guest.

Kevin dropped to his knees, experiencing nothing less than spiritual perdition. The trials of this day would stand alone in his memory, becoming a seminal event of his life. He could not bring himself to face the Major. Not after nearly doing what he thought he'd have to do. His eyes were tilted toward the ground, watching one teardrop after another fall to the frozen turf. They seemed to flow without end, leaving him bewildered by their emergence. It had been far too long since he'd wept and right now he had no desire to stop.

A few moments later, the fires surrounding them became agitated as though they'd been caught in a gust of wind. Snow began to swirl while flaming tree branches rocked in advance of an approaching force. An otherworldly noise soon filled the air, heralding a sight of salvation unlike any ever witnessed. With a mighty blast of its six anti-grav impellers, the experimental X-91 landed in front of them…the Armored Personnel Carrier that had days earlier spared Kevin and his family from a thermonuclear demise at Dreamland.

Reeling from incomprehension, Kevin regained his footing and observed the side hatch slide open. A diminutive scientist emerged into view. Although his face was somewhat shrouded in the darkness, there was no mistaking the man's distinctive nasal voice. It was the sound made by an angel.

"What's with you?," groused Dr. Paul Wirtz. "I travel over

3,000 miles in the middle of the night and you can't even say 'hello'?"

Flustered in near delirium, Kevin bellowed forth a familiar name. "Poindexter!" He ran over, wrapping his arms around him in euphoric relief. "Oh, my God..." They finally separated, at last granting the man's simple request. "Hello...Hello..."

"That's better," he confessed. "C.J. called. He told me you needed help."

Kevin nodded, almost too emotional to answer. "How did you find us?"

Wirtz tapped the athlete's head. "The nanobots. They're still in there, broadcasting at a frequency I was able to home in on. They led me right to you."

Additional conversation was placed on hold, realizing time was of the essence. The men gingerly transferred Osborne into the X-91 and left on a fevered, supersonic path to Anchorage.

Pacing the lobby of Alaska Regional Hospital for several hours, they waited for news on the Major's condition. Finally, an emergency room physician approached the trio with an update.

"He's still in grave condition. We had to remove his spleen, one of his kidneys, half his liver and about two feet of small intestine. He required more than 12 pints of blood during surgery."

"But, he'll make it...right?" asked Kevin nervously.

"No. I don't think he will."

The man's words ravaged his soul. He paused in utter disbelief, waving off the comment as though he'd heard the doctor incorrectly. "That's...That's not possible. After all we went through? After all we did? It can't be true. It just can't. He's alive. He's still alive and you need to make him well. You need to do your job."

"I'm sorry, Mr. Reese," consoled the physician. "I wish I could be more hopeful. But, there's continuing hemorrhage in the abdominal cavity. Bleeding that simply can't be stopped."

"So, what are we supposed to do?" Kevin warbled in shock.

"We've got to be in New York later today."

The man vented a lengthy sigh, mindful of his professional responsibility not to sugarcoat the truth. "It's now in God's hands. If I were you, I'd pray for the best...and prepare for the worst."

CHAPTER FORTY-FIVE

QUANTICO, VIRGINIA — MAY 11th — 4:17 AM EDT

$\mathcal{D}$uring their 1,300 mile trek to Virginia, the soldiers had sufficient opportunity to plan their assault on the military prison. With Lieutenant Hawkins intimate knowledge of the Marine Corps Brig, the men had been fully briefed regarding facility layout, cell block orientation, security measures, guard strength and the scheduled times of personnel shift changes in order to design an optimal attack strategy. Nothing was left to chance and everyone knew their assignments. There was just one problem which threatened to derail the entire operation.

"I don't want anyone getting killed," Shannon ordered.

Hawkins appeared incredulous. "You expect us to walk in there and grab your boyfriend without firing a shot?"

"I can't sanction this if innocent people are going to die."

"They're not innocent!" the irate soldier snapped. "They're prison guards! These pricks made a conscious decision to work there. If they don't wanna get whacked, they need to go to Krispy Kreme and make doughnuts."

Shannon was resolute in her demand. "I want Troy back, but not at the expense of another person's life. I'm sure he wouldn't want that and neither do I. There's got to be another way to do this. If not, then let's forget the whole thing. I'm sorry I mentioned it."

Before Hawkins could express further dismay, Captain Roberts interceded. "Don't worry. We'll come up with something. Just give us a little time."

In light of Shannon's directive, they proposed a new scheme, one she was finally able to endorse.

After collecting all the supplies they'd need, they exited Interstate 95 and approached the main security checkpoint at the Marine Corps Base. One of three soldiers on duty left the guard shack and motioned them to stop. Captain Tejada, wearing what looked like a military dress uniform, suddenly exited the Land Rover from the driver's side passenger door.

"I'm sorry, sir. You'll need to get back in your vehicle," stated the marine.

"I don't think so," Tejada replied, revealing the 30 pounds of high explosives wrapped around his torso. "Wave them through, then escort me into the shack."

The petrified soldier did as instructed, granting the Land Rover access to the base. They walked inside the checkpoint, where Tejada met the other two. After providing another peek at his Semtex-covered vest, the Captain now had their undivided attention.

"This is what's going to happen. I have my finger on the detonator...," taking a moment to display the handheld mechanism. "There's enough explosive here to blow us to hell and back, so don't try anything stupid. We're going to play a little game. It's called, fake out the guy on the other end of those cameras," referring to the four devices trained on the guard shack. "I want you guys to act natural. Let's talk...let's laugh...let's have a really great time. Okay?"

The soldiers signaled their obedience. Monitoring the video feed at base headquarters, the security chief manning the station barely blinked, believing the visit to be nothing more than an unscheduled inspection.

Driving across the complex, the Land Rover began to slow upon entering a tight cul-de-sac in front of the prison. Leaving Shannon inside the vehicle, Roberts and Garza led their cohorts toward the entrance at gunpoint. Hawkins and Murphy, behaving as though they were drunk, stumbled and fell in front of two stoic MPs stationed by the door.

"Come on, get up!" the Captain ordered. He apologized to the soldiers on duty. "Found these two inside the women's quarters... up to no good. We're taking them in to get booked." They reached down gruffly, yanking the Lieutenants from the ground. "Come on, let's go!"

The men came up sober, their act now at an end. "Don't move," Hawkins snarled, their weapons leveled at the pair. "I'd like both of you to carefully look down at your feet...and please do so without shitting yourselves."

They nervously complied, observing two Claymore anti-personnel mines positioned mere inches from their boots. A triggering probe leading from each device was attached to the cuffs on their pants.

"I hope you understand that if you move your legs in any direction, you'll be immediately eligible for the Paralympics?" The two nodded in terror. "Very good. Before we go, I want to personally commend each of you on your anal retention. Well done, men...well done."

Leaving the panic stricken MPs, they proceeded into the lobby where a lone guard was doing a crossword puzzle. Captain Roberts calmly peered over his shoulder. "What's a six letter word for 'screwed'?" The man looked up, startled by the array of weapons trained upon him. "Now you know the answer."

Hawkins frisked him, finding a set of keys in his shirt pocket. They forced the guard from his post, locking him inside a nearby storage room. The four snuck past a sealed metal door which led to the intake area where all detainees were processed. Beyond that, another imposing hatch was the only access to three concrete cell blocks where the prisoners were housed.

"How many guards inside?" Roberts asked.

"At this hour, anywhere from 15 to 20."

They approached a utility room, quickly determining the proper key to yield them access. Once inside, the soldiers donned protective suits, covering their bodies in heavy aluminum mesh from head to toe. Captain Garza ran back to the vehicle, gathering two large boxes with Shannon who was already adorned in similar gear. The two strode past the quivering MPs, prompting the woman to engage them in momentary greeting. "Hi, there."

Captain Roberts had finished dispersing an odorless gas into the air vents of the compound. The vapor was filled with hornet alarm pheromone, a chemical derivative processed from the insects' venom sacs. The smell, undetectable to humans, acted as a biological cue to attack and send the normally docile creatures into a frenzied swarm. Their plan was simple. Inject the hornet colony into the air ducts of the prison and let the ensuing mayhem create a clear path to Troy's cell. All that was needed now were the insects themselves.

Lieutenant Hawkins found a prisoner list hanging from an office clipboard. "Troy Garrett's in Special Quarters 2, Cell J."

Garza and Shannon arrived with the boxes, placing each at Captain Roberts feet. Five pairs of eyes glanced at one other, all begging the question if this was the smartest of ideas. In spite of some inevitable second guessing, they knew they'd come too far to back down at this stage. He positioned the first container directly into the foot wide air duct and released a plume of angered hornets. The buzzing insects flew chaotically down the shaft, detecting traces of the strewn pheromone throughout the building. Roberts dumped the second wave into the vents, sending over 300 of the flying beasts into a full scale search for enemy flesh.

The expected reaction did not take long. Within seconds, they detected prolonged squeals of terror, followed by a rampage of guards heading for the exit. Their aural distress was strident and sustained, with many pounding their fists upon the six-inch thick security hatch. The portal finally slid open, unable to contain the gush of humanity. More than a dozen soldiers bolted into the lobby, flailing their arms and legs in a maladroit dance of fear. Amidst their uncontained screams, a thick cloud of hornets descended about them, stinging the marines repeatedly upon every exposed bodily area. Their faces, necks and arms were already becoming grotesquely swollen from the onslaught, as their manic contortions sent them crashing into walls and side chairs. The traumatized victims stampeded through the main doors, running indiscriminately in all directions. Still tethered to the Claymore mines, the MPs swung their arms at the maddened swarm, desperate to remain in position.

After cautioning Shannon to remain in the lobby, the men forged their way into the intake room, coldcocking two remaining guards. Hawkins entered the security control room where any door in the facility could be opened by electronic circuit. He located the release mechanism for Special Quarters 2, Unit J and activated the switch. The soldiers surged through a hallway and into a nearby stockade, spotting an imposing metal hatch that had been sprung free. Making their way into Troy's cell, they witnessed a body cowering under a blanket, trying to stave off attack from a multitude of hornets.

"Are you Troy Garrett?" Roberts yelled. He attempted to remove the bedding, but the man refused to cooperate, keeping a firm grasp upon his only barrier of protection. "Are you Troy Garrett?" he again bellowed.

"Yes!"

The Captain shoved an empty suit beneath the covering. "Here! Put this on as fast as you can!"

As the others stood sentry, the anxious prisoner complied. After contorting his body into the aluminum mesh, Troy swiftly emerged from the blanket. "Who the hell are you guys?"

"We're here with your girlfriend," Roberts explained. "Let's go!"

Expressing shock at the answer, Garrett rose to his feet and followed the soldiers into the common area. To the surprise of all, Shannon was at the portal, running full speed toward the liberated man. Shrieking in relief, they melded into a passionate embrace, trying to kiss one another through the protective netting. At this instant, nothing else mattered. Not the incessant buzzing of the hornets… not the fervent cries of the soldiers…not even the prospect of being caught would prevent them from having this special moment together. Their eyes were aglow with the warmth of their spiritual connection, aware without words of what each had endured. If she'd ever doubted her true feelings, the woman could do so no longer. Shannon knew she was in love with this man.

"Come on!" the Captain squawked. "You can get a room later! Move!"

The six dashed back through the hallway, returning to the intake area. Lieutenant Hawkins broke formation, once more entering the security control room.

"What are you doing?" his unit commander asked.

"Letting the others out."

"Why?" wondered Shannon.

He smiled mischievously. "'Cuz that's just the kinda guy I am!"

He threw the main switch, opening every cell door in the complex. They immediately heard a torrent of shouts and obscenities coming from a stampede of onrushing inmates. Sprinting ahead of the manic escapees, the six jumped inside the vehicle and maneuvered their way through a sea of jubilant humanity.

Noting the Land Rover's return to the main checkpoint, Captain Tejada removed his explosive vest, placing it in front of the soldiers he'd held captive. "Well, it's been fun, guys. You've been very nice to work with. I'm going to leave this here…it has a range of over a mile, so don't think about coming after us. Have a great day."

He leapt into the vehicle. They sped off, swiftly assuming a northerly course up Interstate 95 toward Washington D.C. It was later determined that the Semtex vest and Claymore mines used during the brazen escape were inert, devoid of key ingredients to make them functional as explosives. As per Shannon's instructions, the entire operation had been executed flawlessly without any overt violence or bloodshed.

As they cast off their protective suits, Captain Roberts stated the obvious. "We've got to ditch this thing. They'll have an APB out on us before we can spit."

Entering the city limits of Washington, the Land Rover cruised into the short term parking garage at Reagan National Airport. They grabbed their weapon satchels and made a quick dash to the arrivals area, where a van then transported them to a nearby rental car agency. Within minutes, the seven were safely ensconced inside a new Ford Expedition. The soldiers huddled toward the front of the vehicle, so that Shannon and Troy could have some alone time in back. Although these men of honor never turned to look, each stole furtive peeks in the rear view mirror. Shannon was in full throttle mode, grasping at her lover's arms, chest and every inch of bulging manhood. Their hyperactive lips were engaged in a slurping serenade that left the others blue with envy. The heated festivities continued for several miles before Captain Roberts timidly interrupted.

"Excuse me. I'm sure you couldn't care less, but where are we headed?"

Shannon parted from her man with a smile. "The nearest hotel's fine by me. After all, I still owe you a rain check."

"Take us to the Hyatt Regency on New Jersey Avenue," Troy implored, amused by his decadent choice. "I've got some membership points I haven't used in a while."

She ran her fingers through his unkempt hair, still not trusting the reality of his presence. "I have to go to New York later today. I promised my sister I'd be there."

His surprise was palpable. "Since when do you have a sister?"

The woman sighed, aware of just how much Troy had missed. She gave him a crash course in recent history. Shannon told him about meeting her mother and siblings...the Las Vegas earthquake...the death of her brother Sean...and the assassination of President Webber at the hands of a secret group known as the MAJIK-12. She concluded the update with word of the scheduled United Nations conference regarding the Roswell conspiracy.

Having been held in solitary confinement for the past six weeks, Troy had heard nothing about these momentous events. Not even a few stray words whispered amongst the guards. Proving his sense of humor was still intact, he concluded the briefing with a question. "So, busting out of a military prison won't make the front pages anymore, huh?"

She grinned at the thought. "I don't think so."

"I'd like to go to New York with you," he stated. "I'd love to meet your family."

"I was hoping you would."

Captain Roberts interjected. "What kind of evidence are you planning to present at the U.N.?"

"The data on the CDs, along with the weapons from Dreamland," elaborated Shannon. "Maybe some eyewitness testimony."

The soldier lingered in silent deliberation. "Wouldn't it be nice if you had something more compelling?"

"Like what?"

"Those of us in the military have always heard these rumors... about this cryogenic hanger at Wright-Patterson Air Force Base near Dayton, Ohio," Roberts explained. "They say they're just storing meat in there. But for years, no one on that base is allowed to go in that facility, not even the Commanding Officer. That's an awful lot of security for a bunch of hamburgers, don't you think?"

"What are you suggesting?" Shannon probed.

"Nothing much," he answered coyly. "Once we drop you off, we'll have some time on our hands. I'd like to go see my sister. She lives right outside of Dayton, you know."

"What an amazing coincidence," she smirked. "Make sure to take lots of pictures, Captain. I'd love to see them when you get back."

The decision was made. Shannon and Troy would take an Amtrak train to New York City later in the day, while the soldiers traveled to Wright-Patterson AFB in Ohio. There they would attempt to locate the secret cryogenic hanger and discover once and for all what was contained therein.

CHAPTER FORTY-SIX

*A*riel informed his pupil that they would have to leave Fort Huachuca before noon. The two had used the morning constructively, executing a battery of tests that would further hone his paranormal skills. Benjamin opened the gateway on three separate occasions, but still wouldn't venture through. It had become a psychological barrier that he couldn't seem to overcome.

Aware of the United Nations conference set to begin in under three hours, the Israeli knew that a dramatic public demonstration of the gateway would be critical in convincing global skeptics. It would also serve their immediate needs well, eliminating the necessity for booking a flight to New York. He had shown Benjamin several pictures of the United Nations complex in Manhattan, as well as interior images of the General Assembly stage and podium dais, in the hope this would trigger his curiosity and swagger. But, the child was having no part of it, digging his heels in and displaying a frustrating stubbornness.

They were packing up their personal items when Captain Parnell entered Building 23, sporting a look of genuine terror. Ariel intercepted the officer in the hallway. "What is it?"

"We're too late. The Garrison Commander just arrived. He's already being briefed by the Provost Marshal."

"Can we still get out?"

"Not a chance," he declared. "The word just went out to the MPs to seal the base."

They decided that it was safer for them to remain inside Building 23 and wait for the Captain to determine a proper course of action. Sheltering the two inside the lab, Parnell left to gather further intelligence and prepare for the possibility of a bloody siege. Events were now conspiring against them, making it clear the gateway was their only way out. Once more, Ariel pleaded with Benjamin to abandon his fears, informing the child of the deteriorating situation. The more pressure his tutor applied, the less willing he was to try. It was a paradox without answer, leaving the Israeli to wonder if the boy's crisis of faith could be resolved in time.

Captain Parnell returned a few minutes later, disturbingly spooling out electrical wires across the wooden floor. He crouched down, attaching the slender filaments to the electrodes of a detonation plunger. His lack of communication spoke volumes.

"Are you doing what I think you're doing?" inquired Ariel.

Parnell finished rigging the charge. "We've got to stall for time," he announced. "I've got 50 pounds of RDX out front and another 50 under the building. They'll think twice about storming the lab. I know they want this room left intact."

Mouths dropped, realizing just how serious their predicament had become. "Is this the only way?"

"You tell me," the officer probed. "The two of you have the power to get out of here. I don't."

Benjamin appeared stunned by the man's actions. "If we leave, what'll happen to you?"

A slight smile emerged. "Don't worry about me. I've made my decision and I'm prepared to see it through."

"I don't want you to do this," the child claimed. "Not for us."

"I'm not doing it for you. I'm doing it for myself. I don't expect you to understand, at least not until you're older. If the President thought this was worth dying for, then that's good enough for me.

That's what being a soldier's all about…sacrificing everything you have for the sake of what's right, regardless of the consequence." He paused to gather his emotions, looking upon the misty-eyed youngster with concern. "I don't want to die kid, but I've got to buy you the time you need to get out of here. You've got to dig down and find the strength to go through that thing, whatever the hell it is. I'm sure you've got some great destiny awaiting you. I don't know what it could be and I'm sure you don't either. Just promise me this. When you finally arrive at that special place in your life…remember me. That'll make this all worthwhile."

Benjamin was deeply affected by the man's passion. Before he could respond, they heard the rapid movement of soldiers taking up position around the building. Dropping to the floor, Ariel and his student huddled behind a metal desk, trusting its bulk would spare them from a hail of bullets. Captain Parnell bellowed out with resolve, informing the forces arrayed against them that the building was booby-trapped and to move back at once. Upon sighting the explosive charges, the soldiers retreated to a more discreet distance. Lines of communication were opened via cell phone and the standoff officially commenced.

A worldwide audience, estimated at over two billion people, were now glimpsing the first televised moments of the United Nations conference. The hour was selected to provide for the largest global viewership possible during normal waking hours. The General Assembly was packed with delegations from every member country. There was not a seat to be had and standing room was at a premium. The United States Ambassador had used every procedural and parliamentary tactic in a futile attempt to derail this meeting which he likened to a modern day Inquisition. Although the U.S. maintained veto power in the Security Council, the Secretary General had skillfully avoided any involvement with that body, so as to ensure the conference would proceed as planned.

Barbara Pinder was seated on the platform, just to the right of the speaker's podium. Most of her siblings were with her on stage, having traveled to New York earlier in the day. Last night, C.J. had taken possession of the Dreamland CDs from Lynda Knight at Roswell Airport. Once he and his brother Moses arrived at the U.N., the salient information was hard copied and made ready for each of the delegations to review. Casey and his sisters Kimberly, Roberta and Hope were also present along with Shannon and Troy Garrett. The vast assembly became hushed as the Secretary General of the United Nations assumed the podium. His words were spoken in English, but the message was translated into over 90 different languages around the world.

"I would like to welcome the delegations of all 192 member states, as well as our global television audience, to the United Nations General Assembly. Our agenda today is to present you with both physical and anecdotal evidence of a preeminent event in human history which occurred more than 60 years ago, but until now has been shrouded in secrecy...to the detriment of all. This incident specifically involves one of this body's founding members, the United States of America. I have assured the U.S. Ambassador and his delegation that they will be given every opportunity to explain or rebut the charges, evidence and testimony that will be presented here today. Before we proceed, I would like to caution the delegates to not only keep an open mind, but to refrain from jumping to premature conclusions until this conference has officially concluded. The information you are about to receive is beyond comprehension. It will most certainly change your perception of the world we live in, as well as our significance as a species. At stake...is nothing less than the future of the human race. I would like to turn the podium over to Ambassador Barbara Pinder, head of the Bahamian delegation to the United Nations, who will address the particulars with the Assembly. Ambassador Pinder..."

Barbara approached the lectern with anticipation, looking out upon her rapt audience. "Thank you, Mr. Secretary, both for your opening remarks and making these proceedings possible.

My fellow delegates, each of you are about to be handed a 126 page summary of the information that I am about to discuss." She paused, observing numerous orderlies now ascending the aisles, distributing the documents to hundreds of outstretched arms. "This data has been selected to highlight the material found on these eight CDs," she stated, holding the box for all to see. "Copies of these CDs will be made available to world governments and media per request."

An angered voice erupted from the crowd. "You can't do this!" the American Ambassador fumed. "It's possible those CDs are United States Government property and we have a sovereign right to protect that data for national security purposes!"

The Secretary General returned to the podium. "That's enough! There will be order in the Assembly! You'll be given your turn to speak. Restrain yourself from further outbursts or I'll have you escorted from the building." He ceded the floor back to Barbara.

"Once you read this material, I believe you'll understand why the U.S. Ambassador is so agitated about its dissemination. It details what happened the night of July 4, 1947 in the town of Roswell, New Mexico, a remote area in the southwestern portion of the continental United States. At approximately 11:00 pm local time that evening, the history of our world was altered forever. A craft carrying three beings was recovered, along with some mind-boggling technology. The American military began a systematic cover up of the incident, ostensibly to hide their attempts at reverse engineering the onboard computer and the resulting technological breakthroughs from foreign governments. The modern conveniences that we take for granted today, owe their creation to that craft in Roswell. It was later determined that these beings were actually human and had traveled here from Earth's distant future. The U.S. Government established an organization in September of 1947 consisting of 12 individuals selected from military, political and scientific backgrounds. This group is known as the MAJIK-12. Their original charter was to analyze the crash data and prevent misinformation and hysteria from spreading to the populace. But, the cabal soon mutated into a hellish regime of almost omnipotent power, silencing anyone that threatened to expose its secrets. Hundreds of innocent people have been murdered to keep the data you are now reading classified. Included in that list are prominent world scientists and leaders, such as Albert Einstein, Enrico Fermi, J. Robert Oppenheimer, along with U.S. Presidents John F. Kennedy, Andrew Petersen... and Susan Webber, who was assassinated by the MAJIK-12 just two days ago." A wave of incredulous gasps cascaded through the Assembly, the sound of which caused Barbara to interrupt her train of thought and realize just how incendiary this news truly was. She took a sip of water before continuing, mindful that her emotions were beginning to swell. "This issue is deeply personal for me. For you see, there was an eyewitness to the crash that evening. A woman whom none of you know...and who I spent only a short time with before she perished in the Las Vegas earthquake. The MAJIK-12 tried to silence her and her children, but they weren't successful. This woman was perhaps the bravest person that ever lived..." Barbara paused as her voice started to crack. "In the face of monstrous evil, she drew upon her strength from God and was rewarded for her faith and sacrifice. I know this to be true, because I am her eldest daughter and remain a target of the MAJIK-12 to this very moment."

The situation had become intense. Captain Parnell had witnessed more than 30 sharpshooters surrounding Building 23, all waiting patiently for a split second view of their target. The dedicated officer sat on the floor, having positioned the detonator between his legs. Convinced he would be shot on sight, he wanted to make sure that when his body collapsed it would fall upon the plunger mechanism and thereby claim the secret room that the Army wished to preserve.

Ariel had been trying desperately to get the child's attention. It was now imperative for Benjamin to use the gateway to save his life, but the boy was not ready to leave. His eyes were riveted upon Parnell, amazed at the man's conviction and stoic nature. He wondered how the Captain could so easily accept his given fate and what would motivate someone to risk everything for another.

The youngster pleaded with the Israeli, asking him to alter the unfolding event. "You could go back a few hours," the child suggested. "You could stop this from happening."

His tutor assured him otherwise. "No, Ben. It has to play out like this."

"But, why?"

"He's here to show you there are things worth dying for... things more important than self-preservation. This is something you have to learn, to achieve greater spiritual strength. Elohim has conferred this task upon him. I can't interfere."

Benjamin expressed his concern. "If we leave, they're going to kill him."

"That's going to occur no matter what," Ariel whispered. "His name's already been written into the book of life. He overcame his fear and found inner peace. You also have to conquer your fears. It's time to let his strength become yours. Open the gateway and step through. You can't deny your destiny any longer."

The boy bowed his head, wanting to cry but finding no tears. He felt embarrassed for his inaction and made sick by the escalating stress he was being forced to endure. Benjamin begged for a way out. "I don't want to do this."

"I can't do it for you," claimed his mentor, physically shaking with urgency. "It's a step that only you can take."

The youngster lamented his choice, mired in phobic apprehension. What happened next was a visceral reminder of the fragility of life and his obligation to a higher calling. In an eruption of violence, the floor heaved open as a Special Forces soldier emerged from underneath the building. Before the Captain could react, three rounds penetrated his body, the severe recoil thrusting him clear of the detonator. Over Benjamin's shriek of horror, Ariel toppled the metal desk onto the shooter, splitting his head open on impact. A maelstrom of frantic images now caused the youngster to lose focus while reality blurred before him. Parnell was dead, his blood merging with that of his killer's. The Israeli pushed another desk up against the door, barricading them from a group of onrushing soldiers in the corridor beyond. Shouts and obscenities reigned freely, echoing from every direction. Ariel spun to his knees, clutching the U.N. photograph. With his eyes swollen in alarm, tutor met pupil face to face.

"We've got 10 seconds! This is where we're going! Look at this and open the gateway!" A crush of humanity struck the closed door, shattering the wood jamb around the lock. "Do you hear me?" he shouted. "This is it, Ben! This is it! There's no more time! Do it now!"

As the soldiers began bulling their way into the room, the boy ran the tonal cues in his mind. The portal appeared, its black heart beating with esoteric life. In a loathsome primal cry, Benjamin surrendered his body to the unknown, allowing the generated suction to transport him into a dark and foreboding realm.

During Barbara's emotional speech to the Assembly, the eyes of billions caught glimpse of a spatial distortion a few feet from the podium. It happened in an instant and sent shockwaves throughout the world. The dual chasms opened wide, depositing Ariel and Benjamin upon the elevated platform. Screams of hysteria reverberated through the crowd, in utter disbelief over what they'd just witnessed. Their vocal agitation crested when United Nations security personnel ran to subdue the pair.

"Ben!" his sister cried into the microphone.

The boy was now slackjawed in amazement, coming to realize what he'd finally accomplished. "Wow!" he howled. "What a blast!"

Barbara saw the guards approaching the dais and tried to restrain their advance. "It's all right! This is my brother and friend!"

They grabbed both of the intruders, but Benjamin would have none of their strong armed tactics. No longer fearing his new found power, he opened the gateway and slipped from their grasp, reappearing in the visitor's gallery overlooking the main floor. "Here I am! All the way up here!" the youngster bellowed, clearly enjoying the audience's stunned reaction. Further shouts of dismay rumbled through the assembly as two more guards rushed his position. Again he slipped away, materializing at the back of the room. "No, I'm over here!" he taunted the authorities. Other security officers tried to corner the child, flailing at empty air upon his sudden departure. He arrived back upon the dais and chided his would be abductors. "Forget it guys! You're way too slow!"

Ariel looked upon him with annoyance. "Now you're just showing off."

Ben's siblings joined him on stage, welcoming him with loving hugs. Attempting to quell the confusion, Ariel assumed the podium at Barbara's request. "Ladies and gentlemen, there's nothing to be frightened of. Please, let me explain." The aural chaos began to abate. "What you've just observed is a gateway into a larger world, one which has been deliberately concealed by the U.S. Government. Years ago, I was at the center of an experiment. It was a plan to mate human females with visitors from Earth's future. A handful of children were conceived, of which I am one. I was essentially held captive for the first 30 years of my life, conducting paranormal research at various military installations around the United States for a secret program called Project Destiny. Because our fathers were more genetically advanced, we have the extraordinary power to manipulate space and time, allowing us free movement within those constraints. We also discovered that we were highly intuitive and able to communicate directly with the future human race. As you become familiar with the information that you've been provided, I'll be available to answer your questions regarding the ulterior motives the military had for Project Destiny, the breadth and scope of the paranormal activities, as well as some of the benefits to humanity from this clandestine research."

Ariel stepped away from the podium amidst a tumultuous

clamor of questions. Reassuming her place at the lectern, Barbara sought to calm the boisterous multitude. "The information that you're being exposed to today is astounding in nature and is beyond our current scientific understanding and comprehension. In order for us to proceed, we need to determine how best to investigate these areas in depth. We can continue to have a general discussion and answer your inquiries one at a time, or we could break into various focus groups for more detailed deliberation then reconvene with our reports to the Assembly as a whole. Perhaps we should take the time to vote on a desired course of action."

The U.S. Ambassador rose from his seat, challenging the proceedings and expressing further outrage. "I wish to raise a formal protest, not only against any vote of this Assembly, but also to the questionable legality of this conference. If these documents that we've been provided are genuine..." holding the papers above his head, "...it begs the question, how were they obtained? If they were stolen from my Government, then a crime has been committed and the United Nations is culpable under international law. I think any member nation here would be incensed over a similar theft of their sovereign property. To distribute this information without telling us where it came from is tantamount to a conspiracy against the United States of America and should not be allowed."

Barbara engaged him in debate, trying to maneuver the cagey diplomat to go on the record. "Mr. Ambassador, are you now saying these documents are bona fide transcripts of the United States Government?"

"That's not what I've represented," he maintained, careful to avoid a legal quagmire. "I'm speaking hypothetically. How can we take a vote or analyze this data if we have no assurance of its authenticity or lawful possession?"

"We would have had such knowledge if President Webber had lived long enough to tell the American people," Barbara squawked with recrimination. "But, your military saw to it that she never got the chance."

"That's a reprehensible charge and my Government demands an immediate apology!" the man roared in fury.

"You'll get no such concession from me. What I've said is the truth. It's you that should be apologizing to us."

The Ambassador was beside himself with indignation, now turning side to side to directly address the other delegations. "This is a travesty of justice! Do you expect me to remain silent while our military leaders are accused of willful assassination? President Webber was an unfortunate victim of an Al-Qaeda terrorist plot on our soil. She died a hero and is being honored as such tomorrow. I find it interesting that these scurrilous charges are coming from the same sources that claim these documents to be valid. I submit that these transcripts are fraudulent and part of a conspiracy to cast the United States Government in the worst possible light. In fact, all we've seen and heard here today are a litany of uncorroborated stories along with an entertaining magic act done with obvious smoke and mirrors." He stole a dramatic breath, taking the pulse of his audience. "These charges are the hallucinations of radical fanatics. There has not been one scintilla of physical evidence that we've been shown that would help prove this ridiculous theory. I therefore move that we adjourn this conference and..."

His voice was overwhelmed by an acoustic disruption in the plaza outside. Dozens of people left their seats to determine the source of the commotion. Television camera crews raced to the scene, capturing the event for the world to witness. Kicking up a swirl of dust and stray litter, the X-91 hovered above the bewildered onlookers on a forced stream of gravitons. It descended with ponderous intent, making certain its arrival was well covered by the media. The craft finally landed, kissing the concrete with a delicate thump. As its aural whine diminished, the side hatch opened releasing three individuals onto the plaza. Kevin was brandishing a sonic gun with one hand and a magnetron in the other. The weapons were trained upon Pierre LeClerke, coercing his entrance into the building. Following the two was Dr. Wirtz, transporting the coveted weapons satchel. To the amazement of all, the men continued their march through the lobby and into the confines of the General Assembly. Kevin took note of the large number of delegates milling about the room.

"You can take your seats," he admonished. "Nobody's leaving."

Barbara smiled at the approaching trio. "You said you wanted physical evidence, Mr. Ambassador. Well, it just arrived."

They marched in single file, stepping onto the dais. Kevin's siblings acknowledged his presence with high fives and fist bumps. The room became hushed as LeClerke assumed the podium, a leveled magnetron in his ribs. He hesitated, leaning away from the microphone to express his apprehension.

"What you're asking me to say will seal our fate. Do you have any idea of the forces that will be brought against us?"

Dr. Wirtz spoke with resolve. "If you don't tell them, I will."

The man released a sigh of defeat and turned to face the Assembly. "Ladies and gentlemen, my name is Dr. Pierre LeClerke. I'm the Chief Executive Officer of GG&E Corporation, headquartered in LaJolla, California. My company works closely with the U.S. military on various secret programs...the largest of which is our research and development contract at the Groom Lake Test Site in the Nevada desert. Since 1958, GG&E has been actively involved in the reverse engineering of highly sensitive technology recovered from a crashed UFO in Roswell, New Mexico." A distinct feeling of unease began to percolate through the crowd, announcing their dismay with a chorus of audible gasps. LeClerke knew there was no turning back and that full disclosure was his only sane option. "The documentation you've been provided is accurate and irrefutable. This data was contained on CDs which were taken directly from a security vault at the Groom Lake complex. Those CDs were not stolen, but were made available by a conscientious and exceptionally brave GG&E employee," he remarked, tendering a nod to Dr. Wirtz. "I wish I could've found such courage in myself and to not have been brought here against my will. For the past few years I've been a member of a shadow government, so perverse and brutal that you couldn't possibly fathom. This group is known as the MAJIK-12. For the past 60 years, they've ruled this country with an iron fist...with no Congressional oversight, no Executive Branch privilege and no judicial review. A totally autonomous entity funded entirely by illegal arms sales from the U.S. military. They have systematically killed hundreds of people to protect a secret that should never have been hidden." Another cleansing breath forced him to pause. "President Webber tried to enlist my support in challenging the inherent evil of this group. Unfortunately, I wasn't as bold as she. Now, her body lies in state as a hero, while I stand before you as a coward. The MAJIK-12 ordered her assassination...just as certainly as they are now ordering mine. If you read my obituary in the next few days, you'll understand who was responsible." He purged any lingering trepidation with an extended sigh. "I've never been a brave man. But from this moment forward, I will no longer live in fear."

He stepped away from the podium, bowing his head in obligatory prayer. The unexpected response started slowly, first with one delegate then another. Finally, the entire Assembly was on its feet, providing LeClerke with a standing ovation for the eloquence and emotional depth of his speech. The man was overwhelmed by the warmth of their tribute, shedding tears of relief now that his onerous burden had at last been lifted.

As the applause continued its throbbing cadence, Kimberly pulled Kevin to the rear of the dais. "Where's Robert?"

He knew this conversation was inevitable, but remained ill-prepared for its occurrence. His stumbling words betrayed any attempt at soothing her fears. "Well, we, uh, had a crash...in Alaska. The Major...he...he had some injuries. But, don't worry. We got him to a hospital."

Kimberly's eyes swelled with panic. "How bad is he?"

His visible gulp answered her question. "Bad."

"Where is he?" her voice cracked. "What hospital?"

"Alaska Regional...in Anchorage."

She probed her brother's face for the truth, furious that he would no longer look upon her. "He's dying?" she screeched. "How could you leave him like that? You left him there to die?"

"I didn't know what to do," revealing his inner conflict. "I made a promise to bring this guy here. That was important."

"And, he's not?"

Kevin tried to explain. "Kim, the doctor's are doing all they can…"

"You son-of-a-bitch!" The enraged woman slapped his face with as much force as she could muster, storming off the platform to exit the building in haste. Within the space of two hours she was on a non-stop flight to Seattle with a further connection to Anchorage. Kevin's family hugged the shaken athlete, assuring him that nothing he could've said or done would have made the situation any easier for Kimberly to accept. He blamed himself, wondering if there was some other way he might've handled this no-win situation.

After a General Assembly vote, the delegates decided to break into focus groups to gain greater insight into several areas of investigation. Some were shown the Dreamland weapons and received demonstrations of their awesome capability. Others were granted an understanding of the inner workings of the MAJIK-12 with LeClerke acting as mentor. Still more delegates were entranced by Ariel's story and seized the opportunity to examine the gateway with greater diligence. During this period of analysis, global television and radio correspondents read the incendiary information contained in the released transcripts to their astounded audience. The data was almost too much to absorb, coming in wave after wave of startling disclosures.

Hours elapsed and still the General Assembly had yet to reconvene. For much of this time, Troy Garrett had been watching the U.S. Ambassador, taking delight in the man's evident distress. His countenance and demeanor were the epitome of defeat. The wily diplomat sat with head in hands after being subjected to the total evisceration of his rebuttals. Having been the recipient of several cell phone calls, the Ambassador failed to register surprise when a lone messenger arrived at their table.

"That's interesting," whispered Troy to Shannon.

"What is?"

"That guy talking with the U.S. delegation," he pointed. "I know him. He's a Bureau agent. We graduated at the academy together."

The entire seven member diplomatic corps suddenly left their seats, striding from the chamber with urgency. Troy's curiosity was peaked, compelling him to follow. He bolted down an aisle running along the perimeter of the room and emerged into the glass walled lobby. There he observed the American contingent boarding an awaiting helicopter, its rotors churning frantically in the plaza beyond. As the craft went airborne, they banked over the East River, accelerating from the area at a high rate of speed. Troy approached a nearby security guard who was watching their unorthodox getaway.

"Have you ever seen a chopper land there before?"

The man shook his head. "The helipad's on the roof. I don't know what those guys were thinking."

It dawned upon Troy that their rapid evacuation had to have been orchestrated by higher authority in Washington, with either the State Department or U.S. Military being the logical suspects. He placed himself in their mindset and the deliberation rendered him pale with dread. *The abject humiliation. The global scorn. Why would they allow this to happen? Why would they let decades of lies evaporate in one televised evening?* The answer was simple. *They wouldn't...*

Troy once more addressed the guard. "Could you escort me to your Chief of Police? I've got a bad feeling about this."

After identifying himself as an agent for the FBI, he expressed his concern to the appropriate individuals in charge of United Nations security. Acting upon a hunch, he asked to see a list of all shipments that had been received within the past 48 hours. As his eyes scanned the manifest, he stopped upon one that marshaled his attention. It was a 370 pound parcel, containing a sleeper sofa destined for the office of Bahamian Ambassador Barbara Pinder.

"Was this a scheduled delivery?" Troy asked.

"I would assume so," reasoned the Chief. "They've been doing extensive renovation up there since the fire."

"What fire was that?"

"About six weeks ago there was an explosion on the 28th floor...in Ms. Pinder's office. She must have ordered new furniture to replace what was destroyed."

"I doubt she's had the time for that," he mused. "I think we should check it out. Can you take me up there?"

The Chief consented to the search, leading him toward a bank of lobby elevators. Minutes later, the two arrived in Barbara's newly restored office suite. They could discern the smell of fresh paint, but the pastel colored enamel had only been partially applied. Drop cloths were in evidence across the floor while a roll of plush carpeting was awaiting installation. Troy found it strange that the only piece of furniture in the room was the brown leather sleeper sofa in question.

"They're not finished yet," he remarked. "Why did they deliver this now?" Approaching the eight foot couch with caution, the agent viewed the item from multiple perspectives. He bent down, trying to lift one end to experience its oppressive weight. "This thing's heavy as hell. How did they get it up here?"

"It was brought in on a hand truck," answered the Chief.

Troy punched through the plastic shrink wrap to lift the bottom cushions. To his surprise, they were attached to the frame. "How does the bed open out?" he murmured, more to himself than the officer with him. Probing the plump seats with his fist, the central cushion did not depress like the others. He spotted a carpet knife on the floor lying next to a roll of foam padding. Without seeking permission, Troy carved the seat at the stitch line and pulled back the material. What he discovered was a 50 kiloton nuclear device with a frequency detonator. After an initial spasm of terror, he called Shannon on her cell.

"What is it?" she wondered, detecting the panic in his voice.

"Tell your brothers to get up here!" Troy barked. "We've got a sofa to move!"

The rampage was on. C.J., Kevin and Casey were at a full gallop, dashing to the elevators for their ascent to the 28th floor. Still hobbling from his surgery, Moses made his way to the plaza with Dr. Wirtz. They entered the X-91 and swiftly brought the craft to life. Word had been sent over two-way security radios to evacuate the diplomats to an underground bunker in the thought it might shield them from the blast. Hysteria swept through the building as thousands bolted into the streets of New York, all captured on television to an incredulous world.

The brothers arrived in Barbara's office to find Troy straining with the couch. Each sighted the explosive lodged in the sofa's core and immediately shared a common thought.

"Can't we just cut it out of there?" Casey suggested.

The agent informed them of the danger. "It might be booby-trapped! The whole thing's got to go!"

Making his own dead lift attempt, Kevin expressed his doubts. "This damn thing weighs a ton! We'll never get it out of here!" He gazed out the picture window and noticed the X-91 maneuvering into position. "Poindexter, you're a genius!" he yelped. "Bust that glass open! Let's shove the sofa onboard!"

C.J. grabbed a nearby step ladder, ramming it into the wall length pane. Disgorged shards broke away from the casement, finally clearing a path to the vehicle beyond. The room gushed with the free exchange of air while the generated noise added to the urgency of their task. Moses stood by the open hatch, providing Wirtz with directional cues in their attempt to dock flush with the building. Utilizing subtle bursts of the motion thrusters, the X-91 closed the required distance, now remaining buoyant against the ruptured façade.

Amidst a chorus of groans, the frantic four hoisted the cumbrous sofa above the roll of carpeting and over to the breach. Kevin was lifting the lead end, flinching upon awareness of the 300 foot abyss beneath his feet. Crossing the threshold, he inched his way inside with guidance from Moses. The sudden weight caused the craft to wobble in midair, requiring Wirtz to increase the negative G-forces flowing through the actively engaged impellers. With a few extra pushes and tugs, the furniture was finally aboard, its massive bulk preventing the others access.

"Get us outta here, Poindexter!" clamored Kevin.

Executing a graceful banking angle, the X-91 left the area on a surge of gravitons, headed away from the city over the muddy waters of the East River. The brothers eyed one another in breathless horror, speculating as to when they'd be consumed within the blast. Now gliding 250 feet over the river's midpoint, Wirtz tried to communicate with the petrified pair.

"How much time do we have?"

"I don't know!" shouted Kevin. "It could go any second!"

"Isn't there a timer?"

Moses bent down for a detailed inspection. "I don't see any!"

"Troy said something about a radio detonator!" his brother recalled.

The comment sent Wirtz into an extended period of reflection. Agonizing over the decision, he blared out an ominous command. "Drop it in the river!"

"What?" the two exclaimed in synchronous disbelief.

"Don't argue with me!" the man squawked. "Just do what I say! Drop it!"

Too frantic to debate the issue, the brothers pooled their strength and soon had the sofa teetering on the leading edge of the hatch. With a final muscular thrust, the prodigious piece of furniture toppled out of the craft and accepted its gravitational fate. It struck the water with a towering splash, submerging instantly beneath the murky veil.

From Barbara's office window, Troy witnessed the sofa being jettisoned into the river. "Take cover!" he ordered.

The men dashed for shelter within an interior stairwell, hoping it would provide some measure of protection from the imminent shockwave. They phoned their sisters and told them to prepare for the explosion and resulting tsunami. Their breaths were shallow and resonant. Sweat-drenched palms grasped metal handrails with fevered anticipation. Hearts throbbed in percussive rhythm. The passage of time was excruciating. They knew it would be bad, but they had no idea to what degree.

The Navy helicopter carrying the U.S. Ambassador and his entourage was currently hovering 10 miles to the south, beyond the potential burst zone. The diplomats had been instructed to leave the building, but were left to ponder the reason. Receiving final clearance directly from Admiral Holliman in the Ft. Meade bunker, the pilot sank his thumb into the activation switch of a handheld igniter. A radio signal operating on a secure frequency was beamed directly at the United Nations complex to trigger the device.

There was no explosion. No fireball. No decimation of midtown Manhattan. The pilot once more triggered the switch, this time over and over. New York's iconic skyline remained. The chopper closed to within a five mile range to target, hoping the minimized distance would establish the desired contact. It was not to be. The mighty city withstood their every attempt to bring it down. Cursing with frustration, the pilot contacted the Joint Chiefs alerting them that their plans had failed.

Those inside the stairwell were awash in confusion. The men couldn't understand why they were still alive, cradled inside a building that had somehow miraculously survived. It was a most welcome, but baffling conundrum. Believing that sufficient time had elapsed, they made their way back to the open breach and spotted the X-91 touching down in the plaza below. C.J. phoned Moses on his cell to gain some insight.

"Hey! What happened?"

"Thank our resident scientist," his brother explained. "Once he figured out the kind of bomb it was, he had us drop it in the drink. Radio waves can't travel through water."

A lengthy sigh followed. "Let him know about 10 million people want to personally shake his hand. You guys okay?"

"Yeah. We'll meet you in the lobby."

With the danger over, the delegates began filing back into the chamber, ready to hear reports from various focus groups and to render votes of censure against the United States. It was during this time when the family realized that Barbara was curiously absent from the proceedings.

"I saw her about an hour ago," declared Shannon with mounting concern. "She asked if she could hold the baby. I don't know where she is now."

C.J. located the Secretary General who was being interviewed by a group of television correspondents. He waited respectfully for a chance to speak with the sought after official. "Excuse me, Mr. Secretary. Have you seen Ambassador Pinder?"

"Oh, I suppose she's still in my suite."

"Your suite?" he asked quizzically.

"Yes. She had a headache and wanted to lie down for a few minutes, so I gave her the keys to my office. I'm sure she'll be here soon." He watched as C.J.'s face began to swell in terror. "Is there something wrong?"

"Where's your suite located?"

"It's on the 39th floor."

"Would you be kind enough to escort us up there?" C.J. implored. "We need to check on her right away."

Fearing the worst, her elder siblings followed the Secretary General to his penthouse apartment. Their concern was justified. If Barbara had drifted asleep with Hope by her side, an already dicey situation could turn tragic. They knew the insidious power of Lucifer's dreams and shuddered to think of the consequences.

Arriving on the 39th floor, they entered the suite in search of their sister, calling out Barbara's name. Receiving no response, an abandoned guest bed with rumpled sheets confirmed the obvious.

"She fell asleep all right," C.J. announced. "But, where the hell is she?"

Kevin pointed at some steps ascending to a metal door. "What's this?"

"That's a private staircase," the Secretary General revealed. "It leads to the helipad."

A moment of indecision evaporated in a swarm of bodies scrambling for the rooftop. Surging through the metal hatch, they suddenly beheld a sight which left them nauseated. Barbara was standing atop the retaining wall with Hope nestled to her breast. She looked straight ahead, her face absorbing the rays of the setting sun. The woman appeared to be in the midst of a daydream, exhibiting no outward concern. Standing next to her was another individual whom Kevin recognized immediately. He was the African-American paramedic that he'd encountered in Alaska. Grinning with malevolence, the archangel Mulciber now did the unthinkable. He placed his hand on Barbara's back and pushed her over the rail...casting the sisters into a certain death freefall. The demon turned to the family, basking in their squall of anguish. As they charged, he disappeared through the gateway, leaving them in catatonic shock. Kevin peered over the ledge, observing the two spinning to the plaza below. In a manic tempest of screams and shouts, the group dashed for the elevators and prayed as they never had before.

Barbara experienced a serenity that was most welcome. A peaceful end to her physical existence that caused her to lament all that had come before. The woman looked upon the babe in her arms and was assured that everything would be fine. She awaited the transition. That split second of exquisite pain and blessed pleasure, which buffered this realm with the next, allowing her soul to continue on its journey to enlightenment. *Don't worry. It won't be long now...*

Upon gaining access to the plaza, the terrified siblings rushed to the site, forging their way through a tight cordon of humanity. They expected to come upon a scene of gruesome carnage. But, what they found was nothing less than a miracle.

Barbara and Hope were curled into a fetal position, suspended in midair approximately five feet from the ground. An active anti-grav mine was positioned underneath, providing life sustaining negation of gravitational forces. Alongside them stood Ariel, preparing to cradle them back to the bonds of Earth. Once safely in his arms, he set them down and switched off the device. As the crowd around them applauded, the siblings expressed their infinite relief and appreciation for what their Israeli friend had done.

Kevin confronted him with a question. "Are you always at the right place at the right time?"

The man smiled, revealing the front page of different editions of _The New York Times_. Each bore tomorrow's future date and reflected his multiple trips through the timeline. As they perused the catastrophic stories that could have been, Ariel found his voice. "It's not easy making everything turn out the way you want," he boasted. "Let's hope this time, I got it right."

CHAPTER FORTY-SEVEN

They prepared themselves for a climactic showdown. Here on the grounds of Consolidated Edison's East 14th Street power plant in lower Manhattan, the forces of good would confront the minions of evil. The Archangels waited for the Grigori to appear, convinced this encounter was not only inevitable, but necessary. They could no longer accept the status quo. If their sleep deprivation continued, it would only be a matter of time before a disastrous event claimed the lives of one or all of them. The family decided to be proactive and embrace a radical idea they fervently hoped would work.

C.J. had spent the evening with Ariel, discussing the functional characteristics of the gateway and its known limitations. Their plan of attack had been conceived by Dr. Wirtz, who'd proposed this location for the decisive rendezvous. Access to the facility was made possible through the influence of Pierre LeClerke, due to his long-standing friendship with one of ConEd's corporate officers. For their part, the Archangels were prepared to do the unthinkable, placing on display a deep and extraordinary faith.

Shannon crept to C.J.'s side, mindful of the time that had already elapsed. "What if they don't come?"

"They'll be here," he assured her. "They're not going to pass up a chance like this."

"Maybe they don't know we're here."

C.J. answered in hushed, reverent tones, his eyes darting through the darkness. "They know. The Grigori are 'The Watchers'. They watch everything. That's what they live for. Watching... waiting...lurking in the shadows...so they can claim the lost souls of humanity."

Arranging themselves in a flared formation, they scanned the midnight shroud for any trace of their adversaries. Behind them was their infant sister Hope, her naked body having been laid across the top of an inactive power transformer. She appeared content, looking up at the heavens and cooing at the stellar display. It wasn't lost upon the family that the baby's perch was reminiscent of a sacrificial altar. As strange as it seemed, the siblings now embraced her perceived vulnerability.

A gentle breeze began to caress their backs, propelled ahead of a thunderstorm to the south. While discarded candy wrappers and coffee cups skipped past them on the ground, their eyes kept scanning the petulant void waiting for the Grigori to emerge. C.J. finally felt the need to force the issue. He took a few strides forward and addressed the swirling night sky.

"We know you're here!" he shouted. "Show yourselves! It's time to settle this once and for all!"

The response was swift and dramatic. Five fissures soon parted the curtain of reality, blossoming like ebony flowers from a netherworld garden. Materializing before them was the sinister quintet, prepared once more to engage the Archangels in battle. Blinded by their insatiable hatred, the Grigori cared little for the motivations of their enemy, waiting impatiently for a chance to strike.

"It'll never be over, Michael," growled Mammon. "This fight is eternal."

C.J. huffed in reply. "So I've read. John Milton...*Paradise Lost*. Don't you think that story's getting a little old?"

"Why waste time reading ancient history, when the final chapter has yet to be written?"

"You won't prevail. Vengeance will end up consuming you."

"Yes," he paused wistfully. "But it's such a delicious meal... we don't ever want it to end."

Their physical condition left much to be desired. Belial's right arm had been severed at the elbow, still weeping blood into a makeshift bandage. The flesh on Azazel's face was charred beyond recognition, with singed pieces flaking off in the breeze. Unable to contain himself, Kevin took note of their grievous infirmities. "Gee, you guys are looking mighty good."

They refused to acknowledge his snide remark. Casey delivered a special message for Belial. "So...do you still love pain?"

The demon's eyes narrowed. "I'm starting to get used to it."

"To what do we owe the displeasure of this encounter?" Mammon probed.

"We'd like to live the rest of our lives in peace," C.J. pleaded, "Without further interference from you."

The Grigori's reaction was predictable, as a chorus of insolent laughter filtered through their ranks. "I'm sorry, but that won't happen."

"You'd be well advised to consider it."

Mammon grinned at the cowardice on display. "You want us to leave you alone? In exchange for what?"

C.J.'s disclosure caught them by surprise. "Immanuel."

Not a word was spoken. Not a breath exhaled. Their optic gaze fell firmly upon newborn skin, coveting the one thing they desired above all else. The baby lay beyond, fidgeting in the shadows. It was now vulnerable and alone. Contained within that flesh was the spirit of spirits. The soul that millennia before had condemned them to eternal damnation. Their bodies tensed in expectation, aware that their chance for retribution might have come at long last. The group began discussing the offer privately using their unique and indecipherable language. After prolonged deliberation, they remained skeptical.

"You're just going to hand her over?" Mammon wondered. "Why?"

C.J. issued a sermon of faith. "It's human nature for adults to protect their young. For the past few days, we've been trying to keep her from harm. But, that wasn't necessary. This is no ordinary child. You know it and so do we. If you really believe that she's God in the flesh, then you should be far more afraid of her than she'll ever be of you. We had to overcome our fears and realize she can take care of herself. It wasn't easy to find that kind of spiritual assurance, but we finally did. She draws her strength from us, because we believe in her divinity. There's nothing that'll harm that child. Not you. Not anyone. But, if you still think you can…" The Archangels parted on cue, allowing the Grigori a clear path to the infant. "Go ahead. She's waiting for you."

The loathsome five were left amused by his theological psychobabble, anxious to prove him wrong. Hardly believing it could be this easy, they commenced a slow, deliberate march toward the baby. Although wary, the enticing bait proved more powerful than an opiate, drawing them in like flies to fruit. The Grigori were emboldened by the fact that if this were an ambush, they could still escape through the gateway in a microsecond. As the Devil's own closed upon the child, C.J. held Shannon back, silently reminding his sister to let go of her maternal instinct. Lightning from the fast moving storm was surging through the clouds, illuminating the area with a vivid strobe effect. Sonic thunderclaps became more frequent, booming with percussive force. Tension was exceeding tolerance and none of them were sure what would happen next.

The demons surrounded the infant, amazed at their current proximity. Eons of festering hate bloomed anew, causing them to visibly shake with rage. Taking care to restrain their primal urges, they spoke amongst themselves, attempting to determine which of them would receive the honor of the kill. A heated debate ensued, appearing as though they'd never reach a consensus. Hopelessly deadlocked, Belial refused to wait. He bent down to grasp a metal shank from the ground and plunged the jagged piece directly into child's belly. An extended scream of agony left her family traumatized and nauseous. C.J. squeezed Shannon's hand as each of the siblings closed their eyes in collective prayer. They visualized Hope in their mind, siphoning the pain from her body and infusing her with renewed strength. Feeling a spiritual rapport which dispelled any doubt, the Archangels now bore witness to the awesome power of God.

Belial continued to issue a manic laugh, his hand still firmly on the blade. His amusement ceased when he detected the infant peering up at him, devoid of torment. In a ghastly spectacle that defied the senses, the Grigori were soon snared in Jehovah's wrathful web.

The blood of the child suddenly morphed from a fluid mass into an ever-expanding legion of fire ants, advancing up his arm. Their numbers expanded exponentially, multiplying through division like malignant cells. Within seconds, Belial's flesh was covered with the voracious beasts, stinging him repeatedly and entering his body through every orifice. His sickening squeal of anguish stunned his comrades, causing them to back away in fright. Frantic to depart, they ran the tonal cues in their minds waiting for their individual escape routes to appear. It was not to be. A series of dysfunctional misfires occurred as the spatial chasms refused to fully open. The generated electromagnetic pulse from the surrounding power transformers and overhead high voltage lines had rendered the gateway useless. Terrorized beyond comprehension, Belial spun wildly into the others, contaminating each with the invasive horde. Entering through their ears, nose and mouth, the ants spread inside them with the speed of a viral infection, devouring their brain tissue at an astounding rate. The five performed a delirious dance of death, crashing into arcing voltage regulators, distribution buses and high tension cables. They soon became nothing more than oscillating shells of scorched flesh, their organs eviscerated from within. With their clothing ablaze, the skeletal remains sank to the pavement, turned to corruption within a flaming communal pyre.

The Archangels stood immobilized at the scene, their vacant expressions left intractable as stone. As the wind-whipped fire cast its noxious embers skyward, they observed the child kicking her legs in agitation. Overcoming their paralysis, they dashed to her side, certain they'd have to immediately transport her to the nearest hospital. What they beheld sent them into a swoon of veneration. The infant was uninjured. There was no blood. No wound. Nothing to indicate that any act of violence had occurred. Shannon ran her hand over the baby's stomach, stroking her skin in amazement. Hope cooed, lifting her arms toward her sister. Gasping in relief, she swept the newborn to her breast, unwilling to contain a torrent of tears. The others were equally affected, a sense of emotional catharsis enveloping them all. There was nothing they could say that would express their true feelings at this moment. Words were instruments of the physical world and unnecessary for the connection they shared.

A beneficial aspect of this encounter was their exposure to the strong electromagnetic pulse emanations from the power plant. The generated EMP was sufficient to incapacitate the nanobots that had bedeviled the Archangels since their bondage in Dreamland. Their manipulated dreams were finally over.

As the thunder continued to peal through the heavens, the endless reverberations seemed to announce the tidings of a great victory. They allowed the fire to burn, slowly transforming their enemies into ashes. It was a time for celebration, as well as reflection. This had been yet another battle in an eternal war. Each of them knew that the enraged spirits of the Grigori would live on...seeking vengeance forever.

CHAPTER FORTY-EIGHT

$\mathcal{S}$teven Yeager came to his feet. After three days of drug-induced hell, the Secret Service agent finally embraced reality. He'd not seen or heard his odious captors in more than 24 hours and was left to wonder what had become of them. The intravenous narcotics had run their course, allowing him to regain his memory and mental faculties. Yeager had kept abreast of recent events through the radio which was still reporting the tragic news of Susan Webber's death. This time he was fully aware of why the announcement affected him so deeply. The man not only remembered his professional responsibility to the fallen President, but also his role as the woman's secret lover. Never an emotional man, he still found himself fighting back tears. He blamed himself for his incarceration, considering it akin to dereliction of duty. He reasoned that if he hadn't been taken captive, he would've been there for Webber at the fatal moment. With his period of self-incrimination officially over, he retreated to an adjoining bathroom where bodily functions took precedence.

Hardly recognizing the man in the mirror, he did what he could to make himself presentable. In desperate need of a shower and a shave, Yeager found the facilities for neither. Locating a sliver of soap in the medicine cabinet, he bathed himself in front of the pedestal sink and used a spare bed sheet as an emergency towel. Feeling a bit more human, the agent searched in vain for the clothes he was wearing when abducted. In spite of his naked state, Yeager realized there was probably no better time to break out of this cage. The man placed an ear to the door, trying to ascertain if anyone was present outside the room. He detected nothing and tried the knob to confirm he was locked in. Yeager noticed that the hinge pins were on his side of the portal. He rummaged through the room for something to help dislodge the hardware. Disconnecting the radio, the agent used the electric plug's metal prongs to slowly lift the pins from their housing. Once removed, there was enough space between the door and its jamb to wrench the portal free.

Yeager entered a dimly lit room which he soon determined to be the living area of an apartment unit. Looking out past the drawn shades, the man was able to identify his surroundings as the Foggy Bottom area around George Washington University, just a few blocks from the White House. The elevated view suggested he was in a high rise complex about five floors from the ground. Detecting no one in the vicinity, the agent barricaded the door to prevent a surprise entry by his captors.

The search for his clothing began in earnest. He entered a back bedroom and turned on the overhead light. A television had been left on with the sound muted. On screen was coverage of President Webber's state funeral now being held in the Capitol rotunda. With curiosity getting the better of him, he located the remote, increasing the volume of the broadcast while he checked inside a nearby closet.

"It's just inconceivable that the American people are being forced to go through this again," the anchorman stressed, his voice appropriately somber for the occasion. "Only six months earlier, we awoke to the tragic news of President Petersen's heart attack and here today, in the same hallowed building, we pay our final respects to President Webber who was killed in that horrific bombing in El Paso three days ago. Her death was so appalling in nature, that the casket remained sealed and no officially viewing of the body was allowed. You can see that the dignitaries have arrived…the entire Congress of the United States is present…so are the nine justices of the Supreme Court…all the surviving members of the President's cabinet…most of the White House staff… foreign heads of state…as well as three of our former Presidents… not to mention the man who would be President, Vice President Jacobs, who has been prevented from taking the oath of office by military edict. We've been told that his swearing-in ceremony will be held in the next day or two, once the perceived threat from Al-Qaeda terrorists has been neutralized." A lengthy pause occurred, making clear the anchorman's contempt for the situation which he and millions of others considered patently unconstitutional. "There's the ceremonial Guard of Honor, representing the five branches of the Armed Services as they surround the bier. Those young men and women have been on 30 minute shifts of duty since the casket arrived. You might recall, they stayed at their post during an evacuation of Capitol Hill when it was determined that a commercial jetliner had wandered into the no-fly zone around the city. The military lauded them for their dedication…as do we all."

Although unable to locate his apparel and personal effects, Yeager came across an article of clothing that he thought would fit him. It was a U.S. Navy dress white uniform which had been carelessly tossed upon the closet floor. He quickly donned the pants and determined that the size was adequate. After slipping on the shirt and matching shoes, he discovered another pile of clothing laid inside a laundry hamper. To his surprise, the first item he inspected was another dress uniform, a three-button pocketless coat in Air Force blue. Digging deeper, he unearthed formal attire for the U.S. Army, Marine Corps and Coast Guard. These were not the type of uniforms that could be purchased over the counter by civilians, but made and distributed exclusively for the military to be worn only during ceremonial occasions…*or for duty as part of an honor guard.*

His idle speculation caused him to look back at the television.

There on screen were five servicemen, each adorned in uniforms identical to the ones in his possession. The agent recalled his quintet of captors and began to shudder at the disturbing parallel. He understood this could be a coincidence, but that prospect seemed less remote by the minute. *Was I kidnapped by the military? Could it have been part of a plot to kill the President? Why did they keep me in this place? Why were those five guarding the casket?*

Yeager shook his head in confusion, encountering far more questions than answers. As he strode toward the door, the reflection in a dresser mirror caught his attention. He spotted several empty boxes lying within the tub of the connecting bathroom. The man's inquisitive nature came to the fore, compelling him to investigate. Inside the oval basin he discovered the ingredients for terror. There were more than a dozen discarded containers, all of which were labeled with the same markings. The letters PETN. Yeager was familiar with the substance. Pentaerythritol tetranitrate was one of the world's most powerful explosives and it appeared they had enough raw materials to bring down any building in the city. The agent noted that a heavy residue of the chemical was lining the walls of the tub. While considering the alarming implications of his find, Yeager's attention was soon directed at a wadded sheet of graph paper located in a neighboring wastebasket. Unfurling the page, he saw a detailed schematic for the design and molding of a bomb with the exact dimensions of the bathtub. The explosive would be detonated by timer and the designated hour was listed as 11:00 am. He wasn't exactly sure what triggered his epiphany. It might have been the approaching time of day or perhaps the unique shape of the device. Whatever the reason, a sense of pure horror overwhelmed his thoughts, leaving him gasping in shock.

"My God," he mumbled. "They've put a bomb in the casket. They're going to kill everybody. The entire United States Government."

In his mind's eye, he could see the Grigori entering the rotunda, dressed in their military accouterments, relieving the honor guard in place...their slow, synchronous salute to the fallen leader...and when Capitol Hill was evacuated, they used the opportunity to place the explosive within the President's closed coffin...the last place on Earth anyone would look. Their insidious plan was about to be realized. Yeager was the only one who knew. *18 minutes remained.*

Dashing from the apartment, the agent refused to wait for the elevator, opting instead to rapidly descend five flights of stairs. He broke through a fire exit, paying no attention to the ear piercing alarm he left in his wake. The signs on a street corner informed him of his current location. *G Street and 23rd. Just over two miles to the Capitol.*

Starting his extended run, he bemoaned the loss of his possessions. Without a cell phone or Secret Service ID, it would be almost impossible to convince anyone in authority of the imminent threat. His lack of spare change was equally disturbing, having no means to pay for the Metro which would get him to Capitol Hill in half the time. There was little point in wishing for the things he no longer had. The agent was now in a desperate race to save the Government from extinction.

Proceeding south on 23rd Street, he bolted past throngs of onlookers and adjusted course down congested Virginia Avenue. The thoroughfare placed him on a diagonal tangent toward The Ellipse and the National Mall beyond. Yeager sprinted across busy intersections with barely a pause in his gait, staring directly through pedestrians as though they weren't even there. His intent was purposeful and focused. The man would allow nothing to stand in his way. Calculating the remaining minutes from a bank's outdoor display, he reasoned that he'd have just enough time to either disarm the device or at the very least warn the dignitaries to flee. With his physical condition enhanced by youth and training, the agent was moving with efficiency, his pulse and respiration steady. The only regret he allowed himself to ponder was the lack of a pair of running shoes.

He was now approaching Constitution Avenue, a mere four blocks from the White House. For a brief moment, Yeager gave serious consideration to changing tack and heading for his Secret Service office where he could alert the Capitol Hill police. However, he knew if there were any delays at the security gate, or if anyone wasted time questioning him, the result could be catastrophic. It was better to press on, keeping his original plan intact.

His frantic crossing at Constitution and 17th was aided by significant vehicular gridlock spanning all six lanes of the avenue. Nonetheless, he was still the recipient of numerous car horns and driver wrath. Now safely on the green expanse of the National Mall, Yeager found himself with plenty of unobstructed space to run. Sprinting past sightseers, sun worshippers and kids with kites, the only daunting aspect of the park was its sheer size. It was another mile and a half to the base of the Capitol steps. On his immediate right was the Washington Monument. The 555 foot obelisk towered over the scene, silently watching the lone man's manic dash to save the soul of America. He crested over a small hill and down an embankment where several tour buses were waiting to collect their passengers. The agent was compelled to pause for a convoy of limousines driving by the monument on 14th Street. During this ill-timed delay, he noticed a National Park Service van on the opposite side of the road with a female Park Ranger leaning against its hood. Thinking he might have a chance to convince her, Yeager recklessly snaked through oncoming traffic and arrived before the woman in a state of panic. She looked upon the disheveled naval officer with a jaundiced eye, believing him to be under the influence of a controlled substance.

"Do you need help sailor?"

"Yes! Listen to me…very carefully," he stated, gasping for air. "My name's Steven Yeager. I'm a Secret Service agent…working on the Presidential detail. I've just come across information…that a bomb's going to explode inside the Capitol…during the state funeral at 11:00."

The woman's incredulous gaze fell to her watch. "That's 9 minutes from now."

"I know!" he bellowed in frustration, his labored breath

making it difficult to speak. "You can save everybody in there... but you've got to get on your radio and call it in! Contact the Capitol Hill police! Tell them the bomb's in the casket!" The agent observed her idle response with dismay. "What are you waiting for?"

She was leery at first, but his sense of urgency seemed genuine. Placing a call to headquarters, the Park Ranger asked the dispatcher to connect her with the Chief of Police for the Capitol District. While she was waiting, Yeager bent to his knees, trying to gain his second wind. Finally, the woman achieved contact with a subordinate in the Police Chief's office. After properly identifying herself, she attempted to pass on the crucial information.

"We don't have time for bomb threats!" the man admonished her. "We've got an emergency here. Five armed soldiers just shot their way inside the East Entrance."

Hearing the news, Yeager mistakenly believed it was his captors, arriving on Capitol Hill to make a desperate last stand. "Oh, shit! I've gotta get down there! They're all gonna die!" He once more began to run.

"Wait a minute!" she cried. "Come back here!"

There was nothing the woman could say that would make him stop. His singular purpose was to get to the Capitol on time. Scolding himself over the interruption, he knew that precious seconds had been lost. The only thing he could do now was to push his body harder and hope that God was with him.

On the floor of the Capitol rotunda, the solemnity of the state funeral was shattered as concerned millions watched live on television. During Vice President Jacobs heartfelt eulogy to the memory of Susan Webber, a wave of consternation surged through the assembled mourners, percolating with audible gasps and yelps long after the danger had made itself known. Captain Roberts and his former SEAL team members moved swiftly to the podium, located just feet from the casket. They swung their weapons in wide, fluid arcs ensuring that all the dignitaries were paying attention. Directly behind them were Captain Tejada and Garza gingerly transporting a zippered body bag.

"My fellow Americans," Roberts began, unable to resist the clichéd opening line. "We're here today to speak for someone who can't. President Webber tried to tell the world about Roswell, but the Joint Chiefs wouldn't allow her to disclose the truth. She was assassinated for that reason. In order for her courageous spirit to live on, we decided to take matters into our own hands. We're going to show you irrefutable evidence that the alleged UFO crash actually occurred. In order to do that, we went to Wright-Patterson Air Force Base...and raided the Government's fridge."

He motioned his men to open the bag. The crowded room became hushed as the biodegradable container was promptly unzipped. Once the outer shroud had been folded back, the body within was revealed to the world. Amidst extended shrieks of astonishment, several of the mourners were overcome by the sight and collapsed to the marble floor. The alien corpse was perfectly preserved, having been frozen for more than 60 years. The audience could clearly discern its black, almond-shaped eyes... its enlarged head...the curious absence of a mouth or genitalia. It was anatomical oddity unlike any ever witnessed. A distorted figure from our past, as well as our future. This was the father of Mary Ellen's children.

As television cameras zoomed in for a closer inspection, Captain Roberts once more addressed the spellbound congregation. "The game's over people. There's no way the MAJIK-12 can lie their way out of this."

Yeager had lost track of time. He would keep running until he could run no more. The Capitol building now loomed before him, the massive edifice known as "Democracy's Greatest Symbol". He continued to sprint down the center of the National Mall, passing other monolithic structures of the U.S. Government. The Smithsonian Institution. The IRS Building. The Justice Department. The Federal Court House. The National Archives. All arrayed in row after row of monumental self-importance. Every office was empty. Every door shut. This was a national day of mourning and millions of civil servants remained home, watching on television as Washington's top officials honored their fallen leader.

As he traversed 3rd Street to enter Union Square, the agent could feel himself beginning to tire. His legs and feet had become wobbly, unresponsive to mental commands. A jackhammer heart could find no relief. Lungs heaved for air, desperate for rest. He wiped clear his sweat-laden face, taking sight of the barricades assembled on the opposite side of 1st Street which led onto the Capitol grounds. The man bore to his right, negotiating his way around the opulent reflecting pool. Carelessly crossing the road in front of two oncoming vehicles, Yeager surged through the cordon and shouted to a nearby police officer.

"I'm a Secret Service agent!" he claimed in respiratory distress. "There's a bomb in the casket! It's going to blow any second!"

The cop dismissed his breathless declaration as the ravings of a lunatic. "Yeah, sure. Get behind the line before you get hurt." He placed a firm hand on Yeager's chest, trying to force him back. Infuriated by his refusal to listen, the agent grabbed the officer's arm, flipping him to the concrete without remorse. He took off toward the west front of the Capitol which triggered a frantic call on the policeman's two-way radio. Racing past the assembled television trucks and satellite equipment, he bounded over large power cables strewn across his path. The networks suddenly went live with an outside camera feed, showing Yeager's fevered approach toward the building. Before him were the imposing steps that would elevate him into the rotunda. As he began his ascent, a swarm of police converged from all angles, tackling the agent to the ground. He screamed as loudly as he could, forcing everyone within earshot to hear his manic plea.

"THERE'S A BOMB IN THERE!" he cried, feeling the oppressive weight of the officers holding him down. "RUN FOR YOUR LIVES! LET ME GO! GET OUT OF THERE!" He issued a protracted final screech, his body convulsing in fear. "NO…"

The sound of his voice was soon eclipsed by an acoustic orgy of death. It rang forth from Hell's heart and resonated throughout the American spirit. The President's casket had exploded. Snared within the prodigious blast were over a thousand souls, each experiencing their ultimate release into the ether. Yeager looked up to behold a rolling cascade of flame balloon over him with propelled force. Fire erupted through the cupola, cracking open the Capitol's iconic dome. As the inferno burst through three tiers of ornate stained glass, it formed a searing umbrella that mushroomed over the venue of carnage. Dozens of neo-classical columns began to splay open amidst the woeful sound of cast iron beams vibrating from the intense pressure. The circular colonnade finally broke apart, separating from its stone entablature. Structural debris rained down into the squealing crowd, covering the plaza along with mounds of bloodied clothing and severed body parts. Seconds later the metal superstructure caved in, collapsing inside a billowing cloud of concrete dust and particulate matter. A climactic roar engulfed the survivors, finally dissipating into a strident chorus of inconceivable hysterics. Hundreds had either fainted or become violently ill. Ambulances and fire trucks raced to the scene from across the city. Television had transmitted the horrifying images into the living rooms of a thunderstruck nation. News correspondents waded through the decimated ruins, trying to maintain some semblance of professionalism. It was a scene of surreal devastation that left the United States without any of its duly elected leaders.

Steven Yeager had watched the death of the Government from a unique perspective. He was aware of the five responsible, but still mystified by their motives. The agent's emotions were raw, swelling beyond his ability to contain them. Tears streamed down his face, unable to comprehend what had occurred or submit himself to endless speculation. All he knew was that his heroic attempt had failed and the American people would be forced to endure further psychological trauma.

CHAPTER FORTY-NINE

FORT MEADE, MARYLAND — MAY 12th — 1:46 PM EDT

$\mathcal{T}$he members of the MAJIK-12 were huddled in their bunker, rendered aghast at recent events. Not only had the group's existence been exposed at the U.N. conference through the betrayal of one of their own, but they seethed at their inability to prevent Pierre LeClerke's damaging disclosures. The explosion at the Capitol further undermined their grip on power. Although it had all the earmarks of a MAJIK-12 operation, it had none of the provocation. The last thing they needed was for the American people to think they'd ordered the demise of the Government. Each of them were now marked men. It was only a matter of time before they were hunted down and vigilante justice would prevail.

They'd taken consolation in the fact that no competent authority figure had yet come forth to substantiate LeClerke's claims. But, that was all about to change. World broadcast and cable networks went live to the Vatican where the Pope was holding a news conference. As he'd promised Mary Ellen's children, the Pontiff had spoken with the Roman Curia about Church acknowledgment of the Roswell incident and the religious implications thereof. After this morning's tragedy on Capitol Hill, the Pope knew he could no longer remain silent. The man spoke from the heart, informing an anxious world of the incredible story, and how a young girl had managed for years to elude the insidious forces of evil.

The conspirators sat dumbfounded, scarcely believing the level of detail that was being so openly discussed. It was clear that the Pontiff was shoveling the final scoops of dirt onto their collective graves.

"Jesus!" Langlois whined after another incendiary revelation. "This is a goddamn nightmare!"

Leonetti sought refuge in denial. "Maybe no one will listen to him."

The CIA Director gazed at his colleague in disbelief. "What do you mean no one will listen to him?" he bellowed, preparing himself for a sustained vocal outburst. "HE'S THE POPE! THE FFFUUUCCCKKKING POPE!" With the veins in his neck swelling into view, Langlois felt his blood pressure soar to an alarming level. He became woozy, clutching his head in the fear that it might explode. The man caught his breath, then quickly strode to an adjacent bathroom without risking another word.

After splashing his face with water, he knew the end had come. Having weathered many trials in his career, Langlois was convinced this one was insurmountable. He reflected upon the decisions that were made and gasped at their appalling consequences. There was only one thing left to do. The man wiped his hands dry, mentally preparing to take his own life.

He returned to the bunker, arriving upon a scene of indescribable savagery. His six comrades had been murdered, all shot through the skull at point blank range. Their lifeless bodies registered the spasm of astonishment each had suffered at the moment of death. Admiral Holliman's mouth was agape as though killed in mid-scream. He saw General Connolly slumped in his chair and Defense Secretary Roth lying across a console with his arms outstretched. Blau and Leonetti were sprawled across the floor as pools of their blood oozed toward his feet. General Stevenson seemed to have been the only one to recognize the danger, shot dead while removing his sidearm. The swiftness of the kill was stunning. As Langlois attempted to make sense of the slaughter, he spotted a familiar figure lurking in the shadows.

"Oh, my God. Where the hell have you been?" He noticed a gun leveled at his chest, arousing his basic instinct for survival. "No!...No!"

An instant later he joined the others, becoming nothing more than a wretched character from history. The assassin walked onward, callously stepping over his earthly remains. A pervasive silence announced their fate. The MAJIK-12's reign of terror had finally come to an end.

CHAPTER FIFTY

*A*fter extensive questioning by Capitol Hill police, Steven Yeager was positively identified by the Secret Service as one of their agents. The man told the authorities everything he knew. He was released on his own recognizance and taken to a nearby hospital for medical evaluation.

While awaiting a doctor's report on his condition, Yeager sat in the Emergency Room watching a wall mounted television. His eyes were glazed over, suffering from chronic incomprehension. As expected, the networks coverage of the explosion was ubiquitous, reported at length from every angle. There were already erroneous claims of Al-Qaeda responsibility being circulated by the press. Only one thing was clear. The elected Government of the United States had been eliminated in a singular, massive strike and the foreboding tension among the American people was palpable. The country needed a leader.

In a startling change of policy, the Pentagon issued a statement that the next President of the United States would be sworn in at an official ceremony, to be held in the Rose Garden at 3:00 pm. Surviving White House staffers prepared for the unprecedented event which would be broadcast live to a nation reeling in anguish.

Speculation was rampant as to whom the military had chosen to assume the role of Commander in Chief. Reporters and pundits alike were amazed by the secrecy of the announcement.

"We haven't been told much yet," the anchorman confessed. "But, we understand that the individual is a high ranking Washington insider...someone who obviously wasn't in attendance at the state funeral this morning. This isn't unusual. For years, the Government has maintained a doomsday scenario, keeping at least one person isolated from any event where a disaster could wipe out all of our assembled leaders. Until today, it had merely been a precaution. Unfortunately, it's now become a sobering reality..."

Soon, the identity of the individual became known. He emerged from the Oval Office to a smattering of applause from the assembled witnesses. It was at this moment that Yeager leaned forward, his eyes dilating as never before. A spark of recognition ignited the agent's psychotic rant, causing him to vault to his feet in shrill, uncontrolled delirium.

"I KILLED HIM!" he screamed, pointing at the television. "I KILLED HIM! HE'S DEAD! THIS CAN'T BE HAPPENING! IT CAN'T BE! HE HAS TO BE DEAD! I KILLED HIM!"

Three nurses and a doctor rushed to his side, thinking the man was in the throes of a violent seizure. The five fell to the floor as others came to their aid. Yeager convulsed in a breathless caterwaul, flailing his arms and legs in hysterics. Another doctor administered a potent sedative as the country's new leader was given the oath of office.

The presiding judge held out a bible for the man to place his hand upon, which he never actually touched. "Repeat after me...I, Richard Marcus Stern, do solemnly swear..."

The National Security Advisor answered, the star-shaped bullet wound in the center of his forehead now covered with makeup. "I, Richard Marcus Stern, do solemnly swear..."

"That I will faithfully execute the office of President of the United States..."

"That I will faithfully execute the office of President of the United States…"

Yeager writhed on the floor, fighting the effects of the potent drug. "I killed him," he moaned in distress. "He's dead…I shot him…He's got to be dead…"

The ceremony continued on screen. "And will, to the best of my ability…"

"And will, to the best of my ability…"

"Preserve, protect and defend the Constitution of the United States…"

"Preserve, protect and defend the Constitution of the United States…"

The agent's extended, baleful cry crested over the televised proceedings, his vocal distress evoking the spiritual agony of America.

"So, help me God."

Lucifer smiled, slowing his response to fully savor what would become his crowning achievement. Each articulated syllable was uttered in a bass throb, saving the final word for his evident contempt. "So, help me…GOD!"

The Master's magnificent plan was fulfilled.

To follow the latest news regarding the Archangels novels; production updates for the Archangels motion pictures; local book signings; author blogs or to purchase autographed copies of *The Archangels* of *Dreamland* and *Archangels II: The Grigori*, please visit our website at *www.archangelnovels.com*.